I0584814

At All Costs
Brett Kihlmire

MATG
PUBLISHING

Copyright © 2024 by Brett Kihlmire

All rights reserved.

No portion of this book may be reproduced in any form without written permission from the publisher or author, except as permitted by U.S. copyright law.

Ebook ISBN: 979-8-9943646-1-1

Hardcover ISBN: 979-8-9943646-0-4

Paperback ISBN: 979-8-9943646-2-8

This novel is a work of fiction. Any references to historical events, real people, or real places are used fictitiously. Names, characters, and places are products of the author's imagination.

Dedicated to my beloved wife, Kaylyn

Without your unending support, patience, and willingness to read outside your preferred genre, this novel and many others may have never existed.

I love you with all my heart.

Special dedication to my son, Elliott

Much of this novel was written while waiting for your grand entrance into this world.

I'll never forget the first time I laid eyes on you, my boy.

You make me so proud.

He who digs pits for others will fall in them himself

Polish Proverb

Chapter 1

Gdynia, Republic of Poland, Slavic Federation

I t was a cool autumn day down at the Naval Shipyard Gdynia in northern Poland. The guided-missile destroyer and flagship of the Polish fleet - the mighty ORP Warszawa - had arrived and dropped anchor in the early hours, but not a soul was allowed to disembark until the captain gave his orders. The ship and its crew had just completed a nine-month tour of duty in the Adriatic Sea as part of an international task force aimed at bringing the long-running Yugoslav Wars to a close.

While the main crew toiled inside with their final duties, those approved for leave quietly packed their seabags with personal belongings and awaited their dismissal from the ship after a long and grueling campaign. When the order came down from the bridge that all men authorized to leave were to report to the quarterdeck, the sailors eagerly made their way there.

Standing in lines from the lowest rank to the highest, crewmen waited their turn to salute a deck officer before heading down the gangway toward a roaring crowd of proud parents, siblings, children, and complete strangers. They were greeted like heroes returning from some glorious crusade, but truth be told, not one of the men who saw combat would call this last tour anything close to glorious. Regardless, they made their way down the gangway with reserved smiles, waving to family and friends as they made their way down to the concrete dock and into an open area made possible only by steel barricades. This didn't stop eager loved ones from vying for the attention of their returning sailor, but they wouldn't be allowed to reunite until the last man was off the ship and assembled at a designated point at the naval base.

While most who left the ship would be doing so for a few days, weeks, or even as long as a month, a handful of men were disembarking from a Polish naval ship for the last time. Among them was Senior Sergeant Aleksey Rybinski, one of a few dozen 'guests' from the Special Troops temporarily stationed aboard the Warszawa.

At first glance, Aleksey blended in with the sailors in his vicinity, but a sharp observer would quickly notice several items that separated him from his naval counterparts. First and foremost, he wore the rank of senior sergeant rather than the Navy's equivalent rank of bootsmann. Secondly, while the sailors wore a golden cord on their dress uniforms, Aleksey and his compatriots wore a grey cord. In addition, his uniform bore numerous campaign ribbons on his chest detailing a highly active career in the Polish Army. However, if one piece of his uniform stood out from the rest, it was the insignia on the front of his steel-grey beret – a diving eagle holding a lightning bolt.

Anyone with a working knowledge of the Polish Special Troops would instantly recognize him as a member of the elite JW GROM, Poland's premier special operations unit. Given his presence on the ship, it was reasonable for one to correctly assume that he was a member of GROM's maritime unit, which was based in the nearby city of Gdansk. However, there was one last thing about his uniform that made him stand out from all the others, but only the most keen-eyed and sharp-witted would not only catch it but also make the connection. It was his surname – his uniform bore the surname of the national hero and current General of the Army, Aleksander Rybinski. In fact, he was the legendary General's only son.

Clearly born with large boots to fill, Aleksey grew up idolizing his father and his extended family for their efforts in the war that ended communism in Europe. Thus, barely a week after completing his secondary education at the age of seventeen, he enlisted in the army rather than accept an appointment at the military academy of his choosing. He did so to pursue his dream of military service without the burden of living under his father's watchful eye as he carried on the family tradition of military service.

A brilliant student, Aleksey was always a goal-oriented person, and from the day he entered military service, he planned to pursue it as a career. While his initial goal was to simply serve with distinction and let his record speak for him, his career took an unexpected turn near the end of his first contract. His above-average skills in the field and with the rifle earned him a spot at the army's sniper school, as well as an opportunity to earn his place amongst the army's elite JW Komandosów.

After earning his sniper tab and the right to call himself an army commando, Aleksey continued to serve with honor and dignity. He proudly rose through the enlisted ranks, attending every special training program he was allowed. By his seventh year in the service, he had amassed a legendary resume that opened the door to Poland's most elite unit, JW GROM.

Through a rigorous selection program, Aleksey pushed his limits and overcame the odds to earn the coveted eagle and lightning bolt upon his beret. His excellent swimming and navigation skills led him to be assigned to Squadron B, where he had served ever since. However, as he neared a decade in service and a fresh contract loomed, he found himself fighting a private war within.

For months, things had been strained between him and his long-term girlfriend, Tatiana. She wanted a family, and she knew he was close to the end of his current contract, so she delivered an ultimatum. He could have a family with her, or he could serve the remaining ten years until retirement. This put Aleksey in a tough spot, and though he assured her that this would be his final tour of duty, he wasn't so sure. He loved the Service as much as he loved Tatiana. So, when he departed for Yugoslavia, he had a hard decision to make, but the mission ahead gave him little time to contemplate his situation back home. In fact, the only thing he could think about was staying alive and safe amidst the nightmare that was Yugoslavia at war.

Haunted by the bodies he saw in the pits and the actions he took against the perpetrators, Aleksey was thinking of nothing more than leaving the service and marrying his sweetheart in a bid to put it all behind him. While he was encouraged by his executive officer to hold off on declaring his intent to resign too soon, each subsequent mission hammered the nails of resolve. By the last month in Yugoslavia, he wanted nothing more than to put down his rifle, unlace his boots, and never leave camp again until it was time to head back to the ship.

While things weren't exactly at their best between him and Tatiana when he left, the thought of holding her in his arms and whispering into her ear that he was home for good was enough to get him through deployment. Unable to call home, he had high hopes she'd be waiting for him when he got back. After all, she stood by him all this time, and he was sure that she wouldn't decline his proposal if he returned a free man. However, there was always a chance that things might not go as planned. So, despite informing his squad that he intended to resign at the end of his enlistment contract, he was still mulling over another two to four years of service as a backup plan. In fact, if he did return, he'd fully consider joining his departing teammates at the special interservice training program they had been selected to attend after their scheduled leave.

Officially on leave for one month, Aleksey left the naval base on foot with his rucksack over his shoulder. Heading over to a nearby bus terminal, he marched with a crowd of sailors now on leave or heading home for the last time. Upon entering the terminal, he spotted a bank of payphones and made a beeline for them. While he was certainly close with his family, the first person he thought to call was Tatiana.

Dropping a few coins into the slot, he dialed the number for their shared flat in Gdansk from memory. He soon heard the ringing, and he held his breath in anticipation. He had been thinking about this moment all day, and now he could hardly believe it was finally here. However, after six rings, he heard her voice through a recorded message from her answering machine. A little deflated that he couldn't talk to her after so many months overseas, Aleksey took a breath to replace the stale air in his lungs and waited for the promised beep to leave a message. Keeping it short, he told a little white lie that he was required to stay on base until a specific time and that he'd be home that evening. In actuality, he was hoping she'd get the message soon and that he could surprise her much earlier than promised.

"You better not be calling home to tell your sweetie you're on your way. You still owe the boys a beer and a shot," said fellow GROM frogman, Mikołaj 'Miko' Zielinski.

Hanging up the phone, Aleksey turned to his friend with a grin. "I don't recall owing anyone drinks," he said, but Miko grinned in return.

"There's a price to pay when you part ways with your squad. Lucky for you, you only have to cover three of us. Of course, I get top shelf all night since I'm going to greener pastures after leave is done," Miko said slyly, but Aleksey just glared as if he knew his friend was full of crap. "Come on, it's tradition."

"Yeah, right. You made that up," Aleksey said with a chuckle, and Miko shrugged with a smirk.

"Yeah, I did. But think of it as paying your respects to the boys you're abandoning over a woman," Miko replied, but Aleksey resisted the urge to roll his eyes. "Besides, this may very well be the last time any of us will be seeing you in uniform. Word has it, Command is going to throw you into the reserves for your remaining time in service."

Looking past Miko, Aleksey saw more of his fellow frogmen – all were in their dress uniforms and wearing a grin for their soon-to-be former squad leader – and given the fact that he had heard that rumor too, he figured it might very well be the last time he'd see any of them. Even if it wasn't true, Miko was certainly gone, so a drink was entirely necessary.

"Alright," Aleksey said. "I'll buy a round, but it's just a beer, and it sure won't be top shelf. We're too close to a base to act like savages."

"Then let's get out of here and go to a neighborhood bar," Miko said, but Aleksey appeared hesitant. "Come on, Aleksey. You've got the rest of your life to go home to your woman. Some of us might not see retirement, you know."

Seeing his point, for the next time he might see all these men together was hard to predict, especially considering the danger of their duties, Aleksey folded.

"Alright, but it's got to be somewhere near my place. I need to make my flight home tomorrow, and I don't want to be hungover."

With a wide smile on his face, Miko ignored Aleksey's concerns and looked at his squad, then waved them over. "You hear that, boys? Rybinski is buying shots and beers all day!"

Rolling his eyes, Aleksey knew he was in for an expensive afternoon, but it was fine. So long as he got a hold of Tatiana and got to hold her in his arms at some point that day, he didn't mind blowing a small stack on one last outing with his friends.

Piling into a cab, Aleksey and his compatriots asked to be dropped off at the nearest bar off-base but far enough away to avoid the Shore Patrol. Their destination was an establishment modeled after an authentic British pub of all things, but so long as the beer was good, no one cared. Considering it was a Thursday afternoon, the pub was relatively empty, leaving a wide spot for the frogmen to occupy and banter.

Keeping his promise to Miko and the boys, Aleksey agreed to a round of beer, but he drew the line there. While he would have preferred a draught of Tolstiak and a shot of potato vodka, Miko placed the order, leading to a round of Guinness draught and Jameson Irish whiskey. Aleksey wasn't much for whiskey, but the stout, while a bit flat on the tongue, was good and cold, so he didn't complain. Besides, he was only there for a quick shot and a beer. So, after choking down his whiskey, he excused himself and headed to the bathroom. Along the way, he spotted a payphone and decided to give his girlfriend another try. Like before, he would get no further in contacting her. This time, he didn't bother to leave a message. Instead, he cradled the phone and went into the bathroom to relieve himself of the burden he'd been dealing with since leaving the ship. On his way back, he considered giving her one last call, but he decided against it and went back to the barroom where the boys were getting ready to play a game of 301 on the dartboard.

Noticing a change in Aleksey's demeanor, Miko handed him the steel-tipped darts and told him he could shoot first. Aleksey nodded and took the darts. Taking his place at the line, he threw all three darts in quick succession, but his mind was elsewhere, so the sharpshooter failed to score very well. This didn't go unnoticed, so when his turn was over, Miko stood back and asked him what was bothering him.

"It's nothing," Aleksey said, not wanting to discuss his personal problems.

"You sure about that? You went to the bathroom feeling good and came back looking like your dog ran away."

"I said it's nothing," Aleksey said firmly, and his friend backed off.

Standing back as another man took his turn, Aleksey took a long sip of his beer and eyed a poster for an upcoming martial arts tournament in the federal capital of Senatgrad, northeast of Poland, on the Sambia peninsula. He was always a martial arts fan, often dreaming of stepping into the arena as a fighter when he was a boy, but that dream was long dead, and he had no regrets. After all, the Blood Games – the top professional fighting league in Eastern Europe – was little more than a modern equivalent to the pankration tournaments of Ancient Greece and Rome. The only difference was that no one died, and very few left the arena crippled. However, the resulting medical expenses of a particularly nasty bout could often cost a fighter more than he earned for winning. Nonetheless, there was a chance to accrue a small fortune in just a few fights, but that was all subject to luck and skill. Many believed the matches were rigged to an extent, especially the amateur invitational tournaments such as the one advertised. Yet, that didn't stop fortune seekers from taking their chance.

"Did the alcohol go straight to your head? You've got that look," Miko said.

"What look?" Aleksey asked, his brow furrowed.

"The look you get when you're about to do something crazy," Miko said, and Aleksey chuckled. He was aware of the fact that he always got a distinct expression when he went into what the other guys called 'cowboy mode.' However, this time it was nothing, but he decided to play around.

"Yeah, maybe you're right," Aleksey said. "I'm just thinking about that tournament coming up in Senatgrad.

Miko grabbed his shoulder tightly. "Not...fucking...worth it," he said, and Aleksey concurred.

"No kidding. It's all rigged, I'm sure. Just bread and circuses for the masses." Aleksey said, but then paused and recalled his childhood dream of being a fighter born from going to amateur matches with his father for a moment. He cracked a smile. "Nonetheless, it's fun watching modern gladiators go to war for our amusement."

"You're damn right it is," Miko said with a smile of his own. "What do you say we go to that tournament? Senatgrad is only a couple of hours away if we drive. There's always the ferry, too. What do you say?"

"Unfortunately, I think I'm going to have to pass. Something tells me Tatiana is going to want me all to herself for a while," Aleksey said before setting aside his half-empty glass of beer. He then held out his hand to shake. "That being said, it's been fun. Unfortunately, I need to hit the road."

"What's wrong with that beer? You know it's against policy to leave an alcoholic beverage unfinished while off-duty."

"Good thing there's no patrols around," Aleksey said, his smile widening as he backed toward the door. "Finish it for me, will you?"

"What? Scared you'll get too drunk to fuck, old man?" Miko asked, but rather than argue that he was two months younger, Aleksey waved him off and hit the door with his backside. He was halfway through the door when he stopped suddenly and turned back for a moment.

"Hey!" Aleksey called out, approaching Miko with his shoulders square and his expression firm. Reaching out, he grabbed his friend by the hand and gripped it tightly. "You take care of yourself. Don't go doing anything stupid that might get yourself sent home in a body bag now that I'm not around to save your ass."

"Go home to your girlfriend, Rybinski. I'll be fine," Miko said with a smile.

"Alright then," Aleksey said, freeing him from his grip.

As if Aleksey were still his squad leader, Miko threw up a salute, but instead of saluting in return, Aleksey grabbed his abandoned beer and chugged it down with a straight face and piercing glare expected of a tough-as-nails.

"There, no laws broken, but if I can't take care of business, I'm coming right back and kicking your ass!" Aleksey said playfully. He then raised his hand as if he were looking for a high five, but Miko grabbed it in a brotherly fashion, clenching his hand while looking him deep in the eyes.

"Thanks for watching my back all these years. I wouldn't have made it through this last one without you," Aleksey said, tightening his grip. "I'll make an effort to get out to Senatgrad for the fights if that's where you're headed."

"Then I truly hope to see you there," Miko replied. "Strength and honor—"

"For you, Fatherland!" Aleksey declared loudly, finishing the motto of their unit. The pair then broke their grip and shared a brotherly hug before parting once more.

Chapter 2
Gdansk, Republic of Poland, Slavic Federation

Hailing a cab after leaving the bar, Aleksey gave his home address and was taken to the nearby city of Gdansk. A thirty-minute ride in a personal car, the ride took a bit longer in the cab, but it gave him time to sober up and think. The last time he spoke to Tatiana, she had been cold and distant, and he left her clinging to what was a lie at the time. Wanting to make amends, he thought long and hard until he had just the right words to say to make things right between them.

Dropped off a block away from home at his request, Aleksey made a quick stop at a flower shop to pick up a bouquet of assorted flowers before heading to his flat in the Old Town neighborhood. Though the lease was in his name, he wanted to maintain the element of surprise and rang the doorbell. When no one came, he rang the doorbell again and knocked loudly. As before, there was no answer, so he abandoned the idea of surprise and dug into his pocket for his key ring. Slipping the keys into the locks, he opened the door and was met with stale air. A little concerned, for it smelled as if the windows hadn't been opened in weeks, Aleksey stepped inside. Standing at the bottom of the stairs leading up to the flat, he called out to her.

"Tati?" he called out, using her sweet name. "Tati? It's Aleksey!" he continued, but there was no answer. A little unnerved, he headed up the stairs, and upon reaching the landing, he found the living room devoid of life and the couch perfectly set. Taking a few steps, he called out to Tatiana again and looked around for anything out of the ordinary. The flat was well-cleaned and had an almost showroom quality, but this only caused him to worry. He was beginning to wonder if she had left him, and when he went into the bedroom, he had his answer.

Like the living room and kitchen, the bedroom was perfectly cleaned with the bed made, but there was certainly something out of the ordinary. While the room still had the lingering scent of Tatiana's favorite perfume, all her knick-knacks were missing from atop the two dressers they had pushed together. His heart racing as he walked over to her dresser and began pulling out drawers. Inside, he found nothing but open space. His stomach knotting, he didn't want to believe that she had left, but it was obvious she no longer lived there. Still, he held onto hope that there was a benevolent reason behind her absence, and in an instant, he had an idea of how to get an answer.

Returning to the kitchen, Aleksey picked up the telephone from the wall receiver. Turning his attention to a short list of important numbers tacked to the wall beside the phone, he scanned for Tatiana's office number. Punching in the number, he double-checked the time using his wristwatch and waited for someone to answer. In about four and a half rings, he heard the voice of a young woman, but it wasn't Tatiana. Confused, he was quiet for a moment, but he quickly regained his composure.

"Oh, my apologies, I was attempting to reach Tatiana Vishnyova. I must have dialed wrong. Could you transfer me, please?" he said, but there was a somewhat lengthy pause. "Hello?"

"Yes, I'm here, I was just looking up her name in the employee directory," the woman said. Another pause followed, and he soon heard puzzled murmuring. "Excuse me, sorry, but can I put you on hold for a moment?"

"Yes, of course," Aleksey said politely, though he had trouble understanding what the problem could be. Tatiana had worked at the same marketing firm since moving out of Gdansk with him three years prior. Nonetheless, he waited patiently until the woman returned.

"Sir?"

"Yes, I'm here."

"I apologize for the hold, but I was having trouble finding that name in the directory," she said, giving Aleksey a renewed feeling of worry. "I spoke with my manager, and he said that Tatiana Vishnyova had transferred to our Moscow headquarters several months ago."

"Oh, well, that's interesting," Aleksey said, unsure of how to feel about this revelation. "Well, thank you for that information. Have a good day."

Hanging the phone back on the cradle, Aleksey was stunned by the news. Immediately, he tried to conjure a reason why she would have taken a job in Moscow, but it wasn't as unbelievable as he initially thought. She was a Moscow native, after all, and she often lamented about being a fish out of water in Poland. He just didn't want to believe that she would have put in for a transfer without telling him, but even that could be explained. He was abroad for the last nine months and was part of a covert unit for most of that time. Even if she wanted to talk things over, he would have been unavailable.

Feeling sorry for himself, Aleksey retreated to the bed and sat on the edge. Staring at the empty dresser, he resisted the urge to cry but couldn't help but feel sorry for himself. After everything he had gone through, the last thing he needed was to come home to an empty apartment. However, Aleksey wasn't the type to sit around and mope. He was a man of action and integrity, and he didn't give in without a fight. Though it was likely his relationship was over, he needed closure.

Forcing himself to his feet, Aleksey went back to the kitchen and dialed the special prefix for Russia, followed by a number he had memorized long ago. Within three rings, he heard the voice of a woman, bringing a smile to his face. This was his mother, Katarzyna 'Katrin' Rybinski.

"Hello, Mother," Aleksey said with a smile, for the only time he referred to her as mother was when he was being funny.

"Aleksey?" Katrin asked, and he nodded as if she were right there with him.

"Yes, it's me. I just got home a few minutes ago," Aleksey said, and his mother gasped with surprise and excitement. "No, not that home, Gdansk," he was quick to say.

"Oh," she said, her voice deflated. "I was hoping you meant you were at the airport."

"Well, that's kind of why I'm calling," he said, building the anticipation.

"You didn't!" she said in such a way that Aleksey knew she was smiling. "You're out?"

"I haven't yet declined reenlistment, but all things considered, I'll be a civilian in three months. Let's keep that between us for now," Aleksey was quick to say, though he knew there was a good chance his father was already aware. "Also, I have some good news. I'm about to take a ride down to the airport and take the first flight to Moscow."

"Really?" she asked with surprise and excitement, for he wasn't expected until tomorrow. "But wait. What does Tatiana think?" she asked, but Aleksey was quiet. "Aleksey?"

"I don't think it matters too much what she thinks," he said, giving his mother pause.

"Is there something you want to tell me?"

"I came home to an empty apartment," Aleksey admitted. "Everything belonging to Tatiana is gone, and I found out that she transferred her job to Moscow months ago."

"I see," Katrin said slowly, giving Aleksey a feeling that she knew something. "Well, maybe it's better this way."

His brow furrowed, Aleksey felt like something was off. "What do you know?" he asked.

Though Katrin spun her wheels, Aleksey could sense the tension in her voice as she tried to find the right words.

"Mom, what's going on?"

"I don't know anything, Aleksey," Katrin said calmly. "I just know that she's back in Moscow. Maybe she did take a job, and that's all there is to it. I really don't know. It's not like we were ever close. Something tells me that she disliked me as much as I disliked her."

It was at that moment that Aleksey felt his mother had something to do with his present situation. By her own admission, she was never Tatiana's biggest fan. In fact, she told him on more than one occasion that she would have preferred him to find himself a more traditional woman. A homemaker with long dashed dreams of veterinary school, Katrin had a low opinion of modern high-maintenance businesswomen like Tatiana. Further, she much preferred her children to marry someone of Polish ancestry. And though he knew all of this, Aleksey didn't want to accuse Katrin of anything. Instead, he worked toward dropping the subject.

"So, she's really in Moscow?"

"As far as I'm aware," Katrin said. "I thought I saw her on the streets downtown a few times, but you know how looks can be deceiving."

"And you swear you didn't talk to her and say something you shouldn't have?"

Backed into a corner, Katrin folded and finally admitted the truth. "Look, I don't know if things are over between you two, but she called your sister of the blue a few months ago."

"What did she want?"

"She said she had a promotion opportunity at the marketing firm. She said she was going to take it and that she would have talked to you first. However, considering you were overseas, Lena was her next best option."

"That's it? Nothing more?"

"That's what I was told," Katrin said, and as if she could sense the pain and anxiety tearing at her son's heart, she did her best to reassure him that she wasn't lying.

"I didn't say you were," Aleksey said. "I guess I'm just feeling sorry for myself, that's all. Then again, I should have seen this coming."

"Don't blame yourself, Aleksey. It's not your fault. Besides, she knew what she was getting into following you around all these years."

"Thanks, but it kind of is," Aleksey said, knowing that his extended stay in the military was at the center of his relationship problems. "Well, it is what it is. I'll call you when I get to Moscow, all right?"

"Let me know when your flight takes off, so I know when to expect you."

When their conversation ended shortly thereafter, Aleksey returned the phone to the cradle with a bitter sigh. He had a nasty feeling that there was more to the story than what he was being told, but on the same token, he appreciated that he didn't learn anything devastating over the phone and a thousand miles away.

Leaving the kitchen, he took a short walk into the hallway connecting the living room to the bedroom and the bathroom. Stopping at the center of the hall, he walked down memory lane with the visual aid of a dozen or so framed photographs of him and Tatiana taken over the years. In every photograph, they were either locked in a loving embrace or flashing a happy smile in front of some monument or place of interest at that moment in time. Nothing in those photos signaled either was unhappy or looking for an out, so he adjusted his grip on his hope that things weren't as bad as they seemed.

Deciding he had tortured himself long enough, he went into the bedroom to pack a change of clothes and a book to entertain him on the flight home. When he was done, he headed back to the kitchen. With the help of a phone book, he looked up a taxi service and scheduled a trip to the nearby international airport, where he'd purchase a one-way ticket to Moscow. Unfortunately, the only flight available left well after the dinner hour, but there was a silver lining – the airport was a short ride from the bar where he had been drinking earlier that day. Considering the shit they went through back in the Yugo, he had no doubt Miko and the boys would still be there.

Chapter 3

Berlin, Germany

Following a particularly stormy night, it was a cool though dreary spring morning in the German capital. The sun was barely rising and poking through the gray clouds, but Gustav Hagen was already out of the apartment and going about his daily business. A semi-pro kickboxer with aspirations of going fully professional sooner rather than later, he was no stranger to the doctor's office. Fortunately, this visit was a simple checkup to see if he was clear to fight again.

Sitting on the exam table in a private room, Gustav dangled his large feet out of boredom, tapping the heels of his worn leather work boots against the body of the table while he stared at the swirling gray splotch on the white tiles. Eventually, he heard the echo of heavy footsteps in the hallway, followed soon by the sound of the door handle twisting in place. His eyes met the doctor a moment later, but she was too hard to read, for even when the news was good, she wore a stern, if not grim expression.

"How's it looking, Doctor?" Gustav asked, his eyes locked on the X-rays in the doctor's right hand. "Am I good to fight?"

"Your ribs are healing nicely, but I'm afraid you won't be fighting tonight," the Doctor said, crossing the room and placing the X-ray sheets on a backlit screen.

"Well, are they broken or not?" Gustav asked, frustrated by the news.

"They're mostly healed, but I implore you to treat them as if they're still broken," the Doctor said. "I'd recommend at least another two weeks away from any form of physical contact."

"While I appreciate the advice, I have bills to pay," Gustav said in mild frustration. He soon dropped from the table, taking a few steps toward the door before reaching for his leather riding jacket hanging on a nearby hook.

"If this is your primary means of making money, perhaps you should begin to consider a safer profession. Your body will thank you when you're older."

"Not going to happen," Gustav said, zipping up his jacket. "I make more money in one fight than I do in a whole night stocking the bar."

"I'm sure, but bartending doesn't carry a high risk of injury."

"Broken bones heal," Gustav replied, reaching for the door handle.

"Of course, but fighting too soon can cause more serious problems. A punctured lung would be catastrophic," the Doctor warned, but Gustav shook his head. "I'm also worried about your brain."

"It was a lucky shot. It won't happen again."

"At least for another two weeks, right?"

"Sure," Gustav said, causing the doctor to sigh, for she had seen him almost weekly for the last two years and was worried about the damage he was inflicting on his mind and body. However, he was a stubborn man, so rather than try harder to convince him to stay out of the ring, the doctor surrendered and told him to take care. After all, there wasn't anything she could do to stop him. She just hoped his girlfriend would be another voice of reason for once.

While her reckless boyfriend was out visiting the doctor's office, Audra Rozek left her bedroom with a frazzled mane of walnut hair that fell just below her shoulders and slightly obscured her tired green eyes with shaggy bangs she'd later tame. Heading straight for the kitchen, she fetched herself a yogurt and went to the table where her sketchpad was waiting. Taking just one spoonful and setting the yogurt aside, she picked up her pencil and got back to work right where she left off the night before.

A bit of a loner due to the fact she worked odd hours tending bar most nights to pay the bills, Audra didn't have too many friends, so she spent most of her free time at home. However, rather than sitting around the house watching television or playing video games for hours, she read epic novels and historical biographies, listened to a wide array of music, and even tried her hand at poetry and short stories over the years. However, her passion was always art. She had a visual mind and a steady hand, giving her a natural ability to create life-like images with both the pencil and the paintbrush. Having been working at her craft since she was barely a teenager, her work was impressive to most, and though she dreamed of making it her profession one day, she knew better than to think of her work as anything other than a hobby for the moment. Still, she was dedicated to her craft and consistently challenged herself to do something different.

Her current project was creating a cast of characters for a graphic novel she hoped to craft one day. The character slowly coming to life on her pad was a young woman modeled after herself. Of course, the character's features were exaggerated to be a slimmer, more attractive version of herself with an alternative style inspired by her appreciation of the Berlin art scene and Japan's Visual Kei movement.

Particularly proud of this sketch, Audra began filling in the colors using an assortment of colored pencils she kept in a small plastic box. As she carefully selected the colors for her heroine's clothing, she heard the scraping of metal on metal. A few moments later, the lock on the apartment door gave way, and Gustav stepped inside. He was surprised to see that she was awake since she was a notorious night owl.

"I couldn't sleep anymore," Audra replied, never taking her eyes off the sketch.

"How long were you up last night?" he asked as he took off his jacket, but she didn't answer. "Well, alright. Any plans for today?"

"Drawing and painting mostly," she replied, her attention still glued to the character transforming before her eyes.

Appreciating her dedication to her art, he walked to the table and leaned over her shoulder to see what she was drawing. "She's hot," he said, and she looked at him with a smirk.

"She's me."

"Then when do I get to see you in that outfit?" he asked, for she had drawn her character quite sexy, but she shrugged.

"Probably never with the way our finances are looking," she replied, setting down her pencil and sighing as she turned to him with sullen eyes. "Rent's due next week. Are you going to be able to help out this time?"

Avoiding contact, he asked, "Do we have to do this right now?"

"No time like the present," she said, for the household finances were why she couldn't sleep. As expected, he shook his head, turning her mood from calm to angry in an instant. "Dammit, Gustav! I can't keep paying for everything. I'm working myself to death."

"What the hell! I didn't even say anything," he defended, as he stomped away to the living room. "And yes, I'll pay this month. Fuck."

Feeling bad for losing her temper with him, Audra was quick to apologize. The feeling was mutual, so he walked over to her and looked down into her emerald eyes as she looked up at him from her chair.

"Look, I know things suck right now, but there's a tournament tonight. If I win, I'll have enough to pay two months of rent. How does that sound?"

"What did the doctor say?" she asked, but he gave her a bullshit story that he was cleared to fight. This incited her to poke his affected ribs, causing his face to contort, though he kept quiet in hopes of getting her off his back. "Play tough all you want, they're still broken."

"They're bruised," he said. "I'm good to fight."

"Did the doctor say that, or are you just desperate to get me off your ass?"

Sighing, because he was tired of her constant barrages, he asked if she wanted him to pay his share of the rent.

"I'd like that, yes, but I'd also prefer you to limit your trips to the doctor's office. You're causing serious long-term damage to yourself."

Her words echoed the sentiment of the doctor, but Gustav didn't want to listen to her either. "It's just a couple of bruised ribs. They'll heal in time."

"I was talking about your brain," she said. "I know you're a good fighter, and you'll win the tournament if you can fight through the pain, but if you don't go pro soon, you might have to consider hanging it up and getting a real job."

"Hang it up? I'm twenty-six years old, Audra. I've got time left. Besides, am I not helping put food on the table?"

"When you're not sidelined with an injury, sure, but it won't last forever. Most semi-pro fighters retire by thirty. What happens then? Are you going to keep working at the Kitty Kat, stocking the bar and making sure no one roughs up the girls in the VIP room?"

Shrugging, he said they'd figure it out, but she was tired of that line.

"Of course," she said, rolling her eyes. "Look, I can't be the one to carry the burden for the rest of time, Gustav. You need to figure something out, and sooner rather than later."

Feeling like he was going to be badgered if he stayed any longer, Gustav said nothing before he turned and walked to the front door of the apartment.

"Where are you going?" she called after him, and he replied over his shoulder.

"To get my paycheck. Maybe that will get you off my ass for a while."

"Whatever... dickhead," Audra muttered to herself before calling out to him again. "On your way back, could you get more yogurt? The stuff in the fridge went bad."

Ignoring her, he stepped out of the apartment and slammed the door behind him. This prompted Audra to shake her head and wonder why she bothered to put up with him anymore. After all, he was far from the charming young man she had fallen for in her first year at university. In many ways, he was the opposite of that sweet young man, and he didn't seem to want to make any meaningful changes. As far as she could see, he just spent all his free time working out, training at her uncle's gym, and prize-fighting. To make matters worse, she felt as though he was getting dumber and cruder by the day.

Sighing, Audra wondered if she would be better off alone. Then again, if that were the case, she'd have to give up her apartment on the west end of the city and move back to the old neighborhood. Just the thought of going back to live in a dingy plattenbau apartment in the middle of gang territory made her skin crawl, even if she was untouchable there.

Heading over to the Marzahn neighborhood where Audra grew up, Gustav stepped through the front doors of the Kitty Kat Club. Given the time of day, the gentleman's club was devoid of life, save for a crew of cleaners tasked with making the whole place shine before service resumed at noon. Unable to spot the day manager, Gustav quietly made his way to the back office to see if he was there. When he stepped into the office, he found the room was deserted. Shrugging, he knew where the paychecks could be found, so he helped himself. However, he was barely able to get a finger on his paycheck before he heard someone clear his throat behind him. Turning to look over his shoulder, he saw Stefan - one of the owner's bodyguards - standing in the doorway. He had no idea why anyone but the cleaners would be there at this hour, but he had no choice but to hear the man out.

"Can I help you?" Gustav asked, and Stefan spoke like a noble servant.

"Mr. Rozek would like to speak with you," he said. "He's waiting upstairs."

Though wanting to sigh, for he simply wanted to get his check and go, Gustav accepted his orders without question. He then followed Stefan back into the public space and up a flight of red-carpeted stairs leading to the owner's private office. It was there that he was left alone with Richard Rozek, a man he deeply feared and loathed. While Richard was Audra's brother and Gustav's employer, Gustav's fear and dislike of this man went far deeper than the casual disrespect he was treated with daily. It was the way Richard presented himself to the world and how he ran his business empire.

Richard was an undeniably attractive man in his early thirties. He was a powerhouse real estate mogul, and he wore his wealth like a badge of honor. He had a fake tan, bleached blonde hair, perfect teeth, and often wore a fancy Italian suit and a pricey watch. However, underneath the suit was a ruthless gangster who didn't bat an eyelash at the thought of killing anyone who crossed him or posed a threat to his business empire. Making matters worse, he was backed by a notorious outlaw biker gang, The Huns, and was rumored to be in bed with the Russian Mafia. For those reasons alone, Gustav kept his mouth shut and spoke only when spoken to, for it was a rare occasion to have a private audience with the infamous Mr. Rozek. This left Gustav scared to death, for considering how bad things were going with Audra lately, there was a chance he might not walk out of that office. Regardless, he faced the man with dignity and respect.

"You're ten hours early for your shift. The place isn't even open for another three hours. What are you doing here?" Richard asked, sulking in his chair with his hands in a flexing steeple formation near his chest.

"I was at the doctor's office and figured I'd pick up my check while I was out."

"Good news?" Richard asked, his pale green eyes staring directly into Gustav's own deep brown orbs.

"Doctor says the ribs are healing nicely."

"So, are you good to fight, or can I lean on you for an extra shift or two? We parted ways with Nils last night."

Unsure what the bouncer in question had done to be fired, but unwilling to ask, Gustav replied truthfully.

"Doctor says I need to keep it quiet for a while, but I need the money."

"So what are you telling me?"

"I can work any night but tonight," Gustav said, and Richard nodded.

"You know that if money is that tight, I have extra work for you outside of the club."

Not wanting to get himself involved with Richard any further than being an hourly employee at one of his legitimate businesses, Gustav politely declined. "There's a tournament with a big purse up for grabs tonight. If I win, I'm set for a couple of months," he said, but Richard glared at him.

"Those ribs are only going to get worse if you don't listen to your doctor, and my sister can't keep carrying your weight," he coolly warned. "I'll pay you handsomely for the work I have available. Otherwise, I can always give you a loan."

The offer of a loan resonated in Gustav's mind, bringing him back to his childhood when his father made the mistake of borrowing money from the Russian Mafia to cover his expenses for the month after spending it all to bribe himself out of a run-in with the Stasi. That debt took years to pay off and tore his family apart.

"I appreciate the offer, but it was a lucky kick. I should have kept my guard lower," Gustav said, trying to keep things calm. "Besides, you know I'd rather earn my keep."

"That's why I offered you extra work before I offered a loan," Richard said. "I'd just hate to see you end up in the hospital, leaving Audra to pay all the bills for that fancy Tempelhof flat. It's not fair, nor is it manly, to leave the burden on your woman."

Unnerved by the shift in Richard's tone, for he was fiercely protective of his sister and not afraid to show his disapproval of him, Gustav swallowed hard.

"I'm doing best," he started, but Richard called his bluff.

"Doing your best is not chasing that stupid dream of yours while my sister works her ass off behind a bar instead of using that degree she worked so hard to earn. Unless you shape up, she's going to realize you're not worth her time or effort."

Biting his lip, for his greatest fear was losing Audra after so many years together, Gustav boldly asked what kind of work he could take on. However, Richard smirked and waved his hand at him.

"Come after your fight, and maybe we'll talk," he said slyly. "Unless, of course, those ribs give out and you end up in the hospital."

Frustrated by how quickly Richard could go from friendly to cruel, Gustav swallowed his pride and nodded in acceptance. He was then told to "kindly fuck off."

Chapter 4

Moscow, Republic of Russia, Slavic Federation

Taking an early night flight home after a few hours of drinking and several heated games of darts, Aleksey arrived in Moscow shortly before midnight. Keeping his promise to his mother, he called home as soon as he could, but he declined a ride home. It was late after all, and though his mother was a homemaker, he didn't want her to have to drive an hour round trip. Opting for a taxi, he arrived at his family home in the Manor District, where he received a quiet but loving welcome home from his parents while his sister remained in bed, seemingly unaware that her brother had arrived.

Spared a hangover thanks to his method of drinking a glass of water between each beer or shot, Aleksey opened his eyes the next morning and found himself in his old bedroom. Despite hitting the pillow in the early hours of the morning, his body was so well-tuned to his work schedule that he had risen with the morning sun. Of course, he would have enjoyed a few extra hours in bed – a privilege rarely enjoyed while on active duty – he was a notoriously light sleeper, and the house was active with the heavy footsteps on the stairs and the clanging of pans in the kitchen.

Unable to fall back asleep, he lay on his back and just enjoyed the calming songs of the birds just outside his window. He soon got to thinking about the dilemma at hand with Tatiana, but his mind soon drifted to the comforting thought of seeing that pretty smile as he appeared at her door unannounced. He soon forced himself out of bed, for there was a lot to accomplish before that moment, and he wanted to see her as soon as possible. But first, he had to see his family for the first time in almost a year.

While Aleksey finished toiling in the bathroom, the rest of the family was seated at the breakfast table, waiting for him to make his appearance. While Aleksey had seen his parents the night before, Lena was in bed due to having an important academic exam in the morning, so she was eager to see him. Soon enough, he made his way down the stairs at the front of the house and made his way to the table. His father was the first in his path, but he simply patted his shoulder and approached his mother. Hugging her warmly from behind, he gave Katrin a quick kiss on the cheek before laying his eyes on Lena.

"There's my baby sister," he said, though Lena was a young woman nearing the end of her undergraduate studies at the prestigious Moscow State University. Of course, he'd always think of her as his sweet little sister, no matter her age.

"Lena starts her final exams today," Katrin said, her face and voice brimming with pride.

"That's right. How are you feeling?" Aleksey asked as he walked around the table to hug his sister.

"Scared shitless," Lena said, just as Aleksey hugged her from behind. She then heard him whisper some brotherly advice into her ear.

"If you studied hard, you'll do fine," he said. "If not, marry someone rich. You're pretty enough."

"Aleksey!" Katrin scolded. "What kind of advice is that for your sister?"

"I was just kidding, Mom," Aleksey said, grinning as he took his seat across from his father. "Besides, she's a brain. She's going to do fine."

"Fine won't cut it," said Aleksander. "Lena still has her sights on veterinarian school. Isn't that right, sweetheart?"

"That's the plan," Lena said with a smile, for it had always been her dream to work with animals.

"That's quite the goal," Aleksey said, clearly impressed with her aspirations. "What schools are you looking at?"

"Wroclaw, preferably, but Warsaw is my close second," she replied, causing their mother to cast a muted smile while Aleksander remained silent.

"The old country, huh?" Aleksey said. "Why not continue in Moscow?"

"Because as soon as she graduates, we're moving back home," said Katrin, bringing Aleksander to look at his wife with contempt.

"We're not going anywhere," Aleksander said, annoyed that she had even mentioned such a thing, but his wife disagreed.

"We're going to win, Alek," she said, but Aleksander ignored her.

"The polls haven't even opened yet," he grumbled, before he reached for a nearby bowl of fried potatoes.

"Secession is really popular back home, Dad," Lena said, but Aleksander didn't want to hear it.

"This is your home, Lena," he said firmly, before looking at his wife. "Now let's eat our breakfast and talk about something more important than politics. God knows I hear enough of that drivel at the office."

Despite being stuck on a base or operating in a foreign land for much of the last decade, Aleksey was keenly aware that his home country was voting to secede from the Slavic Federation. Though he was surprised to see an independence referendum happening, he wasn't surprised to see his mother eager to return to their homeland, while his father was not. This wasn't because Aleksander had no love for his homeland, but because of his profession. He was Chief of the General Staff, thus by extension a trusted advisor to the Premier. Many believed Sergei Medvedev was leading the Slavic world back to the imperial age, so men like Aleksander had to be careful. Aside from the death of communism, little had changed in Russia since the fall of the Soviet Union, especially with a former KGB colonel holding the reins of the federation. So, hoping to put things at ease, Aleksander turned to Aleksey.

"Why don't you tell us about your latest adventure abroad?"

"Not much to talk about. Spent a lot of time at my workstation or in the water, dreaming of better things," Aleksey said, somewhat distantly, for he didn't want to discuss what he really had been up to. "When we went ashore, it was rarely somewhere I wanted to be."

"Has the service lost its appeal?" Aleksander asked, but Aleksey just picked at his food. "I'll take it that as yes."

"I'm just tired of being away so much," Aleksey said, continuing to pick at his food, though he wasn't all that hungry at this point. He then looked up with a reserved smile. "It's good to be home."

Feeling like something was bothering Aleksey deep down, Aleksander put his fork down and looked at his son with calm, fatherly eyes. "If there's something you'd like to say, we can step away."

Looking at his father, Aleksey silently accepted the offer with a nod. Aleksander wiped his mouth and pushed back from the table. The two men then headed down the hall and around the corner, climbing the rear stairwell to the second floor.

Now standing in Aleksander's study, the two men stood just a few feet apart with the door closed. Aleksander motioned for Aleksey to sit, but he didn't want to be long, so he spoke directly.

"I'm thinking about leaving the service," Aleksey said, expecting a reaction from his father, but he was silent. "This last tour was hell on me and I--"

"This is about Tatiana, isn't it?"

"Partially, yes," Aleksey admitted. "I didn't have a whole lot of contact with her this time, and I'm concerned we're growing apart."

"That's natural for someone in your shoes," Aleksander said, giving Aleksey the feeling there was something that needed to be said. "Did she say something?"

"Not that I'm aware of," Aleksander said, shrugging.

"What about Mom or Lena?"

"If she did, they didn't say anything to me." Aleksander said. Just then, there was a knock at the door, and Katrin let herself in a moment later.

"Everything all right in here?"

"We're fine. Just having a man-to-man," Aleksander said.

"Well, your breakfast is getting cold, and Lena needs to get to school soon."

"I'll take her," Aleksey said, for it was an opportunity to get answers.

"Fine by me," Aleksander said, knowing what Aleksey was up to. "We'll finish this conversation later."

Feeling like something was amiss, Aleksey quietly left the study before his parents, giving Katrin concern. Before Aleksander could leave, she gripped him by the arm and asked what they were talking about.

"Girl problems," Aleksander replied, and his wife's eyes lit up.

"You didn't tell him, did you?"

"No, and it's best he sees it for himself first," Aleksander said, for the last thing he needed was to get involved in another man's personal life. "I have a feeling he's going over there after he drops off Lena."

Sighing, Katrin dreaded the outcome, for she had seen Aleksey's girlfriend in public with another man. She hoped her eyes had deceived her, but she was certain, so she swore not to say anything. They then left to return to the breakfast table, but by then Aleksey was already in the garage, warming up the engine of his mother's sedan as Lena gathered her study materials. Not long after, Aleksander headed out for the city, for though he commanded from behind a desk in the Russian capital, his job remained demanding of his time and attention.

Chapter 5

Moscow, Republic of Russia, Slavic Federation

Host to many spacious homes and manicured plots of semi-forested land, the crown jewel of Moscow's Manor District was Premier's mansion, Medvedev Manor. The largest home in the entire district, it was set atop a piece of land more than three times the size of the other lots afforded to the Premier's closest allies. The manor doubled as the official residence of the Russian President and the unofficial residence of the Premier of the Federation, both of whom were Sergei Medvedev. Of course, due to the Medvedev administration's uncompromising position that the upper echelons of armed forces be headquartered in the most populous city in the Federation, the President's official residence in Senatgrad was essentially the secondary residence. This move, as with many made by the seemingly permanent head of the federal government - such as the abolishment of political term limits and intervention in Yugoslavia - made some wonder if Sergei Medvedev was slowly transforming the Slavic Federation into a new Russian Empire. Fortunately, the people of the Federation's many autonomous republics hadn't forgotten the revolution they had won against the Soviet Union and its allies just twenty-odd years prior. Hence, Poland was boldly defying the 'tyrant in Moscow' by making a spectacle out of their bid for secession for the entire world to see. After all, the Slavic Federation was still a democracy on paper, and secession remained a right of the individual republics guaranteed by the constitution Sergei had sworn to uphold at each of his inaugurations.

Seated in his home theater with his wife by his side, Sergei Medvedev sulked on his side of a black leather loveseat. The large projection screen before them was displaying a news program from the Russian state news corporation, and the image was distressing. Countless Polish citizens, young and old, rich and poor, had lined up double-file by the hundreds at a Warsaw polling center. Some were waving small replicas of the Polish national flag or the banner of the Home Army; one man even wore a full-sized flag like a cape. Meanwhile, others either remained stoned-faced or smiled in sweet defiance as the camera panned past them. It was clear that secession was overwhelmingly popular; that angered Sergei deeply. If he had his way, the mere suggestion of seceding from the Federation would have been the death knell for any politician willing to champion such an insult. After all, the reasoning for the secession was largely claimed to be a response to his third term as Premier, following a hotly contested victory over the only politician able to keep pace with his propaganda machine and emerge as a popular figure in the election.

Despite all accusations of voter intimidation and fraud being proven false in a court of law, the Polish president-elect, Filip Bednarz - the man that Sergei had narrowly defeated in pursuit of his third term - had remained a constant thorn in his side in the two years since with his constant call for secession. He played a leading role in the formation of the populist Polish Liberation Party and had recently captured the office of the President of Poland by a landslide. Sergei did not doubt that Bednarz would not let his presidency go to waste. He would surely use his position as Poland's head of state to ensure Poland's entrance into NATO and the burgeoning European Union. Such moves would be catastrophic to the reigning Premier's ambitions for a united Slavic people.

Powerless to stop the Polish populists and their successful attempts to turn an economic downturn into a rallying cry for independence, Sergei could only stand by and allow the law to be carried out as it was written. However, he never expected Bednarz and his cadre of nationalist firebrands to get as far as they did. Never in his life did he expect to see such enthusiasm for breaking away. It was a painful reminder of the events known as Prague Spring and the multi-national war of independence that followed the Warsaw Pact's decision to invade Czechoslovakia to end the nation's reforms. To further rub the salt in the festering wounds of his ego, Russian reporters echoed the political language of his Polish adversaries, bringing his blood to a boil.

"They keep calling this thing a fucking independence vote," Sergei groaned. "This is a referendum. They'll still have to plead their case before the Senate."

"What do you expect from a free press?" said the First Lady, Viktoriya Medvedeva, with a shrug. "Then again, if we still had state-run media, they'd say we're no better than the Soviets."

"Yes, but there's a benefit to having journalists under your thumb," Sergei said, but Viktoriya rolled her eyes. "I can't believe a group calling itself the Polish Liberation Party could gain so much traction. Did no one question how radical that sounds?"

The Premier gritted his teeth in frustration. "We should have crushed the bastards when we had the chance."

"Easy now, we can't play into their hands," Viktoriya said, resting her hand soothingly on her husband's leg. "And yes, people do recognize them for what they are, but we need to let them have their vote. It's how our system works."

"Democracy is bullshit. We should have never given the republics so much power," Sergei grumbled, so his wife gripped his leg tightly, grabbing his attention.

"You worry too much," Viktoriya said. "Even if they win today, they won't make it past the Senate, and that's a promise," she said with a devious smile. "And when they lose, we'll make sure no one hears from these radicals again."

While pleased to see that his wife saw eye to eye with him on the matter, Sergei couldn't help but wonder aloud how the secessionists were able to secure so much power so quickly.

"Their people were hit hardest by the recession. They're desperate and angry with a charismatic leader at the helm, but this is just a vocal minority lashing out," Viktoriya said. "I highly doubt the majority believes Poland would be better off on its own."

"I certainly hope you're right. It would be a terrible embarrassment if Poland secedes."

"They won't," Viktoriya said confidently. "Like I said, even if they vote to leave, their representatives must face the Senate, and that's where this foolishness will end. There's no way they'll earn a majority vote in their favor."

"What makes you so sure?" Sergei asked curiously, and his wife smiled once more.

"We've been in this damn recession for nearly two years now. How many republics have argued for independence?"

"Just Poland."

"Then we must be doing something right, no?"

"Perhaps, but if the radicals get their way—"

"It'll be by a slim margin, and we'll crush them on the Senate floor," Viktoriya said with an almost arrogant confidence.

While he certainly appreciated his wife's enthusiasm and confidence, Sergei's attention had been drawn back to the television, for one of the public faces of the Polish Liberation Party had arrived to cast his vote.

"Look at that smug bastard," Sergei said, referring to Roman Wilczynski – a firebrand senator from the Zielona Góra region and a prominent secessionist. "Arrives in a limousine and cuts the line like he's—"

"You?" Viktoriya asked with a smirk, causing Sergei to frown. "Don't throw rocks in glass houses, dear."

"That wasn't necessary," Sergei said lowly. "You know I'm a man of the people."

"And he is, too, but he's also a very important figure in Polish politics. He doesn't have the time to stand in line," Viktoriya said. "But again, don't you worry. As soon as this little spectacle is brought to an end, he'll fade into obscurity. I assure you."

"Let's hope so," Sergei said as he sank into his seat, nervously watching the television until his wife shut it off. "What are you doing?" he asked with a slighted tone.

"Enough of that for now. You're going to drive yourself mad," she said, remote still in hand. "Let's go about our day. We'll get the results tonight."

"Perhaps you're right. I can't run half a continent from my living room," he said, forcing himself up from his seat. "I should head to the office. I'm sure there's a media circus forming by now."

Reaching out and taking her husband's hand as he passed, Viktoriya looked at him with soft eyes. "Today is an extremely important day for this grand experiment of ours. Please, don't let your anxiety drive you mad today, especially in front of the cameras. We need you calm and composed. The whole world is watching, Sergei."

Looking down upon his wife with lustful eyes, Sergei suggested a quick rendezvous in the bedroom to calm his nerves. Unfortunately for his ego, she turned him down for a more pressing matter – her daily visit with her personal trainer before heading into the office.

"I think Marko can wait," Sergei suggested, but Viktoriya was steadfast in her resolve.

"You know that I'm punctual," she said calmly. "I'll be right here for whatever you need tonight. Now get going, the people are waiting."

"The people can wait, and so can Marko," Sergei said rather forcefully. "In fact, I'm starting to wonder what's more important in your life."

"Alright, that's enough," Viktoriya said calmly, for she could hear the anxiety in her husband's voice. "You have nothing to worry about. It's purely platonic between us. If it weren't for him, I wouldn't look this good at my age. Now, would I?"

Looking at her in hopes his spy skills hadn't dulled to the point he could no longer sense a lie through a person's expression, Sergei watched his wife closely. Yet, as he stared, he found himself admiring the beauty before him and cracked a smile, for despite closing in on forty-five years, she didn't look a day past thirty. Her all-natural diet, regular exercise, and a bit of cosmetic work did wonders for her in more ways than one., Of course, she was more than just a trophy wife, but the love of his life, so his anxiety never truly left him. Regardless, he put up a front.

"Tonight then," he said, and she smiled. "After today, I'll surely need the comfort."

"I'll tell Marko to go easy on me," she said with a wink, but he wasn't amused.

"If there's something unprofessional going on between you two, he's a dead man," Sergei warned, but Viktoriya kept her cool in the face of her husband's sudden shift in mood.

"You know what? You're right. You need to be on your best behavior today. Let's calm those nerves," she replied, before getting up from the loveseat and taking his hand.

A smile creeping across his face, Sergei was more than happy to oblige his wife's sudden decision to please him. However, despite Viktoriya putting his needs before her own in a fairly one-sided bit of lovemaking, he left the manor still unable to shake the idea that his wife was going behind his back. He had heard far too many rumors to think otherwise. It didn't help that she had a naturally flirtatious personality and tended to dress young for her age, but he didn't so much mind her fashion choices. She was a beautiful woman blessed with a body that seemed to defy age and turn heads of all ages. However, something he struggled with was the fact that she was nearly twenty years his junior and his mistress during his previous marriage. All of this, coupled with the fact that Sergei was well past his prime and had let himself go due to the nature of his work, kept him anxious about his wife's loyalty despite never seeing a shred of evidence to confirm his suspicions. However, as soon as he stepped out of his manor and headed for the helicopter waiting on the south lawn, his attention was locked on the business at hand. His concerns about his wife would have to wait until that night, for he had an empire to run, or so he liked to say.

Chapter 6

Moscow, Republic of Russia, Slavic Federation

Dropping his sister off at the university campus two hours ahead of the exam, Aleksey took some time to quiz her on some of the tougher material to ensure she was ready. Living up to Aleksey's belief that she was a brain, she was well-prepared. Not even the toughest of questions staggered her, giving him the feeling that she was going to do well enough to land her name on the shortlist for entry into the veterinary program at whatever graduate school she decided to attend. So, with studying out of the way, Aleksey decided it was a fine time to discuss what Tatiana had said to her while he was overseas. At first, Lena was hesitant to speak, but after some pressure, she furrowed her brow and got defensive.

"Wait, how do you even know she talked to me?" she asked, but Aleksey's expression was more than enough for her to draw a simple conclusion. "Ugh, thanks, Mom."

"It's nothing personal, she means well," Aleksey said, but Lena was growing agitated.

"Yeah, that's because Mom hates her," Lena said, but Aleksey shrugged, for it wasn't a secret that Katrin disliked Tatiana. "But look, I really didn't want to be the one to tell you this, but—"

"It's over, isn't it?" Aleksey asked, and Lena nodded. "Fucking hell."

"I'm sorry, I really am," Lena said, but Aleksey was quiet. "She didn't say why. She just said she couldn't get a hold of you, and that she was going home."

"Wait, did she break up with me, or not? Sounds more like she was just homesick."

"I think it's best that you consider it so."

"What's that supposed to mean? Either she told you to tell me we're through, or she didn't."

"Look, she just told me that she did a lot of thinking since you last left and she needed to follow her dreams, or some crap like that. I told her to think it through, but she said she already made the decision, and she was following through with the transfer."

"So, did she imply we were breaking up or not?" Aleksey pressed, making Lena appear visibly distraught as if she was holding something back. "Lena!"

"Look, she didn't say it then, but she did later, ok?" Lena said, and though she wanted to tell him straight, she knew it was better that he saw it all for himself. So, reaching into her bookbag, she pulled out a notebook and a pen. Scribbling down an address for an apartment in the upscale Christye Prudy neighborhood, she handed it over with anxious eyes.

"This is her current address as far as I know," she said, and Aleksey accepted it. He immediately recognized the street and wondered just what kind of promotion she had gotten. "Can I go now? I need to focus on my test."

"Sure, go ahead," Aleksey said with a cool demeanor, for he was actively plotting out how he'd approach Tatiana and attempt to salvage their relationship. "Thanks."

"Yeah, no problem," she said, and she hugged him briefly, wishing him the best of luck before leaving.

Waiting until his sister disappeared into a nearby building, Aleksey fired up the car and put it into gear. Knowing the city quite well, he headed over to Tatiana's new neighborhood and drove around until he found a florist. Purchasing a bouquet for his estranged sweetheart, he wandered over to a phone booth and attempted to call her cell phone, but the number had been disconnected. Though this was a bad sign, he went back to the car and made his way to Tatiana's new home street. When he found the address, he was impressed that the building towered over the neighborhood's namesake ponds. Clearly, she had gotten quite the promotion to afford such a lavish apartment, but an expensive apartment didn't translate to ease of parking in Moscow. Even in the warm seasons, parking was extremely tight, and Aleksey spent a good deal of time circling the neighborhood in search of a single open space. When he finally found an open spot, he was several blocks from the apartment. However, he didn't mind the walk so long as he was able to see his darling Tati and convince her to give him a second chance if he didn't reenlist.

His back moist from the long march from his car, Aleksey approached the luxury apartments where his sweetheart now resided. Still a bit surprised that she was living in such an expensive part of the city, he wondered what could have changed in her life. He pondered this thought through a long climb up the stairs to the sixth floor of the complex, but he couldn't rationalize how she could afford such a place. While her career in marketing certainly kept her bank account in the black, she had never mentioned a big promotion or even pursuing a better job. Then again, their time to talk was always so limited, he reckoned she just never had the chance. After all, he tended to dominate their conversations due to her reserved nature.

Reaching the sixth floor, Aleksey made his way through a fireproof door into a brightly lit corridor lined with stylish doors and fresh gunmetal gray carpeting. His senses were soon struck by the fading smell of fresh paint and carpeting still lingering in the air. He found it to be a refreshing alternative to the scent of the sea, the stale air aboard a ship, and the acrid stench of a warzone.

Now making his way through the hall, her apartment number memorized, Aleksey's head swiveled left to right with each passing door as he eagerly closed in on his target. When he finally found her door, he faced it straight on and took a deep breath. He had no idea if she'd be happy to see him or not. Their last phone call was unnervingly blunt and short, but it was too late now. He didn't come this far to walk away now. So, with a deep breath held in his lungs, he raised his fist and tapped it firmly against the heavy door.

His muscles tensing, Aleksey eagerly awaited the long-awaited sight of the flaxen-haired beauty he dreamt of so often. Smiling brightly while he clutched the flowers in one hand, holding them to his chest, Aleksey listened for signs of life beyond the door. Though he heard a rustling inside, there was a long pause, and his smile soon faded. He was sure someone had seen him through the peephole by then, and he started to wonder if she was pretending not to be home. For a moment, he thought to leave, but then he heard the working of the locks beyond the door. A moment later, he was faced not with the woman he hoped to marry but a tall, handsome man with a chiseled frame that his white undershirt and gym shorts could barely conceal.

Taken aback by the presence of such a beautiful man, or anyone but Tatiana for that matter, Aleksey said nothing. Instead, he just stood there and stared blankly at the man before him. It wasn't long before the stranger broke the silence.

"Can I help you?" the strange man asked, one hand on the doorknob from the inside while the other rested on the doorframe.

His mind raced as he tried to justify the man's presence without resorting to the absolute worst-case scenario, but it was impossible. This man was far too attractive to be a simple roommate, and he was sure he had the right apartment. So, with his swirling emotions threatening to crack his voice and make this otherwise hardened soldier look weak in front of this stranger, Aleksey kept his words brief. Of course, his words came out softer than normal.

"I'm here to see Tatiana. Is she in?" Aleksey asked, but the man just stared at him with skeptical eyes.

"Who are you?" the man asked, seemingly completely ignorant of his status in Tatiana's life. "Are you a friend or something?"

Before Aleksey could answer, he saw his sweetheart appear in the background. Though it was only a brief glimpse, he was able to see that she was well along with a pregnancy that was certainly not his doing. Though he toiled inside, he kept his emotions in check and spoke calmly.

"My name is Aleksey," Aleksey began, but the man had noticed the flowers and cut him off before he could say more.

"What's with the flowers?"

"They were meant for my girlfriend, but I guess I was mistaken," Aleksey said. Turning on his heels, he began marching away, leaving the stranger dumbfounded.

"Is this some kind of joke?" the man called out as Aleksey continued to walk away, the flowers still in his hand.

"Good day, sir," Aleksey called back firmly. Doing well to keep his emotions in check, Aleksey marched down the hall, refusing to shed a single tear even though his heart had just been ripped from his chest and shredded before his eyes.

Leaving the building without incident, Aleksey made it halfway to his car before he realized the flowers were still in his hand. Though they were unquestionably beautiful, and his mother would have appreciated them, they stood as a stark reminder of the insult he had just endured. Finally letting his anger get the best of him, he threw the bouquet into the street and continued his bitter march back to the car. When he got inside, he sat there quietly for a few moments and tried to think of when his relationship could have died. The moments that came to mind seemed innumerable, and he felt sick from the shame and anger that threatened to overwhelm him. Standing strong, he refused to allow himself to cry. He couldn't let her have the last laugh. She was a coward for what she had done to him, but he wasn't going to let her win. She was in the past now, and all he could do was force himself to move forward. However, that would prove easier said than done, and it was a long drive back to the Manor District. At some point, he was going to break down, but he was too proud to face his parents at his lowest point. He needed to regain control of his emotions and face them like a man, so he fired up the engine and joined the flow of traffic. Where he was headed was anyone's guess, but he wouldn't return home to face his parents until he could do so in a calm, dignified way.

Chapter 7

Berlin, Germany

Dressed only in tight-fitting boxing shorts and cloth hand-wraps, Gustav's fists clenched tightly as they smashed into the practice mitts held steady by his trainer, Jens Groth. One after another, Gustav's fists collided with a mitt in a well-rehearsed combination of strikes and evasion techniques. His hands flowed from pure muscle memory built up from hours of training leading up to every fight. His combination went as follows: jab-cross-jab-cross-duck-weave-right hook-left hook-duck-weave-left uppercut-right uppercut.

A tall, well-built man, Jens stood about a head over Gustav and would be ranked in a higher weight class, yet each blow rattled his resistance. Gustav wasn't the biggest, nor was he the tallest man in the light-heavyweight division, but he was a powerhouse and quick on his feet, and his punches were far from his only weapons. The deadliest weapon in the young fighter's arsenal was a pair of thick legs that gave his kicks the force of a sledgehammer. However, Gustav had spent the morning working on his punching, giving Jens some concern that his best fighter wasn't quite up for the tournament that night. Of course, Jens was a tough-as-nails trainer who believed wholeheartedly in the philosophy that weakness cannot be tolerated. So, in the interest of seeing his gym take the big win that night, he told Gustav to take five and come back prepared to work the legs.

Doing as he was told, Gustav backed off and wandered over to a row of benches along the back wall of the dingy gym space. Fumbling with the lid of his water bottle thanks to his sweaty hand wraps, he spilled a bit of water on the mats, but he wiped it away with his foot. Then, with both hands holding the bottle as an infant would, he drank more than he could handle. The cool water washing over his hot, sweaty body felt great, but the feeling wouldn't last. So, taking a seat on the bench, he leaned forward and observed his surroundings.

A small gym owned and operated by Jens, the place had a nasty reputation among the martial arts community for being home to some of the most vicious fighters in

Berlin. While this wasn't exactly false, the reputation stemmed from the fact that it was frequented by members of the outlaw motorcycle club, The Huns – a group that Jens led as National President. However, most of the fighters who trained there, Gustav included, were not Huns. Of course, all were friendly with the club, and a chosen few were prospective members – 'prospects' in the club's lexicon.

While Gustav certainly had the qualities the Huns looked for in potential prospects, he never seriously entertained the thought of joining. He was there to chase his dream of becoming a professional fighter, not to become a gangster. Truthfully, the only reason he trained there was because of the reputation the gym had for training winners. In fact, Jens was once a revered champion in the former East Germany's professional kickboxing circuit. The only reason he stopped fighting and focused on training was a career-ending knee injury. Of course, that didn't mean he couldn't spar, and judging by the gear he could be seen putting on, Gustav had a feeling he was about to throw down with the 'Rottweiler' himself.

Head to toe in sparring gear, Jens squared off with Gustav in the training ring at the center of the gym. While it wasn't exactly a spectacle to see the head trainer get into the ring with a high-level student, a few of the fighters and staff gathered around to watch.

"This is just a test to see if you're in fighting shape," Jens said as the two touched gloves. "Hit as hard as you want to be hit."

Nodding, Gustav backed off four paces and dropped into a fighting stance. His left hand held out a few inches from his face, while his right hand was held in a guard position by his chin. It was a standard fighting stance, and Jens did just the same, even as he began to close the distance.

Circling each other like a pair of sharks with blood in the water, the two men locked eyes and threw shadow punches and kicks to lure the other into an opening attack. Neither would take the bait, so Jens stood still and ordered Gustav to give him his best shot.

Smirking at the order, Gustav advanced with three feigned jabs followed quickly with a snap kick from the right. Seeing the move coming, Jens easily blocked the kick with a lift of his leg and countered with a hard right cross that Gustav dodged and countered with a nasty head kick. While the blow met its intended target, Gustav felt a powerful bolt of pain run through his body as his midsection stretched to execute the technique.

While the pain was manageable, he nonetheless backed off while Jens stood his ground in a defensive stance.

"Are you good?" Jens asked, watching as Gustav rubbed his side and twisted his core as if trying to mask the source of the pain.

"Tweaked a muscle. I'll be fine," Gustav said, and he immediately took up a fighting stance, but Jens didn't move. Knowing he was being tested, Gustav moved in and tried a quick jab-cross combination followed by a push kick to the belly to put some space between them.

Pushed back by the basic kick to the abdomen, Jens bounced back with a spinning heel kick aimed at the midsection. Gustav caught the leg with both hands and retaliated with a hard side kick that barely missed Jens' sternum. Unlike the head kick, Gustav felt no pain, so he pushed the leg away with a mighty thrust. Knowing what would happen, he ducked just in time to avoid taking a jump spin kick to the face. He would return fire with a rising uppercut that purposely missed Jens's jaw to throw him off balance enough to leave him open to another head kick, and it worked. But just as before, the kick sent a searing shot of pain down Gustav's side, prompting Jens to call for a timeout.

Walking to the corner, Gustav draped his arms over the top ropes and leaned against the turnbuckle. As he did this, Jens walked over and removed his mouth guard to speak clearly.

"Your ribs are hurting you pretty bad yet."

"Only when I reach too high," Gustav said. "They're not broken anymore... just tender."

"It's still limiting," Jens said. "Maybe you should sit out tonight."

"No fuckin' way!" Gustav said suddenly. "There's going to be scouts tonight. This could be my chance! Besides, I need the money. Audra has been on my ass lately."

"I understand that, but I'm worried about those ribs getting broken or worse."

"I'll survive," Gustav said, but Jens shook his head.

"I admire your determination, I really do, but you're risking your entire career fighting like this. Do you even have a backup plan?"

"You know I don't," Gustav said. "I've been training my whole life to go pro. Nothing is going to stop me."

Knowing Gustav's determination was often coupled with arrogance until he was put in his place, Jens sighed and nodded.

"Alright, you want to fight tonight, you're going to have to earn it," he said, and without turning his head, he called out to another of his best fighters. "Stahl!"

Glaring at Jens, Gustav asked if this was a sparring match or an exhibition, but he only got his answer when his rival, Dieter Stahl, stepped into the ring a few moments later.

"You'll fight until I say no more," Jens said. "Standard rules of combat apply. Don't kill each other but fight like there's money on the line. Square up!"

Never ones to back down from a fight, Gustav and Stahl marched to the center of the ring with Jens serving as referee for this unexpected bout. Ordered to touch gloves, they did so quickly and backed off into a fighting stance. As with all fighters in the gym, they were both experienced kickboxers, but Gustav had more skin in the game than Stahl. He needed to prove he could win the tournament injured, while Stahl had nothing to gain but a bit more clout around the gym and the Huns. This would lead to fierce competition that ended when a determined Gustav knocked the sparring helmet free from his opponent's head with a vicious uppercut and struck his exposed head with a powerful roundhouse kick. Jens had no doubt that the kick rattled the outlaw prospect's brain like a church bell, so he called off the fight.

"That's enough!" Jens cried out the moment he saw Stahl's eyes roll back moments before he fell limply onto the mat.

Backing off as Jens rushed to check on the fallen fighter, Gustav watched as his trainer tried to wake Stahl with the sound of his voice and gentle taps to the face. It would ultimately take smelling salts to wake the fighter, but even then, he was dazed.

Enraged by the unsportsmanlike conduct of Gustav, Jens marched over and backed Gustav into the ropes with a furious expression.

"You'd better pray like hell you didn't give him a concussion, or it's going to be hell to pay."

"I've taken worse. He'll be fine," Gustav said unapologetically, but then Jens punched him in the solar plexus, driving the wind from his lungs and sending his brain into disarray. As Gustav struggled to breathe, Jens jabbed a crooked finger into his chest and stared him in the eyes.

"If he's too fucked up to fight tonight or even ride his bike home, you're in deep shit," Jens snarled before marching off to return to Stahl.

"Am I good to fight or not?" Gustav called out, but Jens just looked back at him with a snarling glare.

Chapter 8

Moscow, Republic of Russia, Slavic Federation

Despite the importance of this day in his homeland, Aleksander left his home at his usual time and went about his normal routine. His day at the office began with a quick stop at the officer's café on the third floor, followed by an hour alone in his office to prepare himself for a lengthy meeting with the Premier and the General Staff of the Slavic Federation. However, his mind couldn't focus fully on the war in Yugoslavia or the Premier's imperial ambitions. All he could think of was the referendum back home.

Though he promised himself he'd keep the referendum out of sight and out of mind for the good of his duty, Aleksander could not escape the subject. At multiple points in his meeting with the General Staff, he was asked if there was reasonable cause for concern that the Polish separatists might stage an insurrection if they didn't get their way at the polling booth. Aleksander balked at such questions, stating it would be a war that the secessionists could not possibly expect to win. Therefore, he believed the worst that could happen was small-scale rioting. Truly, it was nothing the local police forces couldn't handle, so he made it clear that the Polish Secession movement was the least of their concern. This allowed him to get the meeting back on track and voice his opinion that the Slavic Federation had done all that it could to end the Yugoslavian civil war. As expected, a heated debate broke out.

When cooler heads prevailed, the General Staff appeared to be evenly split over the idea of further involving the Slavic Federation in the growing conflict that threatened to topple the last bastion of European communism. While Aleksander was as fervent an anti-communist as the rest of the heads of the uniformed services, he was firmly in favor of ending their involvement. He saw too many risks in involving foreign troops in another country's civil war. His rationale was that there was no value in liberating Yugoslavia from the communists since the goals of the rebel factions were clearly to establish independent nations. Therefore, there was little reason for the Slavic Federation to be involved if they couldn't accomplish their goal of absorbing the region.

Despite Aleksander's calm and well-thought-out stance regarding the ongoing intervention, the men and women of the General Staff made passionate arguments of their own. While the group appeared evenly split over intervention and non-intervention, the interventionalists were fractured. Some called for a full-scale invasion aimed at ousting the Serbian-led Yugoslavian government, while others suggested the continued use of strategic black operations. This led to yet another drawn-out debate, but Aleksander stood his ground as the de facto leader of the group. Nonetheless, he left the meeting mentally exhausted.

Returning to his office, Aleksander eased his exhaustion with a stiff cup of coffee before getting back to work. However, as soon as he logged back on the intranet, he found that the Federal Security Service – the notorious FSB - had other plans for the Chief of the General Staff.

Via email, Aleksander was informed that a high-level security breach of the army's intranet server had been detected. As expected, the FSB's cybersecurity division requested that Aleksander vacate his office over the lunch hour to allow a systems specialist to inspect his terminal. Aleksander had a feeling this was just a ruse to get him out of the office so that the FSB could try to dig up information that might implicate him as sympathetic to the secessionist cause in Poland. Though a patriot at heart, Aleksander was a very private person and would never allow himself to leave even a trace of personal politics on a government server. So, given that he had nothing to hide, he took this as an opportunity to go home for a few hours and relax.

The drive home from downtown Moscow usually took Aleksander around thirty minutes, if traffic was good, but leaving the office at noon meant he could expect an extra ten to fifteen minutes in the car. Regardless, he made the journey home pleasurable with a Beatles album that never seemed to leave the CD player. The crooning of the Fab Four always seemed to lift his spirits, and by the time he got home, he was secretly hoping only his wife was home. It had been quite some time since they had last made love, and he could certainly use a few minutes of bliss. However, when he stepped into the house from the garage, he found Katrin sitting on the couch. Her auburn hair was tied back in a messy bun, she didn't appear to have on any makeup, and she was in her lounging clothes she usually reserved for after dinner. In fact, had she not changed out of her nightgown he would have suspected she had just rolled out of bed. To make matters worse, she was staring at the news program on the television so intensely that she didn't even turn to look to see who was coming in from the garage. He figured she just assumed he was Aleksey, especially after the surprised reaction she made when he walked up and placed his hands on her shoulders and kissed her neck.

"Did you go back to bed after everyone left?" he asked, but she looked at him with glee.

"I've been right here all morning," she said with excitement in her voice. "We're up by twenty percent." Her smile then faded into a frown. "Still, I just can't believe how many people actually want to remain."

Turning his attention to the television, Aleksander saw the currently projected percentages based on exit poll data collected around the major cities. While he was surprised to see a strong percentage in favor of remaining in the Federation, he was quick to offer his wife consolation.

"Exit polls aren't a good metric to go by. A lot of people are afraid to publicly express their approval of secession," he said, so she turned to him with confusion.

"Why would someone be afraid to show their support for independence?" she asked, but Aleksander shrugged.

"Some are like me and have prominent positions in government. Others are afraid they might be targeted, and perhaps a few really do want to remain."

"I just don't understand why someone would be against independence," Katrin said with mild frustration. "We fought so hard to free ourselves from the communists just to fall under the boot of fascists a few years later."

"A fascist government wouldn't allow a secession to happen," Aleksander said, for he felt the popularity of referring to the Slavic Federation as fascist was hyperbolic and ignorant. "Nonetheless, I imagine there's a lot of people that are terrified of the prospect of their country being left to fend for itself, Hell, there's a lot of first-time voters who don't even remember the days of the Free Republic," Aleksander said, airing out his concerns about a successful referendum. "It wasn't all sunshine and rainbows, remember? We'd be far weaker militarily, too."

"Sure, but wouldn't we just join NATO?" she asked, but Aleksander shook his head.

"That would be a dangerous move," he said. "Besides, national defense isn't the only thing people have to be worried about. Poland isn't exactly an economic powerhouse just yet."

"Then we'd join the European Union," Katrin said, seemingly having all the answers thanks to a steady diet of Polish-language news and pro-secessionist propaganda. "I've spoken at length with my brother about this. The Liberation Party has a solid plan."

"I'm sure they do," Aleksander replied dismissively. "But you're putting too much faith in politicians, sweetheart."

Feeling the tension in the air, Katrin jumped to a bold conclusion. "You don't want to leave, do you?"

"I never said that."

"Just because you won't say it doesn't mean you don't believe it."

Not wanting an unnecessary verbal sparring match, Aleksander let off a frustrated sigh and spoke his personal truth. "We have a good life here, do we not? Were we not given a big, luxurious home with round-the-clock security, and more money than we could have imagined when we were young and struggling back home?"

"Just say it, Alek. I won't hold it against you."

"Fine, I didn't vote," he answered honestly, bringing a frown to her face.

"Why would you do that?" she questioned, seemingly hurt by his inaction.

"Because as much as I wanted to vote to leave, I realized how much we'd lose."

"We had a good life back home," Katrin challenged. "We didn't have an indoor pool, or a weight room, or private security, but we had a good life."

"We did, but do you really think they would just let us leave? I'm Chief of the General Staff. I know far too much for them to allow me to leave my post and join a new nation."

"You're afraid of them," she said, almost tauntingly. "This is why I told you to turn them down in the first place."

"You're right, I am afraid of them. Have you forgotten that I work for the man whom you believe stole the election from Bednarz? A man you call a fascist."

"Do you really think they would hurt you for voicing your opinion?"

"They'd call it treason."

"More reason to leave," she said distantly. "It should have never been like this, Alek."

Sighing through his nose, for there was clearly no getting through to his wife at this moment, Aleksander silently turned his back to her and headed off. However, he was only a few steps into the kitchen, which was adjacent to the living room, when he heard the garage door activate. Ignoring the sound, he went to a nearby cabinet for a water glass. A few moments later, the door to the garage swung open quickly and slammed hard. Aleksander hardly had a chance to turn his shoulder to catch a glimpse of the anger in his son's face.

"Everything alright, sweetheart?" Katrin called out from the living room, but Aleksey said nothing and proceeded down the hall leading from the kitchen to the front of the house.

Having no doubt that Aleksey had gone to see Tatiana and learned the terrible truth firsthand, Aleksander set the glass aside and walked back over to his wife's side.

"I think he knows," Katrin said, and Aleksander nodded quietly. "Maybe you should go talk to him."

Though Aleksey was a grown man hardened by a decade in the military, Aleksander knew the worst thing his son could do was be alone at that moment. So, accepting his fatherly duty, he promptly left the living room and headed up to Aleksey's room.

☐

More angry than sad, Aleksey patrolled his room in search of anything that reminded him of Tatiana, so that he could dispose of it with impunity. The first to go was the collection of photographs he had stuck to a corkboard over the course of their relationship. For a moment, he intended to gather them in a box to burn, but he was barely able to tear them all down before Aleksander stepped into the room.

"Everything alright in here?" Aleksander asked from the threshold of the only door to the room. "You looked a little upset down there? Something bothering you?"

Turning to his father with a strained face, Aleksey told him what had happened when he went to see Tatiana. Though he was aware that Tatiana had stepped out on him, Aleksander made himself appear surprised but kept cool and shared his sympathies.

"That was a cold-hearted thing to do."

"You're telling me," Aleksey replied sharply. "Fucking bitch could have told me, you know?"

"Some people don't have the guts to face the judge," Aleksander said. "But listen, someone like that isn't worth crying over."

"I'm not crying!" Aleksey snarled. "I'm fucking pissed!"

"And you have every right to be, but don't do anything stupid."

"You don't understand, Dad," Aleksey said. "I came home with a plan. I was going to ask her to marry me. We were going to settle down and start a family. I left the service for her, dammit!"

Though he never really cared for Tatiana, Aleksander felt for his son. He clearly loved her deeply to consider such actions. Though he wasn't the most affectionate man, Aleksander knew he had to console his son in his time of heartache. However, when he hugged

Aleksey, he didn't hear or feel him break down. It was very clear to him that Aleksey was truly angry and nothing else. So, stepping back, he asked what he was planning to do about the situation.

"I don't know yet," Aleksey said, his tone showing that he was thinking with anger and not reason.

"Then I need you to take a few breaths, calm down a bit, and meet me in the sunroom."

"Why?"

"Because we need to talk this out, but I can't reach you like this. I can see a wild man in your eyes, Aleksey. I've seen that look in men before, and it only means one thing."

"I'm not going to hurt anyone," Aleksey said, but Aleksander wasn't taking any chances.

"Just calm down a bit and meet me downstairs when you're ready. The best thing we can do right now is talk."

"Alright," Aleksey said. "Just give me five minutes."

□

At the sound of heavy footsteps echoing from the hall, Katrin turned in her armchair and saw her husband enter the kitchen alone. With concerned eyes, she approached him, and he nodded as if knowing what she was going to ask.

"Just let me handle this," Aleksander said, upon his wife's embrace. "He's angry, but I know how to reach him."

"You didn't tell him, did you?"

"No, he found out for himself. For his sake, please don't bring it up again," he said in a firm whisper. "Just go back to your news program. I'll handle this."

Accepting her husband's wishes, Katrin returned to the living room while Aleksander made his way down the hall into the weight room that led to an indoor pool room to which an all-seasons solarium was attached.

A few minutes would pass before Aleksey made his appearance in the solarium. As promised, Aleksander was alone and waiting near the window with his hands folded at the small of his back as if observing the battlefield from afar. Aleksey thought nothing of it, for his father was always like this, so he shut the door and took his place by his side. Like his father, he folded his hands at the small of his back and took on a stoic expression despite still toiling inside over his heartbreak.

"The forest is beautiful this time of year," Aleksey said calmly. "It's a nice change of scenery from the empty expanse of the ocean and urban sprawl."

Turning his head slightly to look upon his son, Aleksander's expression was stoic, but his voice was warm and fatherly. "Feeling better?" he asked, and Aleksey shrugged his shoulders.

"Calmer, but certainly not better," Aleksey replied. "It's going to hurt for a long while."

"I can only imagine," Aleksander said. His words couldn't have rung truer in his son's mind, for by all accounts, Katrin was Aleksander's first love. "But it's good that you're calming down. Anger isn't going to help anything."

"The Army trained me well," Aleksey replied. "But if you wouldn't mind, I'd like to stop talking about it."

"Yes, of course," Aleksander said respectfully. After a long pause, he asked a question that had been on his mind since Aleksey returned home. "Were you seriously planning to leave the military for her?"

His body tense at the thought of him leaving the military to have a life with Tatiana, Aleksey felt foolish even considering such a bold action. Still, he saw no reason to hide it, so he came clean.

"That was the plan," he said regretfully. "But don't worry, I'll be reenlisting now."

"Well, that won't make your mother very happy, but I think it's the right decision," Aleksander said, silently shuddering at the thought of his son throwing away a decade of honorable service for a woman who had betrayed him. "And if you're tired of life on the razor's edge, there's still time to change. Put in for a transfer to greener pastures."

"Yes, of course," Aleksey said coolly, as his mind wandered back to the hall of Tatiana's apartment. "I have a few options in mind and a few weeks to decide, but I honestly didn't give any of them much consideration. I thought I was going to come home today with good news."

Wanting to keep his son from falling back into despair, Aleksander asked what Aleksey had considered as a backup plan should his proposal not go as expected.

"Well, first and foremost, I was going to reenlist," Aleksey said, but before the words could leave his lips, his father seemed to know what he thought was a tightly guarded secret.

"Word has it you were tapped to try out for a new unit within the Special Troops. Are you going to take them up on the offer?" Aleksander asked, and Aleksey nodded, expecting his father to explode in fury, but Aleksander was calm. "That would be a mistake and a waste of effort. At best, it'll be a lateral move. You're better off staying with GROM."

"Maybe, but what do I have to lose? My best friend is trying out, and if we fail, we go right back to our old unit," Aleksey said. "Besides, if I'm going to serve another ten years, I need a change of pace."

"I can understand that, but this isn't the answer. I looked into this new unit and frankly, it's a waste of money and manpower," Aleksander said with clear disdain for the new unit. "They're selling this unit as a rapid response force. That tells me it'll be nothing more than a special operations expeditionary force. First to fight, and if shit goes sideways, the first to die."

"Easy, Dad. I never said I accepted the offer. I'm just considering all my options."

"In that case, why not pursue becoming an officer? With your grades back in school and your stellar service, you're more than qualified."

"I graduated from school ten years ago. I'd be the oldest cadet in history," Aleksey said with a chuckle. "Besides, I spent the last decade as a combat diver and a commando. I have no business leading armies."

"You'd make a fine officer. It's in your blood," Aleksander said proudly, for their family had a proud military tradition with many officers to their name, including Aleksey's grandfather, who had served as a field officer of the Polish People's Republic. "I can make some calls and get things rolling."

"That's alright. I'd prefer to earn my way, you know that."

"Yes, of course," Aleksander said with mild pride. "But you only have a month to figure out where you're headed before you finish out your contract. Knowing you, I'm sure you've already made up your mind, and you're just blowing smoke up my ass."

"Yes, but no," Aleksey said, greatly confusing his father. "I wasn't expecting things to fall apart with Tatiana."

"Don't tell me you already made it clear you won't reenlist."

"Well, yeah, I kind of did," Aleksey said, causing his father to sigh deeply and shake his head.

"Good god, Aleksey. Did I really raise a son foolish enough to throw away a career for a woman?" Aleksander asked in bitter frustration. "There's a reason we told you to break it off when you enlisted."

Not wanting to hear this, Aleksey grit his teeth and boldly asked if there was a point to this discussion anymore. In response, Aleksander pivoted his entire body to face his son.

"You have a month to fix this, so don't be an idiot. You can always transfer to the reserves if you're tired of the special operations life. But, in my opinion, your best option is going to the academy and doing something greater."

"Why are you so bent on me becoming an officer?"

"Because I'm the General of the Army, and look at the life it afforded us," Aleksander said calmly, and it was a statement Aleksey couldn't argue against. Despite being born in rural Poland, he was raised in wealth and prosperity. However, he had one last option to reveal.

"I know what you're going to say, but what about Alpha Group?" Aleksey asked. "I'm sure you're aware I was invited to their upcoming selection program as well."

"To hell with Alpha Group!" Aleksander thundered suddenly. "You may live in Russia, but you're Polish, through and through. You have no place in their ranks. To them, you're nothing more than a pshek."

Though he had endured a good deal of harassment for his heritage while living in Russia, Aleksey had worked alongside many Russians and saw no real reason why he couldn't serve with Alpha Group. He was invited to attend their upcoming selection program, after all. But rather than argue with his father, Aleksey dropped the subject and entertained the idea of becoming an officer, even if it was just a means of appeasement while he figured things out for himself.

"Look, I'm just trying to get some feedback on my options. Maybe you're right about Alpha Group, but I'm an enlisted man. It's all I've known for the last ten years. I need a gun in my hand and an objective to accomplish, not a platoon behind me."

"You said you're looking for some change. I'm offering that change," Aleksander said. "You're an excellent diver and an outstanding marksman, there's no arguing with that, but I sincerely believe you'd find a better life as an officer than a commando."

"Maybe you're right, but maybe you're wrong."

"You know I'm right," Aleksander said a bit arrogantly. "You wouldn't have wasted all that money on a ring if you didn't want a family. I'm offering you a way to advance your career while enabling you to have a family, too. Don't waste this opportunity, Aleksey. No woman would want to marry a commando. An officer on the other hand--"

"Alright, you win. Make some calls."

A smirk stretched across Aleksander's face a mere moment after Aleksey caved.

"I already have," he said. "You'll be meeting with Colonel Kolchak in person."

"In person? But the academy is out near Senatgrad."

"That's correct," Aleksander said with a nod. "I have business coming up in Senatgrad, and your mother insisted on a family vacation. You'll be meeting with Colonel Kolchak then."

Aleksey thought about the sudden shift in direction the conversation had taken. A few moments later, he had a smile of his own.

"What?" Aleksander asked suspiciously.

"There's a Blood Games tournament coming up. Three days of blood and sweat."

"I'm aware," Aleksander said before turning back toward the window. A satisfied grin soon returned to his face. "We just so happen to be heading out to Senatgrad that week, so I acquired tickets. We'll be sitting in a private skybox for all three nights."

While certainly impressed that his father would take time out of his busy schedule for three nights at the arena, Aleksey wasn't all that surprised. He and his father had a shared passion for combat sports. It was one of the first things they truly bonded over after he started to grow into a man.

"Now you have something to look forward to," Aleksander said. "In the meantime, I want you to keep your head clear and your mind focused on enjoying your limited time as a free man. What happened today was a low blow that you certainly didn't deserve, but you need to pick yourself up and carry on. Is that understood?"

"Of course," Aleksey said, and without much else to say, he held his hand out to shake his father's hand. "Thank you for this. I really appreciate it."

"My pleasure. No son of mine is going to be a knuckle dragger forever," Aleksander said, taking his son's hand in a firm grasp. "Besides, we're going to need grandchildren eventually. Maybe you'll find someone out in Senatgrad... a good Polish girl, perhaps."

Aleksey chuckled at the statement, for considering Tatiana had left him, he wasn't bringing forth the next generation anytime soon. However, there was no reason he shouldn't seize the day and get back out on the market. Of course, he knew better than to go on the prowl in the middle of the day, so he decided to blow off some steam in the weight room until nightfall.

Chapter 9

Berlin, Germany

It was another grim and cloudy night in the German capital as Gustav and Audra made their way through a light spring drizzle that stung any bit of exposed skin. Though it wasn't quite evening, the sky had grown dark, and the streetlights had come on. As they walked, a cold droplet would descend at just the right angle to land upon the thin line of exposed skin between his hairline and the collar of his leather jacket. Due to the rain, his jacket was moist and shimmering from the lights of the city, and his short, sandy blonde hair was damp. Meanwhile, Audra, dressed aptly for the weather, was bone dry, for unlike her beau, she thought ahead and brought an umbrella. Though she offered it to him, Gustav said he wasn't bothered and kept walking with his head low and his hands in his pockets. She wasn't sure if he was still angry from their argument that morning or if he was just focused on the tournament, but she really didn't care.

For much of the walk from their apartment, Audra said very little. She was mentally exhausted from working on her art all day and thinking about her future, and whether she was better off alone. Normally quick to forgive, she was deeply frustrated with Gustav's reckless decision to fight against his doctor's wishes, but this was just the tip of the iceberg. She was far beyond sick of his reckless and selfish ways, especially his inability to hold down a good-paying job due to always being 'on the edge of glory' in his pursuit of going professional. She had heard this excuse for so long that she was beginning to wonder why she was still in a relationship with him, or if he was just some loser roommate that she occasionally had sex with when she could be convinced. While she had felt frustrated for years, this feeling of being out of love with him was relatively recent, and she was beginning to wonder if she really was better off on her own. In fact, this was the thought that was presently on her mind, causing her to fall behind a few steps and miss much of what Gustav had said to her. In time, he stopped and looked back with an annoyed expression.

"Try to keep up with me. This is a dangerous neighborhood," he said, his voice sounding condescending rather than protective as intended.

A resident of Marzahn since being placed in her uncle's guardianship at the age of ten, Audra rolled her eyes at the notion that she was unaware of the neighborhood's dark side. Regardless, she quickened her pace until she was beside him once more, the umbrella partially shielding his body.

"Happy?" she asked, her voice distant, almost loathsome.

His eyes staring straight forward, he told her he didn't want to argue with her, but she didn't reply. She kept an even pace with him and scanned her surroundings for signs of danger, as her brother and uncle had taught her long ago.

"Look, I'm just nervous about this tournament, alright?"

"Okay," she said dismissively, for she didn't see a point in speaking her mind at that moment since it likely wouldn't make a difference.

"Alright, what's on your mind? You seem like you want to fight or something," he said with a glaring side-eye, but she ignored him, so he rolled his eyes and muttered, "Fine, whatever."

Without another word exchanged between the pair, Gustav grew more eager to get to the venue and out of the rain, so he quickened the pace. Audra did well to keep up, but her legs were tired from so many hours on her feet that day. When she finally caught up with him, the look in Gustav's eyes told her that he was either grossly anxious about fighting with an injury or getting lost in memories. Neither would surprise her, for fighting was in Gustav's blood. It was something of a family tradition, as was the failure to go professional, but Audra couldn't let him dwell. He needed to be in the right headspace before the tournament, so she touched his arm and smiled. When he looked at her with curious eyes, she told him she loved him, even though she wasn't quite sure she did anymore.

Their short journey to the beer hall hosting the tournament coming to an end, Gustav held the door for Audra. Though saying nothing, she gave him a brief smile and entered ahead of him. The entrance hall was largely empty, but there was a faint smell of tobacco smoke. When they stepped into the main hall, they were hit with a blast of sound. The beer hall was loud with echoing chatter from the dozens of people crammed inside the main room where a large boxing ring stood. Though the building was an all-purpose event hall, the place hosted wrestling and kickboxing matches most often. As a result, the hall smelled strongly of smoke, spilled beer, and sweat. Gustav was used to this, but Audra flared her nostrils at the smell. Though she was used to the smell of stale beer and smoke, the combined odor was noxious and the air choking, but she didn't complain. She just followed Gustav through the crowd, which was quite sizeable despite the first match not starting for another forty minutes.

Leading the way through the crowd over to a bare folding table manned by the stocky fight promoter, Gustav was stopped short of the table by a pair of burly security guards. Acting casually, Gustav spread his legs and held out his hands. He was then frisked thoroughly for weapons before being allowed to approach the promoter.

"Fighting, betting, or just observing?" the Promoter asked, just before Gustav slapped down a sizeable sum that had Audra quietly fuming.

"That's my buy-in and her ticket... the rest goes on me," Gustav said boldly. "Who's fighting tonight?"

Pushing the roster list across the table so Gustav could see, he saw him smirk.

"I've beaten all of them at least twice."

"You really should check your attitude," the Promoter said, but Gustav shrugged. "I'm serious. This isn't your typical prize fight. There's a lot of money to be made tonight, and most of these guys have been training hard. Word has it there are scouts in the crowd, too."

"I know, and I'm going to catch their eye," Gustav said with a cocky grin. "I'll be back in a couple of minutes for the schedule."

"Give me twenty minutes. I have two more slots to fill."

"Let's make it simple. Give me the first fight of the night,"

"What makes you so fucking special?" the Promoter asked sharply, and Gustav grinned.

"Book me first and I'll show you," Gustav said, pulling out another large bill to bloat his ego further. "Put that on me, too."

Shaking his head, the Promoter warned Gustav that he had better put on a good show. He then penciled in Gustav's name in the blank slot at the top of the sixteen-man bracket.

Seemingly satisfied with himself, Gustav turned toward Audra with a smile, but she was gone. He looked around the room in search of her but failed to see her making her way to the bleachers. She was well beyond pissed after seeing him wager more than a month's rent on a fight, but she couldn't bring herself to leave. She needed to see him fight, for as she stomped away from the betting table, she made a bold decision. If he lost that first match, he'd be on the streets with nothing but the shirt on his back until she was calm enough to let him clean out his belongings. She couldn't believe the nerve of that man. After so many months of living largely on her dime, she couldn't believe he'd be so bold to wave around that kind of cash in front of her, especially in the form of a bet.

Chapter 10

Moscow, Republic of Russia, Slavic Federation

Keeping to his plan to hit the town after dark, Aleksey lounged around the house until after dinner. Dressing sharply in club attire, he took to the streets atop his old IZH sport motorcycle, but each club he approached had a long line for entry. Though he had a famous surname, that did him little good outside of the military. Besides, he didn't feel like waiting for the chance to go into some stuffy dance club. So, hopping back on his motorcycle, he drove down to his favorite sports bar. Upon pulling up to the curb, he noticed the loud pipes had turned some heads, and he got a smile from a couple of pretty ladies having a cigarette out front. With a smile of his own, he headed inside, feeling like he had made the right choice going there.

A place he had frequented more so in his early twenties, Aleksey found the bar was just the same as it was back when he first stepped inside. Modeled after an American sports bar, the place was heavily decorated with local sports memorabilia and furnished with a sizeable bar, a pair of pool tables, and a row of dartboards. If he were with friends, he would probably participate in a few games, but since he was alone, he quietly found an empty stool at the center of the bar and caught the bartender's attention.

"What can I get you?" asked the tall, heavily bearded man behind the bar.

"A cold shot of vodka and a beer," Aleksey replied, not really caring what he got so long as it chased away the blues and gave him a decent buzz.

Opting to give Aleksey a mid-priced shot and a bottle of Russia's most popular beer brand, the bartender asked if he wanted to pay in full or start a tab. Figuring he'd stay for at least two beers, Aleksey opted for the tab. He then took the shot down quickly, slamming the glass down hard before looking up at the television screens. Strangely, the screen directly in front of him was fixed to a news program discussing the Polish referendum. The numbers on the screen declared the estimated final percentages of ballots counted.

To his amazement, the secession referendum had passed with an astounding eighty-one to nineteen percent landslide victory.

"Fuck me... could this day get any worse?" Aleksey groaned just as the bartender poured him a second shot.

"Having a rough day?"

Aleksey nodded and took hold of the second shot. "You have no idea," he said, and he took down the shot quickly. This time, he set the glass down and waved his hand to decline a third.

"Are you sure?" the bartender asked. "You're sounding pretty rough."

"You would too if you got home from leave and found out your girlfriend is pregnant from some prick at the office, only then to learn your homeland is seceding," Aleksey said, his frustration heard loud and clear. "On second thought, give me another, but no more after that."

Pouring the third shot, the bartender told him he was only charging him for the first on account of his misery. While Aleksey appreciated the generosity, he took down the final shot and soon turned his attention back to the hockey highlights. As if to rub the salt deeper into his wounds, his favorite hockey team was ranked dead last in the league. This brought him to shake his head and reach for his beer, but the quick succession of shots had already gone to his head, and he nearly knocked over the bottle with his wobbly hand. Feeling slightly embarrassed, he stared straight forward and spotted a familiar face in the mirror behind the bar. It was none other than the son of a bitch who had stolen his woman, and lo and behold, he was with someone else.

With a furrowed brow and drunken intrigue, Aleksey watched the man having the time of his life with a skinny little thing. By the looks of it, he wasn't there with a friend but rather a lover, for soon enough they were locking their lips in an aggravating display of public affection. Though Aleksey should have just paid his bill and left, his raw emotions caused him to be confrontational.

Pushing back on his stool, Aleksey stood up and flagged the bartender to inform him he had left his cigarettes in his coat. After receiving a nod, he went to the coat rack and checked his corners. Pretending he had chosen his jacket, he dug around and found a work ID tucked inside an interior pocket. The bastard's name was Kirill Miranchuk, and he was in middle management at Tatiana's firm.

Returning to the bar, Aleksey shrugged when he locked eyes with the bartender. "Forgot my cigarettes at home," he said, but the bartender didn't say anything. Instead, he motioned for a fresh beer, but Aleksey declined. He then looked over at Kirill and his lover and smiled. Turning back to the bartender, he flagged him down.

"Change your mind?" the bartender said, but Aleksey smiled.

"None for me, but I'd like to buy a round for the happy couple straight back."

Looking past Aleksey, the bartender observed Kirill and the blonde continuing to make out as if they were somewhere private. However, he had to know if Aleksey had a reason to buy them a round.

"That's the prick that stole my woman," Aleksey said bluntly. "And that isn't the woman he stole."

"Alright, I don't want any trouble here. Why don't you just pay up and go?" the Bartender said, but Aleksey shrugged.

"No trouble. I just want to have a good laugh."

Though wondering if he was going to regret following through with the request, the bartender fixed the drinks and headed over to the table under Aleksey's watchful gaze via the mirror behind the bar. With a grin, Aleksey turned on his stool just as Kirill looked his way. Raising his glass in a cheerful, yet sarcastic fashion, he bid him good health and a happy life. However, this only incited the usurper to walk over and confront him.

Leaning on the rail of the bar counter, Kirill looked Aleksey in the eyes and asked what he wanted. Aleksey took a long drink of his beer, but Kirill's intense stare showed he wanted an answer.

"Does Tatiana know you're out with someone else?"

"That's none of your business," Kirill said strongly, but Aleksey shrugged.

"I don't know about that. I seem to remember finding you in my girlfriend's apartment."

"Fuck, this again," Kirill said. "Look, I didn't know about you until today. I'm sorry."

"That's fine, I don't care anymore," Aleksey said, breaking eye contact with the home-wrecker before turning to face him again with a curious expression. "We're about done here, but I have a question for you."

"What?"

"Is she pregnant?" Aleksey asked, vividly recalling that Tatiana's figure had changed exponentially since he last saw her.

"Unfortunately," Kirill admitted shamefully.

"Then why aren't you home with her right now?"

Smirking, Kirill said again that Tatiana was supposed to be a one-night stand. This prompted Aleksey to ask if he planned to stick around and play with her heart, or if he was going to grow some balls and do the right thing.

"That's none of your business," Kirill said firmly, but Aleksey clearly disagreed.

Pushing off from his seat in a drunken manner, Aleksey stared the taller man in the eyes and told him he had no respect for people without a sense of honor. This only provoked a mocking smile and a taunt to see if Aleksey was really going to defend a woman who cheated on him. This proved to be the wrong move, for Aleksey replied silently with a heavy punch into Kirill's gut, causing him to keel forward in pain and surprise. While Aleksey should have just left the man with wounded pride, his anger got the best of him, and he grabbed his head with both hands. Forcing him to look up, Aleksey brought his forehead down hard on the bastard's nose, crushing the cartilage before shoving him to the ground.

While Kirill rolled on the ground, clenching his shattered nose as it poured blood like a faucet, Aleksey turned to the astonished bartender. Throwing down two large bills to cover his tab, he apologized for the mess. He soon left, feeling justified for his actions, but the moment he laid eyes on the motorcycle, he knew driving would only make a bad situation worse. So rather than take the risk of driving drunk, he started down the sidewalk, fully willing to face the music for his disorderly conduct. Fortunately, he was able to disappear into another bar before the police arrived. Counting his blessings, he would ride out the alcohol in his system in this second establishment by sipping mineral water. When he felt good enough to ride, he headed back to his motorcycle and took off before anyone could raise an alarm.

Chapter 11

Berlin, Germany

Seated among a crowd of blood-drunk spectators, a middle-aged man with slicked-back hair and strong facial features watched the last of the semi-finals with intensity. If one were to judge by his expensive suit and stone-cold demeanor, the man would likely be assumed a member of the local crime syndicate, or its sister organization based out east. In reality, he was affiliated with neither. Rather, he was a talent scout for the Combat Sports Entertainment Group – the parent company of Eastern Europe's premier mixed martial arts league, the Blood Games – and had spent the last two months traveling Europe in search of prime competitive talent. Berlin was among the last stops on his schedule, but considering what he was seeing from Gustav, there was a chance he might be returning to Senatgrad early.

Out of the sixteen fighters that entered the tournament that night, Gustav was the most promising of the bunch. Though a light heavyweight, he was surprisingly fast on his feet and quick with his strikes. Not once did Gustav allow his matches to devolve into a slugfest like some of the others. He clearly fought for the entertainment of the crowd, and the variety of techniques he utilized ensured all eyes were on him throughout his matches. However, the offer the Scout was prepared to give him required Gustav to win the entire tournament. Simply commanding the audience and putting on a good show wasn't enough. He had to win it all that night, or the Scout would walk out with the others. So, with high hopes, the Scout leaned forward and watched with anticipation as the final two fighters were called to the ring to decide the big winner through one last fight.

Having watched each fight closely, the Scout analyzed the final two fighters. Gustav was the shorter of the two, but what he lacked in height he made up for with brawn and a variety of techniques, telling the Scout he was highly trained. Conversely, his opponent was tall and wiry with a long reach, which put Gustav at a disadvantage if he couldn't get inside the fighter's reach. And if he did, there was no concern for Gustav. He displayed a great deal of power behind his strikes. If he could get inside and land a stiff blow or two, Gustav could very well set up a knockout in short order. Of course, if the fight dragged on, there was a good chance Gustav could get gassed and lose his momentum. Fortunately for him, Gustav came out swinging with ferocity in his dark eyes - a quick finish was clearly on his mind.

Three rounds through and the fourth set to begin, Gustav walked back to the center of the ring with his hands up and his head tilted downward slightly. His hair matted and his face glistening with sweat, Gustav's chest rapidly expanded and sank from exhaustion. For three rounds, he sought the night's ultimate victory, fighting hard and fast. While he was dominant and aggressive the entire match, he was having difficulty getting inside his opponent's reach thanks to a pair of long, powerful legs. This caused Gustav to rely on bait techniques to draw out an attack so he could move in for a quick hit or a clinch. Whenever he did score a hit, he threw his weight behind it, but even his most devastating attacks were lacking their usual power. He was getting exhausted from the drawn-out battle and was in danger of losing the tournament, and he knew it. He had to get meaner, and perhaps a little reckless, if he was going to break this man and win.

Battling his opponent just as well as he had in the first round, Gustav scored a few good hits while eating a punch to the face before the fifth round was through. He wasn't going to let this go to a judge's decision; he not only needed but also demanded the knockout. So, in a bid to finish the match with flair, he changed his tactics from moving in slowly and shooting in for a clinch to charging hard and absorbing a blow in hopes of getting in close and launching a flurry of uppercuts and haymakers, followed by a head kick for the knockout. However, the moment he charged, he misinterpreted his opponent's movement and blocked high to avoid a head kick, but that wasn't the intention. Gustav took a fierce kick to the side and found himself stumbling back into the ropes. The fighter quickly moved in with the intent to launch a striking combo aimed at ending the fight there and then, but Gustav wasn't through.

To the roaring amusement of the crowd, Gustav bounced off the ropes and thrust forth with a fierce left hook to the chin, followed by a low right uppercut to the gut. A split second later, he threw a spinning back fist across the jaw. The sheer force brought about by the spinning of his body allowed the blow to land with enough force to stun the fighter and send him stumbling back. Seeing his opportunity, Gustav rushed in and threw his left leg sloppily into the air for the knockout, yet all he felt was the rush of air. His opponent had ducked under his swinging leg, and the force behind the kick caused Gustav to spin to his right, leaving him open for a punishing straight punch to his ailing ribs in retaliation.

His nerves screaming furiously from the blow to his ribs, Gustav doubled back in agony, but his opponent saw his opportunity renewed. Like a shark smelling blood in the water, he rushed out a quick punching combination followed immediately by a snapping roundhouse kick at Gustav's ribs. Fortunately for Gustav, his elbow held firm, and the kick was blocked, allowing him to counterpunch and sidestep away from the ropes to avoid being cornered and beaten into submission.

Seemingly driven mad by the pain shooting up from his side, Gustav launched a short offensive, starting with a step-through sidekick to the midsection. Though his kick was blocked and almost captured with a cross block, he pulled back and spun on his opposing heel to land a risky back fist to the temple. His opponent stunned and staggering from the blow, he lost his grip on Gustav, allowing him to recover quickly and dart forward. Three steps and a bold jump later, Gustav was soaring through the air and throwing a punch at his opponent's chin, knocking him onto the mat after a powerful collision.

Remaining on his feet, Gustav backed off but didn't hold any sort of fighting stance. Rather, he stood by and quite arrogantly watched as the referee rushed in to check the downed fighter. The opposing fighter was limp and staring blankly. It was clear that he was stunned and on the verge of passing out, but the referee had to run through his mental checklist. A few seconds later, he motioned for the bell to be rung, and Gustav threw up his arms in victory. However, the cost of his victory was quickly realized, for just lifting his arms caused him an incredible amount of pain, but the pain would prove worth the risk he took that night in just a few moments.

Thoroughly impressed with the final match, the Scout made his way from the stands and into the expected path Gustav would take to the locker room. When the two men crossed paths, he tried to introduce himself, but was ignored in favor of Audra. Not the least bit offended, he stood off to the side and let the couple have their moment. When they were done, he approached to introduce himself.

"That was some excellent fighting tonight, Mr. Hagen," the Scout said, speaking in deeply accented English as he thrust his business card toward Gustav. "Michał Kwoznik, Combat Sports Entertainment Group. Do you have a moment to talk?"

Looking at the card together, Audra and Gustav learned quickly that this man was a recruiter for the sports entertainment group, which billed itself as the home of Europe's premier professional fighting promotions. However, before either of them could speak, Kwoznik reached into his coat to retrieve a folded brochure.

"We have a big tournament coming up. My colleagues and I are scouting for talented fighters like yourself. While I've never heard of you before, I must say that your fighting tonight was very impressive."

Taking the brochure, Gustav and Audra looked it over carefully and found that Kwoznik was recruiting for a semi-pro invitational tournament. Fighters would have the chance of winning a lion's share of prize money with cash awarded on a per-match basis. What caught Gustav's eye was the ultimate prize - a one-year contract with the Blood Games organization.

"Holy shit, this is my chance!" Gustav exclaimed to Audra, and though she agreed, she looked at Kwoznik with a firm expression.

"What's the buy-in?" Audra asked.

"Who is this, your manager?" he asked Gustav. "Never seen a lady manager before."

"No, I'm his girlfriend," Audra said dryly, for she got the feeling she was talking to an old school, set-in-his-ways misogynist. "What's the buy-in?"

"Five thousand rubles," he said, causing Gustav to sigh, for the Slavic Federal Ruble was on track to rival the American Dollar. "I know it's a lot, but we will cover your food and travel expenses. We'll also provide luxury housing and twenty-four-seven access to training facilities."

"How do we know this isn't a scam?" Audra asked, her eyes sharp as if watching for any hint of a lie.

Smiling, Kwoznik asked if she had access to a videotape player. She nodded, so he reached into the knapsack he kept at his side and handed her a promotional VHS tape.

"This will provide you with everything you need to know," he said. "Any other concerns, feel free to call me. I'll be in Germany for a few more days, but I recommend you make your decision sooner rather than later. I have a limited number of open slots left for the tournament, and there's no guarantee I won't find better talent between then and now."

Holding the tape firmly in her hand, Audra nodded and told him that they'd watch the tape that night and call him in a day or two with their decision.

"Very good," Kwoznik said. "Hopefully I'll hear from you soon."

Parting ways with the scout to get his money for the night, Gustav had a smile from ear to ear. "I can't believe we just met a recruiter for a major promotion," he said, earning a concerned eye from Audra.

"Don't get too excited. Anyone can make a fancy business card and a convincing videotape," she warned, but Gustav rolled his eyes and took a firm tone.

"The Blood Games is the real deal, Audra. This could be our ticket out of here."

"Alright," she said, not wanting to spoil his mood. "Let's collect your earnings and get out of here."

"And then what?" he asked with a smirk.

"We watch this stupid tape and debate whether or not we should risk a year of rent on you."

"I wouldn't call it a risk."

"Yeah, then what would you call it?"

"An investment," he said with a grin, but she just rolled her eyes.

"Well, it's hard to invest money we don't have."

"We'll find a way," he said confidently, and though she felt like she was going to end up financing this endeavor, she didn't say anything. She just let him ride his wave and followed him to the promoter's table to collect his winnings. At the very least, he could hold to his promise of covering the next couple of months of expenses.

Chapter 12

Moscow, Republic of Russia, Slavic Federation

Sergei Medvedev woke up early that morning, exhausted from a restless night driven by his anxious mind. Unable to bring himself to watch the live coverage of the vote counting, he turned in early and did his best to avoid the subject as he went about his morning rituals. He went so far as to openly threaten the job security of any staff who discussed the referendum within his manor for the next twenty-four hours. This, of course, worked exceptionally well on the staff, but the lady of the house was immune to such orders. After all, there was no job for him to threaten, and he certainly wouldn't threaten her with divorce over something so petty. However, out of respect, Viktoriya kept mum on the subject throughout the morning, but a slip of the tongue sent him off to the office knowing he was about to face a long, dreadful morning of damage control in the presence of his most trusted advisors.

Arriving atop Fort Malitrov in his personal helicopter, Sergei arrived in his office within five minutes of touching down. The words of his wife drove him mad throughout the short flight, so his first order of business was to retrieve that morning's newspaper. While he was tense as he crouched down to retrieve the neatly folded newspaper from the floor before the double doors leading into his office, he did not hesitate to lay his eyes upon the headline. However, when he saw the bold letters declaring 'Poland Votes Leave,' he felt his stomach churn, followed shortly by shortness of breath when he saw the final percentages. He was expecting a tight race that would narrowly favor the Federalists. Instead, the numbers loudly declared the secessionists had won a landslide victory.

The Premier suddenly became uncomfortably warm under his fine suit, prompting him to reach for his collar and tug it rapidly to allow the hot air to escape from its confines. This only worked so well, so he headed for his desk, where he removed his suit jacket. Placing the jacket on a coat rack tucked away in a corner of the cavernous office, he eventually took his seat and got straight to business. The tool at hand was his phone, and the first person he called was his personal secretary to order the assembly of his political advisors. When the call was through, he had roughly half an hour before he needed to head down to the meeting. Rather than waste the time letting his anxiety gnaw at him, he picked up the phone once more to summon the man he trusted most regarding the situation in Poland.

Within minutes of his summoning, Aleksander entered the Premier's office through the double doors. Placing his right fist over his heart, he bowed his head in a show of respect. He then closed the distance between the two men and took his seat in a leather chair across the desk from the Premier. Eschewing a formal greeting, Sergei was quick to have the first word between himself and Aleksander.

"You've seen the results of the referendum, I trust?"

"I have," Aleksander said, keen on keeping his answers brief. "I'm as surprised as you are."

"Is that so?" Sergei asked, and Aleksander nodded. "You weren't expecting a landslide?"

"No, sir," Aleksander said. "I expected a Federalist victory, though by a narrow margin."

"Then let me ask you this. Do you believe the counting has been compromised?" Sergei asked, but Aleksander shrugged quietly. "It's a yes or no question, Alek."

"With all due respect, it really isn't. While I'm not saying there's not a chance the ballot counting was flawed, I have trouble believing there was large-scale fraud."

"How could you say that? Surely, you saw the exit polls last night. The majority proudly declared their opposition to secession."

"I wouldn't put too much stock in what people tell the media. Secession may not appear popular in the news, but it was very popular behind closed doors."

"And how do you know that?" Sergei asked with a narrowed glare. "You're not a secessionist, are you?"

"Absolutely not," Aleksander was quick to say. "While I have a deep love for my homeland, I consider myself apolitical so long as I'm an officer in this man's army."

"And if you were a civilian?" Sergei challenged with a sharp eye.

"I'd vote to stay. Poland has nothing to gain from secession," Aleksander said, speaking quite truthfully, leaving Sergei seemingly convinced, for he nodded in approval.

"Then what are your thoughts on a recount?"

"I feel that a recount is expected, but it should be done quickly and transparently. Any political nonsense will fire up the secessionists. That could very well lead to the extremists among them to get violent."

Smirking, Sergei rubbed his bearded chin in contemplation. For a moment, Aleksander thought he'd make some snide remark, but he was pleasantly surprised.

"I'm going to present your advice to the political council," Sergei said. "The last thing we need is more conspiracies about political corruption."

"I couldn't agree more," Aleksander said. "However, I'd implore you to take a hard line with your advisors. It's well known that the majority is against secession and would favor dirty tactics to keep the vote from the senate."

"Don't worry about them. This meeting focused simply on damage control. We don't even know what the rebels want yet."

"Secessionists," Aleksander said disapprovingly. "Until they take up arms against the rule of law, they're secessionists."

"Semantics," Sergei said, brushing off Aleksander's correction. "Nonetheless, it's your job to ensure things stay peaceful in Poland. I trust you've nailed down a date for the negotiations, yes?"

"Of course, I'll be meeting with the Polish Liberation Party's leadership next week in Senatgrad. I have a full agenda planned, and I won't return until I know exactly what they have planned for an independent Poland."

"Then I hope you don't mind that I send Viktoriya to oversee the discussions."

Though he was a little skeptical, Aleksander didn't argue against the First Lady sitting in on the negotiations. In fact, he felt it would help public transparency. Not only was she the wife of the Premier, but she was also quite skilled as a diplomat.

"Very good," Sergei said with a nod. "Now, I hope you don't take that request the wrong way. It's not that I don't trust you, it's just that the room would be overwhelmingly Polish. If you catch my meaning."

Taking Sergei's meaning as that he wanted to ensure the negotiations were balanced, Aleksander showed no distrust toward his leader. "Viktoriya is a brilliant negotiator. She's a welcome addition to my team," he said, and Sergei nodded in agreement.

"Very good," the Premier said, his voice trailing slightly as if he was contemplating something. Aleksander was keen to pick up on this and asked if there was something more. "Yes, a small favor."

"Of course, what is it?" Aleksander asked, assuming it had something to do with the looming negotiations.

Strangely hesitant, the Premier began to speak, but only a syllable crept out before he paused in frustration. Forcing himself to say the words, he explained the other situation that weighed heavily on his mind. "Some vicious rumors are circulating about my wife," he said. "I'm not sure if it's just a pack of lies spread by my enemies, or if it's true, but I'm told Viktoriya is unfaithful."

A look of surprise washed over Aleksander. He wasn't quite sure what to say, but Sergei didn't need him to speak just yet. He carried on.

"I want you to keep an eye on her throughout your time in Senatgrad. If you see anything suspicious, please make a record of it."

"I'll do what I can, but I'm not sure my wife would appreciate me following Viktoriya around."

"Katrin will be joining you?"

"My whole family will be there," Aleksander said. "We're using the trip as something of a family vacation. It's Aleksey's first time home in almost a year."

Nodding, Sergei considered retracting the favor, but decided to double down instead. "Katrin and Viktoriya have always been friendly. Perhaps she could help in this endeavor."

While reasonably uncomfortable with spying on the First Lady, let alone asking his wife to help, Aleksander knew better than to say no to the Premier. So, to hopefully end this conversation before the favors being asked were compounded further, he asked what Sergei was looking for exactly.

"I want you to study how she engages with the Polish representatives. She's always been a flirt, but there are telltale signs when someone is trying to seduce instead of manipulate."

"Indeed," Aleksander said. "Anything else?"

"I'd like for your wife to join her for a night on the town at some point. According to the rumors, when she goes to the nightclubs, she's often very friendly with the younger men and has a knack for disappearing from the watchful eyes of her guards for lengths of time. If she does this, I want to know immediately."

"I'll see to it," Aleksander said dutifully. "I can't promise I'll find hard evidence either way, but I'll do my best."

"That's all I ask," Sergei said. So, with little more to say, he casually ended the conversation and took to his feet. Thanking Aleksander for his apparent neutrality through this secession movement and his willingness to help in this personal matter, Sergei shook

Aleksander's hand and bid him adieu. The two men soon left the office together. While Aleksander headed back down to the army offices, Sergei went to his meeting with his team of political advisors. Though the meeting would run short, the Premier returned to his office with a plan to handle the situation at hand.

By the noon hour, he took to the podium to address the people and share his concerns that the results of the referendum may have been fraudulent and would be subjected to a thorough recount. Knowing this bold, though predictable, move would anger much of Poland, he stood by his decision and attempted to save face by stating he would gladly sign the articles of secession if the results were found legitimate. In reality, he had no intention of signing the documents that would set Poland free. He was simply buying his government time to figure out a means of preventing secession.

Chapter 13

Berlin, Germany

Giving himself a couple of days to contemplate his opportunity to join the tournament that could finally allow him to go pro and the associated cost, Gustav woke up late that morning with an answer. He was going to join the tournament despite Audra's reservations about his chances of winning. Of course, this wasn't because she didn't believe he was a great fighter capable of ascending to the professional circuit; she was worried about the no-holds-barred nature of the league he was trying to join and the high cost of entry. Because of these concerns, he spent the last week trying to convince her to lend him the money, but she wouldn't budge. Over time, this brought him to the point of desperation, for while he wasn't completely penniless, his financial situation wouldn't allow him to take the chance alone. However, when he was just on the brink of accepting defeat, an opportunity presented itself at the gym. Unfortunately, he couldn't tell Audra the truth, fearing it would be cataclysmic to their relationship. After all, what he was considering was akin to selling his soul to the devil.

While the Kitty Kat Club didn't open until noon, this wasn't a problem for Gustav. He was a night owl and often stayed up well into the early hours watching videotapes or playing video games. On this day, he woke up around ten and was at the door of the club just minutes past twelve.

Stepping into the gentleman's club through the front door, Gustav found the place to be a dead zone. Only a single bouncer was working the door, and only a handful of degenerates stood around the center stage as a much too skinny young woman danced for their pleasure and money. Of course, Gustav wasn't there to watch an exotic dancer or partake in her premium services in the champagne room. Rather, he was there to see the man commonly found upstairs in the office that overlooked the public area.

Walking up to the suited bouncer standing behind a reception desk, Gustav nodded silently and was told the price of entry. Gustav shook his head and told him that he was there for a meeting with Mr. Rozek. However, given that Gustav wasn't on duty, a member of the owner's entourage, or even on the VIP list, Gustav was prevented from entering for free. Not defeated yet, Gustav gave his name and told the bouncer that Jens Groth had told him that Mr. Rozek would meet with him just after noon. This seemed to work, for Jens was a notable member of Mr. Rozek's entourage – after all, he wasn't just the man's uncle, he was the head of an outlaw motorcycle club closely tied to the Marzahn Syndicate – the unofficial name for Rozek Enterprises crafted by the German national media.

Upon hearing the name of Jens Groth, the Bouncer told Gustav to wait one moment and picked up a phone. Gustav watched him type in a short extension and listened closely as he spoke with someone on the other end. The conversation was brief and when the Bouncer looked back to Gustav, his face was grim. Gustav had a feeling he was going to be denied and made to pay, but he was pleasantly surprised – Mr. Rozek would see him immediately.

Crossing the public area, Gustav made his way to a stairway draped with a red carpet and a serpentine stairwell secured by brass rails. Upon reaching the top he found a burly pair of bouncers guarding the double doors. A few feet to the left of the door stood a lengthy floor-to-ceiling window of tinted glass. From his knowledge, this was commonly used by Mr. Rozek and his cronies to observe the action below without being easily seen. However, he didn't spend more than a moment observing the glass, for he was immediately ordered to spread his arms and legs for a frisking. Gustav complied and was thoroughly checked for weapons and other contraband. When he was cleared for entry, he was given a short list of rules to abide by while meeting with the boss. When the guard was through and Gustav assured him that he understood, both doors were opened, and he was allowed inside alone. However, Mr. Rozek wasn't behind the large desk that sat at the center of the room. In his place, standing before the desk, was the mogul's lawyer and consigliere, Karl Hess.

Like all members of the upper echelon of Richard Rozek's organization, Karl was well-dressed and perfectly groomed. Blessed with natural good looks, especially his perfect pearly white smile, he had the appearance of an A-list movie star. However, like his boss, his appearance was deceiving, for inside Karl was a ruthless gangster. Despite his ruthless nature, he had qualities that separated him from the rank-and-file gangsters under Richard Rozek and Jens Groth's command. Karl bore the gifts of charisma and above-average intelligence, but most of all, he was a skilled lawyer and was second-to-none in the art of negotiation. Because of Karl, Mr. Rozek and his inner circle were free men and virtually unstoppable by law enforcement. For this reason, he was the most trusted man in Rozek's tight-knit circle.

"Mr. Hagen, welcome," Karl said with a deep, manly voice that seemed to belong to a larger man than Gustav was facing. "Mr. Rozek will see you in the lounge. Follow me."

With a silent nod, Gustav followed Karl through to a pair of double doors at the far end of the office. Once through these doors, he found himself in a small room that was furnished like a private champagne room. While there was a well-stocked wet bar and soft lighting to set a relaxing mood, the centerpiece was a large horseshoe-shaped white leather couch situated at the center of the room. It was there, sitting with his Italian loafers resting on the mahogany coffee table, that Richard Rozek was waiting.

While Richard was Audra's older brother by about five or six years, Gustav hardly knew the man, as the siblings were barely on speaking terms. However, when he did fraternize with the gangster, Richard wasn't shy about his disapproval of him. Strangely, this time around, Richard was warm in reception, going so far as ordering a waitress he had on standby to fix Gustav a drink of his choice before they got down to business. This gesture was certainly appreciated, and Gustav knew better than to turn down the offer, so he requested the first thing that came to mind that wasn't a beer – he didn't want to appear lowbrow at that moment.

Drinks in hand, Gustav and Richard sat across from each other while Karl sat at the center of the horseshoe. Given their history, Richard's warm demeanor was off-putting, but Gustav tried to look past it and explained his situation carefully. In turn, Richard listened attentively. When Gustav was done, he spoke with a smile.

"So, the rumors are true. Jens made you quite a fighter. Congratulations, Gustav," Richard said.

"Thank you, sir," Gustav said, but Richard raised his finger as if to say he wasn't finished.

"Of course, I've also seen the Blood Games firsthand, and that's not the kind of fighting you're used to. Kickboxing has rules, and lots of them. The Blood Games, on the other hand, well, its name isn't just for show."

Allowing for a long pause so as not to interrupt Richard again, Gustav replied carefully. "I'm aware, but I believe I can win."

"Of course, you're undefeated. You just need the buy-in money, right?" Richard said with a grin, and though his expression gave Gustav the feeling he wasn't getting what he came for, he was soon surprised. "Well, your reputation is something I can put my money on. I'll loan you the buy-in fee."

Expecting Richard to continue, so that he could reveal the worrisome conditions of the loan, Gustav thanked him quickly and under his breath.

"Of course, I am a businessman," he said coolly. "Though I'm taking the fact that you're my sister's boyfriend into consideration, what I'm offering is a loan, not a gift. I expect my money back with interest."

"Yes, that's understandable," Gustav replied calmly.

"Good," Richard said, his attention turning to Karl. "Karl, if you wouldn't mind."

Saying nothing, Karl reached down for the briefcase at his feet and put it on the coffee table. Opening the briefcase, he pulled out a document and handed it to Gustav for him to read.

"These are the terms of the agreement my client has just discussed with you," Karl said, pointing to the front page. "You will be loaned the sum of ten thousand Deutsche Marks in cash to be used for the entrance fee and the accompanying expenses for the upcoming Blood Games tournament in the city of Senatgrad. By signing this contract, you agree to pay back this loan within one month of the conclusion of the tournament. Failure to do so will result in a penalty in the form of twenty-five percent interest per month until the loan has been repaid in full."

The color draining from his face at the sound of such a steep penalty, Gustav grew nervous. "What if I can't pay it back?" Gustav asked, his voice turning sheepish as he feared he might have queered the deal. "Hypothetically speaking, of course."

Seemingly ignoring the question, Karl continued. "To ensure the loan is paid in full, we have designed an installment payment plan based on your vocation. Should you fail to pay the loan back by the end of the first month following the tournament, you will be required to compete in as many local fighting tournaments as possible. All earnings will be surrendered to the estate of my client until the loan is repaid in full."

"I believe that's fair," Richard said with a cool stare. "Do you agree, Gustav?"

"Yes," Gustav said, catching both men by surprise. "I've done the math. All I have to do is win two matches, and the debt is repaid."

"That's easier said than done," Richard said, but Gustav was resolute.

"You've seen me fight. I may not win the tournament, but I'll go far."

Smiling, Richard was impressed by Gustav's will and invited him to sign the contract if he truly found the terms of the contract agreeable. Then, seemingly without a second thought, Gustav bent over and retrieved a pen with which he signed the contract.

"Very good," Richard said brightly. "You've either just secured yourself a career in professional fighting or damned yourself to a miserable life in my debt. I'd say I'm pulling for you, but I'd rather make money on this deal."

"Then I'm afraid you'll end up disappointed, Mr. Rozek," Gustav said with bold determination. "As I said, I may not win the tournament, but I'm going to make it far enough to pay you back without interest. Along the way, I'm going to impress at least one of those scouts and finally give Audra the life she deserves."

"That's quite the vow, but let's not get ahead of ourselves here, Gustav," Richard said, his once warm demeanor reverting to the cold, calculated personality of the gangster he truly was. "You're a good fighter, but you'll be going against some of the best in the world. Even if you do win enough to pay back this loan, don't kid yourself with Audra. The moment she finds out where you got this money, you'll be out the door."

"That's my business, not yours," Gustav said boldly, though he secretly feared Richard had lured him into a trap aimed at ruining his relationship for good.

Chuckling, Richard assured him he had no intention of informing Audra of their deal. After all, he was a businessman, not a gossip. "Just keep your head in the game and your lies straight," Richard said with an outstretched hand. "Now let's seal this deal like men."

Wanting to finish the deal quickly, Gustav clenched Richard's hand in an iron grip and shook it firmly. When he was freed from the gangster's grasp, Karl left to secure the contract and retrieve the money. When he returned, Gustav was shown a briefcase lined with one hundred Deutsche Mark bills. When he was assured that it was all real cash, the briefcase was locked, and he was given the combination on a slip of paper. The pair then parted ways, with Karl leading Gustav out through Richard's office, down a private set of stairs hidden in the back wall by a hidden door, and out the back door in a hallway near the champagne room and kitchen.

Stopping only to deposit the money at the bank, Gustav returned home to find Audra sitting at the table. As expected of her, when free time was available, she was hard at work on her art and lost in her own world. Considering things had been tense between them the last few days, he didn't say anything after stepping in and locking the door behind him. However, when he passed by her to go into the kitchen and find a snack, she called out to him. Of course, she didn't bother to look up from her work.

"Where were you?" she asked with mild curiosity, as she carefully detailed her latest character.

"Out," he said, knowing she'd roll her eyes.

"No kidding. Out where?" she asked with a tense but distant tone. This was common for her when she wanted to make peace, so he abandoned his quest for food and walked over to the table. Though he didn't take a seat, he was willing to converse.

"Trying to find the right things to say," he said, looking straight at her so that when she looked up to him, they would be eye to eye.

"About what?" she asked, finally taking her attention from the drawing.

"The tournament."

Letting off a short humph, she put down her pencil and crossed her arms in subtle frustration. "I should have figured."

"Look, I don't want to fight," he said, but she shrugged and said she hadn't changed her mind. "That's fine, I have the money."

"You what?" she asked with surprise, but he shrugged in reply. "What do you mean you have the money?"

"That's what I said," he replied calmly, secretly hoping he could keep his story straight under pressure. "I've been stashing bits of prize money from each fight for a rainy-day situation. Well, I'd call it a rainy-day situation. Wouldn't you?"

"You have nine thousand marks stashed away?" she asked, and he nodded, throwing her into a sudden rage. "You mean to tell me you had nine thousand fucking marks all this time, but you could never pay your full share of the bills?"

"Audra, calm down," he said, but that was a mistake.

"Get out! I don't want to be around you right now," she commanded, but he calmly refused, so she threw her chair back and shouted. "Get the hell out of here, you selfish bastard!"

"And go where? This is my apartment too," he shouted back.

"Not unless you start paying your share!" she snarled, her heart racing as adrenaline began to course through her veins.

"You need to calm down."

"And you need to get out. You have no idea how hurt I am right now. Don't make me do something I might regret."

Shaking his head, for Audra was prone to letting her emotions get the best of her in times of stress, Gustav didn't bother to argue further. Rather, he waved his hand and turned to leave. On his way to the door, he spoke over his shoulder, promising he'd win enough to cover the bills for a whole year, but she didn't say anything. She just sat back down and glared at him with hurt in her eyes, so he left her alone. When he was gone, she broke down and cried, for as much as she wanted to work things out, she was reaching her breaking point with him.

A man on a mission that day, Gustav rang Jens from a payphone and met up with him at the gym to move things forward with the Blood Games tournament. Because the gym was open for business, the place was filled with fighters of all stripes preparing for an upcoming match or just training. For the sake of privacy, the meeting took place in the office.

"I take it the meeting with Richard went well?" Jens said, and Gustav nodded.

"His terms are stiff, but what was I supposed to do? Not take the money and lose my chance at going pro?"

Being the man responsible for Richard's cutthroat nature, Jens wasn't surprised his nephew wouldn't give Gustav a fair deal. But rather than offer to get him a better deal, he told him he could have come to him instead – something Gustav had never even considered an option.

"What's done is done," Gustav said. "I took his money and I'm going to pay him back the moment I have it."

"Alright, then let's talk about this tournament. I've read over their website a few times, and it's nothing like the beer halls. Do you really understand what you're getting yourself into, or do I need to explain it plainly?"

"Go ahead," Gustav said, crossing his arms.

"As you already know, it's a full-contact mixed martial arts tournament. That means you won't be trouncing the competition like usual," Jens said, but Gustav shrugged. "It's also single elimination and will take place over three days until only one fighter remains. Fortunately, you get paid for each win, but you're going to need to win at least twice to pay Richard back."

"Not a problem," Gustav said confidently, but Jens ignored him and continued.

"There are thirty fighters in this tournament. Give or take, the total earnings up for grabs could be as high as half a million rubles. That's a lot of fucking money to be had."

"Hell yes," Gustav said with a wide grin, but Jens was quick to bring him down to earth.

"Even if you win the whole thing, you won't be taking home that much money. Just focus on your first two fights and getting scouted for a professional circuit."

"You're right, I can't worry about the money too much," Gustav said, but his mind began to wander again. He soon found himself thinking about his situation with Audra. "Am I allowed an entourage, or is it just me going alone?"

"You're allowed one guest and a trainer. I'm guessing that's me and Audra, right?"

"Well, you're my trainer, but I'm not so sure about Audra. She's pretty pissed at me right now."

"About what?" Jens asked, worried she'd be a distraction rather than a genuine concern for his relationship.

"I told her I had the money for the tournament, and she flipped."

"What did you tell her?" Jens asked coolly.

"I told her I had squirreled the money away over time by skimming my prize money. She's just pissed because she thinks I should have used it for bills."

"Alright, that's fine," Jens said, for he was concerned that Gustav had told Audra the truth behind the money. That would have caused bigger problems than Gustav might have expected. Fortunately, that wasn't the case, so he remarked that she'll get over it.

"Yeah, hopefully," Gustav said, but he didn't want to talk about the war at home, so he steered the conversation back to the contract.

"As expected, you'll have access to top-level training facilities. Unfortunately, it's a shared space, so there's a chance your opponents could get a feel for you before a match."

"Shit," Gustav muttered under his breath. "Tell me there's a silver lining here."

"There is," Jens replied. "Fight order each day is randomized, so no one will know who they're fighting until they're called out to the arena."

"That's good, but if it's random, is there a chance someone could fight twice in a day?"

"From the looks of it, the only time you'll be fighting twice in a day is the finals when only eight men are left," Jens said, pausing to think it all through. "From my understanding, everyone fights once on either day one or two, and the remaining competitors fight once on the third day. The finals will go a bit differently, and it basically ends up being an endurance round."

"That makes sense," Gustav said, though he was still trying to make sense of it all in his own mind, and then Jens took a firm tone.

"Look, if you're getting cold feet, you need to take that money back right now."

"I'm entering that tournament," Gustav said with sudden determination. "I don't know if I'll go all the way, but I sure as hell won't walk away empty-handed. I'm just confused about how this is all organized. Thirty men... that's a lot of fights."

"Then let's put it in simpler terms. Round one is fifteen fights over two days, and round two is seven fights, plus a bye, I guess. Round three –"

"Wait, hold on. Who gets the bye?" Gustav asked, but Jens wasn't privy to that information, so he just shrugged.

"Whoever is luckiest, I guess," Jen said. "Anyways, round three is an endurance round with slightly different rules. For one, it takes place the following Saturday and will be televised on pay-per-view. And since there are only four fighters, it's double elimination. If you manage to get to the final round, you'll be pretty exhausted by the end, but so will your opponent."

"Well, I don't see myself winning this thing, but so long as I get to the finals, who cares, right?"

"Exactly," Jens said with a grin as he reached into his pocket for a pen. "All you need to do is sign this contract and you're on your way."

Receiving a pen from Jens, Gustav signed his name on the dotted line. He was officially a competitor in the upcoming Blood Games tournament in Senatgrad. While there was a heap of money to be won, his greatest concern was winning at least two matches to avoid falling into crippling debt to Berlin's most notorious gangster. So, to show Jens he was intent on winning, he left the office shortly after to gear up and spar. He would be spending as much time in the gym as possible until the day he left for Senatgrad, so that when he stepped into that arena, he would be ready to show no mercy and trounce the competition.

Chapter 14

Moscow, Republic of Russia, Slavic Federation

Following a slow and meticulous recount following the Polish referendum, Aleksander went to the office that morning with an unwanted burden on his shoulders. Despite the government's attempt at finding a way to disqualify the vote, Aleksander's first task that morning was carrying out his patriotic duty as asked of him by Poland's President-elect. While Aleksander wanted nothing to do with the secession for fear of his safety, he couldn't escape this terrible burden thrust upon him, for refusal to deliver the Articles of Secession would have branded him a social pariah in his homeland – a place where he was celebrated as one of the nation's great war heroes and would be welcomed back as Marshal of the Third Republic.

Having some time to contemplate his burden before being summoned to the Premier's office, Aleksander had long since swallowed his pride by the time he had left the gilded elevators that led out to the Hall of Heroes on Fort Malitrov's tenth floor. As he walked the crimson carpet that draped down the center of the hall, covering a length wide enough for two men to walk shoulder to shoulder without obscuring the black granite tile beneath, Aleksander glanced at the walls. Carved into the granite slabs situated against the wall was the name, service, and homeland of every man and woman to give their life in the armed service of the Slavic Federation, the confederacy that preceded it, and the revolutionary cause that brought those systems into place. While the names weren't meticulously organized by national origin, Aleksander spotted a handful of Polish names among the dead. He tried to read their names in passing and use their sacrifice as personal justification for what he was about to do, but there remained a deep-seated worry in his soul. While he loved his country more than the federation, he knew the Premier on a personal level and thus was aware of what the man was capable of. It was almost certain that if the Premier came to believe that he had voted for independence or even played some sort of role in the politics of the secession, he, and perhaps his entire family, would suffer greatly just as traitors. Regardless, he stood firm in his objective this day and proceeded down the carpet until he reached the double doors at the end. With one free hand, he weakly saluted the pair of guards standing at the flanks of the door. Aware of the General's arrival, they saluted him briefly before opening the doors and allowing the General into the Premier's cavernous office.

The moment Aleksander stepped into the Premier's office, the doors were pulled shut, and he was left alone with the man himself. Though no words were exchanged in those first few moments, Sergei's grim expression spoke volumes. Still, it was too late to turn and walk away, so Aleksander closed the gap between himself and the man who could ruin his life with a simple phone call.

Speaking only to greet the Head of State at first, Aleksander placed his briefcase on a chair meant for guests. Working the knobs, he opened the briefcase and pulled out a thin stack of documents secured together with paper clips. With a blank expression, Aleksander handed over the Articles of Secession and stood by with his head held high and his hands folded at the small of his back.

Taking the articles in his hands, the Premier looked at the cover sheet with cold eyes, but rather than bother removing the paperclips, he set it down on the space before him. He then looked to his trusted advisor with a mild look of sadness, but Aleksander knew there was betrayal behind those deep brown, almost black eyes.

"So, of all the people they could have sent, they placed this burden on you," Sergei said with a cool, somewhat disappointed tone. "What do you have to say on this matter?"

"It's an inglorious burden," Aleksander replied truthfully. "I did not want this outcome, and I especially did not want this burden."

"I see," Sergei said, breaking eye contact for a moment. "Yet here you are... handing me the Articles of Secession like one of Bednarz's lackeys."

"I assure you, I'm no friend of the secessionists," Aleksander said firmly, but Sergei shrugged.

"It's no secret that your wife dreams of going home, but you, Alek... you surprise me. I thought you were my confidant. My right-hand man, if you will."

"I am still those things," Aleksander said, speaking a little stronger than before. "Just because I'm presenting you these documents does not mean I am a secessionist. At no point have I ever— "

The Premier silenced Aleksander mid-sentence with a simple raise of his index finger. "You're not on trial. I was simply testing you," Sergei said with a calm tone that was shortly followed by a friendly smile that faded moments later. "Nonetheless, I am disappointed that you're the man who delivered this insult."

His heart beating a bit faster now, Aleksander remained silent. The Premier then declared that he wouldn't be signing the articles, at least not immediately. This presented Aleksander with a whole new concern, and his expression alerted Sergei to that fact.

"Something to say about that?" Sergei asked.

"Though I stand opposed to secession, the people have spoken. The majority demands independence. Refusing to sign these documents will set a dangerous precedent. The secessionists will use this for their propaganda--"

"And what? They'll call me a fascist again? The second coming of Stalin?" Sergei asked, interrupting with a terrifying grin. "I believe the law states that I have until midnight to sign these documents or provide a proper case for refusal. Perhaps you should put your fears at rest for a moment and let me speak fully before you conclude my own thoughts."

"Yes, you're right," Aleksander said sheepishly. "Please, carry on."

"Very well, and thank you," Sergei said condescendingly. "As I was attempting to say, I'm not worried about their propaganda. What I am worried about is a failed state at my front door... or worse, a new member of that damn fucking alliance."

"NATO is not our enemy," Aleksander said, but Sergei shrugged. "Then again, they're not exactly our ally either."

"Precisely why I'm concerned about Poland going off on its own without a plan," Sergei said. "But you're still planning to sit down with the secessionists, correct?"

"Yes, of course."

"Good, then you can explain to your countrymen that I won't be signing off on their secession without a solid plan. And I don't just mean installing a new government. I want to know how they plan to provide national defense, a working economy, international trade, and so on."

"I'll see to it, but you have to assure me that you'll sign the articles when I return."

"I make no promises," Sergei said, bringing Aleksander to sigh in frustration.

"Do you want a war, sir? Because that's what you get by making democracy a simple illusion. You're providing fertile ground for extremism."

"Are you threatening me, Alek?" Sergei asked with a sharp stare, but Aleksander stood firm.

"No, sir, I'm advising as your Chief of the General Staff. We cannot give the secessionists the ammunition for an insurrection," Aleksander said strongly, but quickly lowered his tone after a short pause. "Look, you had your recount, but it was a dead end. Don't drag this out any longer than necessary. This was an undeniably popular referendum."

"I won't allow this federation to become the next Yugoslavia," Sergei countered. "If the Polish Liberation Party can deliver a meaningful plan, I will sign the articles. Until then, these documents will sit on my desk waiting for the day I send them on their way."

"Then you'd better give the Polish people a damn good excuse. The last thing I want to do is invade my own country should a rebellion break out."

"Don't you worry, Alek. I'll be giving the people an address shortly after the dinner hour. You can tell your friends back home they'd better tune in before they get any militant ideas. We're done here."

"All I ask is that you avoid doing anything hasty. The last thing we need— "

"I said we're done here, General," Sergei said with a firm tone. "You have an army to oversee, and I have a speech to write."

"Very well," Aleksander said before taking to his feet. "I look forward to your speech. Surely it will be well-articulated as always."

When the Premier said nothing, Aleksander turned on his heels and headed for the door. When he passed through the doors back into the Hall of Heroes, he expected to be called back, but the order never came. The doors behind him closed soon after, and he made the long march down the hall to the elevator, which would take him down to the floor reserved for the offices of the Armed Forces Central Command. He would spend the rest of the day stewing in a mix of frustration and concern that would either worsen or alleviate depending on how the Premier presented his case to the people in that evening's address.

Chapter 15

Moscow, Republic of Russia, Slavic Federation

Despite suffering terribly from a broken heart, Aleksey wasn't the kind of person who could mope around the house feeling sorry for himself. He was a soldier. He was a man of action trained to ignore the pain and see his goals through. So, after just a day of feeling sorry for himself, he set a simple goal for himself. He was going to take his mind off his troubles and make the best of his time home before the trip to Senatgrad. However, given that he had spent the last decade in the Service, his closest friends lived far away from Moscow. The few friends he had locally had either moved away at some point or had prior engagements. Even his sister had other plans, so rather than just go to the city by himself, he hit the pool and swam laps until his body threatened to cramp up and sink to the bottom. Of course, he knew his limits, and when he came dangerously close to the point of no return, he pulled himself out of the water and waddled over to the sauna for a few minutes of relaxation. Before he could get too far on his way to the sauna, his mother poked her head in from the adjacent exercise room to tell him he had a visitor waiting on the patio. Though a little confused by who could have stopped by, he quickly assumed it was one of his close friends, like Viktor Zubov or Yanina Mahlkova. However, neither seemed likely. Viktor was a soldier with the Russian Army and Yanina's fiancé, whom she typically followed on deployment, was deployed. Of course, Kristof was with Alpha Group and there was conflict in Yugoslavia, so there was chance she stayed behind. If it was Yanina, he imagined knew about what happened with Tatiana. Hopefully, she was in good spirits, for he could certainly have a good time in the city.

While some might cry foul at a man visiting with another man's wife while he was away on deployment, this wasn't out of the ordinary for Aleksey. After all, the trio had been close friends ever since meeting in their early teens when they were all relative strangers to Moscow's manor district. And while Aleksey once competed with Kristof for Yanina's affection and lost, he had accepted defeat with grace and humility. Having met Tatiana shortly thereafter helped matters, but that got him thinking the worst. While Yanina was never quite fond of his former flame, he had no doubt she knew about her infidelity. Being that his goal that night was to put his heartache out of sight and out of mind, he wasn't so sure he wanted to see Yanina. Regardless, he convinced himself it wouldn't take much more than a calm request to drop any sour subjects. So, taking a minute to dry off and change into regular clothes, he headed out a door leading to the backyard.

Following a stone path marked with flat circular stepping stones and illuminated by solar lights, Aleksey made his way to the back patio fully expecting to see a friendly face. Unfortunately, the woman he found waiting for him was not the kind-spirited former girl next door, but the bitch who ripped his heart out and ran away without saying a word.

Aleksey's blood ran cold the moment he saw Tatiana sitting quietly on the patio swing that sat at the far end of the patio and faced out toward the backyard. She clearly heard him coming, for her head soon turned and she stood up. Nervously, she twisted the silver promise ring he had given to her before his first deployment. Half-expecting her to remove it, he stopped a few feet shy of her and asked what she was doing there.

"I came to talk," she said softly, but Aleksey shrugged.

"There's nothing to say. The damage is done," he said, but she sighed and shook her head.

"I knew you wouldn't make this easy."

"Easy?" he cried. "I came home to find my girlfriend pregnant and living with another man, and you expect me to talk to you like nothing happened?"

"Look, I fucked up—"

"You're damn right you did."

"Fucking hell, Aleksey. Will you let me finish a sentence?" she cried, so Aleksey crossed his arms and glared at her. "Look, I know this wasn't the right way to end things, but I didn't know what else to do." Letting her talk, Aleksey shrugged and angrily cocked his head. "I was lonely, and I was drunk."

"Here we go," Aleksey said, rolling his eyes. "You think I wasn't lonely? I could have slept with dozens of women, but I didn't."

"Yeah, well, not everyone is made of stone like you, I guess," she said sheepishly. "Anyway, it didn't mean anything to me, but..."

"But?"

"I'm pregnant," she admitted. "I don't know how it happened, but it happened. It's not his fault, it's mine."

"I'm aware, you can stop talking now. We're done here," Aleksey said, and she sighed through her nose.

"I don't expect you to care, but I wanted to come clean with you," she said, but he just shrugged. "Do you have anything meaningful to say?"

"What do you want me to say? I was out there serving my country and saving innocent people from death squads while you got knocked up by some middle-management prick behind my back."

"You just don't get it, do you?" she asked out of frustration.

"What's there to get? You cheated on me and expect sympathy."

"Look, I know you're angry, but the truth is, I never wanted to hurt you. I never wanted to be with anyone else, but being alone for nine months out of the year eventually takes its toll—"

"I get that, but you could have done the decent thing and just broken up with me. Instead, you waited for me to come home so you could rip my heart out of my ass!"

"I couldn't get a hold of you, and you never called!" Tatiana cried, but Aleksey didn't care, so she surrendered. "Fine, you're right and I'm wrong," she said distantly, but then her own resentment surfaced. "You can blame me for this, but it's your fault just the same. This would have never happened if you had been around more."

"I had a duty to my country," he said, but she wasn't interested in hearing that.

"You also had a duty to me. We could have been married and had a family by now, but you put the Service before me. What did you think was going to happen?"

Finding her reasoning to be ridiculous, Aleksey attempted to remind her that he had proposed on two separate occasions, but she countered him firmly.

"Oh, come on, we weren't ready at eighteen. We were just kids," she cried, so he reminded her that he had tried again three years prior, but she had an answer for that, too. "Did you honestly think I'd give up my career to live my life on some base while you travelled the world playing hero?"

"If life with me was so bad, why stay with me for so long?"

"Because I loved you," she cried as her face contorted with pain, and tears began to stream.

"That sure didn't stop you from hooking up with some asshole you met at the office. But let me guess, he's a big name down at the firm, right? Promised you a nice raise for a bit of unpaid overtime, didn't he?"

"Oh, fuck you, Aleksey. Fuck you!" she snarled, her face becoming wet as tears streamed down her face. "You abandoned me! If the Service was so much more important, you should have just let me go. I deserved to be happy, too."

"I'm not taking the blame for your mistakes," Aleksey thundered. "Go home to your backup plan, and don't even come back here again. You sicken me."

Wiping the tears away, she stared at him with a firm and determined expression.

"His name is Kirill, and yes, I met him at the office. I wish I could say I loved him, but I don't. He's an arrogant, self-centered man, but none of this is his fault. I pursued him."

"Good for you," Aleksey said dismissively. "You can stop talking now. I don't care to know the rest."

"Look, I just want you to know that he wanted me to have an abortion and I refused, so now I'm stuck," she said with a shaky voice. "You're the better man in almost every way, and I'm sorry things had to end like this. If I could turn back the clock and set things right, I would."

"You made this stinking bed for yourself," Aleksey said, so she sighed once more.

"Then I hope you find what you're looking for, Aleksey. Again, I'm sorry."

"Goodbye, Tati," Aleksey said blankly, knowing she wanted him to apologize for putting her in the position that got her into this mess. However, he was stubborn and refused to accept any responsibility.

Finally accepting that she'd get nothing from him but hostility, Tatiana quietly nodded and turned her back on him. Though she wanted to admit that she'd go through with the procedure if he'd be willing to forgive her, she knew it would be a waste of breath. Aleksey was a man of honor, and because of that, there was no going back to the way things were. Still, she would have felt a little better if he had just admitted that he put his career before her and accepted that he was at least partially responsible for the demise of their relationship. But with each step along that path that would lead to the front of the house, her hopes were dashed. He wasn't going to see things the same way as she did.

After parting ways with Tatiana, Aleksey went back inside through the patio doors leading into the kitchen. Though the kitchen was dark, his mother was seated in the living room with the live coverage of the referendum recount playing on the television. She was pretending to be engrossed in the program, but he knew she had overheard at least the shouting. So, walking into the living room, he took a seat on the loveseat adjacent to the sofa his mother was sitting on. Looking her straight in the eyes, he asked how much she heard.

"Enough," she said with a nod. "I feel bad for you both. I'm sure it wasn't easy for her."

"Oh, please, don't defend her, Mom," Aleksey asked, but Katrin continued.

"When I met your father, we were in a similar situation. Though we made it work, not everyone has that ability."

"I don't need this right now," Aleksey said, taking to his feet. "I'm not even sure why I came in here."

"Because you wanted advice," Katrin said with soft eyes. "What she did was terrible, but she didn't get away easily. You heard it yourself; you're the better man."

"That doesn't matter much."

"Sure it does," Katrin said. "The only thing that ruined this relationship was her inability to stay honest. You gave her a lot of chances for a life together. This is the path she chose."

"Again, this isn't helping, Mom."

"Then let me finish," Katrin said coolly. "Losing Tatiana like this hurts badly, but this is God's plan in action. She wasn't the one for you, but the woman you're destined for is out there somewhere."

"Somehow I find that hard to believe," Aleksey said dismissively as he took to his feet. "I wasted twelve years on love and look what it got me."

"She wasn't the one," Katrin said again, but Aleksey was through with this conversation.

"Loves for suckers," he said. He was soon marching out of the room and into the hall leading out from the kitchen. For a moment, he could be heard rummaging through the front closet. When he returned, he was wearing a leather jacket.

"Where are you going?" Katrin asked curiously, for that was Aleksey's motorcycle jacket.

"Out for a good, long ride. I need to get my mind off things," Aleksey replied, reaching for the door that would lead into the garage where his motorcycle was stored. "I'll be back sometime before dinner."

"Just be careful. I don't want you drinking if you're going for a ride."

"Don't worry, I had my fill of alcohol the last couple of days. I just need to feel the wind on my face and see some friendly faces," Aleksey replied before twisting the doorknob. "Maybe I'll find the woman of my destiny wandering around town."

Initially just cruising the city to clear his head, Aleksey was finding it next to impossible to force the memory of his final conversation with Tatiana from his mind. Though he felt justified at that moment for his words and actions, he came to regret much of it. While he was certainly heartbroken and angry over the circumstances surrounding the breakup, the ride helped him realize his own faults. Deep down, he wanted to have another talk just so he could admit his guilt, but he saw no point. He knew if he saw the man who stole his girlfriend from him again, he might not be able to contain his anger like he did at the bar. So, dismissing the thought of seeing her one last time, he drove down to their special place.

Leaving his motorcycle parked along the avenue, Aleksey walked the path with his eyes locked on the mirror-like pond. He remembered the good times he had there playing ice hockey with his friends and showing off fancy skating skills to impress the girls. It was at this park that he walked the paths with Tatiana and skated the ice together on cold winter days. They even shared their first kiss and became a couple at this place. While this place once brought him so much happiness and joy, it only served to remind him of times long past. They were moments he'd eventually forget without Tatiana to remind him of their youth as they lay in bed or cuddled up on the couch.

Letting off a bitter sigh, Aleksey stepped off the path and made his way to the edge of the pond. A pair of ducks looked his way as they swam across the water. For a moment, he smiled as the pair reminded him one last time of what he was mourning.

"Hopefully you two make it last," Aleksey said sheepishly, a small bouquet of wildflowers clenched in his hand. He looked down at the pink and white petals and sighed deeply before tossing them into the water. Watching the flowers float away and separate, he took it as symbolic of what he had lost, but then he looked at the ducks and felt a glimmer of hope.

"She's out there," he whispered to himself. "Her name's not Tatiana, but she's out there."

Chapter 16

Moscow, Republic of Russia, Slavic Federation

Returning home in time for dinner, Aleksander ate quietly while Katrin attempted to strike up a conversation, but neither her husband nor son was willing to speak, leaving Lena to carry on the conversation. However, considering her finals were nearly through and secession was on everyone's mind, the subject eventually turned to the events of the day and nationalist politics.

"So, is it true?" Katrin asked, her eyes on Aleksander. "Did he refuse to sign?"

Keeping quiet as he chewed his food, Aleksander let the tension build before finally answering. "He refused for now," Aleksander said, before checking his watch. "He'll be giving an address to the people shortly.

"He has no right!" Katrin sneered, but Aleksander said nothing. "How could you let this happen? We made our choice, Alek. We voted for freedom."

"I know, and it will be honored. The Premier gave me his word that he'll sign, but just not yet," he said coolly, before taking a short pause. "Unfortunately, the burden is still firmly on my shoulders."

"What is that supposed to mean?" Katrin challenged.

"It means our trip to Senatgrad will determine the quickness of the secession."

"So, it's happening?" Katrin asked with a bright smile. "They're really going to let us go?"

"That's what it seems," Aleksander said, his voice showing he had grown tired of politics. "The Premier will be speaking in about fifteen minutes. Can we change the subject until then?"

"Of course," Katrin said with a victorious smile.

Gathered in the living room, Katrin and Aleksander sat at opposite ends of the couch while Aleksey took the armchair, and Lena sat in the middle of the loveseat with her legs crossed at the ankles. There was tension in the air and judging by how irritated Lena made her mother by tapping her fingers nervously on her thighs, Katrin was nervous.

"Do you think he'll sign the articles on live television?" Lena asked, speaking to no one in particular.

"We're talking about the man who stole the premiership and views himself as emperor of the Slavs," Katrin replied, bringing her husband to roll his eyes as their son watched the television intently. "He ordered this recount so they could figure out a way to throw the referendum out and prevent the secession."

"I hope you're wrong," Lena said with worry in her voice, before looking at her father. "They didn't they find anything, did they?" she asked, but Aleksander remained quiet. "Dad?"

"I'm sure they tried, but I think we beat the bastards fair and square," Katrin said, allowing an uncharacteristic swear to slip from her tongue.

While Lena appreciated her mother's spirit, her words did little to ease any concerns. But before anything more could be said, the television roared to life with the sound of clapping. The Premier soon walked across the screen and took his place at the podium.

"There's the bastard now," Katrin said, prompting her husband to tell her to stop with the profanity. The room soon fell silent as the Premier began his address.

For the first few minutes, the Premier spoke of legitimate concerns regarding irregularities in voting and the subsequent counting. While he offered an apology to the Polish people for the need to recount the votes, he claimed that it was all done in the interest of sustaining a fair and balanced democracy. He then went on to explain that the recount was fruitful. This struck fear into the hearts of the patriots in the room as he explained that evidence of voter fraud was discovered. However, there was a sigh of relief as the Premier revealed that the revised voting percentage still gave the secessionists an overwhelming majority. Still, the Premier continued.

"...and while the rate of fraud was negligible, I had used this time to personally assess the situation to make a proper decision. While the will of the Polish people is unquestionable, even after this recount, I cannot in good conscience allow for the cutting of ties without a solid plan."

"That rotten bastard!" Katrin exclaimed loudly. "I knew he'd pull something like this."

Remaining eerily calm, Aleksander and the rest of his family listened closely as the Premier continued his explanation for delaying the signing of the Articles of Secession. However, the address ended only a minute or so later, and the podium was vacated. Still, in that minute, the Premier had made it very clear what the Polish Liberation Party would have to do if they wanted the Premier to even entertain the idea of bending to the will of the people and not his stubborn pride.

"Properly convey a sound plan for independence. What the hell does that even mean?" Aleksey asked, breaking his silence at last.

"He wants to ensure that we can truly survive on our own," Aleksander said. "There's fear that Poland would somehow end up like Yugoslavia without Moscow's leash."

"That tyrant seems to forget that Poland existed for centuries without foreign powers breathing down our necks and dictating our policies," Katrin declared, and Aleksander couldn't help but agree.

"Not entirely true, but I see your point," Aleksander said. "Regardless, this isn't over, and I was somewhat expecting it to go like this. We still have a summit with secessionists. While the agenda is sure to change, my team and I will manage."

"At this point, I don't see them letting us go without a war," Katrin said.

"I certainly hope you mean a war of words because that's the only kind of war we can win," Aleksey said strongly, causing Katrin to sigh. She looked at her husband and asked his opinion.

"You know I'd rather settle this conflict through negotiation or on the Senate floor."

"Yes, that would be lovely, but something tells me Moscow will stop at nothing to prevent our independence," Katrin replied, pausing for a moment. "While I surely hope we can win without violence, I thank Christ we have men like General Krupa and President Bednarz ready to take charge should we be left without any other choice."

Quietly unnerved by the words of his wife, for despite all the tough talk from the old war hawks like General Krupa, a war was not something Poland could win, nor did he want it to happen. So, hoping to calm the mood, Aleksander tried to remind everyone that Poland's best chance for independence was through words, not bullets. To this, Katrin replied with a simple wish of luck to them all.

"We don't need luck. We have the will of the people on our side, and we will prevail," Lena said, echoing her mother's spirits in the lead-up to the vote.

"God willing," Katrin said, clearly distraught by the Premier's speech. She then looked at her husband with curious eyes. "Please tell me you'll fight for your country, and not the fascists."

Feeling as though nothing he could say would reach his wife, Aleksander sighed and took to his feet. This caused her to furrow her brow and ask where he was going. "I've had enough of this for one day. I'm going to my study."

After taking some time to cool her anger, Katrin headed upstairs. As expected, she found Aleksander at his desk, working on one of his model tanks. Not wanting to alarm him, she closed the door gently and made her approach from behind. When she was just a half step away, she stopped and placed her hands on his shoulders. Remaining calm as she touched him, it was obvious he hadn't been aware of her approach and wasn't simply ignoring her.

"What are you doing?" Aleksander asked, as Katrin massaged his broad shoulders with slender hands.

"Apologizing," she said softly, before kissing the arch between his neck and shoulder.

"Apologizing for what?" he asked, while his wife pressed her head to his.

"For bringing political tension into this house," she said, before resuming her massage.

"You don't have to do that. I'm not angry with you."

"Then why are you so quiet?"

"I'm just thinking about a lot, that's all."

"You're always thinking about a lot," she said.

"Of course, but that's the nature of my work."

Rolling her eyes, Katrin backed off a few paces so that he could turn and face her. When he did, he appeared to have a tired, seemingly distraught expression, but he said nothing.

"I'm worried about what happens next, Alek."

"Everything is going to work out," Aleksander said, but it wasn't enough, and she was quick to challenge.

"Work out for whom? The federation or your family?"

"Katrin—"

"We're all going home, Alek. As soon as the Premier signs off on the secession, we're gone. You, me, Aleksey, and Lena."

"Do you really think it's that easy?"

"Yes, I most certainly do. Lena is going to Wroclaw for veterinarian school, Aleksey has a place in Gdansk, and you and I are going back to Slawa. There's no way around this. We're Polish, so if our country leaves, we go with it."

"So, I should just give up everything we've worked for and retire? Bednarz already tapped Krupa to be his top General."

"Roman says they're going to make you Marshal of the Republic."

"Roman says a lot of things," Aleksander said. "All that talk of making me Marshal is a load of crap meant to lure me away from Moscow."

"And if it is, so what? Would you rather stay here and be alone?" Katrin challenged, sending a cold jolt through Aleksander's heart.

"You don't mean that," he countered, and as if to say she didn't, she hugged him tightly and pressed her face to his chest. He would then hold her closely and whisper into her ear. "They're going to fight our freedom tooth and claw, but I'll do everything I can to make sure we win in the end. Just don't make any moves yet and certainly don't trust a soul with our plans."

"I'd never betray you," she whispered. "Just don't make me leave without you."

"Just remain patient. That's all I ask. You have no idea how incredibly careful I must be right now. This could very well be a matter of life and death, Katrin."

Pulling back and facing him with wet eyes, Katrin made her intentions known. "I'll stand by you as long as it takes but swear to me that you're a nationalist."

"You know where I stand."

"Just say it, Alek."

Touching her face, he looked deeply into her eyes and recited the first line of the Polish national anthem. "Poland is not yet lost."

Though a simple gesture, it was good enough, so she kissed him tenderly. She had faith that their struggle would not be in vain, and God willing, Poland would be free once more from the grip of another Russian tyrant.

Chapter 17

Senatgrad, Federal Special Region, Slavic Federation

Days following the Premier's divisive speech to the public regarding Poland's secession, a political summit was held between the Federal Government and the Polish Independence Party. Led by Senator Roman Wilczynski, the secessionists went into the first day facing a formidable federal delegation led by First Lady of the Federation, Viktoriya Medvedeva, and the Premier's most trusted military advisor, Aleksander Rybinski.

Knowing the First Lady was a skilled diplomat with a background in military intelligence, Roman's delegation went into the summit as if it were a battle. However, after a long first day at the negotiation table, little progress was made toward an agreement between the two delegations, largely due to Roman's hard-nosed approach to the negotiation. When the two groups agreed to end the day, Roman was exhausted and wanted nothing more than to have a good dinner and relax. Unsurprisingly, his wife, having spent the day with family visiting from Russia, had made plans for a cocktail party that night. While Roman couldn't bring himself to argue, for they hadn't seen most of his side of the family in months, and in some cases, years, he secretly dreaded such an event. After all, he had just spent the day fiercely debating with his brother-in-law and his Federalist cohorts. However, after taking a shower and relaxing on the balcony alone with a cigar before the guests arrived, Roman saw the good in the party.

Despite how firm Aleksander stood in his resolve, Roman didn't believe that Aleksander was quite the federalist firebrand that he made himself appear. Roman knew he was a patriot, not a lackey, but the man he saw in that conference room was the inverse. If he could, he'd seek a private moment to see if he could reach the patriot hiding within and convince him to acknowledge the value of Polish independence. If not, he'd have to go into the next day knowing their familial ties ended at the door and that the man across the table was his enemy for the duration of the summit.

Hours after hatching his plan, Roman and his family hosted his sister's family in his Senatgrad penthouse. While all seemed well with politics kept to a minimum, Roman eagerly awaited the moment to carry out his plan. His opportunity appeared when Aleksander slipped out onto the balcony while Katrin went into the kitchen, likely to help with the dishes. However, when he stepped outside, he didn't find Aleksander staring out at the skyline longingly. Rather, he appeared to be waiting for him, for just as the moment the door was slid shut, Aleksander approached and delivered a few choice words.

"This isn't the time, Roman," Aleksander said automatically, but Roman said nothing. He soon walked over to the railing and looked out at the bustling city that stretched well into the horizon. He broke his silence when his brother-in-law leaned by his side.

"I'm not here for a fight, but I'd appreciate a few moments to talk like men. A cigarette's worth of time, if you would be so kind."

Rolling his eyes, Aleksander pushed off from the iron railing and stared out at the skyline with his hands folded behind his back as if he were on official duty. "Get on with it then."

Lighting his cigarette, Roman took a deep drag and blew a heavy cloud that appeared bluish gray under the dull porch light. Taking just a moment to savor the taste of the fine tobacco, Roman chose his words carefully.

"I've been thinking about the negotiations today," Roman began. "I know I came off a bit harsh towards you, but you have to understand my predicament."

"You don't need to explain anything, but this isn't the time. It's been a nice night so far."

"And it will remain if you just hear me out," Roman replied. He took another drag and exhaled through his nose. "We're not going to lose this fight, Alek. We're prepared to take it before the Senate if that's what it takes."

"Be careful what you wish for," Aleksander warned, and Roman nodded.

"There's a reason President Bednarz—"

"President-elect Bednarz," Aleksander corrected, but Roman just grinned.

"President-elect Bednarz chose me to champion the cause in the Senate for a very good reason," Roman finished. "I have charisma, an excellent track record in political office, and I'm a war hero. Most importantly, I have no fear of the tyrant in Moscow."

Aleksander shot him a smirk at the self-serving description but said nothing, so Roman carried on.

"While I'm not quite sure what side you're truly on, I know you don't want to be here. You're just doing your job," Roman said, but Aleksander remained still. "You're a patriot, Alek. I am, too."

"You've yet to make a point, Roman," Aleksander said, breaking his silence. "That cigarette isn't going to last much longer."

Chuckling, Roman tossed the shrunken cigarette over the railing and drew another one. "Allow me one more and I'll make my case," he said, lighting the second cigarette.

Looking inside, Aleksander saw his family having a wonderful time. It seemed as if they had no idea that he and Roman were missing.

"Fine. But blow that shit away from me. I breathed in enough noxious fumes in the war."

Chuckling once more, Roman took a long drag and blew the smoke from the right side of his mouth, sending it into an updraft of wind. He then looked at his brother-in-law with a cool stare.

"The Party and I have a solid plan. We're not going to lose this debate, and God willing, we'll keep it from going to the Senate, too."

"Is that right?" Aleksander asked. "I didn't see much of a plan today. Just a lot of arguing."

"That's because we're playing the long game," Roman said. "We're not going to show our hand just yet."

"I suppose that's wise," Aleksander said coolly. Although he possessed a strategic mind, the fine art of political strategy was alien to him, so he pressed the matter. "What are you waiting for? Why not just make your demands known and get this over with?"

"Politics is a lot like fighting a war, Alek. Patience and deception are crucial to victory," Roman replied. "We're going to drag this negotiation out for as long as it takes to force the Russian to fold."

"I see, and what's the object of that?" Aleksander asked, bringing his brother-in-law to smile.

"The object is to get the best possible deal. The longer we drag this out, the more likely we are to have our demands met."

"Good luck with that," Aleksander replied, for Viktoriya Medvedeva was as much a firebrand as Roman. "She may be easy on the eyes, but she's a cutthroat. Don't push her too hard. You won't like the outcome."

"Well, that's why I'm talking to you," Roman said tensely. "You're our only chance at a fair negotiation."

"I'm afraid you're wrong about that. I'm here to negotiate on behalf of the federal government, not Poland."

"Yes, but you're still Polish," Roman challenged, but Aleksander shook his head.

"That doesn't change the fact that I'm your opposition, Roman. I have a job to do and that's to negotiate a secession plan that's beneficial to both sides, or God help us, refer to the Premier that Poland isn't ready," Aleksander said firmly. "But if you want my advice, fine. Tell your people to deliver a solid plan in the next few days or the Federals will walk out, and this whole thing goes to the Senate."

"They wouldn't dare! We voted for our freedom. We followed the law!" Roman cried, but Aleksander was unmoved by his brother-in-law's passion.

"I know, but you know what you're dealing with. Unless you can prove that Poland won't end up a failed state or an adversary, you're only setting yourself up for failure."

"Then tell me what she expects."

"A legal agreement that Poland will remain a neutral power economically and militarily," Aleksander said calmly. "We're aware of your plan to join NATO and the European Union, and that's plain unacceptable."

Roman's expression was frozen, but his eyes showed a degree of surprise; he was at a loss for words. The plan to apply for membership in the European Union and NATO was a closely guarded secret known only to members of President-elect Bednarz's inner circle. Not even their assistants or wives knew what they were planning for the first ninety days of the new republic. However, Roman was a seasoned politician and knew how to keep cool under pressure, so he offered a lie.

"If that's all that's needed to ensure our secession, then this negotiation will be over tomorrow," Roman said brightly. "We have no interest in the European Union. That's just a pipedream. As for NATO, what use would we have for them? The Cold War is over. It's not like the Slavic Federation is our enemy, right?"

"Look, I'm not going to pretend I know all the political tricks, but I do know that the Premier and his cabinet are going to fight this tooth and claw. The worst thing you can do is play your cards close to your chest and blow these negotiations."

"Sounds more like your side already decided this whole thing is dead in the water."

"It's not, believe me. But you need to swallow your pride and understand that it takes more than a majority vote to secede. You need to provide a plan so well thought out that not even a tyrant can argue against it," Aleksander said, his words bringing a smile to Roman's face before taking another drag that consumed nearly half of the already dwindling cigarette.

Blowing the smoke through his nose, Roman smirked as he spoke. "I see what you're saying. You want us to polish our plan. We need to be upfront with what we're planning, so we can iron it all out in the short term."

"Yes, but that's not entirely my point."

"I think it is. You're just playing neutral," Roman said, taking another quick drag. "I'll talk to Bednarz first thing in the morning. If I can convince him to open up a bit more tomorrow, I'll need a favor from you in return."

Though a little skeptical, Aleksander was eager to know what the clever senator could want. "What's the favor?"

Tossing the cigarette over the railing, Roman leaned onto the iron and looked directly into his brother-in-law's eyes. "When you go back to Moscow, I want you to sit down with your boss and make him see things our way," he said. "I'm asking you this not only as your brother but as a fellow patriot. I know you have to play your cards right and keep a low profile, but I know where you stand. You have a part in this revolution, whether you like it or not."

Though he felt that the Premier would never see things the way Roman and his compatriots saw things, Aleksander chose not to be a pessimist at that moment. Instead, he gave Roman his word that he'd do him that favor, but he'd only do it if the secessionists properly made their case at the summit first. "No more senseless arguing and wasted time," Aleksander continued. "The longer this summit is dragged out, the less likely the Premier will sign off on the secession."

Seeing reason in Aleksander's words, Roman nodded and held out his hand, taking his brother-in-law's hand in a firm grip. "You have my word, Alek. We'll have this negotiation ironed out in three days or less."

"I sincerely hope so. The less time we have to spend around a harpy like Viktoriya Medvedeva, the better off we'll all be. Christ, I hate that bitch," Aleksander said, inciting laughter from both men.

Following a hearty laugh, Aleksander clasped Roman's shoulder and bid him good luck the next day but warned that he would be just as tough as before. Fortunately, Roman understood that Aleksander was technically his adversary in the negotiations but an ally behind the scenes. So, when Aleksander went back inside, Roman lit another cigarette and leaned back on the railing to think. A few minutes later, he heard the patio door slide open. When he looked over his shoulder, he spotted his nephew and smiled widely.

"Aleksey, my boy!" Roman said with a grin, blowing smoke like a dragon as he spoke.

"Everything alright out here? Everyone is beginning to wonder if Dad put the fear of God into you."

"Do I look petrified?" Roman asked, but Aleksey shrugged. "I'm fine. We just had a rather meaningful talk, but you know your father. He always carries that stone-cold expression everywhere he goes."

"Yeah, that's about right," Aleksey said, joining Roman at the railing. "Say, can I borrow a cigarette?"

"No sense in borrowing one, but since when do you smoke?" Roman asked, pulling a cigarette from his nearly empty pack. He then handed it off and readied his lighter.

"When my job made it necessary," Aleksey replied, as Roman lit the cigarette pinched between his lips.

"I hear you," Roman said with a nod, for his job offered him a great deal of stress just the same, but he quickly changed the subject. "So, what's this I hear you applied to the Office of State Protection. Life in the Special Troops just not exciting enough anymore?"

Not bothering to lie, for he was aware that his uncle was on the Senate's intelligence committee, Aleksey took a long drag and exhaled a thick cloud before answering. "Honestly, I need some change in my life, so I have a few pokers in the fire," he said. "I've been considering that new rapid response unit or going reserve, but I applied to the UOP on a lark."

"Glad to hear it, intelligence is my bread and butter. Honestly, I got a little nervous when I heard that you were considering transferring to the Russian service. Why on God's green earth would you want to join those zealots in Alpha Group?"

"Well, that's an easy one. I had a Russian girlfriend, and I wanted to be closer to her. The FSB would have given me that opportunity."

"Had? What changed?"

"I came home to find her pregnant by another man and living in his apartment."

"Isn't that some shit?" Roman said, shaking his head. "Fucking Russian cunts."

"It's whatever at this point. I'm technically still a member of GROM for another three months, but unless I get a call from the agency soon, I might transfer to the reserves and earn my pension with a bit of quiet dignity."

"Then let me ask you this – would you rather sit around pulling base duty in the reserves for the next ten years, or would you rather have a cushy job working intelligence inside an embassy?"

"Honestly, I don't know what I want at this point. My life is all fucked up right now," Aleksey admitted, and Roman nodded, but he was keen on making his nephew an offer. Whether you want to stand outside an embassy, put that brain to good use in the intelligence field, or try your hand at field intelligence, let me know."

"Field intelligence?" Aleksey asked curiously, and Roman grinned.

"Interested in being a Polish James Bond, huh?"

"No, I'm just curious as to what that job entails."

"Despite what you're thinking, it's not all espionage and assassination. It's largely breaking codes, deciphering information, you know, boring crap like that. They call it field intelligence because you're not typically stuck in an office all day. Think of it like a news reporter."

"Well, consider me interested."

"Is that right?" Roman asked. "What about officer candidacy school? Don't feel like sitting behind a desk for four years and leading men for another six?"

"Not even slightly," Aleksey said with a laugh. "Honestly, my dad applied for me without my knowledge."

"What's the problem? You've always been a bright one. Why not get a nice pay increase for your troubles?"

"Do I look like an officer's candidate to you?"

Shrugging, Roman told Aleksey it was in his blood to be an officer, but Aleksey disagreed. "I'm thinking it skipped a generation."

"Bullshit," Roman said. "You could have been a general one day if you didn't enlist and let that family name do its job. But hey, we all make mistakes."

"I wouldn't call it a mistake. It's been a hell of a ride. Besides, I made it all the way to GROM. I bet eighty percent of the academy seniors couldn't make it through our selection process."

"You're probably right, but you sound so proud, so why leave it behind?"

Sighing, Aleksey tossed the long since burned-out cigarette over the railing. "Because I need a change of pace. Another ten years charging into the fight and going home to no one doesn't sound too nice anymore."

"I see," Roman said coolly. "Well, I'll tell you what. I'm going to make some phone calls tomorrow and see about getting you considered for an intelligence job with State Protection."

"That's not necessary," Aleksey said, though he was grateful his uncle would do such a thing for him.

"I know it's not, but we're family. We look out for each other," Roman said with a smile. "Don't worry, I'll make sure you have your pick of jobs."

"Thank you, that's much appreciated."

"Just make sure you pick something that makes the time fly and gives you time for a family, alright?"

Aleksey chuckled at this last sentence. "You've been talking to my mom, haven't you?"

"Well, she is my favorite sister."

Aleksey laughed again and then went back inside, his smile never fading. Roman wouldn't follow him inside right away. Instead, he'd look out at the city one more time, feeling pleased with himself. Not only did he turn Aleksander from a wild card to an ally, but he was also about to have some major leverage over his brother-in-law by getting Aleksey on the fast track to a career in covert intelligence. If all went his way, he'd have a powerful ally not only in Moscow but within the Premier's inner circle. If he could get a handle on Aleksander, Poland's independence was essentially secure, and they just might leave with more than they were negotiating for.

Chapter 18

Senatgrad, Federal Special Region, Slavic Federation

It was the dawn of the second day of the tournament, and Audra had been alone practically the entire time in Senatgrad. Though Gustav had not been selected to fight on the first day of the preliminary rounds, he spent all day at the gym conditioning himself to fight, leaving Audra to spend the day alone with nothing to do but sit in her hotel room. Unwilling to continue the cycle of boredom until it was time to go down to the arena and watch the second half of the preliminary round, she went against Jens' orders and left the hotel for a change of scenery.

Having spent her whole life in the hustle and bustle of a capital city, Audra knew how to carry herself in public so as not to appear like a tourist or an easy score for a pickpocket. Blending into the multicultural crowd that flooded the sidewalks, she walked the neighborhood and found that the city offered much to its visitors, especially art lovers. Naturally, she found herself admiring the many churches and bridges that made the city famous, eventually finding her way into a fine arts museum. However, even though the city was founded as German territory and had since become a cultural melting pot, so to speak, Senatgrad was very much a Russian city with most signs still in Russian from the Soviet era. While there were a good number of secondary signs in English, the German influence on the city had long since been sanitized, forcing Audra to rely on her command of the English language to get around. However, once she stepped into the museum, she found herself at a loss – everything was in Russian.

"Well, shit," she muttered in German, though a bit louder than intended as her voice carried, catching the attention of a nearby group of women. Her face reddening, she turned her away from them to head back to the ticket office and request a translator. As she walked off in her private shame, she couldn't help but notice a man speaking to the others regarding her troubles.

Though she understood Polish thanks to her expat father, she didn't quite hear what was being said. She just recognized a few words, so curiously, she looked over her shoulder and spotted Aleksey standing among the group. How she missed him before, she didn't know, but he looked like he wanted to say something. When he did, he called out to her in English, causing her expression to shift from embarrassed to bashful.

Though they spoke a common language, and he was quite easy on the eyes, she had a feeling one of the younger women was his girlfriend and didn't want to bother him by asking for help or to tag along. Instead, she quietly walked back to the ticket office, where she politely requested the service of a translator. What she received was a thick pamphlet that contained an English, Polish, and German translation for every painting and informational placard in the building. This wasn't exactly what she was hoping for. She would have gladly paid for the services of a guide, but she didn't argue, either. She just took the pamphlet and returned to the first gallery to begin a painfully slow self-guided tour.

Making her way through the first few halls, Audra thought she was making decent progress until she found several familiar paintings had inaccurate titles and descriptions. Beyond annoyed, she left the room, muttering aloud, "Christ, I could use some help here. I wonder where that cute guy went." To her absolute embarrassment, he was just a few steps away from her and was looking right at her with a smile on his face. Her face reddened and burning hot, she turned on her heels and headed back to the start of the gallery to put some distance between them.

Intent on just enjoying the paintings at face value, she tossed the pamphlet in the trash bin and stood before a painting with her arms crossed. Losing herself in her admiration of the work, she analyzed it so closely that she didn't notice the echo of footsteps until Aleksey was standing beside her. A little unnerved, she looked at him from the corner of her eye, but he acted casually. She could tell he wanted to say something to her, so she broke the ice.

"Sorry that I've made a habit of making an ass of myself here. I'm not normally this pathetic," Audra said.

"No need to apologize. The translations are a joke," Aleksey said, and she chuckled.

"That's an understatement. They mislabeled everything," she said, before launching into a small rant on how some famous works of art were attributed to artists from completely different eras. His only response was the simple utterance of 'unreal' alongside a friendly smile.

"You're not here on your own volition, are you?" Audra asked with a smile. She could tell everything she had just said had gone over his head.

Smiling absently, for he knew next to nothing about fine art, Aleksey nodded and admitted as much. Audra seemed a little downtrodden by this fact, but Aleksey was quick to offer proper translation from Russian to German. Relieved, she accepted, and they started toward the nearest painting before he realized he had forgotten to properly introduce himself.

"I'm Aleksey, by the way," he said, offering his hand for a friendly shake.

"It's nice to meet you, Aleksey. I'm Audra," she said warmly, as their hands linked for a few short moments.

"That's a pretty name," he said, as he found himself captivated by her emerald eyes. She smiled bashfully at this, flashing a nearly perfect set of pearly white teeth that brightened her face as she bashfully brushed aside a rogue lock of hair. Though she would have disagreed, he thought she looked gorgeous, so much so that he couldn't seem to break eye contact. Fortunately, he was able to blurt something out quickly before things got awkward. "That's an interesting accent you have. Are you from Austria? Switzerland, perhaps?"

"Actually, I'm from Germany," she replied, and he chuckled in mild embarrassment. "Berlin, to be exact. Hence the weird pronunciations."

"Oh, I was way off then," he said with a hint of embarrassment. "To be perfectly honest, you're the first woman outside of the Baltic I've met with that name. Had you been speaking Russian, I would've figured you for Lithuanian."

"Yeah, it's something of a conversation starter," she said, looking away for a moment as the conversation was at risk of getting awkward. Recognizing her cue, Aleksey tried to save the moment.

"I'm sorry, did I say something wrong? German is my fourth language and not my strongest," he said, leaving her speechless at his ability to speak four languages. "It's pretty terrible, isn't it?"

"No, your German is fine," she said kindly. "I was just surprised to hear you speak four languages."

"Yeah, it's a bit of a conversation starter," he joked, but she didn't appear to be amused. "Polish is my native language, but I speak Russian, English, and German."

"Oh, so you're Polish? I'm a generation removed," she said, speaking flawless Polish that brought a smile to Aleksey's face.

"I have a sneaking suspicion you have family from my home region," he said, speaking in Polish. "We speak the same dialect."

"Wielkopolski?" she asked, and he nodded with a sly grin, for it was clear she had roots in Poland. "My dad was born in Konin. He moved to Berlin before I was born."

"Konin? Aleksey asked, making a comically sour face, but she rolled her eyes with a smile. "How does a man from Konin end up with a daughter in Berlin?"

"Dad was Polish, Mom was German. It's not a very interesting story."

"No?" he asked, and she shrugged. "Then why don't we talk about something you find interesting? There's plenty of art to see."

"Sounds lovely," Audra said. So, like a pair of friends or students on a field trip, the pair made their way through the museum. While he started by just translating for her, they eventually got down to small talk. When they passed the museum's café, she suggested they take a coffee break. This allowed for their small talk to evolve into a full conversation. It was through this discussion that they learned a bit about each other, such as his lengthy service in the army and roots in Poland, and how her father ended up in Berlin. By the time their coffee was through, she felt like they had a good connection, so much so that she neglected to mention she had a boyfriend. Of course, this created a small problem, for while Aleksey was still suffering from the heartbreak of Tatiana's betrayal, he, too, felt a connection with his lovely new friend. But unlike Audra, he didn't restrain his desire to see her beyond their tour.

"I know this might sound out of the blue, but would you like to go to dinner with me tonight?"

Bashful that a handsome man like Aleksey would take such a liking to someone like her, Audra's face turned a pale shade of red.

"I'm sorry, did I say something wrong?" Aleksey asked, concerned he had somehow offended her.

"No, not at all," Audra said quickly to break the awkward silence. "It's just... well, I already have plans for tonight, and I'm afraid I can't break them."

"I see, you're not here alone. My mistake," Aleksey said, noticing the tension in her voice.

Feeling remorseful for not letting him know about Gustav, Audra grimaced at the thought of letting him down further, even though she had no intention of being more than a friendly acquaintance. So rather than outright explain that she had a complicated relationship, she boldly sidestepped the problem.

"I'm here with my uncle. He's a trainer in the martial arts tournament," she said, lying only by omission. "Technically, I'm not supposed to be out on the town alone."

"Oh, I see," Aleksey said with a gentle smile. "So, you'll be at the tournament tonight?"

"Yes," Audra said with a nod. "If you wouldn't mind, I'd appreciate your cheers for Gustav Hagen. That's our fighter."

"Gustav Hagen." Aleksey's voice trailed as he tried to put a face to the name. "Oh, the German underdog."

"The German underdog?" Audra asked with a raised eyebrow. "What's that supposed to mean?"

"Oh, it's nothing offensive. I stopped by a betting booth this morning to collect my winnings and saw his odds. He's somewhere in the middle, but his background sounds legit. I hope he wins tonight."

"Me too," Audra said somewhat distantly. Her eyes then shifted from Aleksey to Lena, who was fast approaching from behind him. For a moment, Audra worried that this pretty young woman on a crash course with her was Aleksey's girlfriend, for they seemed to have locked eyes, and she didn't appear too pleased to see her with Aleksey.

Quick to notice the growing concern in Audra's expression, Aleksey shifted in his seat to see his sister marching toward them with a stern expression. Though unsure of what she could be upset about, he turned back to Audra and whispered 'my sister' in German, and Audra nodded in relief.

"There you are," Lena said, frustration in her voice. "I've been looking for you for twenty minutes."

"Well, here I am," Aleksey said, and Lena rolled her eyes.

"Don't be an ass. We're all through here, and we're hungry."

"Then go right ahead. My lady friend and I have more to see."

Rolling her eyes again, Lena turned to Audra, but rather than take her frustrations out on a stranger, she asked if he was wearing out his welcome. Audra chuckled at the sarcastic remark from the fiery woman standing before him and answered.

"Not at all, but don't let me keep you all from your holiday," Audra replied to both siblings.

"Nonsense, we still have half the museum to see," Aleksey said. He turned to Lena. "Go back to the group and tell them I'll catch up later."

"Take the hint, Aleksey. She's not taking you home," Lena said, causing Audra to choke in surprise, for she couldn't believe how brash Lena was. "My point exactly."

Her cheeks a pale shade of red, Audra raised her hand and told Aleksey that it wasn't like that at all. She would go on to fumble her words as she attempted to untangle herself from the web of confusion Lena had spun for them, but the damage was done.

"You don't have to explain. I just hope you had a lovely time," Aleksey said, clearly embarrassed by his sister's sardonic behavior

"I most certainly did, but I should probably get back to my hotel. I didn't sleep so well last night, and the tournament went late yesterday."

While he was still embarrassed by Lena's words, Aleksey was accepting of the fact that it was time to part ways. Of course, he managed to make things a bit more awkward by reaching over to shake her hand as if this were a business meeting. Though Audra accepted the gesture, she smiled awkwardly when he wished Gustav Hagen the best of luck in the arena that night.

Leaving Audra in the café to finish her coffee alone, Aleksey left with Lena, but his sister spared no time ridiculing him for his awkwardness as they walked away.

"Was it the pretty face and curvy figure or ten years off the market that melted your brain?"

Casting her an evil eye, he asked sharply what she was on about. Laughing at his cluelessness, Lena pointed out several awkward moments that surely ruined any chance of going back to her hotel. Aleksey just rolled his eyes and admitted she was certainly his type, but he wasn't in pursuit. Lena shrugged and said he could have had her if he remembered how to talk to women.

"I'll keep that in mind if I see her again," Aleksey replied.

"Hate to say it, but I think that ship has sailed."

"Then so be it," Aleksey said with a shrug. "I'm pretty sure she's taken."

"The way she was talking to you, I doubt it. You clearly had her interested, and I know for a fact you were wondering what she looks like naked."

"All right, shut it," Aleksey said with a laugh, for his sister's sarcastic observations were getting dangerously close to the truth. Knowing this just by his expressions, Lena grinned and headed off toward the exit. Aleksey followed a few steps behind, looking back every so often to catch another glimpse of Audra like a lovesick teenager.

Walking a few blocks, Aleksey rejoined their group at a café and had lunch on a sidewalk patio. As expected, the first thing Katrin asked was how it went between Aleksey and the pretty tourist. Before Aleksey could get a word out, Lena spoke on his behalf.

"He had her attention, but forgot how to talk to women," she said with a smirk, but Katrin wasn't amused.

"Well, she seemed lovely. Thank you for being so kind to a lady in need," Katrin said.

Aleksey nodded quietly, and while the women chatted amongst themselves, Aleksey ate quietly. All the while analyzing his perceived social failure with Audra. Secretly, he hoped he'd see her again so he could have a chance of making a better impression, for if she had a boyfriend, he was sure she would have told him. Of course, going back to her hotel was not his goal, though an invitation certainly wouldn't have been something he'd decline. After all, he found her very attractive, but through their conversation, he found that there was more to her than a pretty face and a curvy figure. She was smart, well-spoken, and quite sweet. He really felt a connection with her, and if Gustav Hagen was really her boyfriend, that wouldn't bother him too much, so long as they could be friends at the very least. There was just something about the way she carried herself and expressed her thoughts that he found so invigorating. She was clearly a brilliant young woman, and he wanted to see her again, even if it was just for a few hours of hearty conversation.

Chapter 19

Senatgrad, Federal Special Region, Slavic Federation

Heeding Aleksander's advice, Roman approached the second day of negotiations with lessened intensity. While he had expected a new level of understanding and for reason to prevail, his new approach was pounced upon by the First Lady. Like a predator, Viktoriya Medvedeva made mincemeat out of his arguments, and the day ended with the summit no closer to a favorable end for either side. As a result, Roman felt betrayed by Aleksander and returned to his office deflated and frustrated.

Eager to learn from his mistakes, Roman ordered his secretary to divert calls from the public to an automated message used when the Senate was in session or had gone home for the evening. This ensured him peace while he studied the recordings of the day's negotiations. However, despite his orders, one call was allowed through, and he knew better than to ignore it.

"Senator Wilczynski speaking," he said, immediately upon pressing the flashing button to open the line.

"Senator, this is Marshal Krupa," he heard the gruff voice of a heavy smoker say.

Rolling his eyes at Krupa's premature declaration of his rank following independence, Roman did not entertain the arrogance of the legendary General to whom he spoke.

"What can I do for you, General Krupa?"

Seemingly ignoring the senator's words, or possibly writing it off as a force of habit, Krupa got to the point quickly. Someone had made him aware of the Polish delegation's crushing defeat that day, and the General wanted answers.

"We took a new approach, and it failed," Roman said calmly, stopping short of admitting that his taking of Aleksander's advice was the cause. "We'll hit them hard tomorrow. They showed their hand today."

"Well, I surely hope you can make them see things our way. A lot is riding on the success of this summit, Senator."

"I'm well-aware of what's at stake, General. One bad day isn't going to be the end of us," Roman said, but Krupa scoffed.

"Don't be naïve. One wrong move and an entire war can be lost."

"Well, then it's a good thing we're not at war."

"That's where you're wrong," Krupa challenged. "The people made their voices heard. It is your duty to ensure they are not ignored or silenced, but if you can't do that, then, well—"

"Yes, yes, things will get ugly. I know," Roman said, knowing just what Krupa was going to say. "Rest assured, I'm actively working to revise our approach. We will see this through to victory. I'm a man of my word."

"I certainly hope that's the case. We're counting on you to prevent a bloody struggle, Senator. But I'm also letting you know that we are prepared for such an outcome."

"War will not be necessary," Roman said quickly. "It's in our best interest that you keep your guns silent until absolutely necessary."

"We've been watching this whole affair closely, Senator. Politics is a dirty game, and a lot of men in uniform are concerned Moscow is going to resort to force if things don't go exactly their way."

"I understand that concern, but I'm begging you to keep your temper cool and controlled. We have allies in Moscow. Just be patient."

"We've been patient, but I'm afraid we're running out of time. As for your ally in Moscow, I don't have high hopes that you can convince someone like Aleksander Rybinski to see things our way. He made his choice a long time ago."

"Indeed, but that was over a decade ago, and you seem to forget that he's married to my favorite sister."

"And you seem to forget that I served shoulder to shoulder with the man," Krupa shot back. "I know where he stands politically, and it isn't with a free and independent Poland."

"My sister says otherwise," Roman replied calmly. "In fact, I saw it in his eyes just last night. The man is a patriot in fascist clothing."

"Then why did he turn down the President's invitation to serve as Marshal of the Republic? At the very least, he could have joined the party."

"He has a career and a family to protect. It's easier to draw a hard line when your enemies are twelve hundred miles away rather than a thirty-minute drive," Roman replied. "Just bear with me. He's our ally, not an enemy."

"We'll see about that," Krupa said gruffly. "The man had countless chances to prove himself a patriot. He's loyal to the fascists, and you're yet to prove me wrong."

"Just give diplomacy a chance. You'd be amazed at how accurate the old saying about the pen and the sword truly is."

"Politics and philosophy are worthless when your enemy is willing to lie, cheat, and kill to keep our people in chains."

"While I'm inclined to agree, my duty is to ensure a diplomatic solution that's favorable to our people. I intend on seeing this through," Roman said carefully. "Sergei Medvedev may dream about being Tsar, but he's still just the Premier of the Federation. His office has its limitations."

"Again, you're being naïve, Roman. You know damn well that Medvedev is a tyrant. He'll stop at nothing to kill the secession, and don't you dare tell me force is not an option for him. Just ask his predecessor."

While the mention of the previous Premier, who had died under questionable circumstances during her reelection bid, struck a nerve, Roman kept calm. He then declared that Aleksander would never allow the use of force against his homeland, but Krupa disagreed.

"You can play his political games, but don't be surprised if things come to a clash of arms. Should it come to that, you'd better be thankful for the fight our true patriots will give to the fascists."

"God willing, it won't come to that."

"God tends to look the other way when it comes to our people. But rest assured, we're prepared to take the fight to the streets and the fields."

"If you want peace, prepare for war," Roman replied, reciting an old Roman proverb that he and Krupa knew all too well from their time serving as revolutionaries. "We'll have our way, General. Just you wait."

"Indeed," Krupa said. "Despite my pessimism, I have faith in you. I know there will be a lot of political games at play, but don't fall into their traps.

"I'll see us through this nightmare," Roman said with determination. "The last thing we need to do is get into an unnecessary clash of arms because of your philosophies getting in the way."

"Then make damn sure you do everything possible to get us a peaceful divorce from the Federation. War with Moscow is guaranteed to be bloody."

"The summit is just two days old. We'll come out on top, you have my word," Roman said, but Krupa had nothing more to add. This allowed Roman to switch gears. "Before

I let you go, I'd like to inform you that I have an ace up my sleeve regarding General Rybinski."

"Is that right?" Krupa asked, and Roman smiled.

"My nephew applied to the Office of State Protection. He's a hell of a soldier. Tier One special operations, qualified sniper and medic, combat diver—"

"You're referring to Senior Sergeant Aleksey Rybinski, GROM Squadron B," Krupa interrupted, showing an uncanny knowledge of Aleksey. "What's your angle?"

"My angle is to get Aleksey accepted and send him to Redzikowo for that fancy new unit you're forming," Roman said, but Krupa was silent. "Look, I know it sounds crazy, but—"

"It's a bold move, Senator, but I like it," Krupa said, knowing that getting Aleksey into his new rapid response force might be enough leverage to bend Aleksander toward their cause. "Send in your recommendation, and I'll do the same, but don't think this is going to be enough."

"Oh, I don't. My plan is two-fold," Roman said. "Not only will this put pressure on the good general to see things our way, but it will also work to our benefit should secession be struck down. We'll have a man close to one of the Premier's chief advisors."

"Don't get ahead of yourself. It's preferable that we win this thing politically. Your boy is a wild card, nothing more," Krupa said. "Nonetheless, I'm doing you this favor for the good of the cause. Don't make me regret putting so much faith in you."

The phone call ended shortly thereafter, and Roman leaned back in his chair and stared at the ceiling. The burden of proving Poland's secession plan was sound was squarely on his shoulders. Despite his plan for getting Aleksey into a politically advantageous position in the intelligence world, he had his concerns. He just hoped Katrin was telling him the truth and that Aleksander was truly a patriot in fascist clothing.

Chapter 20

Senatgrad, Federal Special Region, Slavic Federation

After a thrilling first night of the tournament, the arena was sold out hours before the doors opened for the second night, and an excited crowd was waiting anxiously for the tournament to resume. To pass the time, bets were made, drinks and snacks were acquired, and chants echoed throughout the arena. All the while, those with the ability to afford such luxury waited in fully catered skyboxes situated between the moderately priced floor seats and the so-called cheap seats near the top of the arena. Inside one of these skyboxes, one could find Aleksander, Roman, and their wives, while their fully grown children occupied a different skybox suite.

□

Just a few minutes before the opening match of the night, Roman left the suite section of the skybox and found his seat on the balcony beside Aleksander. Driven by a seemingly successful round of negotiations that day, Roman was in high spirits and had no intention of discussing politics. Instead, he handed his brother-in-law a frosty mug of a fine Czech pilsner and asked if he was familiar with the format and intent of the tournament. Shrugging, Aleksander asked Roman to enlighten him, for something told him this wasn't a run-of-the-mill martial arts tournament.

"It's a single-elimination tournament featuring thirty of the very best fighters the league could find across Europe," Roman began, but Aleksander interrupted him with mild skepticism.

"Thirty fighters from across Europe? That's an impressive number, but how many are really the best in the world?"

"That's to be determined," Roman said with a smirk. "Eight were sent packing last night... some ended up in the hospital."

"I take it this isn't a friendly competition," Aleksander remarked, but Roman shrugged.

"This is mixed-martial arts, Alek. No points are going to be scored here. The only way the match ends is with a knockout, tap out, or a critical injury."

"So, what's the point? Are these men fighting for a prize or just glory?"

"Every match won lands a fighter a hefty sum. The ultimate prize is a contract to fight as a regular contender in the Blood Games."

"And why on earth would someone want to do that?" Katrin asked, leaning over her husband to interject.

"Because this is going to be Europe's premier combat sport," Roman said, before chuckling. "Unfortunately, the only one guaranteed a spot in the league is the winner. Everyone else is being scouted, so they're going to fight like hell to earn their place."

"Which will lead to bloodier fights and more injuries," Aleksander remarked, and Roman agreed.

"They know what they got themselves into," Roman said, smirking. "Unfortunately for the amateurs, there are a few professionals thrown in the mix to give the crowd some much-needed brutality."

"Much-needed brutality?" Katrin asked. "Listen to yourself. You make it sound like a gladiator fight."

"It's not far off. I mean, it is a blood sport. It's in the name, right?" Roman replied. "The only difference here is you'll see broken bones instead of severed heads."

Clearly disgusted, Katrin remarked that she found it hard to believe people came to see such barbarity, but Roman was a true believer.

"Believe it, my dear. The name of the league says it all. If people wanted to see a gentleman's fight, they'd watch one of those sissy semi-contact karate and taekwondo matches."

Wanting to prevent an argument between siblings, Aleksander spoke up, asking for the rules of the Blood Games. After all, he had a hard time believing that this tournament was one step above the ancient Roman blood sport of gladiatorial combat. Of course, the way Roman described it did little to quell his own reservations, even though the tournament had more in common with the ancient Olympic sport of pankration.

"The rules are few and simple: single-elimination rounds, no time limit, no pads. Just pure bare-knuckle fighting until someone falls limp, taps out, or can't fight on. Heavy hits and flashy moves are encouraged both for the excitement of the crowd, and the more blood the better."

"This is certainly a far cry from the martial arts tournaments I've enjoyed in the past," Aleksander said, but Roman shrugged.

"As I said, if you want to see friendly competition for medals and personal glory, then go watch karate. This is designed to be war in a ring, and it's the future of martial arts competition, so don't judge it so harshly. The Americans and Japanese have been running promotions like this for years."

Nodding, for he knew it would be wise to change the subject before Katrin forced him to leave with her, Aleksander asked who would be fighting first.

"Some gutter punk from Germany. Gunnar Hayes, or something like that. He's not expected to go too far. His style isn't versatile enough."

"What makes you think that?" Aleksander asked.

"He's a kickboxer. It's a severely limited style in mixed martial arts," Roman said, and Aleksander couldn't help but agree. "Even if he makes it to the semi-finals, he'll get torn apart by someone like Razin."

"Who's Razin?" Aleksander asked curiously. "The name doesn't ring a bell."

Smirking, Roman said he was an up-and-comer from Ukraine, and easily the most savage fighter he had ever seen in the ring. "I saw him fight in Warsaw a few times. He's absolutely brutal. No mercy whatsoever. I have quite the sum on him tonight."

Overhearing their conversation, Katrin leaned over her husband to address her brother. "You sound a bit too enthusiastic for a man of the people."

"Again, it's a blood sport, my dear."

"Again, it's barbaric, my dear," she replied, before sitting back in her seat, causing Aleksander to silently laugh to himself. Though his wife was an outspoken pacifist, if Roman wanted an argument, he'd find himself on the losing end. Fortunately, Roman knew better and turned his attention back to the ring.

Feeling the need to lighten the mood, Aleksander got up and headed into the suite. Upon noticing he was heading for the door to the public corridor, Katrin called out to him to see where he was going.

"To put a small bet on our German underdog," Aleksander said with a grin.

"I'd advise against that," Roman said. "He's a filler fighter... just here to pad out the roster."

"More reason to place a bet on him," Aleksander said, and he continued through the skybox.

Seeing his chance to have another man-to-man with Aleksander, Roman stood up but felt someone grasp his wrist. When he looked down, he saw his wife looking at him with suspicion. When asked about his intentions, he said he was going to try to prevent the General from pissing away his money on a losing bet.

Stepping out into the public corridor, Aleksander stopped briefly to check his surroundings to find a betting booth. When he spotted one and started on his way, he heard the door behind him shut and soon saw Roman. Choosing to ignore him, he kept walking, but Roman was quick to close the distance and stand shoulder to shoulder with him.

"Before you say anything, I just want to apologize for last night. I was out of line."

"This isn't the time," Aleksander replied. "I legitimately came out here to place a bet."

"I know, but I wanted to thank you for your efforts today. I know it was a rough start yesterday, but it seems like it's going well already."

"Good money was spent on these tickets, Roman. Don't spoil another good time with politics."

"Look, I know you don't want to talk politics, so apologize in advance for what I have to say, but it has to be said."

"You don't take no for an answer, do you?" Aleksander asked, but Roman's expression was serious.

"I'm afraid not."

"Fuck me," Aleksander muttered in frustration. "Fine, speak your piece. But make it quick and don't bring it up again for the rest of the night."

"We need your help, and by 'we,' I mean our countrymen," Roman said. but Aleksander stopped him in his tracks.

"We already had this discussion. You know where I stand," Aleksander said. "I gave you my word that I'd try."

"Yes, you did, but you'd be lying to my face if you told me you didn't think Moscow wouldn't try every dirty trick in the book."

Annoyed with his brother-in-law, Aleksander reminded him that there was a time and place for this kind of discussion.

"Look, all I'm asking is for you to be our champion in Moscow," he said, but Aleksander had heard enough and turned back to the skybox instead of placing his bet. "I only want what's best for our people, Alek. Don't you?"

"This isn't the place, Roman. Now drop it!" Aleksander snarled.

Stopping in his tracks as his brother-in-law continued onward, Roman sighed deeply. He was beginning to fear that his faith in Aleksander as a man he could trust to aid their cause was in vain. A few moments later, loud music began to echo through the halls of the arena. It was obvious the tournament was about to begin and that the time for politics was over for at least the next few hours.

Chapter 21

Senatgrad, Federal Special Region, Slavic Federation

Dressed in no more than his lucky trunks and hand wraps, Gustav stood at the mouth of the tunnel that would lead out to the arena floor. Informed just minutes before that he would be the first to fight and the first to be called out, he hadn't had much time to prepare himself mentally for the battle to come; he wasn't even aware of his opponent. All he knew was that he had to fight hard and overcome the odds, but he was confident in his abilities. Still, Jens took the time to remind him that he couldn't forget the fundamentals and that he needed to keep cool and focused if he was going to prevail.

"I'm going to win," Gustav whispered to himself endlessly as Jens tried to motivate him and prevent his arrogance from becoming a handicap and possibly costing him his first win.

"Did you hear a word I just said?"

"Remember the fundamentals, utilize good footwork, and keep a cool head. I heard you," Gustav said, before starting to hop up and down as the crowd began to roar. "And if all else fails, rip his fucking head off."

"You're damn right," Jens said with pride. "You got this. Go out there and kick some ass!"

Still hopping, Gustav clenched his fists tightly and felt his heart thumping in his chest. Even though he appeared to ooze confidence, he was toiling inside. He had to win this match and the one to follow, or his world would be turned upside down. Of course, he wasn't going to let that happen. He was going to step into that ring, give his opponent the fight of his life, and walk out the winner. God willing, he was going to do that again and again until he was declared the winner of the whole damn tournament. But realistically, he knew his chances of going all the way were slim, but there was nothing wrong with dreaming. So long as he won twice, he would break even. If he could win three, he'd go home with his debt paid and enough money to make good on his promise to Audra. Anything beyond that was a blessing he wouldn't squander. But first, he had to win this fight and send that unlucky son of a bitch home with nothing to show for it but a whole lot of bruises and a fractured ego.

The moment his name was called, Gustav began marching through the tunnel. When he emerged on the other side and stepped into the arena, he was hit with an unexpected wave of fanfare with cheers and shouts aimed in his direction. As he walked down to the ring, hands reached out to him like he was a superstar. He couldn't help but smile at his reception and slapped as many hands as he could on his way down to the ring. However, the moment he climbed into the ring, his glory was stripped from him and transferred to his opponent.

Standing at the center of a traditional boxing ring beside the referee, Gustav watched as a man of equal size marched out from the tunnel. Like him, he basked in his few moments of stardom as the crowd cheered and jeered, but when the two were face-to-face, their smiles turned to scowls. Their brows furrowed as if they were hated enemies and only one man was going to walk out alive.

Staring into one another's eyes, the fighters listened as the referee explained the rules of the fight. For a moment, Gustav had an uneasy feeling after being reminded he had to either knock this man out, injure him critically, or force him to submit. Considering his fighting style, the third avenue to victory was not an option, so it had to be a knockout, as he preferred not to injure his opponent more than necessary. The order was soon given to touch gloves and back up to their respective corners until the signal was given to commence the fight. When Gustav reached his corner, Jens said something meant to be inspirational, but Gustav wasn't listening.

With the sounding of a bell, the signal was given. The two men began their approach, stopping just a short sprint apart at the center of the canvas. His legs spread wide with his left foot in front, Gustav held his left hand out and his right hand back by his jaw, as did his opponent. A short pause would follow as neither man wanted to be the first to take a swing, but the crowd wanted blood. Chants rang out; Gustav's opponent lost his nerve and made his move. It was through this flurry of well-executed strikes that Gustav knew this man was well-trained. His moves came fast and hard, barely giving Gustav a chance to block and counterattack. More than a dozen strikes were thrown with just one breaking his defense before Gustav took his chance and spun on his front heel, throwing a strong sidekick that skirted his opponent's defense and met its mark against his side, all while narrowly blocking an incoming head kick.

Earning himself a bit of breathing room from the blow, Gustav backed off and switched his stance to place his dominant leg back in the front position. Recovering quickly, his opponent threw up his hands and feigned a charge at Gustav, successfully inciting him to shift back a few inches and brace for a takedown. His opponent smirked at this and continued to bait him to study his reactions before finally charging in with a flying knee attack. Barely able to react, Gustav took the blow to the shoulder but caught his opponent in the ribs with a quick left hook - the collision forced both men to the canvas.

His shoulder tingling but not in enough pain to relent, Gustav hurried back to his feet and clashed with his opponent with a furious combination of jabs, crosses, and hooks until he landed a fierce uppercut to the ribs. Seeing his opponent keel over, seemingly stunned, he chose to take the risk and end the fight. Spinning on his heels and thrusting his back knee up like a propeller, Gustav spun himself in a single rotation. The tornado kick was a dangerous move to use in competition, but when used at the right moment, it was a decisive attack.

Knowing the risk he had just taken, Gustav expected to take a surprise hit to the stomach or side as he spun through the air. Instead, his foot connected with the head of his opponent unopposed. His body weight lending power to the technique, Gustav's foot struck with such force that he felt his entire leg shake, causing him to land awkwardly on one foot and fall to the canvas.

Vulnerable on the ground, Gustav hurried to his feet and into a defensive position, but his opponent remained grounded. From what he could tell, his eyes were clenched shut and his breathing was shallow – he was out cold.

I did it! Gustav screamed in his head as he watched his downed opponent wriggle on the ground, but his feeling of glory was short-lived as his humanity took control. He had knocked out plenty of men, but never had he seen them react like that while unconscious. For all he knew, the man's neck had broken from the sheer force he threw at him, and for a moment Gustav was fearful. He stood back and watched as the referee checked the downed fighter.

The ringside physician was called into the ring, and Gustav's heart began to race. Even if it were in the rules, it was never Gustav's intention to critically injure his opponent; he just wanted to win with a knockout. Fortunately, with the use of smelling salts, the defeated fighter would be revived and back on his feet in under a minute. Only then would Gustav's arm be held up in victory to the delight of the crowd.

Chapter 22
Senatgrad, Federal Special Region, Slavic Federation

Seated alone in a private box seat while his sister and their cousins talked and drank wine inside the suite behind him, Aleksey watched Gustav's match with analytical eyes. He was quite skilled and possessed a surprising level of speed and fluidity in his movements for a man who likely fought in the light heavyweight division. However, his fighting style had its flaws, and if Aleksey could see that, surely his future opponents did as well. After all, Gustav was clearly a pure kickboxer, for whenever he hit the mat, he got back on his feet as quickly as possible. That was a flaw that the more-rounded fighters would seek to exploit. However, his saving grace was the power behind his blows. Despite his stocky figure, Gustav was a powerhouse, and he hit like a tank. However, his tendency for flashy moves was dangerous - while his tornado kick was sexy, jumping attacks came with a high degree of risk and left the fighter open to counterattack.

While the crowd roared with excitement as Gustav landed his signature move for the knockout, Aleksey stared at him with intense eyes. As he had done throughout the match, he watched how he carried himself. He had an air of cockiness, and the crowd hated arrogance. This was evident when he threw up his arms in victory and shouted something in German even as his opponent was tended to by medical personnel. They booed him harshly for his lack of tact, and he responded with two middle fingers. Perhaps it was his soldierly sense of duty and honor, but Aleksey found Gustav's behavior to be repugnant. He soon wondered if he was like that in his personal life, and how a sweet woman like Audra could stand by such an ape. He soon shook his head as he found himself feeling a bit jealous for a moment. Smiling, he left his seat and went inside to grab a fresh beer from the fridge and socialize while the ring was being cleaned.

Stepping back into the suite as intermission began, Aleksey placed his empty beer bottle on the counter and headed toward the bathroom. While relieving himself, his phone vibrated in his pocket. Figuring it was just one of his parents calling, he ignored it and moved on to washing his hands. As he washed, his phone began to ring again. Figuring it had to be important, he quickly dried his hands and caught the call before it ended.

"Yeah?" Aleksey said.

"Is that any way to initiate a phone conversation?" Roman asked, causing Aleksey to roll his eyes.

"Sorry, you caught me at an awkward moment—"

"Well, my apologies, but it's important," Roman said, his tone sounding rather annoyed. "Meet me at the executive elevators in five minutes."

"What's this about?" Aleksey asked, but Roman had already ended the call.

Shaking his head, Aleksey slipped the phone back into his pocket and left the bathroom. Stepping back into the suite, he sought out his sister as she was refilling her plate with appetizers kept warm in a chafing dish.

"Change of plans, I have to skip out," Aleksey said, catching a side-eye and a cheeky grin from his sister.

"I heard you having a private conversation in there. Off to meet up with your new lady friend from the museum?"

"Something like that," Aleksey said, playing it cool.

"Well, have fun and be careful, she looks like a heartbreaker," she said, quickly seizing Aleksey by the arm and looking deep into his eyes. "Oh, and don't bring her back to our room. It's bad enough I have to listen to your snoring."

"I don't snore," Aleksey said, but her suddenly annoyed expression said otherwise. Aleksey chuckled at this and bid his sister a good night and then left.

Meeting Roman at the elevators as ordered, Aleksey followed his uncle down to the garage and climbed into the passenger seat of his BMW 7 Series. While not the prettiest car on the road, it was quite comfortable and drove smoothly. However, the luxury car afforded to his uncle by the Polish government was the least of his concerns. He needed to know why he was being dragged away from the arena in the middle of the tournament and where they were going. Unexpectedly, Roman wasn't very forthcoming with that information. Instead, he told him to enjoy the ride and that they'd be there in a few minutes.

After about twenty minutes of travel, the car came to a stop in front of the valet station for a luxury hotel along the coast. Despite his family's wealth and status, Aleksey was unfamiliar with this place, or places like it. Like his mother, he was small-town at heart, but he followed his uncle inside regardless.

As if they were royalty, Aleksey and Roman were led through the luxurious halls of the hotel and up to a third-floor bar and lounge. From the looks of it, the room was reserved for only the most esteemed guests; thus, it was sparsely populated, but Aleksey didn't mind. Following his uncle's lead, he took a seat across from his uncle in a circular booth with tufted red upholstery. Almost immediately, a well-dressed waiter arrived at their table and asked what he could get for them. As if he had become James Bond himself, Roman ordered a very particular martini, shaken rather than stirred, and a charcuterie platter. Meanwhile, Aleksey was a simple man and ordered vodka on the rocks.

While they waited for their drinks and appetizer, Aleksey leaned back and looked at his uncle with curiosity and suspicion. "So, are you going to tell me what this is about?" he asked, but Roman was quiet. "Seriously, I'm out of my element here."

Looking past Aleksey, Roman spotted his other guest and said, "Relax, you're in good company," before raising his hand to signal to his approaching colleague. This caused Aleksey to turn and crane his neck for a look at whomever his uncle was signaling. He soon saw a woman approaching. Though he couldn't get a good look at her from that awkward angle, his first impression was that she was well-dressed and walked with sophistication. Though she was carrying a black briefcase, Aleksey couldn't shake the thought that she was his uncle's mistress as she took her seat. After all, she was somewhere around her mid to late 40s and quite attractive for her age, but then she extended her hand to Aleksey and introduced herself.

"Elena Zmarlak, Office of State Protection."

Though shaking the government agent's slender hand with a semi-firm grip and a pleasant smile, Aleksey was feeling rather surprised by her presence. In fact, he was downright afraid of what was about to transpire. Regardless, he kept his nerve and kindly asked what division she hailed from.

"Special Intelligence," Elena said without hesitation, before easily shifting the subject. "Once upon a time, your uncle was my direct supervisor."

Nodding slowly, surprise in his eyes, Aleksey looked at Roman seeking clarification. "I didn't realize you were in Special Intelligence."

"Closely guarded secret," Roman said, but Elena spoke up before Aleksey could respond.

"It's my understanding that you're interested in joining our field of service," she said, but Aleksey was quiet. "Am I mistaken?"

"No, you're not mistaken," Aleksey said, breaking his silence. "I'm just a little taken aback by all of this. I wasn't expecting to sit down with government officials tonight, especially in a place like this."

"The timing and venue were chosen with a purpose, I assure you," Elena said warmly. "It allows us to avoid suspicion from certain parties."

"Avoid suspicion from certain parties? You mean my parents, don't you?" Aleksey said, and Elena looked to Roman, who nodded.

"Yes, exactly," Elena replied. "Your father is a powerful man, but unfortunately, he's not on our side at this moment in time."

Rolling his eyes, Aleksey was quick to explain that he was well past the age that his father could sway his career choices. However, Elena was quick to admit she wasn't taking any chances around a man of Aleksander's status. Understanding her meaning, Aleksey, growing ever impatient, asked exactly what he was being recruited for.

Appreciating his bluntness, Elena smiled and explained the position she had envisioned for him. "My team and I have been tasked with aiding the creation of a new special operations unit. We're recruiting exemplary soldiers and operatives, and you fit the bill."

"Special Group for Rapid Operational Response, am I right?" Aleksey asked with cool composure, before he sipped his vodka.

"That's correct," Elena replied. "However, we've taken to calling the unit Rapid Response for short."

"Makes sense," Aleksey said, taking another sip and swishing it around his mouth while he thought. "So, what makes me stand out? I'm just a simple soldier."

"Don't sell yourself short, Aleksey," Roman said, and Elena agreed, for she soon produced a short list of achievements from her briefcase.

"Graduated in the top five percent of your class at age seventeen. Combat veteran with ten years of service in the army, six of which were served with Komandosów and GROM Squadron B. Qualified sniper and field medic. Multiple military honors, including the Cross of Valor. You also have standing invitations to officer candidate school and Alpha Group Selection, both of which carry recommendations from high-ranking military officials," Elena said, reading off the short list of Aleksey's accomplishments. "If you ask me, that's one hell of a resume for a simple soldier."

"Yes, but it seems my uncle forgot to inform you that I simply want a quiet guard post at an embassy."

"While I can certainly make that happen, I'm going to be honest. That would be an incredible waste of your talent."

"Sure, but I've had my fill of combat. I want nothing more than to serve out my remaining years in comfort and relative peace," Aleksey said, and Elena nodded.

"You have a sweetheart, don't you?"

"No, not anymore, but I wouldn't mind having a family someday. In fact, I'm told that an embassy job allows for that sort of thing. Hard to get deployed to war when you're paid to stand guard for diplomats."

"Fair enough," Elena said, but she wasn't beaten yet. She had an ace up her sleeve that she was saving. "What can I do to convince you to join Rapid Response rather than waste away on guard duty?"

"Honestly, if I wanted to stay in a combat unit, I'd just ride out my time in GROM," Aleksey said, giving Elena pause. "Look, I'm not saying I'm against transferring over to your service. I just don't see the point in making a lateral move."

"Completely understandable," Elena said. "Then tell me, what do you want? Surely working as an embassy guard wasn't your first choice."

"Actually, it was. Ideally, I'd like a comfy guard post at an embassy somewhere in Europe. I'd be happy to go through spy school and keep an eye on things from my post, if that's what it takes for such an assignment," Aleksey said, giving Elena a reserved smile. "I'm not saying I'm not willing to go into the intelligence world, I'm just done with being gone nine months out of the year and risking my life on missions. Like I said, if I wanted that, I'd stay with GROM."

"Yes, you had mentioned that," Elena said, looking at Roman. "What do you think, Senator? A spy posing as a guard?"

Sighing through his nose, Roman attempted to persuade Aleksey into trying out for Rapid Response by calling him a prime example of an elite soldier, but Aleksey was steadfast. Seeing that his sister's headstrongness had passed on to her son, Roman shifted gears.

"You really want to have a wife and kids, don't you?"

"Yes, sir," Aleksey said resolutely.

"Very well, we'll call it a deal," Roman said, reaching out to shake, but Aleksey was still.

"What are we agreeing upon?" Aleksey asked, noticing that Elena was scribbling down on a notepad with incredible speed.

"We're agreeing that you'll accept reassignment to the Office of State Protection," Elena said, finishing whatever she was writing.

"No, I'm not agreeing to anything just yet," Aleksey said, taking Roman by surprise. "I'll need to know the facts before I make even a hint at consent."

Suddenly, Elena flipped the notepad and slid it toward him. Taking the notepad in hand, Aleksey read through the hastily but legible list she had made. It contained everything he was asking for, but with the addition of a highly generous compensation package. However, he found two things to be off-putting. For one, they wanted him to attend the selection program for the new unit. Secondly, he was expected to pass a covert operations school.

"Haven't I made myself clear?" Aleksey asked, his finger pointing at the bullet points in question. "I'm not interested in your new unit, and I'm done with special operations."

"You misunderstand. This isn't as easy as signing a contract and you're a member of my team. Every recruit must undergo weeks of rigorous physical and mental testing to determine if they're truly the right fit. It just so happens that the new unit goes through the same program as prospective field intelligence officers," she said. "It's all there."

"Yes, I see that. Selection, paramilitary training, covert operations, and intelligence gathering," Aleksey read from the paper, before shaking his head and looking up. "This is a bait and switch. You're trying to get me to sign up for your new special operations unit without realizing it."

"Absolutely not. This is standard protocol for all field operatives."

"Ha!" Aleksey cried, his index finger pointed at Elena accusingly. "Field operative... I asked to be an embassy guard, not a fucking spy."

"Calm down, we don't need to make a scene," Roman said, but Aleksey glared at him. All the while, Elena remained cool, calm, and collected.

"I'm afraid my choice of words may have been confusing," Elena said. "By field operative, I'm referring to all employees in a non-clerical role. Being that you're being considered for an embassy guard position, it is inherent that you understand how to handle yourself in the many tense situations that you might find yourself in. Truth be told, standing at a gate is only part of the job. In the event of an attack or a security emergency, you might find yourself involved in the destruction or transport of sensitive information. We need our people to know what they have and how to protect it."

"Understood," Aleksey said, and Elena nodded. "However, I need time to think. Can I keep this offer?"

"Of course," Elena said. "Rest assured, we're not looking to screw you or your dreams. We're simply trying to find the very best people for our service. We work for the good of Poland, please understand that."

"Loud and clear. I just have a few more questions."

"What is it, Aleksey?" Roman asked impatiently as he figured Aleksey was just wasting time at this point.

"Say I accept this generous offer, but for whatever reason, I fail to meet expectations in one of these trainings. What happens then?"

"You'll return to your former unit, and any record of service with the Office of State Protection will be destroyed."

"Why is that? Unless I sign a new contract, I'll be a reservist in three months."

"Because your transfer is not official until your current contract officially expires," Elena said. "But I don't see that as a problem. Your service record speaks for itself."

"Indeed," Aleksey said, his voice trailing off.

"So, have we come to a decision?"

"Negative, I still need time to think," Aleksey said, and though Roman rolled his eyes, Elena remained friendly.

"We'll touch base in a few days. How about that?" Elena asked, sliding Aleksey her business card. "You can reach me at this number when you've arrived at a decision." She then reached over the table and offered her hand. "It was a pleasure meeting you, Aleksey. I surely hope we can meet again."

Shaking her hand, Aleksey nodded silently. Elena left soon after, and while Aleksey watched her leave, Roman glared at him intensely.

"If I knew you were going to embarrass me, I would have never wasted my time," Roman snarled, as Aleksey took a long sip from his watered-down vodka. "You're throwing away a golden opportunity, Aleksey."

"I know what I'm doing," Aleksey said, but Roman only grew angrier.

"Watch it, you little smartass!" he barked, but Aleksey raised one hand as if asking for the floor or to silence him.

"My mother taught me never to make a deal when drunk, and I had a few beers at the arena," Aleksey said calmly. "I wasn't trying to embarrass you, but I won't be pressured by a spy handler either."

"So, what's the deal, Aleksey? Are you going to think about it, or should I call Elena and tell her this was a waste of time?"

"I'll call you tomorrow when I've had time to think this through," Aleksey said. "The offer is amazing, but I need to sleep on it."

"If I don't hear from you before the tournament tomorrow, I'll write you off," Roman said, and Aleksey nodded. "Don't make a fool out of me."

"I don't intend to," Aleksey said, before reaching over and grabbing a hunk of hunter's sausage from the charcuterie plate. "Thank you for the food and drink."

"You're welcome," Roman grumbled, before taking a long pull from his drink. He then took a handful of nuts from the platter and chewed away his frustration. Fortunately, his anger toward Aleksey softened some as the pair indulged in a second round and put the business with Elena and the intelligence agency behind them.

Chapter 23

Senatgrad, Federal Special Region, Slavic Federation

Having missed the remainder of the fights for the night, Aleksey returned to his hotel with the intention of turning in early and thinking things over with a couple of beers alone on the balcony. However, upon returning to his room, he found a note from his sister urging him to join her and their cousins at a local bar. Figuring he was better off drinking with company than drowning his sorrows alone, Aleksey changed into something more befitting of a night at a dive bar and headed out.

Upon arriving, Aleksey was pleasantly surprised to see Miko hanging out with his sister and cousins. With a smile on his face, he approached his fellow frogman from behind and placed his hand on his shoulder with a tight grip.

"Careful there, buddy. This one's more trouble than she's worth," Aleksey said, nodding toward his sister. "I should know. I had to grow up with her."

Turning around with a wide grin, Miko shook Aleksey's hand and swore that he wasn't trying to pick her up. Lena rolled her eyes, for it was painfully obvious that he was. Nonetheless, she turned the awkwardness onto Aleksey.

"Hey, where's your lady friend? Did she stand you up, or did you give her the old pump and dump?" Lena asked with a cheeky grin.

"Met someone new already, Rybinski?"

"I wish," Aleksey said with a laugh. "I had some business with my uncle that had to be taken care of."

"Business on a Saturday night in the middle of a martial arts tournament?" Lena asked, skepticism showing in her voice. "Christ, you're a shitty liar. Just admit it. You seduced the poor girl, got your rocks off, and ditched her when she went to the bathroom like an asshole."

"There's nothing to admit, but wouldn't Liev like to know you've got the bedroom eyes for a decorated soldier you met in a dive bar?"

Glaring at him, Lena mouthed 'fuck you' to her brother, but Aleksey just smiled. He knew she wasn't the type to cheat, and though he would rather see her with someone like Miko than Liev Medvedev, she had standards too high for a military man. She liked her men cut from the elite cloth, and the only thing elite about Miko was his status in the military, and a soldier certainly didn't make the money to live up to her standards. So, unless he suddenly became a lawyer, a doctor, or a rising star politician, there was little chance he was going to steal his sister from the youngest member of the State Duma.

"Well, this got weird. How about a game of darts?" Miko suggested, feeling like the sibling rivalry on display was going from lighthearted to downright vicious.

Realizing they were going a bit too far with their verbal sparring, Aleksey cracked a smile and pointed at his sister. "Ready to get embarrassed again?"

"Game on, frogboy. I've been practicing."

□

Locked in a serious best-of-three series of darts, Miko, Aleksey, and Lena tried their best to beat the other and claim victory as quickly as possible. All the while, beers and cocktails flowed, and their cousins cheered Lena on and booed the men at every turn. Despite Aleksey's insistence that he was the greatest dart player in the room, he consistently took third place in all three rounds, with the sudden death round going to Lena. A bit on the drunk side by that point, Lena's playful gloating leaned toward obnoxiousness when she scored the winning points. Excusing himself to urinate, but mostly so he could be spared her stupidity for a few minutes, Aleksey headed for the bathroom. Along the way, he took notice of a surprising sight– it was Gustav, and sitting on his lap was a pretty young thing that was certainly not Audra.

Though this wasn't Aleksey's business, he couldn't shake the thought even after using the toilet. In fact, as he took care of his business, he thought about what he had gone through and the pain he felt. When he emerged, he felt the latent fury of his own betrayal bubbling to the surface. However, rather than walking up and punching him in the face as if Audra were a close friend or relative, he returned to his group.

Obnoxious as ever, Lena challenged him to a one-on-one game of high winner vs low loser. Normally, Aleksey would have rolled his eyes at the jab, but he was noticeably distant. Feeling like he was being unreasonably perturbed by one of her more harmless jabs that night, she asked what was with him, but he shrugged it off and grabbed the darts. However, the way he threw his darts told a story all its own, so when it came time for Lena to throw, she pulled her brother aside.

"Alright, what's gotten into you? You can't take a joke, suddenly?"

"I'm fine," Aleksey said, but Lena wasn't stupid. She knew something was bothering him deeply.

"Cut the shit, Aleksey," Lena said firmly. "You went from joking around and being fun for once to a complete dickhead. Either tell me what's going on or go back to the hotel. Either way, you're telling me what's on your mind at some point tonight."

"Look, I said it's nothing."

"And I said you're a shitty liar," she said, before realizing Aleksey was staring past her. She then turned to see what had his attention and saw Gustav with the pretty young thing held tightly. Recognizing him, she turned back to Aleksey with a puzzled expression. "It's that German fighter. So what?"

"Remember that girl from the museum?" he asked, and she nodded. "That's her boyfriend."

Looking again, Lena felt Aleksey's anger, for she, too, had been cheated on, and wounds like that never quite heal. So, with teeth clenched, she glared at Gustav until he made eye contact and gave her a confused expression. Just then, she turned to Aleksey with a devilish grin.

"What's the poor girl's name?"

"Audra," he said, and Lena took off for Gustav's table with her shoulders square and her jaw clenched.

With curious eyes, Aleksey watched as Lena marched over to Gustav's table. Without an ounce of fear in her body, his sister leaned over the table and looked Gustav directly in the eyes. Though the music was too loud for Aleksey to hear what was being said, Gustav's expression went from puzzled to annoyed and finally to angered. All the while, the girl on his lap kept that same pretentious smile until Lena turned her attention to her. With a finger pointed at the bimbo, Lena gave her a seemingly vicious tongue lashing before giving her the finger.

Confused but a little proud of his sister for putting a cheating bastard in his place, Aleksey stood by as Lena marched back with a proud smile.

"That'll show him. Fucking asshole," Lena said, snatching up her darts and channeling her anger and disgust to score an incredible one hundred and ten points in a single round.

"Christ, what's gotten into you?" Aleksey asked when his sister returned to the table.

"I guess I'm feeling a little mean tonight," Lena said with a smile, before taking a long pull from her vodka and tonic. "Have fun topping that round."

"Call it a game. I'm more interested in knowing what you said to that German."

"Oh, nothing too harsh. Just that he had a lovely girlfriend that my brother could have easily taken from him if she weren't such a sweetheart."

"That's it? Seemed a lot worse," he said, but she shrugged.

"Well, I also told him that it was just a matter of time before she realized who he really was and that his lady friend was a dirty whore who fucked half the city already."

"Well, that was certainly ruthless," Aleksey said, looking past his sister to see that Gustav and his adoring fan had already left. "I guess he didn't take your advice."

Turning to see for herself, Lena rolled her eyes. "What a prick. I hope he catches something nasty from her. I bet she has the clap."

"Don't wish that on him. He'd end up giving it to Audra," Aleksey said, but Lena smirked reassuringly.

"Something tells me there's not much going on in their bedroom these days," Lena said, speaking from experience. "Nonetheless, I think you should give her a call. Maybe she knows he's a cheater and might be looking for a little payback."

"That's quite alright," Aleksey said with mild disgust. "I've been on the receiving end of that sort of thing. The last thing I'd want to do is be a tool of revenge."

"Then your morals are stronger than mine," Lena said, giving Aleksey reason to shudder, for he never wanted to think about his sister like that, no matter how old she was. "Come on. I'll give you one more chance to beat me."

Slamming his piss-warm beer, Aleksey told her to bring it before snatching up his darts and losing yet another game.

Chapter 24
Senatgrad, Federal Special Region, Slavic Federation

Waking just before dawn as he had always done since the earliest days of his military service, Aleksander completed his daily routine and left his suite dressed in full uniform even though the summit wasn't scheduled to resume for another two hours. He had been unexpectedly summoned to the presidential suite, where the First Lady resided, and told to go alone. While he knew of the rumors of her extracurricular activities, he doubted she harbored any attraction toward him, as she seemed to like them young and well-built. Regardless of that fact, he didn't believe his early morning summoning was of any nature but political. So, heading down the vacant halls of the hotel's third floor, he made his way to the bank of elevators at the center of the building. Once inside, he pressed the button for the ninth floor and stepped out about thirty seconds later.

A massive suite that was essentially a miniature hotel itself, the Presidential Suite took up the entire west wing of the ninth floor and was secured with state-of-the-art security, including bulletproof glass and reinforced doors. Of course, being that a powerful dignitary was staying in the suite, armed guards were positioned at each entrance, but this was no problem. Aleksander was one of the most famous men in the Eastern Bloc, so when he approached the main entrance to the suite, he was allowed entry with little more than a silent welcome.

Stepping into the suite, Aleksander found himself in a naturally lit atrium of sorts. The ceiling and walls were composed almost entirely of glass, allowing for an indoor garden. It was here in a small lounging space among the flowers and plants that he found Viktoriya waiting for him. As expected of a woman of her prestige, she was well-dressed in a custom lounging outfit from one of the world's premier designers. Befitting her nature, the outfit was a tad revealing and somewhat form-fitting, making it impossible to notice that she had a body akin to a goddess. Of course, Aleksander never had a problem looking past a gorgeous woman, and this would be no exception.

Approaching Viktoriya without ever breaking eye contact, Aleksander greeted her professionally, never forgetting that she was the First Lady. As expected, he was rightfully greeted as 'General Rybinski' before he was presented with her slender right hand. Though he was never a fan of such antiquated theatrics, Viktoriya was a woman who loved to be admired and pampered, so he made no fuss and kissed the top of her hand. He was then told he could be seated, so he sat down on a couch situated across from the pseudo-monarch. His body stiff and his eyes locked on his host, he gave her the clear impression that he was there for business and nothing more. Not the least bit interested in him sexually or physically, she acted as if time was of the essence and got straight to business, making her intentions clear.

"I understand you've been out gallivanting with the enemy," Viktoriya said coolly, catching him by surprise, though he made no meaningful attempt at defense. Rather, he replied calmly and respectfully.

"By the enemy, you're referring to Senator Wilczynski."

"Indeed," Viktoriya said with a nod. "Yes, I'm aware he's your brother-in-law, but he's also a leader and founding member of the Polish Liberation Party. And lest we forget, a profound pain in my ass."

Though he wanted to chuckle, for Roman had verbally sparred fiercely with her throughout the summit thus far, effectively putting the spoiled politician in her place many times, Aleksander kept his composure. However, she could read him like a book.

"You find that amusing, don't you?"

"No, madam," Aleksander said, but her eyes became sharp and her voice catty.

"Then enlighten me as to what's been said between you and the good senator."

Knowing better than to lie or sidestep, Aleksander gave her the truth without hesitation.

"He asked on multiple occasions that I act as an ally in Moscow," Aleksander said, and Viktoriya smirked. "More specifically, he wanted me to convince the Premier to see things their way."

"And what did you say?"

"I told him that I would not endanger my position of authority, but I would certainly seek a mutually beneficial outcome."

"Mutually beneficial outcome," Viktoriya said sardonically. "I understand you're Polish, but so long as you serve as a member of my husband's cabinet, you are a federalist, and I expect you to act as such."

"Permission to speak freely, madam."

"Cut the crap, Alek. It's just the two of us here. You can call me by my given name."

"Very well," Aleksander said, though he never felt at ease calling the First Lady by her given name. "May I speak freely, Viktoriya?"

"You may but do be careful. I'm in no mood for insolence."

"I'm afraid you're carrying yourself too proudly before the separatists," Aleksander began, earning himself an annoyed glare. "It was because of me that the separatists revealed their plans yesterday. In exchange, they expected us to be open to negotiation."

"Was I not open to negotiation? Did I not hear them out and debate the weakness in their plans?"

"You did, but I'm afraid we've lost sight of the purpose of this summit."

"Then enlighten me," Viktoriya said with brewing frustration.

"We're here to ensure the Polish plan is sound, not deny them their right to secession. So far, all we've done is argue."

"And your point is?"

"My point is we're wasting time. The people have spoken, and the separatists have a solid plan. All we're doing at this point is manipulating the plan in our favor."

"Yes, that's the whole point," Viktoriya replied coolly. "As for the people having their say... you do realize that the referendum was little more than a feel-good measure to calm the radicals, correct?"

"With all due respect, I understood it to be a lawful vote. We're still a democracy, are we not?"

Rolling her eyes, Viktoriya proceeded to split hairs by stating that the Slavic Federation was a constitutional union of republics, not a free-for-all democracy like the confederacy that preceded it. Of course, this did little to win the debate, so she shifted the subject to her liking.

"Look, you're making it painfully obvious that you're going to resign and go back home the moment this secession nonsense is done and over with. Given that my husband refuses to believe you'd turn on him like that, I'll let you in on a little secret that you should have already known," Viktoriya said firmly. "No matter how this summit ends, Poland will not be seceding from the Federation."

"Is that so?" Aleksander asked calmly, and she nodded.

"There's a reason the Confederacy became a federation," Viktoriya said. "Too many of these backwater countries lack the ability to stand on their own. History has proven they need Russian leadership. How else did we manage to fall back onto the better aspects of the Soviet system?"

"Then what was the point of all of this, Viktoriya?" Aleksander questioned.

"The point was to provide the illusion of democracy while maintaining the integrity of the system."

"That doesn't even make sense," Aleksander said with a shake of his head. "If we screw over the separatists, there could be a war."

"Surely, you're prepared for that. That is your job, no?"

"I am, but that's an outcome that should be avoided at all costs."

"Avoided at all costs. Spoken like a true patriot," Viktoryia said with a grin that faded into a cold stare. "If the separatists want a war, then they're as stupid as I believe them to be. The combined might of the Federation would destroy their army in weeks, perhaps even days," she declared, and Aleksander was silent. "But don't worry, we won't let it get that far. We already have a plan for crushing this movement without giving the separatists a leg to stand on."

"Interesting, please elaborate."

"Gladly," Viktoriya said comfortably. "We're going to allow these negotiations to fail. In doing so, we send this matter up to the Senate. The separatists can make their case before the entire Federation, and we'll put it to a vote. We'll give them a fresh taste of the democracy they so desire and save the federation from Balkanization in the process."

"I don't believe this will work as intended."

"I don't care what you think," Viktoriya said with a firm tone and cold, calculating stare. "All I need from you is to sit back, shut up, and prepare for war. Something tells me your people won't take no for an answer."

"This is outrageous. I won't stand for it!" Aleksander said with clear disdain for what Viktoriya expected of him.

"Just whose side are you really on, Alek? Because all this time I thought I was talking to a man who honored the law and followed his orders like the good soldier he's supposed to be."

"I'm loyal to the Federation, but you can't seriously believe I'd appreciate your plan. You're playing political games with my people's futures and asking me to prepare for war against my homeland."

"You don't have to like it, but you do have to abide by it," she said calmly. "Of course, I don't really think it will come to a clash of arms. We're going to make them feel like they're getting a fair chance at victory. I think a month is more than enough time for them to try and win allies in the Senate."

"Why a month?"

"It gives them enough time to feel like they've adequately prepared while keeping the rabble-rousers at bay."

Seeing the wisdom in that plan, Aleksander inquired about what the federal side would do to ensure Poland fails before the Senate. Viktoriya smiled for a moment, giving Aleksander the feeling that they would use every dirty trick at their disposal, but then she answered.

"We'll use the time to craft our own arguments to be presented in private to the senators deemed most vulnerable to Polish suggestion."

"Very well, but what happens if it comes down to a tie?"

"The Premier has the final say," she said calmly. "I believe I can say with full confidence that my husband sees things the way I do."

"I do not doubt that, but I have to know what is motivating all of this."

"Have I not made myself clear? The only way to secure the future of the Slavic people is through unity and a strong central government."

"Then let me ask you this one question," Aleksander said coolly. "Do you really believe what you just said, or are you simply attempting to rebuild the Russian Empire with a new name?"

"There's no purpose to a new empire, Alek. The Slavic nations are stronger together, but the last thing they need is an autocrat," Viktoriya replied. "But if you really need to know what's at the core of all of this, it's a collective concern about the eastward expansion of the European Union and NATO. Imagine if a breakaway republic like Poland couldn't quite stand on its own. First, it would be the European Union, then it would be NATO. Surely other republics follow suit and begin to break away one by one until all that's left of our victory over the communists is a cornered, isolated Russia."

"Yes, I've heard of such concerns from your husband. From what I've come to understand, they aim to remain an economic bloc, nothing more."

"Yes, or so they say, but look what happened to our own confederacy," Viktoriya warned. "We can't risk losing Poland to the West, Alek. The Cold War may have ended, but we can't risk an imbalance of power in Europe. NATO and the European Union must remain west of the Oder-Neisse, or one way or another, everything we've worked for ends up in the dustbin of history."

"I see your point, but I think you're misunderstanding the intentions of our cousins to the west."

"No, I don't think I am, but I'm not asking you to understand," Viktoriya said with arrogant confidence. "I'm asking you to follow your orders and trust in your superiors. Can you do that? Or do I need to recommend my husband find someone else to lead the army?"

"That won't be necessary," Aleksander said calmly.

"Then let me do what I've come here to do."

"Yes, madam," Aleksander said in bitter surrender.

Chapter 25

Senatgrad, Federal Special Region, Slavic Federation

Gustav woke early that morning with a beam of light shining through the crack in the curtains. Having overdone his celebration the night before, he felt terribly ill. His stomach was sour, his breath stunk like death, his body was greasy, and his head felt like it had been pressed in a vise. Regardless, he had to recover quickly, so he forced himself out of bed. When his feet touched the cool carpeted floor, the room began to spin. It was immediately obvious that he was still drunk, but he had to soldier on.

Taking short, careful steps to keep his balance, Gustav made his way from the bed toward the bathroom. As he passed by the bed, he didn't bother to turn his head and give Audra even the smallest loving glance. He was plenty mad at her still for what she did the night before, yet he couldn't remember what she did. He surmised the alcohol still coursing through his system was clouding his mind and that he'd remember it at some point. Surely, she had done something meaningful to make him angry, though it was likely his fault. After all, it was usually the other way around with her giving him the silent treatment.

Leaving her to sleep, Gustav kept on his way. Soon enough, he stepped into the small bathroom that barely contained a bathtub, toilet, and sink. The light was blinding and caused his pickled brain to scream in agony, but he adjusted quickly enough. It was then that he noticed a foul smell. Looking around, he immediately checked the toilet, but it was clean. In time, he noticed his shirt was hanging over the side of the wastebasket. When he pulled it out, he found it stained with vomit. Judging from the foul taste in his mouth, it was his own.

Deciding to rinse his mouth out, he stepped over to the sink but got distracted when he caught a glimpse of himself in the mirror. His ribcage was covered in huge splotches of blackish-purple bruises and felt warm when he held his finger nearby without even touching it. It was obvious that he had worsened the damage the previous night, but he couldn't quite remember how. All he could recall on command was dominating the fight and winning with a perfectly timed tornado kick. Everything else was a blur. Even when he closed his eyes to think about the blow that caused his ribs to turn purple or whatever Audra said or did to piss him off, his brain throbbed, and he could recall nothing.

Deciding not to dwell on it and get cleaned up instead, he turned on the shower faucet and waited for the water to warm to his liking while stripping out of his socks and underwear. Fortunately, he didn't see anything worse than his ribs. There were a few cuts and bruises, but nothing serious.

Climbing into the shower, Gustav let the hot water run down his body. As he stood there in the hot rain, he could practically hear Jens bitching at him to drink more water, for if he had not neglected proper hydration after the tournament, he probably wouldn't be in such sorry shape. Then again, he could hardly believe Jens would have allowed him to go out the previous night. This triggered a negative memory - he had an argument with Audra about going out to a nightclub to celebrate. She didn't want to go, but he was riding too high on his victory, so he managed to convince her to go anyway.

Thinking hard about this while he lathered his body with a cheap bar of soap, Gustav recalled having an argument at a club and being struck across the face before seeing her walk away in a rage. Still, he couldn't quite remember what made her so angry that she slapped him. Moving on to washing his hair, though this only took a tiny dab and a bit of lathering to cover his shortly trimmed hair fully. Again, he let the water wash over his head and face, clenching his eyes to avoid getting soap in his sore, bloodshot eyes. A flood of memories of the previous night came rushing back.

Audra had slapped him because he called her a bitch, or something along those lines. Why he called her that, he couldn't recall, but after she left, he went to a neighborhood sports bar alone. That's why Jens wasn't around to stop him from getting pickled drunk. He couldn't recall taking any drugs, but he remembered getting a lot of looks and free drinks from people who recognized him from the tournament. Good-looking girls, even some men, were looking at him with suggestive stares as he basked in his temporary celebrity status. Even though he wasn't the most handsome man on earth, he had his pick that night, and the alcohol was driving his actions with his underutilized dick riding shotgun. Just then, he recalled the mouthy redhead shouting at him as he sat in a booth with the hottest girl in the bar.

Feeling like he might have done something incredibly dumb, Gustav shut off the water and reached out beyond the curtain to grab a towel. Wiping himself dry, he stepped out onto the shower mat and sought out the mouthwash to cleanse the nasty taste still hanging around. Finding the wash right where he expected it, he popped the cap, took a swig, and felt the minty burn as he swished it around his mouth. In doing so, he discovered the presence of several cuts inside his mouth, so he leaned over the sink and spat prematurely. After turning on the water and splashing the stream to wash away the rogue refuse sprayed around the sink, he noticed something out of the ordinary. It was a pink toothbrush and a foreign brand of toothpaste. This struck him as odd, for not only was his toothbrush missing, but Audra's toothbrush was purple, and they used a German brand of toothpaste.

His eyes wide, Gustav's nagging fear that he had done something incredibly stupid came rushing back. He carefully left the bathroom and headed into the dimly lit bedroom. He quickly spotted his pants alongside the bed. As he approached, his fears were confirmed. The woman he spent the night with was certainly not Audra, and if he had made a closer inspection, he would have seen that she was the woman from the bar. Of course, he wasn't interested in knowing what this woman looked like without his beer goggles on; he just needed to get his pants and go. With a bit of luck, he was able to do just that. Unfortunately, his clothes smelled horrid, and his gym bag was back in his rightful hotel room. He had no choice but to go back and face the music of his scorned girlfriend.

Making his way back to his hotel, Gustav was standing at the door to his room. His room key clenched in his palm, he took a deep breath. There was a good chance Audra was still in there, and if she was, she was most certainly going to put him through the roof for staying out all night. Of course, Gustav knew there was no escape. He had to go in there at some point, and he'd certainly have to face Audra sooner or later. Of course, coming clean was never something Gustav did particularly well with. He was a hardheaded individual, but what he did last night was easily the worst mistake he had ever made. Despite being tempted many times over the years, he had never cheated until the night before, and he felt a terrible feeling of regret eating away at his conscience.

Knowing his relationship was about to end if he came clean, Gustav conjured up the best lie he could think of. He'd admit to staying out all night and ending up in someone else's hotel room, but he'd claim he had blacked out. While this wouldn't save him from a vicious tongue lashing, perhaps even a stiff slap to the face, he felt a lie by omission was the best course of action. After all, if he admitted to infidelity, Audra wouldn't just end their relationship; she'd very likely turn to Jens in anger. He very much wanted to avoid the wrath of his trainer until after the tournament. So, he would take a walk down the hall and up to another floor where he'd pace around until he got his story right.

Returning to his room, key in hand once more, Gustav slipped it in slowly and worked the lock. Fully expecting Audra to be sitting on the bed with her arms crossed and her expression cold, he was taken by surprise. The room was lit, but it was empty. The bed had been made, and the bathroom was vacant. Where she was, he had no idea, but he was grateful for the divine intervention that allowed him to avoid her for a little while longer.

Seizing the opportunity, Gustav changed out of his dirty clothes and grabbed his gym bag. In all, he spent about a few minutes in the room, but it felt far longer, for he feared that Audra might return at any moment. To make matters worse, a glance at the alarm clock informed him that he was three hours late for his arranged time at the gym. Suddenly, Audra was just one of his problems, and he'd have to face Jens first, but he knew how to handle him best.

Chapter 26

Senatgrad, Federal Special Region, Slavic Federation

ngry with Gustav for his reckless and insensitive behavior at that club, which earned him a hard slap before she left him behind, Audra barely slept through the night. As much as she hated that man for calling her one of the worst things a man could call a woman for merely suggesting they go back to the hotel so he could rest, she was worried. He hadn't returned by the time she finally pulled herself out of bed, and Jens didn't know where he was either. Several trips down to the gym, and even a stop at the local police station, yielded nothing about Gustav's whereabouts. For all she knew, he got mixed up with the wrong people and disappeared or got so sloppy drunk that he got a stupid idea to climb one of the bridges and fell into a canal. But as each hour passed, she started to worry a little less. She reckoned it was just the terrible loneliness she felt from being essentially abandoned the whole time in Senatgrad, but she was starting to feel like she was better off without him. So rather than sit in her hotel room and wait for him to stumble in, she went out for breakfast, visited a museum and some shops, and then returned to the hotel only to find Gustav was still missing.

Worried that Gustav had gotten himself into serious trouble, Audra called Jens at the gym and learned that he had appeared while she was out. Relieved that he was alive, but furious that he had apparently ended up sleeping in the locker room of the gym after a night of binge drinking, she needed air and a nice atmosphere. Retrieving her backpack in case she caught the urge to work on her drawings, she headed for the door.

Audra walked the city for close to an hour with the sole aim of cooling her nerves while reassessing her life. Along the way, she passed a lovely little café and committed it to memory. She figured she'd stop by on her way back to the hotel, but before long, the air became noticeably colder and thick raindrops began to fall from the sky. Figuring this was a sign from the universe to grab a coffee and do some drawing, she walked back to the café. She stepped inside mere seconds before the wind picked up with heavy gusts, spraying sheets of rain at a nearly horizontal angle. Relieved that she had missed the storm by sheer luck, she scanned the café for just the right spot to claim as her own for an hour or two.

Finding a quiet, cozy spot at the back of the café, she claimed a table meant for two as her own, spreading out the tools of her trade before flagging a waitress to order a strong coffee and a pastry. With her workspace prepared and her coffee and snack on the way, she got down to work. However, having not touched her graphic novel for some time, it took her a few minutes of mental struggle to cast out her frustration with Gustav and summon her creativity. When the spark finally lit, it cast a blazing fire on the figurative deadwood clogging her mind, revealing a fresh wave of creative energy.

Her mind focused and her pencils working at a steady pace, Audra was in her own world. She was breathing life into a character she had long conceptualized in her mind but hadn't yet put to paper. Slowly but surely, lines came together and formed an unnamed anti-heroine in a long black coat and knee-high boots. With the base of the character done, she began to fill in the blank spaces, adding detail where she saw fit. The most striking detail was the decision to draw jester-like black makeup around the mouth and eyes. However, it wasn't until she was done and sat back to drink her long-since cold coffee and appreciate her work that she realized she had basically ripped off the gothic anti-hero from The Crow.

Deflated by the realization that her character had to be heavily reworked, or scrapped entirely, Audra sat back with a sigh. Sipping the coffee, she looked around the room in a bid to clear her head and soon locked eyes with a familiar face across the room. A few moments later, she was greeted by Aleksey with a warm smile.

"Well, hello again," he said, but Audra merely forced a smile.

Though she thought her expression, if not her crowded table, made it clear she was busy, it didn't appear so. Aleksey asked if he could join her, but rather than cast him off in a rude fashion, she waved her hand toward an empty chair.

"What do we have here?" he asked, looking down at her drawing. He soon made an impressed murmur. "This is quite good. Can I have a closer look?"

"Knock yourself out," Audra said with a shrug. She then cleared her pencils and allowed him to flip the sketchbook so he could look at the drawing from the proper angle. "It's just a rough draft. It won't stay like that," she said quickly, but Aleksey was quiet as he analyzed her work.

"This is really good. I love the detail in the costume. It's very realistic," he said. He then looked at her with curious eyes. "Did you base this one on a photograph?"

"No, just the image in my head," she said, but then she sighed. "I was going for something like Siouxsie Sioux, but I ended up with Eric Draven."

"Maybe a little, but The Crow didn't invent that look. Besides, it's a rough draft, right?"

"Right," she said, feeling slightly at ease, though a little curious about their meeting that morning. "How is it that we managed to cross paths again? You're not following me, are you?"

Noting the sarcasm in her voice, he chuckled and answered truthfully. "I'm staying at the Kaiserhof Hotel. It's not far from here, actually."

"I'm aware," she said. "It just so happens that's where I'm staying, too."

"Well, isn't that a fun coincidence?" he said with a bright smile. "Quite convenient, perhaps."

"I'm not on the market," Audra said bluntly to quickly squash any brewing thoughts Aleksey had regarding a romantic encounter, though she felt bad for her delivery. "Sorry, but I'm just putting that out there."

"Of course, Gustav Hagen, right?"

"Right," Audra said with a tinge of embarrassment, but he remained friendly.

"What I meant by convenient is that you're a fun person to be around. I'm sure Gustav is just the same," he said, but before he could go on, Audra explained her demeanor.

"Look, I'm sorry if I came off a little rude, but I'm naturally defensive around men. It's a bartender thing."

"So, that's how you make your money?" Aleksey asked, but Audra shrugged.

"It pays the bills, and that's about it," she remarked. "Professional artist is my dream job."

"And you seem to be chasing that dream," he said, but she thanked him with an irritated sigh and a roll of her eyes. "I wasn't being sarcastic. You really have talent."

Realizing he wasn't just feeding her a line of bullshit for the sake of her self-esteem, Audra finally allowed a small smile to creep out from her otherwise serious expression that was marked by strong eye contact.

"You really like my work?" she asked, and he nodded. She smiled a little brighter at that and admitted that she needed to hear that. "Well, that's just one little piece. I have dozens more, but to be honest, I was considering shelving the project."

"Why would you do that?" he asked, but she shrugged her shoulders.

"Confidence?" she replied. "Gustav doesn't get art, and most of my artsy friends are more into painting. Granted, I am too, but something inside me yearns to create a graphic novel."

"Sounds like you just needed some convincing," he said, leaning back in his chair. "Glad I could be of assistance."

"Again, thank you, but I don't know if it's really worth carrying on with. I'm a much better painter than I am an illustrator."

"Wait, you don't consider this good?" Aleksey asked with mild surprise.

"I never said that. What I meant to say is that I have a better chance at a career in art if I focus on painting instead of a graphic novel."

"But why? I thought you had a yearning to publish a graphic novel?"

"Because art snobs will pay more than a niche demographic of comic nerds," she replied, but Aleksey didn't want to see her throw away her dream so easily.

"How long have you been working at this?"

"I don't know... six, maybe seven years?"

"So, you have a solid portfolio just for this comic, huh?"

"Yeah, I have the entire story outlined in detail. The main cast of characters is conceptualized and drawn, and I have a couple of early scenes completed for proof of concept."

"If you wouldn't mind, I'd love to see it sometime. Your paintings, too."

"I'd love to, but unless you're planning on visiting Berlin and contending with my jealous boyfriend, you'd have to make do with scanned images and photos."

"I wouldn't mind visiting your homeland. I could bring a lady friend if that would keep Gustav calm," he said casually, but she sighed hard.

"Yeah, well, I don't think that would be too good an idea, honestly."

"Gustav is the type that doesn't like you have male friends, I presume?"

"Well, yes, but also no," she said, trailing for a moment. "Look, I'm not sure Gustav will be in the picture much longer, and I'm really not interested in getting back in the field right away."

"I'm sorry to hear that, but I didn't mean it like that," he said, but she shook her head.

"No reason to be sorry for someone you barely know," she said. "It's a long time coming. Honestly, the only reason I'm even in Senatgrad is that I needed to see for myself if he has a future in professional fighting."

"Not much faith in your boyfriend, huh?"

"He's a good fighter, but he's a rotten partner," she replied, but was quick to stop herself from airing out her dirty laundry to him. "Look, you don't need to hear about my personal troubles, but you seem to be honest, so I'll give you this in good faith," she said, scribbling her email down on a napkin. "This is my personal email. I'll send you some samples, and we can go from there."

"That sounds good," Aleksey said with a nod. "And I apologize if I intruded at all. That wasn't my intention."

"It's fine. I'm just stressed out and worried about a lot of things right now," Audra said, trailing off once more before asking for Aleksey's insight. "You said you watched Gustav fight. Do you think he's any good? I mean, do you think he'll make it in the big league?"

"I think he's got promise, but if I'm being honest, he's not Blood Games material."

"Really?" Audra asked with an inquisitive stare. "You didn't think he was a standout? That knockout was incredible, right?"

"It was a great fight, but I think he's much better suited for kickboxing competitions. Mixed martial arts leagues are much too varied for a single discipline fighter."

"So, you think he'll lose at some point?"

"Unless he can handle himself on the ground, it's pretty much a given," Aleksey said with confidence. He then looked around the room before leaning in. "Truth be told, I have a feeling this whole tournament is rigged."

"Rigged? What do you mean it's rigged?"

"Did you see Andrei Razin fight?" he asked, and her fearful expression told him so. "He's a professional fighter with multiple championships to his name. He's easily the most dangerous man in the tournament."

"I'm inclined to agree, but what makes you think it's rigged? Are they calling matches wrong?"

"No, but they're throwing professionals into the mix," Aleksey said. "I've counted at least four pros, but there could be more."

"So, there aren't that many. There's a good chance a few of them might get eliminated before Gustav might fight them," she said, but Aleksey shrugged.

"Sure, there's a chance that could happen, but I couldn't help but notice his reaction after taking a shot at the ribs. He's injured, isn't he?"

"I... I'm not sure if I should answer that," Audra said, but Aleksey never broke eye contact and gave her a friendly warning.

"Look, if I saw it, then someone like Razin saw it, too. They'll be gunning for that weak spot."

"What are you suggesting?"

"Quit while he's ahead," Aleksey said honestly. "I know everyone in that tournament is looking for a big payout and the contract awarded to the champion, but it's not worth it. They don't call the league 'The Blood Games' without reason. Careers are short, and people get seriously hurt... sometimes worse than they can afford."

"I see," Audra said, her anxiety brewing inside, but then she took a deep breath and sighed hard. "Well, I don't think he's going to listen to me, so we might as well let the dice roll."

"Are you sure about that?" Aleksey asked, for he felt like she should have been more concerned. Surely, she didn't want something terrible to happen to her boyfriend, so he pressed the issue. "Did you see Sykora?"

"Who's Sykora?

"One of the toughest fighters I've ever seen," he replied. "If you think Razin was vicious, wait until you see Sykora."

"Hold on," Audra said with a contemptuous stare. "Do you have money involved in this? Are you trying to get Gustav to quit for a bet or something?" she asked sharply, but Aleksey kept his composure to ensure she didn't think he was a conman.

"No, I'm just familiar with this league, and I don't want to see your boyfriend carried out on a stretcher. It's just not worth it. Take it from someone who's been there."

"So, you're a fighter?"

"No, well, not anymore, at least," Aleksey said, but Audra's expression urged him to explain further. "Look, I don't have any skin in the game. I'm just a soldier on leave with a bit of firsthand knowledge of how these tournaments work."

"So, you fought in one of these tournaments?"

"Yes, but it was several years ago, and it didn't end well," Aleksey admitted. "I thought I was a hotshot because I had a military background and a black belt in Shotokan. I ended up getting eliminated in the first round with a broken jaw for my trouble."

"Alright, I appreciate your concern, but why do you care so much? You don't know him, and you really don't know me."

"I guess I'm just trying to put some positive energy into the world. Make up for some of the bad shit they made me do in the service, that's all. But look, I feel like I crossed the line here, so I'll just leave you to it," Aleksey said, but before he could get further than pushing out his chair before she called out.

"Hey, wait!" she said, catching his attention. "If he drops out, does he keep the money he's earned?"

"I believe so, but don't quote me on it," Aleksey said. "I just figured you should be spared some grief, that's all."

"I appreciate that," Audra said with a nod. "Thank you for your concern."

"You're welcome, and good luck with Gustav," Aleksey said, before he left her to pack up her things.

Leaving the café in a hurry, Audra headed down to the gym rented out by the fighting promotion for the tournament. Finding her way through the small and crowded building, she found Jens coaching Gustav through a heavy bench press set.

Knowing better than to interrupt someone while they were lifting, Audra stood back and waited until Gustav had safely set the bar back in its resting position and sat up. His eyes soon met hers, and she asked what he wanted. She furrowed her brow at the mild hostility in his voice but chose to ignore it.

"Can we talk?" she asked, but he rolled his eyes and lay back down. "Seriously, it's important."

"This isn't the time, Audra," Gustav said, gripping the bar once more, but Audra kicked his leg with force.

"Listen, you stupid meathead. I'm trying to help you!" she snarled, though a little louder than she meant.

Sitting up once more, Gustav glared at her and told her to make it quick.

"Not here," she said, but Gustav wasn't going to budge. "Seriously, we need privacy."

"Too bad," Gustav said, lying back down once more.

"Fine, get your ass kicked, but don't say I didn't try to help," she cried out of frustration before storming off.

◻

Leaving the gym in anger, Audra started down the sidewalk with her fists and jaw clenched. When she heard a piercing whistle from behind, she stopped in her tracks and felt her muscles tense. If it was Gustav, she was going to let him have it, but she soon heard Jens' voice and saw her uncle walking her way with a cool expression.

"You want to tell me what that was about?" Jens called out.

Her body pumping adrenaline as Jens closed the distance, Audra's voice sounded like a frog was in her throat when she tried to address him. Swallowing hard and clearing her throat harshly, she was able to speak clearly on the second attempt. "The tournament is rigged," she said. "There are seasoned professionals mixed in that tournament."

"Is that right?" Jens asked with cool skepticism. "And how might you know that?"

"I met a guy at a café who has insider information," she said, but Jens just chuckled.

"You met a guy? You're that pissed with Gustav?"

"It's not like that!" Audra said sharply. "He recognized me from last night. He says he's an ex-fighter, and he told me Gustav needs to drop out while he still can."

"What? Who the hell were you talking to?"

"It doesn't matter. He said there are at least four professionals in the tournament. The most dangerous are Andrei Razin and a guy named Sykora."

"Interesting. What else did he tell you?"

"He pointed out Gustav's flaws. He noted his rib injury and warned that unless he can protect his weak spot and handle himself well on the ground, he's going to be eliminated or worse."

"Or worse?"

"He said people get injured regularly in this league. It's called the Blood Games for God's sake."

"Yes, but that's because it's a minimal rules promotion. I think you're just pissed with him for something and looking for an excuse to go home," Jens said, and Audra knew there and then that he didn't believe her.

"If I just wanted to go home, I'd be on a fucking train right now!" Audra snarled. "This isn't about me, it's about Gustav. He got hurt last night, and I'm afraid he's going to get carried out on a stretcher if he goes out there again."

"That's not going to happen," Jens said firmly, his index finger pointed at his niece's chest. "Gustav may not win this thing, but there's no way in hell he's going home without a stack of cash to his name."

"Please, Jens. You need to listen to me."

"We're done here, Audra. You obviously don't know what you're talking about. As for that fuck boy of yours, you best keep your distance. He's either full of shit or he's working for the opposition. Whatever the case, you got yourself played for a fool."

"Fucking hell! I'm not cheating on Gustav. I was at a café doing some drawing, and I overheard some guys talking about the matches. When I looked up, I caught his eye, and he recognized me, ok?"

"Whatever you say," Jens said dismissively. "Just get lost and stay the hell away from Gustav until after tonight's fight."

"You know what? Fuck you, too. If he gets hurt, it's on you," Audra cried, but Jens just turned his back to her and walked away, so she did the same.

Chapter 27

Senatgrad, Federal Special Region, Slavic Federation

Eating his lunch alone, Aleksey left the café and headed straight back to the hotel with an important mission on his mind. He needed to stash Audra's contact information in his room safe as soon as possible to ensure he didn't lose it at some point. She was a fascinating woman, and even if he couldn't have her for himself, he wanted to stay in touch. She was a one-of-a-kind person in his book, and he had a feeling their friendship would be something they'd come to cherish. So, with that hopeful attitude driving him, he made his way up from the lobby and down the third-floor hallways to his room. But when he stepped into the room, he found his sister sitting on the bed watching television. The expression she shared with him brought him back down from the clouds, for she didn't look pleased at all. In fact, she was a spitting image of their mother when she was 'not angry, but disappointed.'

"Where were you all morning?" Lena asked, upon muting the television.

"Out," Aleksey replied, as he continued toward the safe.

"What's that there?" she asked, sitting up for a closer look, though it didn't help much.

"Important papers. Eyes only kind of stuff," Aleksey said, but Lena just laughed.

"Well, I sure hope it's a good enough reason for missing the academy tour today. Mom is pissed."

"Shit, that's right," Aleksey said, partially under his breath, though he hadn't forgotten. He canceled at the last minute.

"Seriously, man? Dad stuck out his neck for you, and that's all you have to say," she asked, so Aleksey turned to her with an annoyed expression. "Don't tell me you skipped out on this for that cutie from the museum?"

"I got an important call from my commanding officer. And since when are you my mother?" Aleksey asked sharply, for while he often ignored Lena's maternal instincts, he wasn't in the mood for a lecture from his sister.

Rolling her eyes, Lena told him she was preparing him for the real deal.

"Thanks, but no thanks," Aleksey said. "I don't need to hear it from three people."

"Fine, whatever," Lena said with a shrug. "Mom is over in her room. You should probably get over there before Dad comes back. It'll be easier that way."

"Yeah, you're probably right."

Leaving his hotel room, Aleksey walked one door down and gave the door a heavy rapping. He heard the door unlock from within, but no one beckoned him inside. Still, he gave the knob a turn and let himself in, finding his mother walking back into the sitting area of the suite. She was clearly upset with him, but she didn't say a word until she was seated on the couch, and he was standing before him.

"Where were you all morning?" she asked, her words echoing her daughter. "I got a call from the Academy. They told me you canceled."

"I can explain," Aleksey said tensely, for even at twenty-seven, he still found it hard to face his mother when she was disappointed in him.

"Please do, because your father is going to be furious when he sees you."

"I got a call from my commanding officer. There was important business down at the base," Aleksey replied, but Katrin said nothing – she was trying to detect a lie, but she couldn't see it in his eyes. The military had taught him well.

"What was it about?" she asked, but Aleksey shook his head.

"You know I can't discuss that with civilians," Aleksey said, but Katrin wasn't just some civilian. She was his mother, and she demanded an answer. "Alright, look, it's nothing to worry about. In fact, it's a good move for my career."

Katrin sighed, for she had hoped he had skipped out on the tour due to a plan to leave the military entirely. Regardless, she made it appear as though she was upset Aleksey didn't go. "Better than securing your place at the military academy?" she asked skeptically. "You would make a fine officer, you know that, right?"

Faced with the choice of lying through his teeth to his mother or giving her a half-truth, Aleksey was hesitant to answer, but his mother was impatient, so he went with the half-truth.

"I met up with Miko to talk things over and to consider my options," Aleksey said calmly. "I've been thinking a lot about the future, and well, things with Tati didn't go as planned, so I decided to reenlist. I'm returning to my old unit at the end of my leave."

"Aleksey, no," she said, trailing off with disappointment. "Your father and uncle gave you a golden opportunity. Why would you throw it all away like this?"

"Because this is what I want to do," Aleksey said, despite feeling that it was ludicrous to have to explain himself like he was some pimply kid wanting to enlist for the first time. "And since when are you a proponent of military service?"

"I'm not, I'm just worried about your future," she said. "To be honest, I was relieved when I heard you canceled. I thought you were going to come here with good news... like maybe you were going to finally leave the service and start a new chapter for yourself."

"What makes you say that?"

"Well, just a few weeks ago you were talking about marriage and starting a family."

"What's your point, Mom?"

"My point is that you're twenty-seven years old, Aleksey. You're in the prime of your life, but if you're not careful, there won't be a lot of time left for a family. Not to mention, the likelihood of finding a good woman with your occupation isn't going to help matters."

"I realize that," Aleksey said bitterly. "Unfortunately, marriage and a family don't seem to be in the cards for me."

"That's nonsense. You still have time to find someone... dare I say, better matched to you," Katrin said, speaking out of fear and disappointment. "Don't throw your future away over Tatiana. You can still find a good woman and have a family, even as an officer."

"I'm inclined to disagree," Aleksey said bitterly. "Tatiana was a wakeup call--"

"Tatiana was an unfaithful bitch," Katrin said sharply, surprising her son with a rare use of profanity. "She broke your heart in the worst way imaginable, but that shouldn't be reason enough to throw away your future."

"The Service is my future. Not just anyone can achieve what I have," Aleksey said, but Katrin couldn't disagree more.

"I'll be honest with you, Aleksey. It broke my heart when you left for the first time, and it breaks my heart now to see you carry on like this. I would much rather see you come home and be a civilian than spend the rest of your life in uniform," Katrin said, losing control of her emotions for a brief moment. "It's bad enough I'm going to lose your sister to a damn Medvedev. I'd like to have at least one of my children around to take care of me when I'm old."

"You're not making much sense, Mom."

"I most certainly am," Katrin countered. "You may think the Service will always be there for you, but that's not true. The Service won't be there for you when you're old. It won't love you or give you children, nor will it mourn you at your funeral. It will only use you up and spit you out when you're no longer useful. And by then, it'll be too late for a happy life."

"I do have a happy life," Aleksey said, but Katrin shook her head.

"If you're so happy, then why was your plan to get married and leave the Service?" she asked, but Aleksey was at a loss for words, and she nodded. "Exactly, you're not happy. This is just your backup plan."

"You're right, it is," Aleksey replied, a bit deflated. "But what other choice do I have?"

"You can let your contract expire and make plans to stay home in Poland. While you're at it, you can convince your father that family is more important than another ten years in uniform."

Letting off a sigh, Aleksey had long feared his parents might face a crossroads if the secession went through. The way his mother looked and spoke told him that divorce was on the horizon, so he tried to ease her burden.

"Dad's not going to abandon you, and you're not going to abandon him."

"Sometimes I wonder," Katrin said distantly. "Your grandfather abandoned your father and grandmother for the Army--"

"And he was a son of a bitch for it," Aleksey said strongly. "But Dad isn't his father, and you've stuck by him this long. Why would you think it would end now?"

"He loves his job... sometimes, I think he loves it more than me," Katrin said distantly. "I don't want that for you, or anyone, for that matter."

"That won't be the case," Aleksey said reassuringly. "Dad is well past his time to earn a pension, and I have no doubt in my mind he'd take his wife over his duty. But if you really think he needs convincing, I'll talk to him, but you need to help me too."

"How?" Katrin asked, wiping a single tear from her cheek.

"Soften him up for me. Tell him that I took a long, hard look at my life and realized I belong in the Special Troops and nowhere else."

"But do you mean that?"

"Sometimes, yes," he said with a shrug. "I only need to serve ten more years for a pension, but I swear I won't be a frogman forever. I'm going to apply for a training position as soon as one becomes available. Hell, I'd even take a desk job if the opportunity presented itself."

"And that really sounds better than raising a family? You'd rather yell at recruits or push papers than go home to a wife and children of your own?"

Though he saw his mother's point, Aleksey was down on the concept of love thanks to Tatiana. While Audra was certainly someone he would have liked to pursue, that clearly wasn't an option, at least not realistically. So rather than continue to talk in circles with his mother, Aleksey asked if they could put this discussion to rest and enjoy the day. To his surprise, Katrin accepted his plea to end their debate, but closed with a simple warning to be prepared with a better explanation for his father, to which Aleksey assured her he would be well prepared.

Chapter 28

Senatgrad, Federal Special Region, Slavic Federation

With the third day in full swing, Gustav was standing ready in the locker room. Fully aware that he was next to fight, and that he'd be fighting Havel Sykora, he was dressed down in just a muscle shirt bearing the emblem of his home gym and his fight shorts. Unlike the night before, his hands were unwrapped to allow for better grappling should the need arise. However, his feet and ankles were wrapped tighter than normal to help with ankle stability and grip on a slicker-than-expected mat.

At Jens' instruction, Gustav watched not the ongoing match but a tape of Sykora's fight from the first day. Despite the ferocity he witnessed on screen, the expression on Gustav's face showed that he was cool, calm, and collected. This was rather surprising, for Sykora was one of the apparent professionals, but Gustav was confident in himself and unafraid of the odds stacked against him. However, he knew that arrogance was a weakness and that if he was going to best a professional fighter, he had to fight almost perfectly. Even more so, he had to avoid him where he was strong and fight him on his terms. This meant he had to keep on his feet and Sykora off the mat, but the way the match was going, that was easier said than done.

"Scared?" Jens asked with a smirk, but Gustav said nothing. His eyes were glued to the screen, so Jens nodded in approval. "He's not a god. Just remember that."

Never breaking his silence until the match ended by submission in Sykora's favor, Gustav carefully studied the way Sykora controlled his opponent on the ground. When the bell finally rang, he stopped the tape and looked at Jens.

"He's incredible on the ground, but he's weak on his feet."

"And you're the opposite," Jens replied, and Gustav didn't argue. "He's going to be tough to keep standing. He's got a background in Judo; he likes his throws and sweeps. He will do all he can to get you down to the mat. You need to win this thing quickly or be flawless on defense."

"I'll kick low and work his legs to wear him down. You know how I work. All I need is one good shot to the head and he's done," Gustav said, but Jens shook his head.

"Do you hear yourself right now? You can't afford to get cocky, Gustav."

"I'm not cocky, I'm confident," Gustav said. "You saw that fight. His standup game is weak. All he has are throws and sweeps."

"Yes, so he can get you on the ground," Jens warned. "He has no interest in fighting you on his feet, but don't take him for weak on his feet. If he can catch one of your kicks and get you on the ground, it's as good as over."

Though he was a kickboxer through and through, Gustav felt like he had just been insulted. "Whose side are you on, Jens?"

"Don't be a moron, Gustav. That man is dangerous, and you know it. You can't approach him all guns blazing. Just last night, he tapped out one of the heavy favorites in this tournament."

"Then it's a good thing we did our homework," Gustav said, looking over his shoulder for a fight coordinator. "In the meantime, I should get stretched out. It's about to be my turn."

Knowing that Gustav was right in this instance, Jens let him go off to the practice mats to stretch and warm up in preparation for his looming match. When he left, Jens rewound the tape and watched the fight for himself. What he saw left him worried that Sykora was indeed a professional brought in as a ringer for the tournament. If that were truly the case, he just hoped Gustav could back up his arrogance and not end up a bloody mess on the mat.

Cheered as he entered the arena, Gustav entered the ring and threw up his arms, screaming like a madman. The crowd roared with excitement but went quiet as the announcer waved his hands for silence. This was nothing new, so with a stoic expression, Gustav went to his corner and waited for the announcer to call out his opponent. To the surprise of only the crowd, his opponent was none other than Havel Sykora. Despite his calm exterior, Gustav was raging inside. He wanted blood and war, and he was going to do all he could to flatten Sykora before he could take him off his feet.

"Keep calm and your mind centered, you got this," Jens said, rubbing Gustav's tense shoulders. "Beat this fucker and you can drop out with a lot of money."

"Fuck that!" Gustav growled through his mouthguard. "I'm going all the way."

"Then rip his head off!" Jens snarled into his fighter's ear.

Stepping away from his coach and heading toward the center of the ring to greet his still-approaching opponent, Gustav hopped on both feet and swung his arms. Even when Sykora entered the ring and bowed his head to him, he kept hopping with anticipation. Some saw this as a sign of disrespect, but this was just the way Gustav steeled his nerves. So, when ordered to stand still so that the referee could give the rules, he did exactly as he was told.

Having heard the rules countless times now, Sykora and Gustav stared at one another until ordered to touch gloves and back away. When their gloves hit, Sykora spoke directly to his opponent.

"Give it your all, German. The whole world is watching," Sykora said, but Gustav didn't understand and took it as a warning.

"Expect no mercy," Gustav shot back in his own native tongue, but Sykora simply smiled and backed up the necessary paces.

Waiting patiently as the crowd chanted for blood, Gustav and Sykora didn't flinch until the bell rang and the referee ordered the fight to commence. When he did, the two fighters began circling each other like wolves, stepping in every so often to take a swipe, but Gustav would score the first hit when he successfully faked a kick at the midsection and followed up with a fierce back fist to Sykora's jaw.

Believing he'd be made to pay for the blow in short order, Gustav fell into the habit of sliding back every so often. While this allowed him to evade a few attacks, it also caused the crowd to become frustrated with the lack of action. After thirty seconds without contact, the referee stepped in to enforce a special rule native to the Blood Games.

"Three steps back. On my mark, come out swinging!" the Referee ordered, enforcing a rule known unofficially as 'the Dual' which stated that a strike had to be made within thirty seconds. If no contact was made, the fighters were brought to the center of the ring, made to stand three paces apart with their backs turned. On the count of three, they were ordered to take a swing at their opponent. Failure to attack would result in a disqualification for one or both fighters.

Believing the rule would work in his favor against an outsider, Sykora took his three steps and swung around immediately with his heel high, but Gustav had done the same, and they clashed at the shins, throwing one another off balance in terrible pain.

The crowd cheered as both men fell to the floor and scrambled to their feet to get back into the fight before they were engaged. What would follow was a rather balanced fight that showed the expertise of both fighters. Despite a lack of heavy blows meeting their mark, the crowd was entertained by the fury and skill with which the fighters fought. However, the fight had to come to an end at some point, and someone had to walk away the winner. The deciding factor, it seemed, was overall physique and endurance.

A professional fighter in the light heavyweight division, Sykora was the best built and conditioned of the pair. His professional background allowed him to fight harder and longer than his opponent. This, alongside the lack of timed rounds, all led to Sykora getting the upper hand around the five-minute mark. But even as he began to land blow after blow on his increasingly gassed opponent, Gustav never gave up. He blocked more blows than he suffered and was even able to capture Sykora's leg, allowing him to attempt a painful ankle lock while standing. However, Gustav's lack of experience with grappling allowed Sykora to quickly escape the maneuver with a risky jump kick to Gustav's shoulder, which not only freed him from Gustav's grasp but also allowed him to put some space between them with a quick shoulder roll.

Barely stunned by the kick and seemingly catching his second wind, Gustav quickly closed the gap Sykora had created and charged in to launch a flying knee that would hopefully land just as Sykora turned. However, the maneuver failed to meet its mark, leaving Gustav wide open to a quick punch to the midsection that sent him to the mat and left him vulnerable.

His ankle seized in a tight grasp, Gustav realized he was in a dangerous position and acted accordingly by rolling over onto his back to break Sykora's grasp. When that failed, he used his free leg to strike hard at his opponent's face and chest until he let go. By some stroke of luck, his flailing leg managed to strike Sykora just right, for the better-trained fighter suddenly dropped his leg and backed off. Not wanting to stay in such a vulnerable position, Gustav rushed back to his feet, and when he was faced with his opponent again, he saw a thin stream of blood running down his face. Of course, he had no time to contemplate how he drew blood, though he later considered it was the fault of his toenail. Sykora, though strangely calm, went on the offensive. It was clear he was out for blood and looking for the win as soon as possible.

Amidst his second wind, Gustav sparred fiercely with his bloodied opponent, blocking and checking rapid-fire kicks and punches and countering whenever given the chance. Despite his quick movements and uncanny ability to absorb a full-force punch to the face without stumbling back, Gustav was clearly at a disadvantage. His only chance at turning the tide was scoring a counterstrike at just the right time and location. But the ferocity of Sykora's assault left him unable to breathe, let alone think through his next few steps.

However, when it seemed as though Gustav was close to gassing out again, he ducked a heavy kick aimed at his head, spun on his heel, and threw a sidekick with all his remaining might. The blow met Sykora at the center of the chest, forcing the air from his lungs and forcing him to keel over as he gasped for air. This gave the battered Gustav an opportunity he couldn't pass up.

Sliding forward on his front foot, Gust threw a heavy uppercut at his stunned opponent and followed immediately with a left-hand haymaker before grabbing Sykora's shoulders and driving his face down as he thrust his knee upward in a blind rage. The blow sent Sykora to the ground limply, and the crowd went wild with excitement, but Gustav was lost in the moment. Hardly allowing his opponent to hit the mat, he dove atop Sykora and mounted him. Raining blows, he didn't stop until he felt someone take him in a bear hug and pull him away. He had won the match.

Overcome with joy and excitement, Gustav jumped to his feet and sprinted around the ring, jumping and shouting excitedly. While this certainly earned him plenty of jeering, he was cheered by far more. A nobody from Berlin had beaten the odds and defeated one of the premier fighters in the tournament. However, no matter how arrogant he appeared at times, he was far from a poor winner, so the moment he saw Sykora come to with the aid of smelling salts, he rushed over to help his defeated opponent to his feet. Though he expected at least a scowl and some foul words, he was greeted with a bloodied smile and hugged like a friend.

"Congratulations," he heard Sykora say in English. "Continue to fight like that and you'll be on the roster!"

Touched by Sykora's words, Gustav patted the humbled fighter's back before grabbing his wrist and thrusting their arms into the air. This show of professionalism led the crowd to erupt in cheers so loud that the announcer was almost completely drowned out as he attempted to declare the match's winner and other stats. However, the moment wasn't destined to last, for the two fighters were made to vacate the arena through their respective tunnels, so they touched gloves one last time before departing.

Parting ways with his opponent and heading through opposite tunnels, Gustav was taken to the privacy of the arena infirmary. Still shirtless, the doctor checked his ribs and noted a great deal of redness. He would go on to warn against fighting on. Gustav scoffed at such a move and demanded his ribs be wrapped up, but the doctor argued his point.

"Your ribs were broken fairly recently and weren't fully healed. While I don't believe they're broken, you're taking a terrible risk in continuing."

"I don't care. Give me some happy pills and wrap me up. I'll ice it overnight and be fresh by tomorrow."

Sighing, the doctor didn't bother to argue further. After all, he was just there to patch up injured fighters post-fight. So, doing as Gustav demanded, he went to a cabinet and retrieved two large capsules.

"These should numb the pain through the night, but take it easy tonight. They can cause drowsiness, nausea, and dizziness."

Taking the pills in hand, Gustav tossed them into his mouth like candy and held them between his back teeth, but a bitter flavor soon assaulted his tongue. Hurrying out, he grabbed a sports drink bottle from a nearby cooler and washed the pills and their bitter flavor down with a deluge of limeade. He proceeded to down the entire bottle, and when he tossed the bottle into a nearby waste basket, he saw Jens walking his way with Audra in tow.

"Ah, fuck me," Gustav muttered to himself, but when Audra spoke, she didn't appear angry anymore. In fact, she congratulated him with a bright smile, though she stopped short of hugging him. It was clear that she was aware of the blow he had taken and the damage it may have inflicted on his ribcage. This made him thankful, but when she asked what happened next, he couldn't lie. "I fight on," he replied, and her smile faded in an instant.

"You can't be serious," she said, but he was resolute. "Gustav, please. You got lucky."

"Lucky?" he asked with a pained chuckle. "What fight were you watching? I beat a professional with a ground and pound!"

"You did, and you were great, but you need to count your blessings," Audra said, but it wasn't enough for him to see reason, and she knew it, so she tapped his ribs with the slightest pressure. When she saw him flinch, she sighed and told him, "You can't fight on like this."

"The hell I can't," Gustav said with a furrowed brow.

"Gustav, please. You made a lot of money already. Quit while you're ahead."

"You just don't get it, do you? I'm not fighting for the money anymore. I'm fighting for that contract."

"Who says you're getting a contract if you fight on?"

Taking a step forward, he looked her straight in the eyes. "The league champion I just bested," he said firmly. "Now I'm not going to ask you to come back tomorrow, but I am going to ask you to leave this place. I'd like to watch the remaining fights with a clear head."

"Don't be an idiot, Gustav. You said it yourself, that guy was a professional. This thing is rigged!" she snarled, but Gustav shook his head and crossed his arms. He then took in a deep, slightly painful breath and let it out slowly before asking Jens to escort her back to her seat.

Chapter 29

Senatgrad, Federal Special Region, Slavic Federation

A single match followed Gustav's surprise victory over Havel Sykora before the night's intermission began. Uninterested in watching a professional dance troupe flaunting on the bloodied canvas of the ring, Aleksander went inside to get himself a fresh drink. Following close behind was Roman, and while he appeared pleasant all night, Aleksander knew it was a ruse.

Approaching his brother-in-law slowly as he shoveled ice cubes into his glass, Roman carefully selected his words before speaking. Though he had promised to keep things peaceful for the night, he couldn't get his mind off the order given him by Senator Bednarz earlier that day. Though he wasn't keen on a debate this night, he had a duty to his nation, so he took his chances while Aleksander was only partially inebriated.

"Alek, do you have a moment?" Roman asked, as Aleksander garnished his drink with a twist of lime. The question went unanswered until they were facing one another.

"Unless this is about the fights, I don't," Aleksander said, his highball glass held as firmly as he spoke. However, the expression his brother-in-law displayed told him otherwise, so he shook his head and headed for the door. Roman soon seized his arm just below the bicep and looked to him with a sharp eye. "Let go of my arm, Roman."

"Just a few minutes, that's all I ask."

Looking down at his arm, Aleksander watched as Roman released him from his grip. The pair then squared off as if they were about to fight, but neither had such an intention.

"It's fairly clear the federals are intent on sinking this conference," Roman began, holding up his hand to keep Aleksander quiet for a bit longer. "We'll fight them like the devil on the Senate floor, but there are concerns that they'll play dirty and rig the entire vote against us."

Keeping silent, for he certainly didn't disagree, Aleksander allowed him to continue. Roman silently thanked him and continued.

"There's talk that the military won't take a defeat lying down," Roman said, piquing Aleksander's interest.

"Is that right?" he asked, and Roman nodded.

"I'm not at liberty to give names, but there's a lot of talk about contingency," Roman said, knowing he had Aleksander's attention. "However, I'm afraid I can't say much more, but I assure you that it would be hell to pay if our demands aren't met in full."

"Making a move against the Federation would be the first and last mistake your government would ever make," Aleksander replied, and Roman bit his lip.

"Please tell me you're not planning to keep us by force."

"To prevent secession? Not on my watch," Aleksander replied strongly. "Rest assured, any action taken against the Federation, especially the Special Region, would be treated as an act of war."

"I see," Roman said, his voice seething. "You're not even going to entertain our request for a partition."

"Read my lips, Roman. Poland will not be invaded unless provoked, but those bases will remain with the Federation for the sake of regional security," Aleksander said, for the Polish delegation had insinuated that the military bases in the Sambian peninsula north of Senatgrad were a threat to a free Poland, thus should be transferred to Poland as an act of good faith."

"If an invasion is not an option, then why would they argue so fiercely to keep more than thirty all-weather strike aircraft and a dozen long-range reconnaissance aircraft in the Special Region? Surely, those assets can be moved elsewhere. If not, then Baltiysk should be transferred to Poland."

"I think you're missing the point of those bases. They're critical positions against NATO, not Poland."

"You're joking, yes?" Roman asked out of frustration. "Does Prague Spring bring back any memories?"

"Again, there won't be an invasion unless our hand is forced."

"Of course not," Roman said with a sarcastic grin. "But I'm sure the Premier would be more than happy to find a reason to invade."

Furrowing his brow, Aleksander kept a hard expression and spoke firmly. "Listen to me, Roman. Nothing short of a violent seizure of power or an assault on Senatgrad itself would incite an invasion."

"I beg to differ. Why else are they fighting so hard to keep us a part of this godforsaken union?"

"We're here to ensure Poland doesn't end up a failed state, nothing more," Aleksander said calmly. "The Senate will vote at some point, but when that happens depends on the outcome of the conference. If we walk away in disagreement, there's no telling when the Senate will hold its vote."

"That's bullshit and you know it!" Roman snarled. "We voted for our sovereignty back. This conference stands for nothing more than tying us up with red tape and breaking the public's will."

"Then you haven't been listening," Aleksander said, ignoring his brother-in-law's sudden hostility. "We're here to negotiate the transfer of vital assets to ensure the coming free republic is adequately able to defend itself. Unless we reach an agreement, no vote will happen. Of course, that's unless you want to see our homeland strike out with an underequipped military."

"I stand by our cause," Roman said proudly. "You may think we're fighting over simple matters, but we're looking to the future with the past in mind. Poland has been invaded far too many times to let a hostile power stand so close to our borders without firm assurance of our security."

"I see your point, but the Sambia Peninsula is not Polish territory, and never has been. You have no say in what the Federation does there," Aleksander said, but Roman remained resolute.

"Baltiysk may have never been Polish territory but leaving it to the Federation would put us at an extreme disadvantage. You wouldn't want to leave your homeland at risk of invasion, would you, Alek?"

Growing frustrated, Aleksander shot back with force. "You're already getting a quarter of the Baltic Fleet. Do you have any idea how hard it was to convince Nemsky to agree to that?" Aleksander asked sharply. "You're overreaching, Roman."

"Perhaps I am, but that's what you get from a man who loves his country," Roman countered, but Aleksander rolled his eyes. "Roll your eyes all you want, but come tomorrow expecting a fierce debate. We're not going to let this one go without a fight. In fact, we have a trump card."

"Let me guess, you'll threaten to join NATO."

Judging by the bitterness showing in Roman's face, it was obvious that Aleksander had guessed right. However, rather than continue this debate, Aleksander silently excused himself and went back out to await the second half of the night's scheduled events. This left Roman to contemplate if Aleksander really was the patriot he thought he was, or if he truly was just a lapdog of the tyrants in Moscow. Whatever the case, he would treat Aleksander as an adversary for the remainder of the conference.

Leaving Roman behind, Aleksander returned to his seat, visibly perturbed. Katrin touched his arm and asked what was on his mind, but he remained silent. So, looking over her shoulder, Katrin could see her brother pacing and talking to himself inside the suite. He was clearly upset, so she turned back to her husband and asked what had happened inside.

"He made a fool out of himself, that's all," Aleksander replied, but he knew Katrin wouldn't let it rest, so he gave her a quick summary. "Let's just say he can't accept that we're on different sides of the political divide due to our careers, not personal politics."

"I see," Katrin said coolly. "Would you like me to talk to him?"

"No," Aleksander said quickly yet firmly. "I just need to deal with him for one more day. Let's enjoy the night."

"Then we'll talk about this later," she said, but he just sighed, for he was sick to death of politics surrounding him at every waking moment.

The night would carry on with four more fights, but in that time, no words were shared among the occupants of the skybox. The tension was thick, and when Aleksander got up to use the restroom after the sixth match, Katrin followed him inside to confront her husband. Though he asked her to leave it be, she refused and blocked his path until he finally relented.

"Fine, do you really want to know what's gotten between your brother and me? It's this game Moscow is playing with the secession and your brother's belief that I can make a difference. It's driving me mad."

"What about it?" she asked, and though he wanted to drop the subject altogether, he knew the quickest way to the bathroom was by giving her what she wanted. So, after looking over his shoulder to ensure no one was listening or about to walk in, he gave in to her.

"Viktoriya told me in confidence, so do not tell anyone. Not Roman, not Paula, not Aleksey, no one," he said quite firmly. She quickly nodded in agreement, so he continued.

"The referendum was nothing more than political theater. A means of easing tension and gauging reactions, nothing more—"

"That's bullshit," she said quickly, but Aleksander raised his hand to keep her from losing her cool too quickly.

"They didn't expect the turnout it got, and they realized the mistake they made in letting it happen at all. Poland will have its day before the Senate, but I don't have high hopes, Katrin. I think they're going to rig the results somehow."

"What else is new?" she said with a clear disdain for the corruption of Sergei Medvedev's administration. "But how can they rig a vote? Isn't each vote given in person?"

"Yes, but who's to say they won't manipulate the votes through intimidation?" he said. "I wouldn't put it past Dmitri Sarich and his thugs over in the FSB," Aleksander said, referring to Dmitri Sarich, an old colleague of the Premier from his days in the KGB, and the reigning Director of the Federal Security Service. "Look, we really shouldn't be talking about this here, or at all for that matter, but tomorrow is the last day of the conference. It's going to be a long and grueling day, but in the end, I'm going to see to it that we at least agree to ensure the vote goes before the Senate on time."

"That gives them a month to prepare and win over allies," Katrin said, but Aleksander wasn't so confident.

"Yes, but those are the rules. We may not like it, but it's the law," Aleksander said. "At the very least, this gets Roman off my back. However, I'm afraid of what might happen if the Senate denies secession."

"Really? I'd be more afraid of what Moscow might do to ensure it all goes to shit for the whole world to see," Katrin scoffed, but Aleksander remained cool.

"This entire thing is a mess, Katrin. The Secessionists are making unrealistic demands, but so is Viktoriya, and I'm caught in the middle. Both sides are considering their options, and to be frank, I'm terrified of what might happen if the Senate takes pity and grants the secession with all their demands."

Her eyes narrowing, Katrin thought of all the demands Roman and his compatriots had made thus far, or at least what Aleksander had trusted her with. The only thing she could think that might cause an uproar was the ceding of the naval base at Baltiysk."

"What does that bastard want you to do? Wage war on your own country?" Katrin asked with a sour face, but Aleksander shook his head.

"That's always a possibility, but I swear on my life that I'm going to do everything I can to prevent a clash of arms," he said with determination, but even as he sighed at the thought, she touched his shoulder and looked deeply into his eyes. It was clear that she believed in him and his ability to keep the peace, even if the man he answered to wanted war.

"We'll find a way through this storm," she said lovingly. "No matter what becomes of all this, I'll always know you did your very best despite the circumstances."

"Thank you," he said. "Sometimes it feels like anything is possible with a woman like you at my side."

"I'm your anchor," she said with a slight smile. "I'll always be by your side. Don't you ever forget that."

"Never," he whispered. A short moment later, they shared a kiss.

Heading back into the skybox, Aleksander's heart finally began to ease, but as the tournament continued, he began to toil inside once more. He couldn't shake the thought of feeling like he was a double agent operating behind enemy lines, no matter where he was or with whom he was speaking. He loved his homeland, but he also valued his career, as well as the life afforded him by the Federation. On the same token, he wanted desperately to escape the burden of command and the ever-present threat of social ruin, and perhaps even death, that came with working for a man who clearly viewed himself as a monarch rather than a statesman. Deep down, he would love to leave it all behind and go home to his farmhouse in Sława, never to put on a uniform or attend a high society function ever again. But to achieve that dream, he had to see this terrible burden through and hopefully prevent a war between the land he loved and the government he feared.

Chapter 30
Senatgrad, Federal Special Region, Slavic Federation

Still seething at Gustav, Audra watched the remaining fights with disdain for the entire event. Truthfully, she just wanted to go back to the hotel and turn in to bed early, but the crowd was tightly packed in their rows, with some even standing in the aisles. Stuck in the middle of her respective row, Audra looked around for an avenue of escape. She could have elbowed her way toward the aisle, but with everyone on their feet, many of whom were drunk by that point, she didn't want to risk toppling over the row of seats in front of her and getting hurt. Biting the bullet, she stayed for the remainder of the tournament. Fortunately, most of the fights were quick affairs, and she just had to witness one final bout to determine the last man to go on to the tournament's finals the next day.

Remembering her conversation with Aleksey from earlier that day, Audra couldn't recall seeing Andrei Razin fight that night, so she wasn't too surprised to see him called out for the night's finale. As expected of a man known to the crowd as a world champion, he was given a hero's welcome to the arena, and he soaked up their admiration with a grinning show of arrogance as he walked down the ring. When he was through with showboating, the ring announcer stated that the fighter originally scheduled for this bout had unexpectedly resigned from the tournament. This announcement was met with loud shouts of profanity and boos from the crowd, but Audra was somewhat relieved since this likely meant she could leave sooner than expected. However, the announcer soon stated that the promotion had decided the match must carry on and announced the name of the man chosen to fight against Razin.

The moment Audra heard Gustav's name, her stomach sank. She couldn't believe what she had heard. She tried to reason in her head that this was some mistake, and that the fighter wasn't her Gustav Hagen, but he soon appeared at the mouth of the tunnel that fed out into the arena on the ground floor. Her eyes quickly darted to the massive video display hanging high above the center of the arena. The cameras were locked on Gustav, and the expression on his face told her he was scared to death, and with good reason. He was injured in his bout that night, and Razin was a savage fighter, but this only made things worse. Razin appeared to be grinning as if he knew of Gustav's handicap and was going to send him out on a stretcher the moment the bell rang.

With anxious eyes, Audra watched as Gustav finished his approach to the ring. Unlike the previous bouts, he didn't throw up his hands and let off his battle cry. Instead, he looked at Razin and marched up to him until they were toe to toe and their noses were practically touching. The camera was fixated on this moment, and Audra could see the bloodlust in Razin's eyes and the determination in Gustav's. The referee soon stepped forward to ease them apart and deliver the rules as always. When he was through, the two fighters touched gloves and backed away.

Thanks to the screen hanging from the rafters, she was able to see that Razin kept his piercing eyes locked with Gustav, but it was obvious to her that Gustav was trying not to look nervous. He was clearly hurting from his battle with Sykora barely an hour before and was likely going to try for a quick win. This would most certainly spell disaster, but she knew Gustav too well to believe he'd start on the defensive. His hands were high, his shoulders square, and his feet positioned well. The moment that bell rang, he was going to charge in with something powerful but risky. This strategy won him a lot of matches in the beer leagues, and even a few in the semi-pro circuit, but there was no chance in hell that Razin would fall from just one blow. This man was a seasoned professional; he was conditioned to take even the heaviest of blows without going down or showing pain. He was going to give Gustav the fight of his life. The most Audra could hope for was a quick finish by Razin with minimal damage inflicted upon her foolish boyfriend.

Backed into their corners, an eerie stillness fell over the arena until the bell chimed and the fight was on. Just as Audra had expected, Gustav darted forward with reckless abandon. To Gustav's credit, he was much faster on the sprint than one might expect for a man of his build, but Razin was sharp-eyed and seemed to know what was coming. So, when Gustav launched from the mat, it didn't matter if it was a flying knee or a lunging punch, for he sidestepped at the last moment while throwing a high roundhouse kick.

Though she couldn't hear the crack of Razin's unguarded shin against Gustav's face, she could feel his pain in the form of a wave of terror as Gustav's head snapped back. With wide eyes, she watched him stumble back and lurch forward before finally falling face down on the mat. His arms and legs sprawled out it appeared he was knocked out cold, but he could have been dead, too. Whatever the case, it seemed as though Gustav's strategy had backfired horribly, and he had been eliminated in just one blow himself. However, as the referee knelt beside the downed kickboxer, Audra saw Gustav wave him off in an angry fashion.

"No! Stay down, you idiot! Stop!" Audra cried out, unconcerned with the confused looks she was receiving from those around her. "Lay back down! It's over!" she continued, but Gustav's pride would get the best of him.

Though he was slow to his feet, Gustav wasn't ready to call it a day just yet, even as his nose shone red and bled profusely. Fortunately, Razin was still gloating over his apparent quick victory and had his back to Gustav, blissfully unaware that the fight was still on. This allowed Gustav just enough time to go back on the offensive and score a powerful spinning sidekick into Razin's unprotected side as he turned back to see why the bell had not yet rung.

A smile shot across Audra's face as she saw Razin tumble to the floor, but her joy quickly faded as the seasoned fighter easily recovered by landing on his shoulder and rolling back onto his feet. It was clear that he was frustrated that the fight hadn't been called, but before he could channel his rage on Gustav, the German underdog charged in once more, connecting a stiff roundhouse kick to the right thigh before launching a barrage of high and low punches with full force. From the angle of the camera displayed on the screen, it seemed like Gustav was breaking through Razin's defense. But even after landing several punches to the face, ribs, and abdomen, Gustav made a terrible mistake by trying to tie up his opponent to pummel his affected side with his knees. In doing so, he opened himself up to a headbutt - an illegal move in competitive kickboxing, but common in the Blood Games - followed by a push kick that gave Razin enough breathing room to turn the tables with a circle block that captured Gustav's strong arm and set him up for a shoulder throw.

Knowing Gustav was vulnerable on the ground, Audra's stomach turned the moment he hit the mat, but Gustav apparently had a few new tricks up his sleeve. Not only did he land in such a way that he was able to recover quickly with a back roll, but he also managed to dodge a lightning-fast heel kick aimed at his head and counter with a low spinning sweep kick. The unexpected maneuver borrowed from Karate brought Razin to the ground, but Gustav knew it wouldn't be long and that he had to fight dirty to win this bout. So, the moment he recovered to his feet, he charged Razin and kneed him square in the face as he was returning to his feet. This sort of technique was highly illegal in most martial arts competitions, but Gustav didn't care at this point. He needed to win this match, so seizing the opportunity, he dove atop his opponent. Fully intending to pummel his opponent until he fell limp, Gustav didn't realize he had made a grave mistake until he felt Razin's heels catch him in the gut. A moment later, he found himself sailing through the air and saw the arena spin before his eyes before landing hard on his back.

The look on Gustav's face - projected onto the screen above the arena by way of a close-up shot – told Audra, and everyone else in attendance, that the air had been driven from his lungs. Strangely, Razin stood back a few feet and waited for him to get up. This caused chants that translated to 'Kill! Kill! Kill!' to echo through the arena, but Razin didn't seem to listen. He continued to stand back as Gustav slowly returned to his feet. In doing so, he was analyzing his opponent, for the simple throw shouldn't have caused him to recover so slowly after fighting with such vigor. He was injured, and by the way he was guarding his ribcage, Razin had a weak spot to target, but Gustav wasn't finished yet.

Having landed awkwardly with his wrist under his body, Gustav held his affected limb at a low guard over his ribcage. Given the rules of the match, there was no option to surrender, so he stared at his opponent with fire in his eyes. letting off a battle cry, he charged his opponent, feigning a low kick followed by a high kick that flew over Razin's head, setting up a spinning back fist that met its mark.

With a smile on her face, Audra had a warm feeling of excitement as she watched Gustav go toe-to-toe with the professional fighter. He did well to block and counter every blow thrown his way and even dominated on the offensive for a short while. It even seemed like the crowd was beginning to turn against their champion, for when Gustav rocked Razin with a strong head kick, the arena exploded in cheers. This clearly invigorated Gustav as he pushed harder toward victory, eating a few blows to the face and body as he continued his assault. Throwing fast punching and kicking combinations to wear down his opponent, he'd mix in a few heavy uppercuts whenever possible. In time, Razin looked dazed, so he took his opportunity for a knockout. Leaping into the air, Gustav fired off a lunging punch that would have won the match had he not taken a brutal shot to the ribs in exactly the right spot mid-flight.

Seemingly knowing he was being watched closely by the only person that mattered to him outside of that ring, Gustav ignored the pain screaming through his body and continued his barrage. His final blow – another devastating head kick - caused Razin's hands to drop as he stumbled back, dazed and exhausted from the drawn-out fight. This was the moment he was waiting for, so with a big smile, he looked to the camera, gave the crowd the thumbs up, and got into position to carry out a crowd-pleasing finisher. Yet, when he launched himself into the air and twisted his body around with his leg stuck out straight and firm, he felt only air. His feet soon touched the ground, but when he landed, he felt a surge of pain akin to a burst of electricity shot through his body as Razin – clearly feigning exhaustion to lure him into a fancy technique – struck him in his injured ribs with a sidekick fired off with all his might.

Like the rest of the arena, Audra's jaw dropped in shock as Razin revealed he had been feigning weakness. Her stomach knotted tightly at the thought of Gustav's imminent defeat, but the underdog from Berlin wasn't out yet. Seemingly a force of nature at that point, Gustav regained his footing, and though he took a punch straight to the jaw, he blocked an uppercut aimed at his reddened ribcage. Somehow, he managed to grab hold of Razin's arm and pull him in for a nasty headbutt that opened the professional's brow while causing his own brain to jolt against his skull, bringing about a hazy feeling. Nonetheless, he was resolute. He had to win this fight, but rather than go headlong into another offensive, he backed off and began to circle Razin as half of the professional's face shone crimson with blood. Like a wolf, Gustav stared his opponent down, seeking the right spot to strike. Despite his injuries, Razin didn't appear to be slowing down one bit. Every time Gustav took a shot, Razin was quick to block and counter, but Gustav never allowed more than a glancing blow, for Razin's strategy had become predictable – he was going for the ribs.

Hearing the referee's warning that contact had to be made soon, Gustav ceased his circling and took up a position. Feigning a charge, he expected Razin to make a lunging counter to which he would match with a jumping double motion kick to the face or chest. However, Razin's counter was pulled when he noticed the shift in Gustav's feet, and when he saw him go airborne and flail his legs like a pair of vertical scissors, he dashed sideways to his left and threw a straight punch directly at Gustav's unprotected ribcage.

Screaming in his head, Gustav was paralyzed by the pain shooting through his body. He had no doubt in his mind that his ribs had been broken, if not shattered. Though he wanted to fight on, the pain was just too much at this point. The most he could do was prop himself upon his knees and face his opponent with defeat in his eyes. For a moment, he felt like a man facing the firing squad.

The moment Gustav fell to his knees, Audra felt her heart rising into her throat. She couldn't see his face very well, but if she had, she'd see the defeated expression marked by tired, glazed eyes as he prayed for the referee to signal the bell. Unfortunately, the rules for the tournament were clear. The fight only ended when someone was knocked out, made to tap, or received an injury preventing continued combat. Therefore, Audra could only stand and watch as Razin gloated for a moment before sending Gustav to the mat with a fierce twist kick to the face. Though she couldn't hear the strike connect, the roar of the crowd told her that Gustav had suffered a brutal and humiliating knockout, yet the match had still not been called. For a few moments, she looked around, trying to see if anyone else was as confused as she was. When she looked back at the screen, she saw that Gustav was down but trying to get back to his feet.

"No! Stay down!" she cried out, hoping that by some miracle Gustav would hear her pleas, but it was useless. Gustav's arrogance had cost him the fight, but his pride wouldn't let him give up. He was determined to walk away with a contract.

With terror in her eyes, Audra watched as Gustav threw a desperate punching combination followed by a roundhouse kick. Razin easily dodged the punches but caught Gustav's leg and gripped it tightly with both hands. Though Gustav tried to keep his balance, Razin threw a low kick and swept the load-bearing leg, sending Gustav to the mat. Never releasing the captured leg, Razin shifted his grip toward the ankle and bore a hideous smile. What would follow would leave Gustav screaming in agony and Audra in tears.

Chapter 31

Senatgrad, Federal Special Region, Slavic Federation

Like most people in attendance, Aleksey left the arena amazed, though a little disturbed by how the final match concluded. Gustav Hagen had put up one hell of a fight in Aleksey's eyes, but his determination to fight on even when he was barely able to stand was foolish. However, Aleksey had no ties to Gustav, so rather than mourn his brutal defeat, he went back to his hotel for a quiet night alone to clear his head and reflect on bigger matters in his life. When he got there, he raided the mini fridge for a bottle of beer and headed out onto the balcony to stare out at the skyline to think about his life.

Sitting back in a patio chair, Aleksey looked out onto the city. In the daytime, he could see the Vistula Lagoon in the distance, but the city lights obscured the view, and all he could see was a colorful display of a living, thriving capital city. Letting off a short sigh, he took a long pull from his beer and got down to thinking about everything on his mind. Most importantly, his decision to re-enlist and take his chances with Rapid Response instead of the Office of State Protection.

Sitting back and sipping slowly on his beer, Aleksey thought deeply about the consequences of his actions that morning. However, the more he thought about it, the more he realized not much would have changed. Had he known that Tatiana was unfaithful before he left for Yugoslavia, he would have re-enlisted before shipping out and accepted the invitation to try out for Rapid Response. In a way, he was glad he found out the way he did, for being in the dark on Tatiana's situation was beneficial. Not only did it allow him to make it through Yugoslavia with a clear head, but it also led him to book a month of leave. Had he not taken leave, he wouldn't have crossed paths with Audra. While she was spoken for, Aleksey was certainly smitten with her. As foolish as it might sound, the possibility of getting to know her, perhaps even becoming close, kept him from signing his liberty away for another decade.

Shaking his head at such foolish thoughts, Aleksey easily admitted it was just wishful thinking. Audra was a beautiful stranger, but she belonged to someone else. He had no business getting between them, even if Gustav was a cheating bastard. He didn't know her; for all he knew, she was fine with that. So, shrugging off the thought of a new love for now, he thought about his decision to give two more years to the Service and see where he ended up. Just then, he noticed from the corner of his eye that a light in his parents' suite had switched on. He paid this no mind and set the bottle aside on a low sitting table beside his chair. After a short while, he thought about getting another beer, but then the patio door to his parents' suite opened. A few moments later, he locked eyes with his visibly frustrated father, but with no words shared before Aleksander retreated inside. Aleksey shrugged at this and went inside to get himself that second beer after all. By the time he reached the fridge, there was a knock at his door. He had little doubt it was his father, so he opened the door with a cheeky grin.

"Did Mom throw you out?"

"No, but apparently you and I need to talk," Aleksander replied, his voice eerily calm as his eyes scanned the room through the opening between the door and the frame. "Are you alone?"

"No," Aleksey said, but Aleksander knew he was lying and gave him a stern, fatherly stare. Like a child realizing he'd better face the music rather than the wrath of his father, Aleksey opened the door fully and allowed Aleksander in.

Taking enough steps inside to allow Aleksey to shut the door behind him, Aleksander turned to his son. When their eyes met once more, he shook his head in frustration. "Did you really think I wouldn't find out?"

"Find out about what?" Aleksey asked, considering he had done a few things that day that his father would disapprove of.

"The Academy," Aleksander said. "Your mother says you were a no-show. Care to explain?"

"Well, I'm not going to lie. I got a better offer."

"A better offer than a chance to go to the Academy and become an officer?" Aleksander questioned, and Aleksey nodded, bringing a sour expression to the General's face. "Humor me."

"I decided to reenlist and accept the offer to try out for the new Rapid Response Force."

"You have got to be kidding," Aleksander said bitterly. "You embarrassed me so you could try your hand at joining an expeditionary force?"

"With all due respect, I never asked—"

"Shut it, I don't want to hear your excuses," Aleksander said dismissively, before turning toward the patio door and marching toward the glass. "Follow. It's stuffy in here."

Annoyed that his father was treating him like a misbehaving child rather than a man at the crossroads of his career, Aleksey rolled his eyes. Rather than immediately following his father outside, he grabbed a fresh beer first.

□

Standing by the door while his father leaned against the railing, Aleksey shut the door but didn't go to his father's side. Instead, he stood back and heard him sigh and grumble to himself. Aleksander soon turned to face his son, but his expression was softer than before.

"Look, I'm not angry because you chose not to go to the Academy. I'm angry because of the way you handled it. It was unprofessional and embarrassing, not just for yourself, but for me as well," Aleksander said.

"I understand you're angry, but I didn't ask for anyone to stick their neck out for me," Aleksander said. "I never once spoke of wanting to be an officer."

"Perhaps, but I'm a strategist, Aleksey. I think four to five steps ahead of the common soldier. Two, if you're elite."

"I'm aware," Aleksey said dismissively. "I bet you're going to say you were aware of my consideration for Rapid Response, and thought you'd make a better option available."

"That's correct," Aleksander replied. "And yet you still made a fool out of me."

"Even the best generals make mistakes," Aleksey replied, but Aleksander just gave him a cold glare. "Look, I know you're pissed with me, but I made my choice. I'm not a kid anymore, Dad. I'm an accomplished soldier. I'm a qualified sniper and frogman for god's sake. I'm elite."

"Then what more do you have to prove? GROM is the very best we have. Tier One. Poland's answer to America's Navy SEALs."

"Greener pastures, I suppose," Aleksey said, clearly lacking confidence in his answer.

"Alright, then tell me what happens if you wash out. Do you go back to GROM with your tail between your legs?"

"If I can get through underwater demolitions training, I can get through this."

"Yes, I'm aware that your training was certainly beyond the common man, but you didn't answer my question," Aleksander said. "What happens if you wash out? Do you think you're going to be a combat diver for the next ten years? Or are you honestly considering becoming a trainer?"

"You make training the next generation sound like a bad thing," Aleksey said, but Aleksander shrugged.

"No, I respect the profession, I truly do. However, in my honest opinion, if you're going to be barking orders in your twilight years, you might as well be commissioned."

"And why is that?" Aleksey challenged. "Is it because you're still upset that I enlisted, or did Mom put you up to this?"

"Leave your mother out of this," Aleksander said firmly. "And no, it's none of that made-up horseshit. It's the fact that you're making a lateral move, but mostly because you won't be under my jurisdiction. You do understand that this new unit is controlled by the Office of State Protection, yes?"

"What's your point, Dad?"

"My point is that if you're going to stay in a combat profession, you might as well stay where you are."

"Like I said, it's really just about greener pastures," Aleksey said. "I'd like to get as far from Gdansk as I can. Besides, this new unit is recruiting the absolute best soldiers in Poland. And the pay is incredible, so there's that, too."

"Do you need to go to the bathroom and clean the shit out of your ears, or are you just being an idiot right now?" Aleksander scoffed, but Aleksey was through being pushed around.

"Are you done insulting me yet? Because I'd really like to explain myself further," Aleksey said, uncharacteristically firm with his father. "The main reason I accepted this offer is that I ultimately want to work as an embassy guard."

"A noble goal, I suppose," Aleksander said. "Why do you need to join a new unit for that?"

"Because it would give me a chance to learn some new skills that might set me apart from the rest," Aleksey said. "I may be an accomplished soldier with a few coveted decorations on the record, but there are plenty of others like me in GROM. I need to stand out from the pack any way I can."

"So, you figured trying your hand at a new unit is your ace in the hole?" Aleksander asked with a hint of skepticism, but Aleksey didn't react, so Aleksander cooled a bit. "Look, I'm not being hard on you because I'm angry with you. I'm worried that you don't quite realize what you're getting yourself into."

"I've heard the rumors, Dad. I know my chances of making it through their qualification are slim," Aleksey said, but I need to stand out.

"Yes, I understand that, but I stand by my belief that the Academy is the better path."

"I respectfully disagree," Aleksey said calmly. "But look, even if I do make it through, I only plan to serve for the duration of my new contract. That should be more than enough to turn some heads when I reapply with State Protection, so don't worry. I'm not going to turn into an ultranationalist."

"Let's hope not. You're in for a wild ride once you report in," Aleksander said, before letting a smirk slide across his face. "I suggest you find that foreign girl and enjoy yourself the best you can before then. A couple of good memories will do you good when you find yourself knee-deep in the shit trying to prove how tough you are."

Unsure how Aleksander even knew about Audra, and to what extent he thought he knew, Aleksey said nothing. His father soon walked toward him and patted him on his shoulder before opening the door to presumably get himself another drink. Instead, Aleksander left to return to his wife, for he had accomplished what he had come to do. All that was left now was to finish his business in Senatgrad and enjoy what little time he had with his family before they went their separate ways again. As for Aleksey, he felt the need for another drink, but he didn't want to be alone. So rather than sit around in his hotel room, he headed down to the hotel bar to see if there was anyone around to entertain him for a few hours.

Chapter 32

Senatgrad, Federal Special Region, Slavic Federation

Hours had passed since Gustav was carried out of the arena on a stretcher, but Audra hadn't heard a word of his condition. Though she had waited in the arena's lobby for Jens to come for her, she was left waiting until the last of the tournament's attendees filed out into the night. Mentally unable to wait there any longer, she returned to the hotel and waited by the phone for a call from Jens. However, just like at the arena, Jens left her waiting. She tried him several times, but his phone was either dead or turned off. Even as the midnight hour approached, she held onto hope and waited on the edge of the bed, remaining fully clothed with the television playing quietly in a vain attempt to distract her, or at the very least keep her awake, but it only worked for so long. Eventually, her eyes grew heavy, and she succumbed to the need for sleep despite the intense worry that had been tormenting her since the moment Gustav took that vicious kick to the face. Yet seemingly, the moment she finally drifted asleep, her eyes shot open at the sound of the phone ringing atop the nightstand.

Her bloodstream rich with adrenaline, Audra thrust herself from the bed and hit the ground with shaky legs. Rushing to the phone, she answered with a quick repetition of the phrase 'hello.' As she had hoped, it was Jens, but he didn't have very good news, though he was scant on the details. He just told her that Gustav was alive and taken to the hospital. While Audra was relieved to know he wasn't dead, she needed more details about his injuries.

"You really don't want to know," Jens said, but Audra implored incessantly, and he eventually caved. "Look, his ankle and ribs are wrecked, and his face is pretty messed up, but that'll heal in time. The doctor is more worried about his brain."

"His brain?" Audra said with wide eyes. "What about his brain?"

"He's got a concussion, that's for sure, but there's a concern of brain bleed. He's going to be in the hospital for a couple of days at least," Jens said, but Audra was silent with fear. "He's going to be all right. He's right where he needs to be right now."

"I know, but I can't get the image of that beating out of my head," Audra said, clearly disturbed by the memory of Gustav's vicious defeat. "Why would someone do something like that to another person? This is a sport, not war."

"I don't know, but let's just count our blessings. He could be dead right now," Jens said, before trying to brighten her outlook. "But look on the bright side. He got real far and earned a lot of money in the process."

"Sure, but how much of that prize money is going straight to his medical bills?" she asked, but Jens didn't have an answer. "Of course, you don't know. You don't know anything!"

Unwilling to be her punching bag, but understanding why she was lashing out, Jens made it clear that he wasn't looking for a fight. So, to ease her worries just a bit, he promised to go down and collect Gustav's earnings first thing in the morning. That did little to help matters, so he made another failed attempt.

"Look, even if the hospital takes it all, we'll get them paid up in short order. Gustav will be on his way home as soon as possible."

"How? He doesn't have any money," Audra said, but Jens said nothing, so she jumped to the logical conclusion. "We're not getting my brother involved."

"I doubt it'll come to that, but unless you have money squirreled away, a loan might be our only option if his winnings aren't enough."

"I'd rather him be in debt to a legitimate government than a gangster," Audra said sharply, causing Jens to take a firm tone.

"You watch your mouth. That's your brother you're talking about."

"Whatever, you're no different," Audra said, shaking her head. "Is there anything else? I need a drink."

"Why don't you skip the drinks and get some sleep? Gustav's been through hell. He could really use someone nice to look at in the morning," Jens said. "Visitation begins at eight."

"Looking at the alarm clock, Audra saw that it was well past midnight, so she sighed. "Ok, maybe you're right," she said. "Just tell me he'll be alright, ok?"

"He'll live," Jens said. The call ended soon after, but his words left Audra feeling no better, prompting her to return the phone to the cradle. She would sit there for a few minutes wallowing in her pain, but she couldn't bear to be alone at that moment. She could really use that drink to ease her nerves and a shoulder to cry on. So, with a nervous hand, she reached back for the phone and dialed the front desk. Less than a minute later, she was out the door and headed for the hotel bar.

Wandering into the hotel's bar, Audra scanned the environment for an empty spot or a friendly face. She soon spotted Aleksey sitting at a high-top table near the back corner. With a meek smile, she waved and headed over. In just a few moments, she crossed the spacious barroom and took her seat across from him. Though she toiled inside over what happened to Gustav, and what someone like Jens might think if she were seen meeting with a handsome stranger, she ignored the guilt. Taking her seat, but nearly toppling the table as one of the legs caught a crack in the floor, she shook her head and smiled bashfully as Aleksey waited for her to break the awkward silence.

"Sorry, there's a lot going through my head right now," she admitted. "I hope I didn't drag you out of bed."

"No, it's fine. I wanted to come," Aleksey said. "It sounded like you needed someone to talk to."

"Yeah, that and a stiff drink," she replied with mild exasperation as the vivid memory of a defeated Gustav flashed before her eyes. "Thanks for coming down."

"My pleasure," Aleksey said. He then raised his hand to capture the waiter's attention. "Whatever the lady needs, it's on me. She's had a hard night."

Her face turning a mild shade of red, Audra was quick to say that such generosity was unnecessary, but Aleksey insisted. Appreciating this, she kept things simple and ordered a beer, and he asked for the same. When the waiter left to make their order, she looked at him and thought to insist that he let her pay but decided to let it ride instead. Easing back into her chair, she asked if he was at the arena that night.

"I was," Aleksey said slowly. "It was unfortunate what happened to Gustav."

"Yeah, but thanks anyway," she said, causing him slight confusion.

"Thanks for what?"

"For telling me about the professionals," she said. "I tried to warn him, but he didn't listen."

"I'm sorry," he said, reaching his hand over the table to touch her hand.

Her eyes glanced down at their linked hands for a moment, but she didn't give in to the urge to pull away. She just looked back into his eyes and admitted she didn't think he would have listened, but it was worth a try.

"He sounds prideful," he said, but she shook her head.

"Perhaps, but you don't know Gustav. He's a real arrogant asshole sometimes... well, most of the time. To be honest, he's kind of a shitty person, and I'm not sure why I'm still with him."

"I'm sorry to hear that," Aleksey said, not quite sure what else to say. "I hope I didn't open the floodgates."

"Well, I guess I can just go back upstairs," she said, but he tilted his head in confusion. "Look, call me selfish, but I needed someone to bleed out to, alright?"

"Bleed away," Aleksey said, pulling his hand back and sitting up straight. "I didn't choose my words correctly just now. I apologize."

"You don't need to apologize," Audra said quickly, but silenced herself when she noticed the waiter coming with the drinks. The pair remained quiet until the drinks were placed before them. Audra then took a long sip and savored the grainy flavor as the bubbles danced on her tongue before continuing. "As I said, I just needed someone to talk to. I hope you didn't come down here with some sort of aspiration."

"Not at all," Aleksey replied. "Frankly, after what happened to me, I wouldn't dare mess with a cheater."

Her ears perked at Aleksey's words; Audra was intrigued. "I take it you were on the losing end of something awful."

"Yeah, very recently, actually," Aleksey said, stopping suddenly to take a drink to chase off foul memories of Tatiana's betrayal. "To be honest, I came down here with nothing on my mind but talking with you. I figured there was a reason you called me and not someone you know better."

Stopping short of admitting she didn't have too many close friends anymore, largely thanks to Gustav, Audra thanked him for his apparently pure intentions. She then admitted that what happened to Gustav was awful, but it was an opportunity. She just wasn't sure if she had the guts to go through with it.

"What do you mean by that?"

"I don't know why I'm telling you this, but I've been considering leaving him for a good while, and the way he treated me this afternoon sealed it. I can't carry on like this. I'm not happy."

"Well, I'm sorry to hear that, but don't let your emotions get the best of you. You need to do the right thing."

"What do you mean?" she asked with a cool stare, before jumping to the defense. "Didn't I make it clear that I didn't ask you down here to get drunk and hook up?"

"That's not what I was implying," Aleksey replied calmly. "Even if that was the case, he's been severely hurt. The last thing he needs is for you to break his heart."

Audra rolled her eyes at his words, but after a few moments of silence, she saw the wisdom of his words and admitted she was worried about him.

"Of course, you're worried about him. You've spent a good chunk of your life with him," Aleksey said. "Look, I'm not saying you shouldn't end things, but maybe you should give it some time."

"Maybe you're right," she said, but then she leaned in with curious eyes. "Why are you suddenly so invested in my relationship? We just met."

Leaning back into his chair, Aleksey slouched a bit. "I guess I don't want to see someone go through the same thing as me," he said. "I spent ten years with a woman I thought was the love of my life. I even planned to marry her, but she had other plans."

"What happened?" Audra asked, curious yet cautious. "Don't answer if you don't want to."

"She left me for another man while I was deployed overseas," Aleksey replied, and Audra sighed as if she could feel his pain. "It wouldn't have hurt so bad if she had just told me, but instead I had to find out the hard way."

"I'm so sorry, that's awful," Audra said, but he shrugged.

"The moral of the story is that you can't always choose who you fall in love with, but care should be taken when you decide it's time to end things," Aleksey said, touching Audra with his words. "But let me ask you one thing. Do you still love Gustav?"

There was a long period of silence as if Audra was trying to find the right answer or deciding if she should answer at all. Eventually, she looked down at the table and admitted, "Honestly, I don't think I do."

"Is there anything that can be done to change that?" he asked, but she shrugged.

"We're just too different anymore," she said. "I want to say this feeling is recent, but the more I think about it, the more I realize we were never really all that compatible to begin with."

"I see," Aleksey said softly. "Well, if I were you, I'd take some time to think it all over before making a big decision. Like they drilled in my head in sniper school – timing and location is everything."

"You're absolutely correct," she said after a slow nod. She then saw him raise his glass of beer.

"In the meantime, I offer a salute."

"A salute to what?"

"To Gustav's health."

While Audra appreciated Aleksey's good heart, he didn't know Gustav at all, so his words had only a mild effect on her thought process. While she would certainly heed his advice on not inflicting poorly timed heartbreak on a wounded man, she would simply wait until a more appropriate time to put their relationship to an end. There was just too much negative energy between them for her to carry on with him. Her mind was essentially made up, but rather than ruin a rather pleasant conversation, she politely changed the subject. However, when her drink was finished, she excused herself for the night, but not before thanking Aleksey for his kind advice and generosity. She then left with no lingering suspicions that Aleksey was anything but a good person. She looked forward to chatting with him in the future and learning more about him, perhaps even crafting a meaningful friendship.

Chapter 33

Senatgrad, Federal Special Region, Slavic Federation

Waking up early, Jens threw together an antiquated outfit of acid-wash jeans, a faded black sweatshirt, and a pair of dark sunglasses. He finished the look with a black leather vest emblazoned with patches declaring himself president of the Berlin chapter of the infamous international outlaw motorcycle club, the Huns.

While his wardrobe appeared to have been put together without much thought, it was actually a product of strategy. Jens was intent on securing Gustav's money, and if diplomacy or his intimidating stature wouldn't do the trick, then surely the patches on his vest would. After all, Senatgrad was no stranger to organized crime, especially outlaw motorcycle clubs friendly with the Huns and their Russian rivals, the Werewolves MC. Of course, he wasn't there on behalf of the Huns, nor was he there looking to start a fight with any Werewolves he might come across, but it was a calculated risk. If he got jumped, all he had to do was make a few phone calls, and it would be hell to pay for the offenders. With any luck, he'd go unnoticed, or at least ignored. After all, it was very early on a Sunday morning, and few outlaws got up early without a purpose when they could sleep off their hangovers instead.

Upon leaving the hotel, Jens hit the streets and hailed a cab. It was quite the distance down to the high-rise office building where he could find the regional headquarters for the Slavic Federation's Professional Fighting Commission, but the fare was cheap. When he arrived at the building, he stepped through the glass doors and walked across the polished granite floors. His attire made him stand out like a sore thumb, but not one of the stuffed suits and blouses he passed said a word. They simply piled into the elevator beside him and tried not to make eye contact. This had Jens laughing inside, but he didn't push his luck. Rather, he left the elevator when he reached the correct floor and announced his arrival at the offices with a knock before entering.

Now standing in the office lobby for the fighting commission, Jens made eye contact with the secretary. His heavy leather boots thumping as he approached heel to toe, he placed his large, battle-scarred hands on the counter and leaned in toward the pretty secretary. Despite his intimidating appearance, he spoke calmly and professionally, and in passable Russian.

"Good morning, my name is Jens Groth. I'm here on behalf of my fighter, Gustav Hagen."

Though a little nervous, the Secretary typed the information into her computer and brought up Gustav's file. She was able to confirm that Jens was listed as Gustav's manager, but she needed to see proof of identity, which Jens promptly provided.

"What can I do for you, Mr. Groth?" the Secretary asked.

"I'd like a word with the Fight Commissioner," Jens said calmly. "It's regarding my fighter."

"My apologies, but what is it regarding exactly?"

"The payment of my fighter," Jens answered. "He was eliminated last night and put in the hospital, so I'm here to collect on his behalf."

Appearing perplexed, the Secretary turned to her monitor and made a few clicks with her mouse. She would go on to confirm the number of matches Gustav participated in and how many he won, but Jens was growing impatient.

"Yes, I'm aware of all of that. How much did he win?"

"I'm afraid I don't have access to that information," the Secretary said, so Jens rolled his eyes. "I'll have to phone my supervisor."

"Yes, please do," Jens said, before standing by through a short phone call. He was soon met by a middle-aged man in a mid-priced suit.

"Mr. Groth?" he asked, and Jens nodded, bringing the man to smile awkwardly. "Right this way."

Nodding, Jens turned to the secretary and thanked her for her help. He then followed the manager to his office about midway down the hall from the lobby.

Seated in a basic office chair, Jens watched as the Office Manager ran through files on his computer. From what he could see, there was a detailed profile on Gustav, including fight statistics in the tournament. This gave him the impression he was going to get what he wanted, but the manager was forced to deliver some unfortunate news.

"As you're probably aware, your client was eliminated last night and the tournament is ongoing."

"Yes, I'm aware. What's your point?" Jens asked with brewing impatience.

"My point is that while I can assure you that your client will be paid the premium for each match won, I don't have access to his final total just yet."

Furrowing his brow, Jens quietly demanded an answer. "The totals aren't made available until the tournament is through," the Manager said, but Jens called his bluff.

"Sounds like bullshit to me," Jens said. "Just give me the money that's due to my fighter."

"I'd love to, but I don't have a total."

"Then get yourself a pamphlet and do the fucking math," Jens snarled, but the Manager was silent. "Look, my fighter is laid up in a hospital and can't leave the country until he's paid up, and the bill is going up every day."

"Again, I'm sorry, but I don't have a total," the Manager said.

"Say that again and I'll give you a fucking total!" Jens thundered. He then pointed to a fading tattoo of a sneering Hunnic warrior on his forearm and spoke boldly. "Surely you've heard of the Huns. At the very least, you're aware of our local support club, the Jomsvikings."

Though deeply intimidated by the outlaw in his midst, the Manager kept his composure and repeated the statement. When Jens raised his voice again, he was countered with a nervous declaration that could very well have backfired.

"Perhaps we should take this up with the proper authorities," he said, his finger pointing to a camera positioned in the corner near the door.

Realizing he had been filmed this whole time, Jens didn't bother to bargain or even apologize. He simply let off a sigh and apologized for his short temper.

"My fighter is like a son to me, so I'm a little high-strung right now," Jens said, hoping to smooth things over. "Could you at least tell me when he can expect a check?"

The sudden change in demeanor eased the Manager's nerves enough for him to give a straight answer. "Final totals will be tallied the day after the tournament. Your client can collect his winnings in about five days."

Jens grimaced at the thought of being stuck in Senatgrad for another five days. He was by no means a poor man, but he was needed back in Berlin sooner rather than later. That meant his only option for a quick turnaround was turning to Richard, but even that was going to take some time. So, grimacing at the situation at hand, Jens thanked the Manager for his time, shook his head, and promptly left the office without further conflict. As he left, he shook his head at his own recklessness back there, but it didn't matter so long as he got the job done and left the country without incident.

Making a beeline for the hospital, Jens stepped into Gustav's room to find him sleeping and Audra by his bedside, right where he had left her. The expression on his face told Audra something wasn't right, but she didn't want to wake Gustav. So, stepping outside, they conversed softly in the hallway, but it wouldn't last long before tensions would flare.

"What do you mean they won't pay him for five days?" Audra questioned. "Universal healthcare doesn't apply to foreigners. His debt is going to be astronomical if we don't get him out soon!"

"Yeah, well, it's a good thing he's not critical."

"Have you seen him lately? He's a mess in there!"

"Yeah, but it could be a hell of a lot worse. He's still breathing, he doesn't have brain bleed, and he's going to get paid," Jens said. "He's not out of the woods, but at least he can see the sunlight."

Rolling her eyes, Audra crossed her arms and asked to know just what he said to cause the fighting commission to refuse payment.

"I didn't do anything," Jens lied. "They won't bother calculating the winnings until after the tournament."

Hope in her voice, Audra said, "So we really just have to wait five days?"

"That's what the stuffed suit said," Jens said distantly. "In the meantime, we need to get him out of the hospital as soon as medically advisable. He's already deep in debt."

Furrowing her brow, Audra felt like Jens wasn't talking about the medical bills at this point, but Jens was able to cover himself well.

"This isn't the time for jumping to conclusions. What I meant is his medical debt is piling up every minute he spends in here, and it's only going to get worse if we don't get him cleared."

"Okay, but then what? I already spoke to the billing department. He can't leave the country until his debt is paid."

Gritting his teeth at the unforeseen variable, Jens turned his shoulder to her and began to pace. Despite what his gruff exterior would say about his intellect, Jens was known for his quick thinking.

"We put him up in a cheap hotel until he gets paid and the check clears," Jens said.

"Okay, but who's going to pay the hotel bill?" Audra asked, but Jens just glared, giving her a silent answer she didn't quite like. "Why should I pay for this? I'm not the one who convinced him to come out here. Hell, I even tried to get him to drop out while he was ahead."

"Because at the end of the day, you're the one he goes home to at night," Jens said. "I get that things aren't great between you two anymore, but he needs your help, Audra. The best-case scenario is he spends another week out here and walks away owing less than he won."

"That's the best-case scenario. What if things take a turn for the worse?" she asked, but Jens didn't have an answer. "I don't have a lot of money saved, and I'm not going to my brother."

"Unless you want to leave him stranded and alone, your brother might be your only option."

"I'd rather abandon him here than put him at the mercy of a loan shark."

"What did I say about respecting your brother?"

"To hell with that bastard," Audra said with apparent disgust. She then turned back and went back into Gustav's room, but Jens didn't follow. He just went on his way. As far as he was concerned, his hands were clean of this mess.

Leaving Jens in the hallway, Audra stepped back into Gustav's room. Expecting him to be sound asleep still, she sat back down on the chair beside his bed, but once she did, he turned his head with a confrontational glare.

"So you're going to abandon me here?"

"What?" Audra asked with a perplexed expression. "Why would you say something like that?"

"I heard what you said out there. You'd rather leave me here than take money from your brother."

Considering what he had heard was true, she admitted that he had heard right, but it was out of context. This did little to ease him.

"I'd rather be in debt than abandoned," Gustav snarled, causing intense pain to flare throughout his body. He took a calmer, though hurt tone. "After everything we've been through—"

"Stop it," Audra ordered. "What I meant was I don't want you to fall into debt to gangsters," she said, but he turned his head so that he was staring at the ceiling. It was clear he didn't want to hear more, but she continued anyway. "Jens says it should only be a couple of days until you get paid."

"And if it's longer?"

"It doesn't matter. We'll put you in a hotel as soon as the doctor lets us," Audra promised. "We're going to get you through this just fine." She then touched his arm, careful to avoid the IV snaking up from his hand. "I'm not going to abandon you."

Staring up at the ceiling with unsure eyes, he asked, "And what if the hospital bills cost more than I won? I can't leave the country until it's paid off."

"It won't be," she said, squeezing his wrist lightly. "You won a lot of money. There's no way."

"And if it is?" he asked, growing more sullen. "You heard the doctor. I might not be able to fight again. How will I make the money to go home?"

"We'll find a way," she promised.

Turning toward her again, he had an expression that told her that he had something profound to admit to her, but when asked what it was, he looked at the ceiling again. "Just don't leave me here," he said. "I know we're on the rocks, but I don't deserve to be left like this."

His words pulled at her heartstrings and reminded her of the everlasting pain of her father leaving when she was just a child. Audra again promised that she wouldn't leave him behind. She even went as far as to tell him she loved him, though she still wondered if there was any truth behind those last few words.

Chapter 34

Moscow, Republic of Russia, Slavic Federation

His time in Senatgrad through at last, Aleksander returned to Moscow in the early morning while his family stayed behind to enjoy the city for a few days longer. This was no bother at all, for his homecoming was anything but relaxing. After all, Aleksander had gone to Senatgrad with a specific task, and he was expected to report directly to the Premier within hours of his return to Russia. This gave him time to go home and prepare himself for a return to the same old song and dance.

Initially stopping at home only to drop off his belongings and freshen up after a much too early flight, Aleksander found himself standing alone in his living room. His dark eyes scanned the room as if he were searching for something. Truthfully, he wasn't looking for anything. He was just reminiscing about the good times he had in this room and silently wondered if he could really leave this place behind for the old farmhouse back in the old country.

Stepping up the single step that led into the dining room portion of the kitchen, Aleksander passed through the kitchen and went down the hall that led into the weight room. Passing through this room just the same, he opened the glass double doors that led into the pool room. While the pool certainly looked inviting in the early morning light that came in through the skylights and windows, his attention soon turned to the spa that was built into the floor of the room.

Stripping down to his bare skin, Aleksander stepped into the hot, bubbling waters of the spa and took his usual seat. Easing back into the deep, molded seat until his head sat comfortably on the headrest and the water tickled at his throat, he gazed at the recess typically occupied by Katrin. His relaxed mind quickly conjured an image of his wife, and he thought deeply about the conflict that threatened to destroy his marriage if he chose wrongly.

Aleksander loved his wife deeply, and he understood her desire to return to the old country. However, no matter how well he explained the complexity of the situation he was caught up in as a member of the General Staff, he could never get through to her. Never in his life would he have ever considered divorce an option, but he was fearful of what might happen if he heeded his wife's demands and abruptly resigned from his post the moment Poland was set free. After all, he worked for a dangerous man who may or may not have been a high-ranking spy hunter in the Soviet Union's infamous Committee for State Security. Yet, on the same token, his wife was determined to go home to their old life, with or without him. This put incredible strain on his soul, for though he wanted nothing more than to make his wife happy, he feared for them all. Simply put, one does not reach the highest echelon of a quasi-authoritarian regime and walk away amidst a social revolution. He knew far too much not to walk away with a target on his back.

Sighing, Aleksander was facing a most inglorious burden. Despite his strategic brilliance, he was at a loss for how to win this battle. The Premier was an intimidating man who would surely fight tooth and claw to keep him on his leash. However, Aleksander had overcome greater adversaries and conflicts in his life. He was a war hero in the old country for being the unlikely victor of the Battle of Warsaw when he was just a mid-grade officer who suddenly found himself in charge of an entire division in the middle of one of the most decisive battles of the entire war. If he could overcome those odds, then surely, he could find a way out of this mess without losing the love of his life or suffering the wrath of a government assassin. He just needed to clear his head and think it through, and there was no time like the present. He was alone, and he had a few precious hours to himself before he had to drag himself before the Premier.

□

Strategically reporting to the Premier's office after the end of the daily meeting of the General Staff, Aleksander was now seated across from the man himself with an impressively large mahogany desk between them. Like old friends, Aleksander and Sergei made small talk over coffee - a gesture reflective of their longstanding professional relationship. In time, they got down to business, but despite relaxing at home, Aleksander was still tired from a sleepless night and the flight in, so he asked how much Viktoriya had already shared. Sergei smirked and told Aleksander to give him the main points. It was clear Viktoriya had already given her husband an earful, and he desired to see the facts filtered out from the muck of vitriol she had for the secessionists.

"Where do I begin?" Aleksander muttered, and Sergei answered by asking him if the Secessionists were truly so bold as to walk out on the last day over their refusal to partition the Sambia Peninsula. "Indeed, they did."

"Fucking idiots," Sergei said with a chuckle. "At no point in modern history has that peninsula ever been Polish territory. What do they seriously expect?"

"That's anyone's guess," Aleksander said, but Sergei smiled at his words.

"That's funny. I've heard you have been spending just about every night with the enemy."

"The enemy?" Aleksander asked, but Sergei bowed his head to offer a condescending glare. "You're referring to Senator Wilczynski, aren't you?"

"He's the public face for the secession, is he not?"

"Yes, but he's also my brother-in-law," Aleksander replied. "I assure you that he had no sway over me."

"Let's hope not," Sergei replied. "You're much too valuable to me, Alek. I'd hate to have to part ways."

"I'm not going anywhere," Aleksander said with determination. "In fact, if your wife spoke the truth, then surely you know that I worked furiously to keep the peace and provide an amicable agreement."

"Yes, and I thank you for that. The last thing we needed was to give the secessionists a propaganda victory," Sergei said. "However, I don't see this Sambia nonsense going away."

"It's all political theater," Aleksander said. "Honestly, I don't believe they expect to even win that debate with the Senate."

"Then what's the point?" Sergei asked.

"I think they plan to use our refusal to cede those bases as just cause to join NATO."

"NATO... I fucking dare them," Sergei groaned viciously, but then he grinned. "Then again, how do they plan to join NATO if they're still part of the Federation?"

"Well, that's where we get into murky waters," Aleksander said, piquing the Premier's interest. "While the secession appears entirely political, the outcome of the vote was astonishing. The fact that such a large portion of the population supported secession, I'm concerned about the Polish Armed Forces."

"What are you saying, Alek?" Sergei asked, deeply intrigued. "Are you suggesting a coup d'état in the event of failure?"

"I don't want to rule out the possibility," Aleksander said honestly, and Sergei smiled.

"Did your brother mention such a thing, or is that what you would do if you were in league with the opposition?"

"A coup would be a devastating and messy affair that would do more harm than good. Besides, I believe in democracy," Aleksander said stiffly, but Sergei was quick to challenge him.

"But if your loyalties lay with Poland and not the Federation? What then?"

"Unless there was sufficient evidence that the vote was rigged against my favored cause, I would accept the results without public outcry."

"And if there was a rebellion?"

"I would move to crush it swiftly," Aleksander said boldly. "However, I'd be very careful in doing so. The West could be behind any attempt at a violent takeover."

"Do you believe the West would risk a war over Poland?"

"No, but I wouldn't rule it out either. There are plenty of war hawks in seats of influence that don't seem to realize the Cold War is long over, especially in America," Aleksander said grimly, but his tone soon changed to something more hopeful. "Of course, I don't believe that would be the case if we allowed democracy to prevail."

"What are you implying?"

"I'm not implying anything, but I am imploring you to allow Poland a fighting chance through the democratic process," Aleksander replied, and Sergei remained silent. "We need to show the world that we're not the fascist dictatorship that our rivals and detractors claim us to be. To accomplish this, I simply ask that we allow a clean and transparent political process."

"Well, contrary to popular belief, I wholly agree. Of course, I can't help what radicals might do."

"The negotiations are over, and the vote is a month away. If the radicals among the opposition try anything stupid, they'll sink their own cause," Aleksander said, but before Sergei could concur, he continued. "We need to keep our own radicals in line just the same."

"Forgive me if I heard you wrong, but it sounds like you're accusing me of attempting to sway the vote," Sergei said with a mildly sinister tone. "Is that what you're saying, General?"

"No, I'm simply asking you to lean on people like Sarich and Voychenko," Aleksander said coolly, for he was deeply suspicious of the intelligence services, especially the FSB's infamous Directorate S.

"I'll do that," Sergei said calmly, but Aleksander was not yet free of suspicion. "But should this come down to a clash of arms, I'd like to know exactly where you stand."

"Right where I belong," Aleksander said firmly, "at the head of the Federal Slavic Army."

"Good," Sergei said with a nod. "God willing, it won't come to that."

"God willing."

Chapter 35
Redzikowo, Republic of Poland, Slavic Federation

Taken by bus roughly two hours west along the Baltic coast, Aleksey and more than one hundred other 'candidates' poured out onto the cracked tarmac of a former Soviet airbase outside the coastal village of Redzikowo. When they left Senatgrad, it was a warm autumn day, but a cold, salty wind gusted off the sea to the north and across the tarmac every so often, painting a dark picture of what was in store. However, these men were the very toughest the military had to offer. Therefore, the wind was tolerable to the men, most of whom had the sleeves of their BDUs rolled up, but as time passed, their skin began to grow numb. Some tried to tough it out longer than the rest, but eventually no one stood with forearms exposed, and the chilly wind began to take its toll, causing them to shiver.

"Where's the welcoming committee?" Aleksey heard Miko mutter to him. Though he was surely joking, considering his choice of words, he concurred. It was strange that they were left to stand out in the open for so long, especially with orders to wait on the tarmac.

For more than an hour, the men braved their first test at Redzikowo. Like the men around him, Aleksey stood tall and firm, doing well to ignore the cold and the occasional involuntary shiver. However, he had a growing need to urinate, so when he spotted a small light utility vehicle pull onto the tarmac from behind a row of hangars, he sighed in relief. "Finally," he thought to himself. "Hopefully, they don't take too long with the welcome speech. I need to piss like a racehorse."

Standing at attention as the utility vehicle sped down the cracked, somewhat overgrown tarmac, Aleksey watched with sharp eyes. He saw at least three passengers but assumed there was a fourth hidden by the angle at which he viewed the vehicle.

Coming to a halt before the perfectly formed unit of men, the truck faced the group head-on. The first to emerge was the driver, but if the dark green beret atop his head was anything to go by, he was an officer of the Special Troops Command. The Driver was followed shortly by a pair of similarly dressed officers. What a group of so-called 'desk jockeys' was doing there was anyone's guess, but his attention was quickly turned to the final occupant of the vehicle. Unlike the others, she didn't wear a beret or a battle dress uniform. Rather, she wore a formal uniform with all the trimmings of a decorated combat veteran and the markings of a full colonel. Rightfully assuming she was the commanding officer of this base, Aleksey immediately began to analyze her with respect and curiosity.

A tall woman, about a head above the average Polish woman, she had a strong jawline like a Scandinavian, a steely gaze, and a notable scar that snaked down from the right side of her nose and across her lips at a sharp angle. Had it not been for the scar, she would have been quite pretty for a woman her age, but such frivolous thoughts about this woman were quickly chased away when she addressed the group.

"Recruits, I am Commander Kozak, commandant of this camp. I've been tasked with the formation of a new unit and this is the third class to undergo the first phase of my program. While I intend to add you all to my ranks, only the very best and most dedicated will see the end of this program," Kozak said with a commanding voice and stern expression. "Nonetheless, I expect nothing short of your finest efforts while under my command."

The way Kozak spoke gave Aleksey strong feelings that she had come from the clandestine intelligence side of the military. However, she was not someone who basked in her accomplishments or demanded praise for her service in the revolutionary period. She was a dedicated soldier, and duty always came before pride. So rather than waste time on false promises of glory and brotherhood, she welcomed the men to their worst nightmare.

Setting the bar high, the Colonel declared that the coming days and weeks would be the hardest of their lives, and that everything they would endure was her own design. She was open with her expectation that less than half of them would see the entire program through, but that was also by design. She wanted nothing short of the very best under her command.

"Rest assured, you're all here because you have been flagged as among the best in your respective field of expertise," she said, her stern expression quickly turning to a grin. "We'll put that to the test."

The Colonel's welcome speech through, Aleksey and the others listened closely as she explained that one hundred and fifty men and women from across the special operations community were in attendance. As a result, she had three handpicked officers at her side to lead them through the selection program. Shortly thereafter, the officers began reading names from a list, dividing the group into three units led by a specific officer. Considering the nature of Squadron B, it was no surprise that Aleksey and Miko fell in with the men from JW Formoza under Lieutenant Commander Linetty.

Standing at attention, though not in formation but rather a huddled mass of eager frogmen and naval commandos, Aleksey's eyes were glued to his new commander. Like Colonel Kozak, the LTC spoke with a firm tone and always bore a stern expression.

"All right, listen up. I don't care what you were or what you accomplished before coming here. All I know is that you were handpicked for being among the best the naval elements of the Special Troops have to offer, but don't let that go to your head. The Colonel was not kidding about this place being your worst nightmare. You're going to face, and hopefully overcome, challenges you never thought possible. You're going to get hurt, you're going to get sick, and you're going to want to quit, but I won't let that happen easily," Linetty said. "My job here is to separate the wheat from the chaff, but I want as much wheat as I can get. You're here to prove you're the toughest son of a bitch to come out of the water, and I'll be pushing you through Hell itself to accomplish that feat. I don't want to see a single frogman go belly up. Do you understand me?"

"Yes, sir!" the men shouted with vigor, and Linetty appeared pleased.

From the moment they fell out for the first time under LTC Linetty's command, Aleksey and his newfound compatriots were faced with physical challenges that tested their physical and mental limits. They began with a steady jog around the camp that didn't end until someone fell out of formation from exhaustion. This man was quickly faced with Linetty and asked if he needed a bottle of water. When the man nodded, the LTC pointed toward the front gate of the base and told him how far he had to walk to get to the nearest supermarket. This was clearly a test to see if the recruit was willing to wash out after a few miles of jogging, but he wasn't giving up that easily, so he got back into formation, and the jog resumed. Fortunately, the end was in sight, for the moment Linetty's feet touched the tarmac, he ordered the men to break formation and charge toward the nearest hangar. However, when the men began their charge, they did so at the same pace they had been jogging at. This caused their commander to shout out for them to run as if their lives depended on it. The resulting sprint was a befuddled race to the finish with exhausted men clenching their jaws and grunting through the burning in their legs and core as they forced themselves into overdrive. While some certainly made it all the way without error, others, Aleksey included, found themselves tripping over the cracks in the tarmac and hitting the ground with force. Yet, somehow no one gave up, and every one of the men made it to the rusted shell of a hangar. Inside, they were greeted with desperately wanted relief from the punishing wind that continued to whip off the sea and batter the camp with cold sea air.

Like everyone else, Aleksey stood around trying to catch his breath after what felt like fifty miles of nonstop running. His legs felt wobbly as if the bones within had jellied, his heart was pounding like a jackhammer, and his lungs felt like they were on fire. He was hoping for a bottle of water after so much running, but no one dared ask even as Linetty asked if anyone was thirsty. This brought a smirk to the grizzled former frogman's face, and he called their bluff and told them there was a faucet in the back. Aleksey could have sworn he heard a collective sigh of relief as the group began moving toward the back of the hangar. However, relief for their dry throats came at a price – the faucet was green and rusty, and the water had an off-putting sulfur smell as if it were connected to a swamp or the well was contaminated, but that was the nature of the program. The will to survive was one of the many things that would be tested here, so the choice was painfully obvious. They could choke down the bog water or go into the next phase thirsty and vulnerable. On the same token, they were risking cholera if the smell was anything to go by.

Given all the time they needed to rehydrate and catch their breath, the men were eventually ordered to form a double-file line and stand shoulder to shoulder. When ordered to do so, they turned to face the man to either their left or their right. They were then commanded to take three steps back. This allowed Linetty to walk down the corridor that the men had created as he explained that the body is just as much a weapon as it is a tool. This instantly brought back memories of the intense hand-to-hand combat training each of them had endured to earn their place among their respective special operations unit.

"Expertise in hand-to-hand combat can be the difference between life and death in the event you are without a weapon or you're out of ammunition," Linetty said as he walked the corridor. "Unfortunately, studies have shown that only around forty percent of all active members of the Special Troops hone their skills beyond minimal proficiency," Linetty continued. "Proving you didn't squander this precious gift is your next test. You'll begin sparring on my orders, and you will not stop until I tell you to stop."

Linetty paused for a moment as a look of bewilderment showed on the face of each of the men. They were unsure of what the LTC was expecting of them, but some had an idea. For Aleksey, it wasn't a comfortable prospect, considering the man directly across from him was Miko.

"Do you need further instructions? Take your fighting stance and prepare to demonstrate your hand-to-hand skills," Linetty said, but the men appeared anxious and moved sluggishly. "Are you all deaf? Move your asses! Today!"

Once more doing as they were told, the men of Linetty's company took up an identical fighting stance, save for Aleksey and his fellow GROM frogmen. By order of their commanding officer, all members of GROM Squadron B honed their hand-to-hand skills beyond minimal proficiency through the incorporation of other fighting styles, including krav maga and sambo. Therefore, their fighting stance made them stand out and earn themselves unwanted attention from the Lieutenant Commander. By sheer misfortune, Aleksey was nearest to him.

"You must be from GROM," Linetty said. "What style do they teach you in the maritime division?"

"GROM combat system, sir," Aleksey replied, his eyes staring past the Lieutenant Commander. "It's a blend of jiujitsu, krav maga—"

"Shut it, soldier," Linetty said firmly. "Take your stance and prepare for combat."

Quietly, Aleksey took up his fighting stance and patiently awaited the order to begin sparring. He soon heard Miko call out. "No mercy, Aleksey! Let's give him a show!"

A shrill whistle pierced their ears before Linetty ordered them to fight. The entire company soon closed the gap and began trading blows at half-strength to avoid causing unnecessary injury. Though a few blows managed to land, their collective form was perfect. Each man demonstrated not only mastery while on offense but on defense as well. However, after a short while, Linetty had seen enough showmanship and shouted at them, calling their sparring pathetic before ordering his men to fight like their lives depended on it. He then added the threat that failure to follow orders would result in early dismissal.

Under threat of being expelled from the program if they didn't put up a real fight, the men got more aggressive. Despite their intention of throwing full-strength punches and kicks, exhaustion was holding everyone back. Some even tried to use exhaustion as an excuse, but this was met with a renewed threat of elimination for cowardice and weakness. What followed was a vicious melee like an underground fight club - noses were broken, lips split, eyes blackened, but the men fought with fury more commonly seen in the Blood

Games. In due time, men ended up on the ground either from a blow that landed just right, an unexpected throwing technique, or simple exhaustion.

By the time Linetty blew his whistle and ordered the fighting to cease, not one man failed to impress him. However, one pair that stood out the most - Aleksey and Miko. Though it wasn't because they were fighting more impressively than the others, but the technique Aleksey had applied to Miko after catching a roundhouse kick to his midsection and sweeping his friend's leg for the takedown and a painful ankle lock.

Clenching Miko's lower leg tightly between his bicep as he gripped his boot and twisted just enough to inflict pain, Aleksey was clenching his eyes shut when he felt the warmth of the morning sun disappear. He soon heard Linetty speaking directly to him and saw the LTC standing over him, blocking out the sun with his large figure.

"A submission technique? If this were a combat situation and I was that man's compatriot, you would be dead right now," Linetty said strongly. "Release him and face me at attention."

Fear shot down Aleksey's spine as the words registered in his mind. Doing as he was told, he allowed Miko to go free of his grasp, stood up, and faced his commander, but Linetty was seemingly done with him. Having already made his point, the LTC ordered everyone back into their original lines and to stand at attention.

"While this exercise started out looking like an absolute joke, you all demonstrated your skills well. Some of you certainly need to know when and where to use certain techniques, but the fact of the matter is that not one of you failed," Linetty said. "Congratulations, you've earned your first meal. Fall out after me."

Chapter 36

Senatgrad, Federal Special Region, Slavic Federation

With his campaign to form a pro-secession coalition within the Senate struggling terribly, Roman was becoming more desperate by the day. While he was dedicated to liberating his nation through the pen rather than the sword, he was beginning to feel the pressure from the more impatient members of the Polish Liberation Party. Regardless of this fact, he was able to avoid the de facto leader of the party's hardliners until the man himself made an unexpected appearance at his office in Senatgrad. The presence of General Krupa – a man rarely found beyond the limits of Warsaw where his beloved 2nd Army was headquartered - was certainly a surprise, but to be a good politician meant keeping a cool head in the face of the unexpected. Therefore, Roman chose not to greet General Krupa as an unwelcome intruder but as a friend and a valued ally. Thus, behind closed doors, they sat down to discuss in private.

A stout man with a long, drooping face that was aged beyond his years by the hell of war and a love of cigars, Krupa sat across from the far more youthful-looking Senator. His peaked cap resting on his lap as his legs were held tightly together, his steely gaze analyzed the Senator's unusually calm expression. Truth be told, he thought his visit would have ruffled some feathers, but he could sense a ruse, so he got straight to business.

"We're getting impatient, Senator," said Krupa, a man forever in love with formal titles. "There's a good deal of talk that your campaign to gather allies is flailing in the wind."

"Yes, I've heard that rumor, but rest assured, it's just that."

"Just what?" Krupa challenged. "A mere rumor?"

"Yes," Roman said with a nod. "The Bulgarians have already agreed to stand by us in favor of a military alliance should the time for their own secession come."

"That's one of just six possible allies. We're going to need a lot more than one. We all know where the Russians stand," Krupa said. "Quite frankly, courting the Bulgarians is a waste of time."

"How do you figure?" Roman countered, and Krupa smirked.

"I hope that's a rhetorical question," Krupa said, but Roman was silent, so Krupa explained his reasoning. "They're landlocked with a neutral nation between them and us. Supporting them militarily would be next to impossible considering that fact."

"It was their suggestion, not mine," Roman said calmly. "Frankly, I agree with your sentiment on a military alliance."

"Then consider them neutral and pursue a logical ally like the Czechs or the Slovaks. They're the ones that kicked off the last revolution, after all."

"I've spoken to both sets of senators. Neither was outright willing to align with us, but I have a feeling they're mulling things over."

Wondering if Roman was just playing dumb, Krupa furrowed his brow and asked if he had accomplished anything notable since the referendum was tied up in a legal technicality.

"Politicians are a different breed, Karol. We don't speak the entire truth, even in private. We tend to keep our cards close to our chest and wait for the right time to make our move."

"Yes, yes, I know how your kind operates. You're a slimy barrel of snakes," Krupa said, showing his disgust for the political establishment.

"Then bear with me. These things take time. We can't just go guns blazing and expect the Senate to vote unanimously in our favor. We're playing by Moscow's rules, remember?"

"Yes, I do, but I also recall the last time we played the political long game. It ended with Prague Spring, followed by six long years of war that somehow ended in favor of liberty rather than authoritarianism."

"And yet here we are lying under the heel of a Russian boot once more," Roman said sharply. "We need to give peace a chance. It's the only way for Poland to secure its freedom once and for all."

"Do you really think the people wouldn't rebel if our collective will was denied by the Senate? Do you think our soldiers, some of whom served on the front lines in the revolution, don't know what a little foot-to-ass can achieve?"

"All that I'm saying is that we need to exhaust our political options before we resort to violence. In fact, let's leave violence off the table, shall we?"

"What are you afraid of, Senator? A little blood on your hands?"

"Quite frankly, I'm afraid to see my country on fire for the fourth time in a century," Roman said coolly. "Poland has always fought valiantly against the odds, and we've successfully seen our way through many wars that have threatened our very existence. But one thing that war dogs like you seem to forget is the price of such conflict."

"That's where you're wrong. Every soldier I've ever met knows what they're there to do, and very few would cower in the face of the enemy. In fact, that price you speak of is something all of us should be willing to pay if it means the survivors get to see our country free and independent."

"Then I pray to God it doesn't come to that," Roman said, but Krupa just glared at him with a mixture of disgust and determination.

"Go ahead and give peace a chance, but don't be surprised when your backroom politics fail," Krupa said snidely. "But rest assured, when the people call on my troops for a more direct solution, we'll be ready to step up and get the job done, no matter the cost."

Sighing, because he knew Krupa was planning something big, Roman made a simple request of the grizzled warrior before him. "Just let me have my time before the Tsar," Roman said, bringing a smirk to Krupa's face, for never had he heard the maverick senator speak ill of the Premier in such a manner.

"We'll give you until the moment the bastard rules against us. That'll be the biggest mistake he ever makes, and the whole world will see how determined we are to be free."

"And then what?" Roman asked, but Krupa shrugged and took to his feet. "I want an answer, General. What are you planning?"

Having turned toward the door, Krupa looked over his shoulder and gave Roman his answer in the simplest way.

"If they dare question our resolve, war will be the answer."

Chapter 37

Senatgrad, Federal Special Region, Slavic Federation

It had been nearly three weeks since Audra left Gustav behind due to her inability to extend her leave from work. Gustav had since regained his ability to walk without crutches but was reduced to living in a hostel and working the night shift at the front desk to cover his expenses. It was certainly a cheap way of living while he waited for his check to come from the Fighting Commission, but it was lonely. At first, Audra called him every night to keep him company while he worked the front desk, but the last few days saw their calls becoming irregular and less satisfying. He was beginning to wonder if she was losing hope that he'd return, so he woke up that morning with a plan. He was going to go down to the Fighting Commission's office and see about the check he had been promised for weeks now.

Doing just as he planned, Gustav spared a few minutes to shower and grabbed a bite to eat from a street cart on the way to the offices. When he arrived, he approached the front desk with a friendly face and gave his name and business in English. While it didn't seem like the woman behind the desk spoke English, she nodded the moment she got his name and began paging through a stack of sealed envelopes. A few moments later, he had his check at last, but when he tore it open and unfolded the paper within, his jaw just about dropped to the floor. He was expecting a hefty sum considering the number of victories he had achieved in the tournament, but the sum stamped on the check was about half the amount listed under the gross pay section. Though he couldn't read Russian, he could see that there was a slew of charges that had chipped away at his earnings.

"Excuse me, do you speak Russian?" Gustav asked the receptionist, and she nodded. Pointing to the earnings statement, he asked if she could translate.

Willing to oblige Gustav's request, the receptionist went down the list, explaining that the reason his check was so low was due to the high tax rate for foreigners and the fact that his injuries required an ambulance. As it would turn out, income for foreigners was taxed at thirty percent – a rate that was exactly twice the rate paid by the wealthy class of the Slavic Federation.

His stomach twisting and churning at the thought of being stuck in Poland with no way to pay his medical bills conveniently, Gustav felt a panic attack coming on. So rushing out of the offices, he found a quiet corner in the hallway and took rapid breaths in a vain attempt to ease his chaotic mind and slow his racing heart. He soon took to pacing and tried to come up with a solution to his problem. Looking at his check again, the number struck him differently this time around as he realized he had enough to pay Richard back if he could somehow get home.

A desperate, sly grin slid across Gustav's stubbly face as he hatched a simple but risky plot to walk out on his debt to the local authorities and save his neck from the wrath of an impatient Richard Rozek. Doing so would brand him a wanted man, but the chances of him being tracked down for extradition seemed slim. Besides, he was a desperate man, and he was much more afraid of a ruthless gangster than a foreign government. Prison would be a vacation compared to what Richard Rozek might have in store for him.

His check safely tucked away deep inside his backpack, Gustav stepped into the terminal of Senatgrad-Passazhirsky, the largest train station in the region. Dressed casually to appear like an everyday traveler, he checked the departures and arrivals to see that there was a train leaving for Warsaw, but nothing headed toward Berlin. This was met with a sigh, but getting out of Senatgrad was a good first step, so he walked to the ticket booth and asked for a ticket to Warsaw. The clerk nodded before giving him a price and asking for his government-issued identification.

Gustav reached into his pocket and withdrew his wallet from which he took enough federal rubles to cover the price of the ticket. He then handed over his identification, and the clerk looked at it with a short glance before typing his name into his computer. A few moments later, he noticed a strange look of suspicion on the clerk's face. He was soon asked if he had anything to declare. Finding the question strange but keeping cool, Gustav shook his head and said he wasn't intent on leaving the country. The clerk nodded and handed his identification back. He was then asked to wait while his change was gathered and his ticket produced. Nervous, Gustav waited as his ticket was printed while his change was collected from an old register. When he was given what he was due, he headed toward the double doors that would lead onto the main platform.

Stepping outside, Gustav found an empty bench and slid off his backpack before taking a seat. His legs slightly spread apart, he leaned forward with his elbows resting on his thighs and began tapping his fingers together nervously as he stared at the ground. A sudden blare of the horn from a nearby train caught him off guard, and he sat up. In doing so, he spotted a pair of police officers walking down the platform. A wave of anxiety washed over him as he made eye contact with one of the officers. He began to wonder if the strange look the clerk gave his identification was because his name had come up with a temporary travel ban. He wasn't quite sure what the laws were in the Slavic Federation for someone attempting to leave the country without paying their debts, but he didn't want to find out either. So, grabbing his backpack, Gustav quickly slung it over his back and headed back inside.

Marching across the terminal, Gustav approached the ticket booth once more and asked for a refund. The Clerk gave him a confused stare, but he repeated the request and was challenged when he looked over his shoulder to see if the officers had followed him.

"Is something wrong, sir?" the Clerk asked.

"No, I just changed my mind," Gustav said quickly. "Please give me my money back."

Saying nothing, the Clerk took Gustav's ticket back and exchanged it for the exact amount he had paid for the ticket. However, Gustav was in such a hurry that he didn't even bother to collect the coins he had dropped on the floor after snatching up his cash.

Leaving the train station without incident, Gustav stopped by a bank near the hostel to deposit his check and arrange for a wire transfer to Audra. When he made this request, he was informed that, due to the fact that he was not a client of that bank, he couldn't request a wire transfer without a fee. Annoyed, Gustav asked what the fee was and grew bitter when he learned that it was quite steep due to two factors: he was not a registered client of the bank, and he was a foreign citizen. What this amounted to was a transfer fee equivalent to eighty marks back home – a price he was unwilling to pay. To make matters worse, due to the size of the check, he would need to open an account and wait a week for it to clear, regardless. Fortunately, opening an account knocked off about half the cost of the transfer, but the fee was still ridiculous in his mind. If there was one positive to note, it was that he would at least be out of Richard's debt when he finally got home. However, his troubles didn't end at the bank, as there was a piece of mail waiting for him at the hostel that further soured his day.

Normally able to pass the time until his night shift in some way, Gustav was unable to find pleasure in anything after reading the letter sent to him by the Senatgrad Ministry of Health Services. Apparently, he had been signed up for a payment plan structured for exactly one year. Considering he spent several days in the hospital and required specialized care, his bill was quite high; therefore, his monthly payment was crippling even for someone with a good job. To make matters worse, his first payment was due by the end of the week. His check would have easily covered it, but the bank had his account frozen for a week. This left him spending the day in a whirlwind of anxiety and physical sickness, though the latter was due to his inability to satiate his body's craving for the painkillers he had been prescribed at the hospital. Fortunately, physical pain was something he had long since become accustomed to dealing with, but the anxiety was driving him mad. He needed a plan. Unfortunately, the only idea he could conjure up involved getting himself deeper into debt with Richard, so when Audra finally called that night, he waited for the opportunity to ask for help.

"Is something wrong? You're unusually reserved tonight," Audra said, and Gustav sighed.

"I got a lot of shitty news today," he said glumly. "My check was taxed to hell, and the Health Ministry is ordering me to start making payments at the end of the week, but the bank is holding my check for seven days, and a wire transfer costs sixty rubles."

"Shit," Audra whispered, and Gustav concurred.

"Yeah, I'm not doing too well over here," Gustav replied. "Honestly, I considered just taking the first train home and going on the lam. They wouldn't extradite me, would they?"

"I don't know, but you shouldn't risk it," Audra warned. "You have a knack for making things go from bad to worse unnecessarily."

"Thanks," he said distantly. "I didn't realize I needed to know how much of a piece of shit I am."

Sighing, Audra apologized but stopped herself before she could remind Gustav that this entire mess was his own fault. Instead, she went quiet, and there was a long pause until he broke the silence.

"I know this sounds crazy, but I'm stuck here, Audra. I need help, and I know you don't have the money—"

"I'll do it," Audra said suddenly. "If that's what it takes, I'll do it. Just promise me you won't make this worse for yourself."

"What are you talking about? You'll do what?"

"I'll get you the money," Audra said. "I can take out a loan."

Though he was enticed, Gustav was quick to decline her generous offer. "You shouldn't have to go into debt to help me," he said, but then she spoke a little slyly.

"I have a feeling it would be interest-free," she said, so Gustav rightfully concluded her meaning.

"You're talking about Richard, aren't you?"

"Unfortunately, I am," Audra said, bringing Gustav to sigh deeply in frustration and regret.

"Don't bother, I have a plan," he said, after a sudden change of heart. "Getting in deep with the Syndicate would only make things worse."

"Not if I take out the loan," she said brightly. "He wouldn't charge his own sister interest. I'll come up with a good reason, too."

"I appreciate it, I really do, but you can't do this."

"Well, then, tell me what you plan to do. You're working at a hostel, Gustav. How are you going to pay back your debt in a year?"

"I'm going to join the Foreign Auxiliaries," he said bitterly, but she wasn't receptive to the idea.

"And you think borrowing money from my brother is a bad idea? You're talking about a five-year commitment that could get you killed."

"It's better than getting into debt with your brother. Besides, it's equivalent to fifty thousand marks a year, and it comes with official residency. We could finally escape your fucked up family."

"No, Gustav," Audra said firmly. "You're not joining the Auxiliaries. My brother did that, and he came back the man he is today."

"Your brother went to war. There's no war right now."

"There's a war in the Balkans. Who's to say they wouldn't send you out there like some worthless mercenary? After all, isn't that what the Foreign Auxiliaries are? A band of mercenaries sent to fight and die so citizens don't have to?"

"Basically," he said lowly. "But what choice do I have? I'm in debt to a foreign country, and my options are either to take money from a gangster or take my chances in a foreign army in peacetime. I think I'm better off with the latter."

"You're not," Audra said strongly. "Just give me some time. I'll get the money, I swear."

"Then promise me it won't involve Richard."

Sighing, for she couldn't make that promise in good conscience, Audra simply told him to stay out of trouble and that she would call him again another night. The call would soon end with Gustav unable to shake the feeling that she was going straight to her brother's club to ask for the money. He just hoped she had a damn good story and that her brother loved her more than profit.

Chapter 38

Berlin, Germany

Denied a bank loan that morning, Audra's heart was aching for Gustav, but she was running out of options to bring him home. She would spend the entire morning trying to figure out how to get him home without burying herself in debt or turning to less savory means, but nothing seemed feasible. With her shift at the bar fast approaching, she grew desperate and eventually left her apartment and made her way down to the Kitty Kat. Though she rarely set foot in that place, and never for recreation or work, she was instantly recognized and given the VIP treatment. She thanked the security guards with a smile, then made her way across the public area and to a red-carpeted staircase in the corner. These stairs led up to Richard's office and were guarded by two of the burliest, most intimidating men in her brother's service. Despite recognizing her, she was asked to submit to a frisking, but she told them to frisk themselves and ordered them to inform her brother she was there to see him. However, it was likely that Richard was standing in his floor-to-ceiling window to the left of the stairs, for she soon heard his voice ordering the guards to let her through via the walkie-talkies on their belts.

"Right this way, Ms. Rozek," a Guard said, and the pair opened the heavy carved oak doors that bore the family crest Richard had created – a blue and white heraldic shield emblazoned with a red Germanic rune standing in for the modern letter R.

Thanking the guards, Audra stepped through the open door and immediately saw an empty leather chair behind her brother's desk. The man himself soon walked across her line of sight and told her to follow in an odd tone of voice. Rolling her eyes, for her brother was clearly high, she followed him through a set of double doors that led into his private lounge that sat adjacent to his office. Once inside the lounge, Audra watched as her brother walked over to the wet bar, but was quick to tell him she didn't want a drink.

"Are you sure?" he asked, and she nodded. "Really sure?"

"Cut the shit, Richard. I didn't come here to hang out."

Turning to her with a more serious expression and an empty glass in hand, he asked her quite firmly to state her business as if she were wasting his precious time. His dramatic change in mood told her he wasn't high, though he was probably riding a wave of satisfaction from some other illicit means. Fortunately, the long walk over was more than enough time to iron out her story.

"I'm sure you've heard Heinrich's is for sale," she said, hoping Richard wouldn't catch the lie. "I'd like to buy it."

"Why would you want to buy that hole in the wall?" Richard asked, smirking with curiosity. "Sentimental value for our dear old dad? You know he never owned it, right? All that talk about losing it in a game of Skat was bullshit."

"Yes, I'm aware," Audra said, rolling her eyes, for she knew full well that their father was a degenerate gambler with a habit of telling tall tales, especially when drunk. "But look, I want to put my schooling to good use," she said. "Heinrich said he'd sell it to me, but I need to give him a down payment, and I don't have it. Would it be possible to borrow twenty thousand marks?"

"For my sister, of course," Richard said warmly. "But how will you go about acquiring the rest? I'm not a cash machine."

"We agreed on a lease-to-own plan," she said, bringing a proud expression to her brother's usually conniving face.

"All that time at Uni certainly made you industrious," he said warmly, but he paused as if something suddenly struck him wrong. "You know, there's a lot that can go wrong with a lease-to-own plan. In fact, I think it's a downright dangerous way to acquire a property."

"I'd rather not resort to your methods," she said, and Richard laughed. "Seriously, Richard. I want this to be my own legitimate business. No ties to you or your organization, please."

"Then perhaps you should get the money from somewhere else," Richard said with a sharp tongue and furrowed brow. "I'd hate for the Federals to come knocking at my door after they find out how a young bartender from East Berlin managed to come up with such a steep down payment."

"Look, I didn't mean to insult you. I'm just anxious about things, alright?"

"It's fine, but I need time to think about it. A bar in Marzahn isn't exactly a goldmine investment," Richard said. "Besides, do you even have a business plan?"

Her expression showing her impatience, Audra considered just giving up on the idea and going down to a pawn shop to sell some jewelry to cover Gustav's first payment, but Richard kept her attention.

"Look, all I'm trying to do here is ensure that I don't lose money and fall into debt. It's bad enough you have that paperweight weighing you down at home."

Nodding, Audra admitted she didn't have a business plan, but the timing was crucial as there were other interested parties in the bar. Of course, considering Heinrich's was something of a neighborhood dive bar, Richard didn't believe her.

"Give me twenty-four hours. I need to sit down with Karl and talk finances and legalities," Richard said. "I'm not saying no, but I am warning you not to get your hopes up."

"Thank you," Audra said warmly. "But what kind of interest can I expect?"

Chuckling, Richard asked if she seriously thought that he'd attempt to profit from his own sister. She shrugged, so he furrowed his brow once more and told her that he wasn't that evil.

"Since when?" Audra said in a joking manner, but while he wasn't amused, Richard smiled. She then left feeling like she would have some good news for Gustav very soon. However, as soon as she disappeared behind the two oak doors, Richard reached for a nearby phone.

Waiting for an answer, Richard had a determined expression as he stared at the floor-to-ceiling windows overlooking the club below. When he heard his confidant's voice, he got to business quickly.

"Karl, I need you to open the books and go over my finances. I'm looking to make a bold purchase, and I need to know if it's financially viable," Richard said. As expected, Karl was interested in knowing what his boss wanted to purchase, so Richard leaned back in his chair with a smile. "I'm thinking about buying my sister an early Christmas present for the ages."

Chapter 39

Redzikowo, Republic of Poland, Slavic Federation

Twenty days into Selection, only one man from Aleksey's platoon had given in to the temptation to quit after long complaining of a burning sensation in his foot. Unfortunately, that man was his old teammate, Kalinsky. Despite fighting through the pain for almost two weeks, the line was finally crossed when the GROM frogman suddenly fell to the ground, screaming in agony during their daily 'death march' at dawn. While he showed no outward affliction, Kalinsky told the medic tending to him that he was suffering from acute plantar fasciitis – inflammation of the thick band of tissue connecting the heel to the toes. It was surmised that he had failed to properly tie his boots before marching, or his boots were ill-fitting. Whatever the case, he needed medical attention, and the only way Linetty could allow that to happen was by sending him to the naval hospital at Gdynia. In doing so, Kalinsky would drop out of the program and return for a later selection, if physically able. However, he'd have to restart the entire program should he choose to return. Otherwise, he'd finish out his contract with his original unit.

While the loss of one man didn't do much to break anyone's spirit, morale was beginning to wane among the men as their meals were slowly reduced from three to two per day. This left the men hungry and irritable. When it came time for their midday march, one man made the mistake of arguing with the LTC over the purpose of another death march, resulting in a day at the beach instead. However, in this case, a day at the beach meant spending hours lying in the cold, rocky surf of the Baltic Sea. This was reminiscent of the training all frogmen had to go through, but their lack of sleep and hunger pangs caused five more men to give in to the temptation of coffee and a hot meal in town by the end of their day in the surf. This left their platoon at forty-four, which wasn't terrible considering the hell they'd endured thus far. However, that evening's physical challenge would help shave their numbers down a bit further to an even forty after a particularly grueling assault course.

Their stomachs hurting from having not eaten in almost twelve hours, and their bodies tired from their 'pre-dinner stroll,' the men faced an obstacle course that seemingly had gone up overnight. In reality, it had always been there but had been largely obscured from view by the lay of the land. At first glance, this was a standard urban assault course. The men were given a small amount of time to gear up in their standard loadout for their personal combat specialty and the nature of the course. When they were ready, they broke down into their usual squads and went through the course one squad at a time to avoid accidents due to the use of live ammunition.

By luck of the draw, Aleksey's squad was the first to be called to arms. Though he was the squad leader back in his old unit, that honor went to Miko, but that was fine. Aleksey never liked being the center of attention in a combat situation and was fine taking orders. So following Miko's lead, he and his compatriots made their way through an urban assault course resembling a typical Eastern European rural village. Using squad tactics, they made their way through the village slowly but surely. Their weapons were always at the ready, and their shots were always precise whenever a target appeared. It seemed as though they were going to pass through this scenario with flying colors, but as soon as they reached the end of the town's single block, they found themselves staring at a hellish sight.

Where the concrete road ended began a dirt path cutting through what appeared to be rural backcountry. This was a common scenario in the countryside, but as they approached the dirt road, they found a sign that warned of landmines and snipers. Though quite sure real snipers and landmines wouldn't be used against them, the men treated the situation as if the threat was real. Therefore, the only option was to crawl through the drainage ditches along either side of the road and through a culvert running under the crossroad further down the road. This wouldn't have been too bad had it not been for the fact that the ditches were not only draped with razor wire every few feet, making it impossible to walk or even crouch through ditches, but the air coming from them stunk something fierce.

It was obvious what was expected of them to do, so the men got to it. But when the first pair dropped into the ditch, their boots sank into the grass and weeds, revealing a stinking muck that they would have to crawl through. One man could be heard gagging at the stench, but neither he nor his compatriot opposite of him stopped until they reached the drain pipe. It was at that point that someone yelled out that the pipe stunk like death.

"Move forward!" Miko shouted from the rear, but the men were already making their way through the pipe. "All right, they're in the pipe. Tomashek, Rybinski, you're up."

Carrying out the order like they were in a real-life combat situation with a sniper about to zero in on one of them, Aleksey and Tomashek sprinted and dove face-first into the trench. When they hit the muck, both felt a churning sensation in their stomachs as the overwhelming stench of the watery sludge bombarded their senses, and their gag reflex engaged.

Wanting nothing more than to get out of this trench as fast as he could, Aleksey propelled himself forward with his elbows and knees. Each movement sloshed the putrid muck around, but Aleksey kept his lips tightly sealed and kept going until he was finally at the pipe. Though he couldn't see into the tunnel due to the fading daylight and position of the sun, Aleksey could tell that the man ahead of him was still inside and moving. He tried to call out his name, but opening his mouth and tasting the fumes caused him to gag uncontrollably for a few moments. Though his primal survival instincts demanded that he turn back, he felt inside the pipe and forced himself inside. When he attempted to pull himself up, he lost his grip and threw out his hands to avoid smashing his face into the edge of the pipe. When his hands hit the pipe, he found it too slick and felt his hands move forward, and his body followed with them. He felt his sleeve catch the edge of the pipe and heard the fabric tear away before a sharp pain overwhelmed his right forearm. His eyes lit up in horror as he realized he had just suffered an open wound in a ditch filled with what he had determined to be a mixture of water and excrement. Still, he forced himself forward, gritting his teeth against the pain until his head collided with the backside of the man ahead of him.

"Gurkin, move your ass, I'm wounded!" Aleksey shouted.

"I can't, I'm stuck!" Gurkin called back.

"Bullshit. Suck it in and move, god damn it!" Aleksey shouted, but the man ahead of him shouted for him to back off. Determined to make it through this nightmarish exercise, Aleksey pressed his hands against the man's rear and pushed him hard, but he wouldn't budge.

"I said I'm stuck!" Gurkin called out. "My shoulders are pinned! I can't move!"

Gritting against the pain and frustration, Aleksey told Gurkin he was going to pull him out. He then shouted to the man behind him, who was just about to enter the pipe, to back off because he was going backward. Over the course of the next few minutes, Aleksey worked against the pain in his arm to free his compatriot before forcing himself to trudge through the ditch one last but backward. When all was said and done, Miko and the other men on his side stood at the checkpoint, confused. As it would turn out, the pipe Aleksey and Gurkin attempted had narrowed, making it inaccessible for the average man to pass through. This meant that both men would have to go into the stinking ditch one last time before they could call for help. Fortunately, this was the end of the assault course, but by the time the final man made it through, Aleksey was already being looked over by Linetty. This would be the first time the men saw the kinder side of the LTC, for when he saw the extent of Aleksey's injury, he cried out for a medic.

Rushed off from the assault course by the medic on standby, Aleksey was taken straight to the infirmary, where his wound was cleaned, examined, and patched up. Despite the incredible pain he was suffering, he was returned to his unit shortly after, but this was by his own doing. He knew that if he went to a hospital, he'd be considered a washout and would have to return to his unit as a failure until the next session. Aleksey's face burned red with anger when he was reminded of this by Linetty, but he bit his lip and reassured the Lieutenant Commander that he could carry on. His reward for his determination was another run through the course.

Running the course the first time around was a challenge. Running it a second time with an injured arm and no one to help him through was a lesson in brutality. Every step of the way, Aleksey's arm throbbed as his body fought off pathogens attempting to break through the antibiotic barrier lying beneath the bandages. The pain was almost unbearable whenever he was forced to drop to the ground and crawl beneath an obstacle, but like a true member of the military elite, he forced himself through it all until he got to the cesspit. The first thing that came to mind was the pipe that had sliced him open and the threat the sewage posed to his wound. Looking to Linetty for guidance, he only got a stern expression in return. Gritting his teeth, he mentally prepared to bear the worst of it all, but Linetty was impatient.

"Come on, Rybinski. Get down in that shit before you get shot!" Linetty shouted.

Though knowing no one was going to shoot him, Aleksey acted quickly. Dropping feet first into the stinking muck below, he lowered his center of gravity by crouching. Walking like a duck with his legs spread wide and his feet pointed outward, he crept forward. The once-trivial maneuver learned in basic training proved to be a lifeline here, as he never once lost his footing as he made his way to the drainage pipes. As he approached, he glared at the one that had cut him open as if it were an enemy he was ordered not to kill.

Using only his good arm, he relied on his upper body strength to pull himself into the pipe. With his good arm flat and his wounded arm bent upward at the elbow, he forced his way through the pipe and dropped out from the other side in a tight ball, landing on his knees, soaking himself up to his waist in refuse. Ignoring the added discomfort, he forced his way to the end of the trench and climbed out to face Linetty. As always, he was standing with his hands folded at the small of his back and his expression cold and stern.

"Well done, Sergeant. You earned your right to stay."

Knowing what came next wouldn't be pleasant, Aleksey closed his eyes and tensed his body. A few moments later, he was doused with icy water sprayed from a hose with a pistol nozzle, and the spray didn't stop until he was visibly clear of sludge. He then marched off to the showers to properly clean up before heading for the infirmary to have his wound cleaned and redressed.

Patched up once more and sent on his way again, Aleksey entered the mess hall and found himself the center of attention. Ignoring the stares of his compatriots, he stepped into line, loaded his plate, and sat down at a table with his usual group. As he began to eat, he looked up to see Miko staring at him in awe.

"What?" Aleksey asked, but Miko was apparently in shock. "What? What the hell is your problem?"

"How are you still here?" Miko asked, but Aleksey shrugged. "Seriously, man. You got cut open in a cesspit. Why didn't they send you to a hospital?"

"They gave me a tetanus shot and cleaned the wound again," Aleksey said, but Miko shook his head in disbelief.

"That's it? What the hell kind of doctor do they have working here? That's not going to cut it."

Unsure of what to say, Aleksey quietly picked at his food, but Miko couldn't let it drop. He knew Aleksey was a tough man with an incredible tolerance for pain and the endurance to match, but like all GROM operators, he was trained in field medicine. A blood infection was nothing to take lightly.

"Listen, man, you need to tell Linetty that you need a real doctor."

"I'm not getting tossed out that easily," Aleksey said, but Miko was adamant about his friend's health.

"Would you rather lose that arm or die from the flesh-eating bacteria hiding in your ass?"

"No, but this has to be some kind of test. They're seeing how much pain and discomfort I can take."

"Maybe, but if that's the case, they're all insane."

"Such is the life we chose," Aleksey said, and he again went back to eating. This time, he kept quiet and avoided eye contact with Miko until the bell rang out and they had to head off to whatever physical exercise the leadership had planned for them for the rest of the night.

Chapter 40

Berlin, Germany

Originally scheduled to work just the night shift, Audra was unexpectedly called to work in the early afternoon, forcing her to cancel plans to go to the park and enjoy the nice weather for a few hours before another grueling night behind the pine. When she stepped inside, she expected the place to be empty, save for Heinrich, but she was caught by surprise. There was an unfamiliar woman behind the bar, a group of Huns lining the bar, and her own brother sitting back in a booth with a cocktail in hand.

Considering Richard would never waste his time in a place like Heinrich's, she certainly didn't expect him to be there, let alone have a drink among a bunch of outlaw bikers. Something was clearly off, so she marched over to her brother. Staring down at him with her arms crossed, she watched as he looked the place over like a man with an eye for art.

"What the hell is going on?" she asked of her brother, while the outlaws stared at her from across the room, but Richard was silent. "Richard!"

His eyes locking with hers, Richard smiled and raised his drink to her. "There's my beautiful, industrious baby sister."

"What the hell? Are you high right now?" Audra asked, for Richard was rarely this jovial toward her. "Where's Heinrich, and who is that behind the bar?"

"Heinrich went home, and that's one of my girls from the club," Richard said, taking a sip of his whiskey. "We were just holding the fort until you arrived."

"Well, I'm here, and you better have paid for those drinks."

"Yes, yes," Richard said, pulling out his wallet and tossing a one-hundred Deutschemark on the table. "Suddenly, one hundred marks is chump change around here."

"What are you talking about?" she asked, and Richard flashed her a fiendish grin. Audra's stern expression dropped, and she became worried. "Oh my god. What did you do?"

"Nothing bad, don't worry," Richard said. His gaze soon returned to his surroundings, but Audra grew suspicious.

"What's got you so interested in this place suddenly? It's the same hole-in-the-wall it's always been," she said, and Richard concurred.

"It sure is, but not for long," Richard said with a grin. "I'm confident you'll bring it back to its former glory."

"Oh yeah, like Heinrich is going to allow that," Audra said with a roll of her eyes. "There's a reason this place looks like it belongs in the fifties."

"Well, that's going to change soon enough. So why don't you humor me? How would you bring this place into the new millennium?"

Though suspicious of her brother, Audra indeed humored him with her thoughts on renovation. "Well, for one, I'd update the counters and stools, get some new tables, strip the tacky wallpaper, and replace it with warm colors. Most importantly, I'd install air filters since no one seems to see the no-smoking sign."

"Good ideas," Richard said, but Audra shrugged.

"Of course, it's not like I haven't suggested any of that to Heinrich a million times."

"Don't worry about Heinrich. That old boozehound is done dragging this place down," Richard said confidently, giving Audra a shudder of fear. "You have an appointment at the Notary's office tomorrow morning at nine. Don't be late. You know how those government assholes can be."

"What?" Audra asked with spiking concern. "What the hell did you do, Richard?"

Reaching into his sports coat, Richard removed a check written out to her for exactly the value of the property. He then told her that all she had to do was go down to the Notary's office, agree to the terms of the contract, and sign the document to become the new owner of Heinrich's Platz.

"Or should we rename it Audra's Platz?"

Taken aback by what she had just heard, Audra could only surmise that Richard had done something terrible to Heinrich. After all, the bar wasn't actually for sale as far as she knew. That was just a lie to get Richard to loan her the cash she needed to get Gustav home. She never expected him to finance the full purchase of the bar, let alone risk writing her a check from his personal bank account.

"I know you said you didn't want any ties to me, but I couldn't let you go into a lease-to-own contract," he said. "But you have my word that this will go smoothly. I don't keep dirty money in my private accounts, and the property will be completely in your name," Richard said. "As for old man Heinrich, he's getting a nice sum to add to his retirement account. Everybody wins, but you win the most."

"You didn't have to do this," Audra said, but Richard shrugged in a friendly fashion.

"We're family, Audra. We take care of each other from time to time," Richard said. "All I ask is that you bring this place into the modern era and make it your own."

"But how on earth will I be able to pay you back and update this place without putting myself into serious debt?"

"Consider me a silent partner," he said. "I'm not going to charge you interest, but I will take five percent of your profits until the loan is paid in full."

"Well, that's generous, I suppose."

"It's twenty percent less than my regular rate," he said, but he noticed she didn't seem very happy about this arrangement. He then made a bold conclusion, complete with a sly grin. "You didn't actually want to buy this place, did you?"

Her heart racing as she found herself cornered and unable to come up with an answer quickly enough, she stayed silent. In return, Richard nodded.

"What was that twenty thousand meant for, Audra?" he asked, but she remained silent, so he chuckled and leaned onto the bar. "You wanted that money to bring home your worthless boyfriend, didn't you?"

Judging by her silence and the mild contortions in her face, Richard knew he was right.

"Trust me, investing in this place over that idiot will be the best thing you'll ever do. You're going to go from a starving artist trapped in a dead-end job to a respected member of the community in short order, but don't thank me too fast. I know you get tongue-tied when you're excited."

"Thank you," Audra said lowly, but he wasn't through with her.

"It's going to be alright," he said reassuringly. "I'm going to send my best bartender over to be your right-hand girl. We're going to make this place a jewel of the neighborhood."

"What about Gustav?"

"Forget about that loser and move on," Richard said firmly. "He's been nothing but an anchor on your life. Not to mention, he's in debt up to his eyeballs on two fronts."

"Wait, two fronts?"

"Yes, he owes the Slavic Federation, and he owes me," Richard said, and Audra's stomach dropped.

"What do you mean he owes you?"

"You're better off without him. Let's just leave it at that," Richard said, but Audra demanded an answer, so he gave it to her in the simplest terms. "How do you think that perpetually broke fool conjured up the entrance fee for that tournament in Senatgrad?"

"Son of a bitch," Audra snarled, but Richard shrugged.

"I'm a businessman, sweetheart."

"Not you, him," Audra said, gritting her teeth as the anger took hold. "That stupid bastard! I can't believe he would deceive me like that."

"More reason to leave him to the rubbish bin of your personal history."

"No shit," she replied, absolutely seething at Gustav over this revelation. She then took a deep breath and regained her composure. "Thank you for this, Richard. Truly."

With a smile on his face, Richard warmly replied, "You know I only want the best for you."

She nodded, and Richard soon called for a round of schnaps to celebrate her new chapter in life. Though she wasn't much in the drinking mood thanks to the revelation of Gustav's debt to Richard, she went behind the bar to evict Richard's girl and fix the drinks regardless. A quick shot of schnapps would hopefully cool her anger.

Having just a quick celebratory shot of cherry liqueur, Richard and the Huns left Audra to her busy work behind the counter. This left Audra to sulk for a few hours as she thought of how she would confront Gustav. Though she didn't want to believe that Gustav would be so foolish as to borrow money from Richard, she couldn't think of a scenario in which Gustav would have been able to gather that much money on his own. After all, he was a notoriously bad saver, and though he did make a decent living in the fight clubs, he mostly pissed it away on frivolous crap after paying the bare minimum of his share of their expenses.

By the time Gustav's night shift at the hostel was to begin, Audra thought she had herself under control, but that was wishful thinking. Since Richard had left, she had downed three additional shots of schnapps to ease her troubled mind. While she thought she was calm and collected, her tongue was a little looser than she thought. Regardless, she took advantage of the empty bar and picked up the phone to call Gustav like she had been doing just about every night since she left Poland. When she heard his voice, she had to fight the sudden urge to go ballistic on him right out of the gate. Instead, she started calmly and worked her way to the confrontation by explaining that she was going to be the new owner of Heinrich Platz come Wednesday morning.

"You bought Heinrich's?" he asked, seemingly taken aback by the statement. "I thought you were going to ask for money to get me home?"

"I did, but my brother decided to do things his way," Audra replied, sighing through her nose before taking a firmer tone. "Besides, apparently, twenty thousand wasn't going to be enough to get you out of debt."

"What do you mean?"

"You borrowed money from my brother, Gustav."

"That's a lie," Gustav said quickly, but Audra was quick to call his bluff.

"My brother told me straight to my face!" she barked, the alcohol fully in control of her emotions. "How could you do that? He's a gangster--"

"Yeah, and he also hates my guts. Why would he tell you the truth if it means getting me home?"

"He wouldn't lie about something like that to me," Audra said, somewhat calmer. "I've put up with a lot of crap from you, Gustav. I stood by you even when you couldn't find work and kept a roof over our heads. I even stuck around after I heard you were going behind my back with other women, but this is below the bottom. You made a deal with the devil and look where it got you."

"First you claim I borrowed from your brother, and now you think I cheated on you? Are you drunk right now?"

"Shut up and listen to me, you idiot," Audra snarled, unwilling to admit that she was actually a bit tipsy. "I can't do this anymore. The lies, the aimlessness, the uncertainty, I'm sick of it all. I'm at the end of my road."

"What's that supposed to mean?"

"I think you know what this means."

Driven by fear and anger, Gustav went on a tirade of accusations. First, he tried to accuse her of cheating on him in Poland while he was fighting for his very future. Next, he blamed the struggles of their relationship on her intimacy issues and her obsession with money. None of this worked in his favor as she was through with his emotional abuse and manipulation.

"Stop projecting yourself onto me, you fucking loser!" she snapped. "I wasted seven years of my life waiting for you to get yourself together, and you took me for granted. And how dare you accuse me of being unfaithful! You practically ruined the entire idea of intimacy for me. You can rot alone in the filthy bed you've made for yourself. I'm done with you! Go to Hell, Gustav Hagen!"

Slamming the phone down hard, Audra stepped back until her back tapped the shelf behind the bar, causing the collection of liquor bottles to rattle. For a moment, she thought she was going to cry, but the tears never came. In time, her anger slowly gave way to a feeling of relief rather than sadness. Though she wished things had turned out better for them, she was actually feeling quite liberated. It felt as if a great weight had been removed from her shoulders. She was finally free from a loveless relationship steeped in lies and manipulation. She really was starting a new chapter in her life, and for that, she had her brother to thank. Of all people, her brother.

Chapter 41
Mława, Republic of Poland, Slavic Federation

Desperate to go home but out of options, Gustav took a bus down to the city of Mława. Let off a few blocks from the town center, he wandered the town, taking notice of the baroque influences on many of the older buildings, which clashed with the modern structures sprinkled in between. If he were with Audra, he'd be hearing the story about the architectural style and why it was so prominent in the town, but since he was alone, he only heard the wind whistling in his ears and the patter of the rain against his raincoat as he walked the empty sidewalk.

Reaching the edge of the town, he could see the military outpost in the distance. To his tired eyes, the outpost, shrouded in the mist and fog of the dreary morning, looked countless miles away. Already exhausted from a restless night and an uneasy bus ride from Senatgrad, he dreaded the thought of a long walk in the rain and the bitterly cold wind sweeping down from the Baltic. Regardless, he was determined to make his way to his destination, so he kept walking and increased his speed. A few minutes would pass before the sound of an oncoming diesel truck forced him off the pavement and into the muddy gutter just off the gravel shoulder. A delivery truck would quickly pass but would almost immediately pull over to the shoulder.

Relieved by this random act of kindness, Gustav quickened his pace and made his way to the passenger side door of the truck. First speaking in German, Gustav quickly remembered where he was and asked the driver if he could speak English. The driver nodded and asked him where he was headed.

"I'm headed to the military base down the highway," Gustav said, pointing his arm toward the outpost in the distance. His words brought a grin to the driver's face.

"Looking to join the Auxiliary, huh?"

"Yes, sir," Gustav said. "I need a fresh start."

"Don't they all," the Driver said. Automatic locks were suddenly disengaged with an unseen motion of his left hand. "Hop in. I'll get you there."

Grateful, Gustav tossed his duffel bag into the bed of the truck before climbing into the cab. Hardly a moment after he closed the door, the truck started back toward the road. At first, the driver was quiet and kept his eyes on the road. After about a mile, he glanced over at Gustav, who was staring out the windshield with a nervous expression on his face.

"Regretting your decision already?" the Driver asked.

"I'm sorry?" Gustav asked, and when the question was asked again, he shrugged. "I don't have the luxury."

"I've heard that before. Running from something back home?"

"No," Gustav replied sharply, but a few moments later he answered more politely. "Look, I ran into some bad luck and lost everything... my home, my woman, my dreams... everything."

"That's unfortunate," the Driver said. "Can I ask what got you to this point?"

"No," Gustav said bluntly. "It doesn't matter anymore, and I don't feel like talking about it. It gives me a headache."

"Sorry," the Driver replied. "Well, if it makes you feel any better, there's a light at the end of the tunnel if you make it through to the Auxiliaries."

"That's what I'm hoping for," Gustav said, staring out the windshield and wondering what life would be waiting for him when he got through the five-year commitment that he was about to surrender himself to. He went quiet for a few minutes before looking at the driver.

"Is it true what they say? Do Auxiliaries really get citizenship at the end of their contract?"

"That's not something I'd know," the Driver said. "What I do know is that it's not an easy life. They make you boys earn your place."

"That's alright. I'm accustomed to hardship," Gustav replied. "So long as a war doesn't break out, I'll be fine."

Though he wanted to warn Gustav against joining if he was worried about violent conflict, the Driver didn't see it as his place to speak. Instead, he told him he'd do fine if he learned quickly and followed his orders. The subject was soon changed to something more comfortable for the remainder of the journey. Gustav appreciated the change of pace as it helped ease his nerves.

Dropped off at the main gate, Gustav walked away from the truck with his duffel bag slung over his shoulder. The rain had died down to a miserable drizzle, but the guards tasked with watching the gate remained inside their small five-by-five concrete block shack until Gustav stood around dumbfounded for long enough.

Met with a single guard dressed in a transparent rain slicker over his olive drab standard battle dress uniform, Gustav greeted the soldier with a nod of his head. In response, he was asked to state his business. However, the question fell on deaf ears due to Gustav's lack of understanding of the Polish language.

"Do you speak German or English?" Gustav asked, just as he had with the civilian who had given him a ride from town.

"I asked for your business here," the soldier replied, speaking in natively accented German, catching Gustav by surprise. "I'll ask you one last time--"

"I was told I could join the Foreign Auxiliaries here," Gustav said quickly. "Am I in the right place?"

"Follow me," the German soldier said, and he led Gustav into his shack so that they could tend to their business away from the elements. After a quick frisking by a second man waiting inside, Gustav was ordered to produce his passport.

"It's in my bag," Gustav said, and the soldier nodded quietly.

Dropping to one knee, Gustav unslung his duffel bag and unzipped the front pouch. With one hand holding back the flap, he rummaged around with the other, eventually retrieving his passport. "Here you are," he said, offering the small leatherbound booklet.

With a cool expression, the German opened the passport and paged through quickly, confirming the information within with a grunt. It was all government records, so Gustav had no problem with being asked to confirm things such as his birthplace, birthname, and most recent residency, but didn't see the point of the questioning. When the soldier was through, he was asked if he was a fugitive from the law or convicted of a felony. Gustav was neither, so he answered without hesitation. Suddenly, the second man broke his silence, revealing an accent that Gustav couldn't quite figure out.

"Why do you want to join the Auxiliaries? You should have it good in the West, no?"

"I'm in debt and need a new start," Gustav answered, but before he could say more, the German soldier told him to step outside.

Fearful that he had somehow gotten himself disqualified, but not wanting to take any chances, Gustav stepped outside with the German leading the way. He was soon led to an awning above a rusty steel door and told that physical strength was a core requirement for a soldier of the Auxiliaries.

"Show me how many pull-ups you can do," the German said. "Use that crossbar. I'll keep count."

Taken off guard by the demand but remembering the Driver's advice, Gustav accepted the order without question. He soon took the necessary steps over to the awning and observed the crossbar in question. Though the rain was flowing down from the awning, the bar appeared dry under the fluorescent light fixed above the door leading to the other side of the gate. So, with a quick hop, he took hold of the crossbar and pulled himself up until his chin had risen an inch above the bar. He did five more without much effort before the soldier told him that was enough. Knowing he had passed this test, Gustav dropped back to the ground and looked over at the soldier with curious eyes. The soldier didn't say anything to him. Instead, he raised his radio to his mouth and spoke in Polish. After a few moments, someone replied, and Gustav was told to stand by.

Standing at proper attention, at least what he assumed to be as such, he waited patiently under the awning until told otherwise. In time, he was granted access to the outpost by a new pair of soldiers and marched off to the administration building for processing.

Seated in a small office occupied by an administrative clerk, Gustav went through the motions of enlistment. Once more, he was asked to provide proof of his identity. As the clerk checked his papers, he was informed that he would be subjected to a criminal background check and a medical examination before he could be considered for enlistment. None of this came as a surprise, though he was curious as to why they wasted time explaining the perks and benefits that came with enlistment in the Foreign Auxiliaries. However, he was pleased to know that the brochure he had acquired was up to date – for a five-year commitment, he would receive all the amenities a modern professional soldier could expect, plus the added benefits of permanent legal residency within the Slavic Federation and an untaxed salary of forty thousand federal rubles per year of service.

What he didn't know was that this meeting was just one of the many social and psychological tests he would be subjected to during the pre-enlistment process. In this case, the clerk was attempting to see if he understood what he was attempting to sign up for and if he was worth the investment the Slavic Federation would put into him. After all, life in the Auxiliaries was harsher than in the regular army, and they would be among the first to the front should an armed conflict ever break out. So, when the clerk had finished his work, he told Gustav he had two options. He could follow Sergeant Grech to the medical clinic or have him lead him out the main gate.

Faced with the options of carrying on down the path of joining the Auxiliaries or leaving with his tail between his legs, Gustav saw only one real option. He was there with a purpose, so with a determined tone, he made his choice in an instant. The clerk nodded, and Sergeant Grech was called in to escort Gustav on his way.

Leaving the offices, Gustav followed the tall, lanky Maltese sergeant to the outpost's medical clinic. It was here that he was met with an English-speaking doctor, who was quite friendly despite his gaunt appearance. The visit began with a questionnaire regarding medical history. When the questioning had completed, Gustav hadn't reported anything negative, which proved fortunate, for even a curable venereal disease was grounds for denial of enlistment. He was next subjected to a routine blood draw and urine collection to check for a host of things, from undeclared disease to the presence of drugs in his system. As with all other tests, Gustav didn't think anything of this and quietly submitted to whatever was asked of him.

When all was said and done, he was escorted from the clinic to a two-story concrete building that resembled the plattenbau apartment buildings found around Berlin's east side. This building served as temporary housing for prospects, and it was here that he was stripped of his personal belongings, given surplus olive drab army BDUs leftover from the Soviet era, and cut loose with a motley collection of men of varying ages, yet strangely of similar complexion. It seemed that the Auxiliaries only took men of European descent, for there was not a single man tanner than an islander from the northern region of the Mediterranean. However, he was too tired to think much about it, nor did he really care so long as he proved worthy of enlistment. He came to join the Auxiliaries, earn the money needed to pay off his debts, and move on with his life. Until he was officially sworn into service, he didn't give a damn about a single man in that room but himself.

Chapter 42

Redzikowo, Republic of Poland, Slavic Federation

After four exhausting weeks, Selection was coming to an end. This final week – colorfully referred to as 'The Culling' – was expected to be the worst nightmare for anyone who made it this far. Strangely, the week wasn't much different than the others that had preceded it. In fact, the only thing that appeared out of the ordinary was the fact that every so often, a single man would be called aside and disappear for a few hours. While most returned, others quietly made the long walk to the gates in bitter defeat. Those who refused to surrender and returned to their unit were dead silent about what they had gone through, as if petrified or sworn to secrecy.

By the fourth day of the culling, Linetty's company was cut down to half its original strength, with Aleksey hanging in the balance due to a nasty infection taking root in the days after the incident at the assault course.

In just twenty-four hours, the infection had given him a debilitating fever. Though he was given medicine to keep him well enough to get out of bed, the doctor on site urged him to go to a hospital to ensure he was properly tested and treated. However, he knew the rules of the program. Under no circumstances could he leave before the program was completed, or he'd suffer the penalty of disqualification. Therefore, he refused the doctor's suggestion, but he suffered greatly for this decision. Feeling worse than ever, he was struggling through the morning's physical training and was urged repeatedly to surrender by Linetty and Miko. Despite this, he fought against the urge to give up and forced himself through that morning's agenda. Though he proved himself tougher than the average soldier, when it came time for the midday death march, Aleksey looked to be on the verge of collapse.

"I'm not giving in," Aleksey said to Miko through a bout of chills as his friend urged him to ask for a medic as they marched.

"You're going to lose that arm or die from sepsis if you ignore it any longer," Miko argued, but Aleksey looked away and fought against the spasms throughout his body.

"I came here... for a... reason. I'm not... giving up," Aleksey said, speaking in short bursts. "They'll call... on me... soon. I'm going... to pass," he continued. A piercing whistle was soon blared, and the men were ordered into proper formation for the run.

His jog no better than a weak shuffle, Aleksey took his position and tried to avoid eye contact with Linetty, who seemed to be staring directly at him. In actuality, he was looking past him toward a pair of medics fast approaching with a collapsible stretcher carried between them at length.

"Sergeant Rybinski!" Linetty called out. "Fall out and go with these men."

Slowly turning to see to whom Linetty was referring, Aleksey was relieved to see the medics and looked to Miko with a weak smile. He then broke formation and went off with the medics, believing he had bested one of the most brutal tests yet.

Promised medical attention for his wounded arm and the fever ravaging his mind and body, Aleksey was taken away on a stretcher due to his inability to march at a regular pace. He was then given an injection to help with the pain and medicine for the fever, but his eyes grew heavy, and he drifted off while being carried to a truck. When he came to, he found himself tied to a chair and faced with a masked man who accused him of being a spy.

Confused as to how he could be accused of spying, Aleksey tried to defend himself verbally but was struck across the jaw with the back of his interrogator's hand. The Interrogator repeated his question regarding Aleksey's handler and struck him once more when he declared his innocence.

For the next three hours, Aleksey would be faced with accusations of espionage and treason. Remembering the training he underwent with Komandosów, he gave them basic information, such as his name, rank, and unit. However, each response only turned up the heat, so to speak.

Each time Aleksey failed to answer a question with a relevant answer, the interrogator climbed the ladder of progressive torture. It started with verbal threats of violence. When he failed to answer adequately, the interrogator began with physical torture. At first, he smacked him on the back of the head and the face, hoping to wear down his resistance. When they didn't work, he resorted to punching his shoulders, back, and gut. When that proved insufficient, more radical approaches were taken, such as snuffing out a cigarette on his forearm, bending his fingers back just far enough to cause excruciating pain, and hooking his nose and mouth with his fingers. All of this was done in an effort to force a false confession, but Aleksey stood strong against the torture, dutifully declaring his name, rank, and unit.

As expected, the more Aleksey resisted, the worse the abuse became until finally a knife was placed against Aleksey's throat. Just a soft press against his skin was enough to prove it could make his throat smile with a bit more pressure, but Aleksey was resilient. In fact, he dared his interrogator to kill him, claiming it would be a favor considering he would surely lose his arm or suffer brain damage if his sickness continued to go unchecked.

"We can cure you just as soon as you confess to your crimes," the Interrogator declared, but Aleksey wasn't buying it, nor did he possess the strength to raise his voice at that point.

"I'll die... before... I... betray," Aleksey said, his last bit of energy expended. His head soon slumped. Though he wasn't unconscious, he was fading fast and held a slipping grip on reality. He soon felt the blade pull away and wondered if what he was hearing was a figment of his imagination. Though he lacked the strength to look up at that moment, he could see that the legs of a second person belonged to a woman. Before he could ask who had joined them, he heard the voice of Colonel Kozak. This was the first time he had seen her since the first day, and though he should have been relieved, what he had endured had left him bitter and resentful. Regardless, he was too tired and sick to put up a fight. He was defeated, so he sat quietly, hunched over and suffering as the Colonel kneeled before him and looked up into his eyes.

"Congratulations, Sergeant Rybinski, you've been selected. Welcome to the unit," said Kozak, but Aleksey was too weak and out of sorts to reply. In fact, his body had become so weak that a bloody drool was oozing from his mouth. Seeing this, the Colonel looked up to the interrogator and ordered him to summon the medic at once. The same medics from before soon marched in to render the necessary aid.

Returned to his unit cleaned and patched up as best as possible, Aleksey took a seat beside Miko in the mess hall. Upon seeing the sorry shape Aleksey was in, Miko quickly noticed the distant look in his eyes and instinctively asked what had happened. Like a zombie, Aleksey's head turned slowly, and he looked at his friend with defeated eyes.

"I've been... selected," he said with a gravelly voice, unable to form full sentences from exhaustion and sickness. "But... I'm done. Get that... bastard... Linetty."

"Come on, man. Don't do this," Miko said, but Aleksey just stared at his hot, throbbing arm and shook his head.

"I'd rather... keep... my arm."

His eyes widening at the sight of Aleksey's infected arm, Miko couldn't believe that he hadn't been given medicine. So, jumping up from the table, he rushed over to Linetty and pleaded for him to get Aleksey medical attention. Though he said nothing, Linetty approached Aleksey and took him forcibly by the arm. Upon inspection, he looked into Aleksey's eyes and asked if he wanted to drop out.

"Sir!" Miko cried, but Linetty told him to shut up and fall back into formation. "But he needs help. He's dying!"

"And he'll get it... in Gdynia," Linetty said to Miko, prompting Aleksey to grumble something unintelligible. "What was that, Rybinski?"

Seemingly dying in his seat, Aleksey summoned the strength to look Linetty in the eyes and boldly repeated himself. "I said... fuck you... sir," Aleksey said, his voice so tired that he appeared to be on the verge of passing out, but Linetty simply grinned.

"Alright, let's go. You've suffered enough."

Despite the muscle spasms and the inescapable feeling of cold throughout his body, Aleksey marched shoulder-to-shoulder with the man who had pushed him through a living hell all these weeks. Though he had proven worthy of the unit, he couldn't bring himself to face another day in this nightmare. If that meant risking washing out and serving out his contract with his old unit, then so be it. GROM's training was brutal with a purpose. This was just plain barbaric.

Chapter 43

Gdansk, Republic of Poland, Slavic Federation

Spending just a few days at a naval hospital in Gdynia to get his infection under control and his fluid levels back to normal, Aleksey was essentially a free man until he received a clean bill of health from a military physician. Given that he was due to return to his old unit in Gdansk, he decided to ride out his recovery at his flat in Old Town.

Returning to the flat after breaking up with Tatiana was anything but easy, but thanks to wise words from Audra, he was able to drum up the courage to purge the place of her memory. He did so by tossing out any of her possessions, burning old photographs from their time together, and lighting incense to purify the air of her lingering perfume. In the days that followed, the infection had been purged from his body, and his bruises were starting to fade. However, his spirit was crushed by his refusal to carry on through the end of Selection. Even so, he was managing well enough by spending his days alone in his flat, entertaining himself with television, spy fiction novels borrowed from the library, and conversations with Audra over an online instant messenger program. Of course, he knew deep down that the day would come for him to report back to duty to serve out his contract. As well, he would have to call home and break the news of his status to his parents. He figured they would be relieved to know he washed out and wouldn't be serving with the shadowy faction. This would certainly help with the shame he felt for failing to achieve his goal, but he surely wouldn't have the heart to tell them what he went through in Redzikowo.

Strangely, the only person he felt comfortable talking to about his experience was Audra, as she was quickly becoming something of a confidant to him. He wasn't sure what it was about her that made him so trusting of her, but something was brewing between him that went beyond the skin-deep attraction he had for her since they first met. However, he was still working up the courage to break his silence on his more brutal experiences, particularly the incident on the assault course. Yet, when the opportunity arose to share his story further, he held back as usual. Something inside him told him that the story of his crawl through the collective excrement of the camp was something she could do without. All she needed to know regarding his injury was that he was recovering and would be back on his feet in a few more days. This statement hopefully put her at ease, for like a good friend, she had asked him every morning about his condition and how his recovery was going. He appreciated this, and when the chance for a change in the subject came, he gladly took it. However, the way their conversation ended that morning felt abrupt. He wondered if he had been too eager to see her again and if she wasn't too keen on seeing him as a result.

Dwelling on this thought through a long shower, he eventually emerged with the belief that he was overthinking things. What helped him come to this conclusion was her use of emoticons to convey her emotions, which always seemed to show her as a warm, caring person, and not at all impatient or uneasy, as his brain often defaulted to in their absence. So, believing that things were going well with Audra and that she might make the effort to see him before he went back to active duty, he went about his day just as he told her he would.

After his shower, Aleksey would sit down in his easy chair, prop up his legs, and get lost in the final James Bond novel authored by Ian Fleming. When he grew tired of reading, he turned his attention to the television until his alarm rang, informing him that it was time to head out for dinner with Uncle Roman. Though he wasn't exactly looking forward to dinner, for he knew it would be more business than casual, it was just one more hurdle he had to make on his way to normalcy.

Chapter 44
Mława, Republic of Poland, Slavic Federation

After days of living under a figurative microscope, Gustav was beginning to wonder what the point of all of this was. He came to this place to join the Auxiliaries - to be a soldier and earn money. Instead, he spent his waking hours stuck with a motley collection of social misfits. While most were happy with just sitting around and talking about what they'd do after they got out, Gustav was doing everything he could to stand out from the pack. Whether it meant working out on broken-down exercise equipment or using the limited library of books available in a language he could understand to study tactics and military history, he was keeping busy. This seemed to serve him well, for every day he woke up, he'd find that someone was missing, never to be seen again. Of course, rumors would circulate that the missing man got fed up and left or got cold feet. Gustav liked to believe that the authorities kicked them out. After all, since the day he arrived, he had been subjected to a variety of medical tests, drug screening included. Therefore, he clung to the idea that most of the people who got booted in the middle of the night failed their drug tests, which he was fine with. After all, the last person he wanted to be beside in a foxhole was someone battling addiction or withdrawal symptoms. As for him, he had nothing to fear but the fear of the unknown. He hadn't had a drink in weeks, and he never took hard drugs, so he kept right on his path of righteousness until the day came that he was ordered out of the gym and quietly escorted to the administration building.

Brought to the very same room where he met with the administrative clerk - now known to him as Staff Sergeant Rodic - but was instead met with the big boss himself, Lieutenant Colonel Radanovich, the regional commander. As with anyone of higher rank, Gustav knew better than to avoid eye contact and not give his respect with a salute and a short greeting. However, Radanovich didn't seem to care and ordered him to take a seat. As Gustav did as he was ordered, the Colonel took a seat and opened the manila folder he was holding.

"Hagen, Gustav. Born on the seventh of January 1972, in Bremen, Federal Republic of Germany. Last known residence: Berlin, Germany. Is that correct?" the Colonel asked, his forehead forming several creases as he looked up from the document before him.

"Yes, sir, that's correct," Gustav said, nodding slowly.

"Very good, and congratulations on making it this far," the Colonel said. Still, Gustav resisted the urge to smile, even as he believed he was about to be welcomed into the Auxiliaries. "You've proven quite dedicated to joining our ranks. However, I had you brought here to discuss some concerns with your character."

"Concerns with my character, sir?"

"Yes," the Colonel said lowly. "Tell me about your affiliation with the Marzahn Syndicate."

"There is none," Gustav said quickly out of fear.

"Is that so?" the Colonel asked curiously. "According to my sources, you're quite close to a woman by the name of Audra Rozek. Those same sources tell me she's the sister of a rather notorious real estate mogul, Richard Rozek. According to the Federal Security Service, he's a known ally of the Savyolovskaya Bratva, and the de facto leader of their German branch, the Marzahn Syndicate. Is the FSB mistaken, Mr. Hagen?"

"That's true, but neither of us has connections to the Syndicate," Gustav said calmly, but quickly breaking face with a nervous smile. "You can't pick who you're related to, right?"

"No, but you can pick who you associate with," the Colonel said. "Tell me how you met Ms. Rozek and how you ended up in Marzahn."

"We met at uni. I believe that was seven years ago," Gustav said, and the Colonel nodded, so he continued. "After graduation, we moved to Berlin. Oh, and for the record, her brother never liked me."

Seemingly ignoring Gusatv's nervous choice of words, Radanovich continued as planned. "What is your opinion of the Marzahn Syndicate?"

"Gangsters and scumbags, the whole lot of them," Gustav said quickly, but the Colonel smirked.

"Then tell me why you would associate yourself with a known syndicate enforcer," the Colonel challenged, but Gustav was puzzled. "You're aware of Jens Groth's membership in the Huns motorcycle gang, yes?"

"Yes, I'm aware, but he's simply my kickboxing coach. What he does in his personal life is none of my business," Gustav said. "He's a good coach, but he's not my friend or business associate by any stretch."

"Yet, he managed your run in a recent martial arts tournament in Senatgrad. Sounds like he's a business partner."

"He's my coach," Gustav said firmly. "In fact, he's the reason I'm even here at all."

"Is that right?"

"Yes, he took my earnings from the tournament and left me stranded. Excuse my language, but he's a dirty son of a bitch, and I hope to even the score one day."

"That's quite enough," the Colonel said, raising a hand to silence Gustav. "Let's shift gears for a moment. How about you tell me why you're even here?"

"I'm in debt to Polish government," Gustav answered, quickly explaining himself. "I owe for my medical expenses following the tournament."

"I can see how that would be a predicament, but why not ask Richard Rozek for the money? He has a reputation as a private banker, does he not?"

"You mean loan shark, and I'd rather be crucified, but I see what you're trying to do," Gustav answered with a hard expression. "I'm not affiliated with them, sir. I'm nothing more than a washed-up kickboxer with an ex-girlfriend who happens to have criminals in her immediate family. So, to better answer your question, I'm here for a fresh start. I want to pay my debt and start a new life as far from Berlin as possible. Is that too much to ask?"

"Not at all," the Colonel said. There was a brief pause before he cleared his throat. "I believe that is all for now. Sergeant Grech will be with you shortly."

"So, what happens now?" Gustav asked, but the Colonel remained silent and left the room, shutting the door behind him.

Left alone for around five minutes, Gustav wasn't sure what to think of the situation. He knew he raised his voice to the Colonel, and that wasn't a good thing in this scenario, but he felt justified. If that's what it took to convey his innocence, then so be it. However, when Sergeant Grech stepped into the room, his high spirits faded and his anxiety took hold, for held between the Sergeant's hands was a cardboard filing box with his name on it. For a moment, he feared the worst, but he quickly overcame his anxiety and told himself that his time had come. He was about to be given the official training uniform that he'd wear through basic training. However, when the box was presented to him, all he found inside was the small collection of personal belongings he had surrendered on the day of his arrival. His stomach sinking, he looked to Grech for answers, but the Sergeant was stone-faced as ever.

"Please, don't throw me out. I'm not a criminal," Gustav pleaded, but Grech remained silent. "I swear on my mother's life," he cried, but it made no difference.

Put out on the street for his apparent connection to organized crime, Gustav walked the streets of Mława, wearing the clothes he had originally arrived in while carrying his few personal belongings in his rucksack. The only thing that had changed was that he now had a wallet filled with enough cash to get him wherever he was going. However, unable to go home and unwilling to return to Senatgrad, he walked until he found a payphone. Reaching the operator and paying the additional fee, he was able to call Jens back in Berlin.

"Where the hell are you?" Jens asked after a short opening exchange.

"Someplace I can't even pronounce," Gustav said. "But look, I'm in trouble, man. I tried joining the Auxiliaries, but they threw me out."

"You did what?" Jens asked, but Gustav didn't bother to explain.

"It doesn't matter. I have enough money to get back to Senatgrad, but I'm stuck in Poland until I pay my debts. Audra dumped me, the Auxiliaries are a dead end, and I'm out of ideas. I need help, Jens."

"How desperate are you?"

"Desperate enough to sell my soul," Gustav said, knowing full well where this conversation might go. "Please help me. I just want to go home."

There was a brief silence before Jens asked if Gustav had a pen and paper handy. Of course, Gustav didn't have paper, but he had a pen, so pinning the handset between his shoulder and ear, he asked for the number and wrote it on his left palm. When he had it down, he asked who it belonged to, and Jens told him to take a guess. Gustav sighed at this revelation and thanked him regardless.

Hanging up the phone and taking a deep breath, Gustav took the handset in hand. Holding it against his shoulder, he raised the operator and paid the long-distance fee. He then punched in the number given to him by Jens, and within a couple of rings, he heard the voice of the closest thing to the Devil he'd ever met.

"State your business," Richard Rozek said with a stern voice.

"Mr. Rozek, it's Gustav Hagen."

"State your business," Richard repeated.

Unsure if Richard somehow knew about his predicament, perhaps waiting for this call to come at some point these last few weeks, Gustav swallowed hard before speaking.

"I'm in trouble and I need your help. I have nowhere else to turn. I'll do whatever it takes to get you paid back, I swear."

There was an eerie silence, but Gustav could have sworn he heard a chuckle. Sighing, he asked if Richard was still there.

"Yes, I'm here," Richard replied. "What do you need?"

"I need forty thousand Deutschmarks," Gustav said, but there was only an eerie silence once more. A few long seconds would pass before Richard replied quite simply.

"I'll consider it. We'll be in touch," Richard said, ending the call before Gustav could say another word.

"Fuck!" Gustav cried, slamming the phone back onto the cradle, for he had a reasonable suspicion that Richard had just written him off and would leave him to rot.

Chapter 45

Berlin, Germany

Taking to the single life well, Audra got into a workable routine of waking up with the sun and seizing the day, especially when she wasn't scheduled to work that day. She would often head straight to the bathroom to get cleaned up, clearing the way for her to utilize her free time most effectively. She would follow that with a quick, and usually simple, breakfast that she ate at the computer while chatting with Aleksey while he recovered. Of course, he didn't tell her what got him in the hospital, but she didn't care. She just enjoyed having someone to talk to.

Her shower out of the way and a simple breakfast of apple slices with peanut butter and a cup of black coffee atop her desk, Audra logged onto her computer. By force of habit, she logged into her instant messenger program and saw that only one friend was online – Jomsviking71. By the time she turned her attention to her email desktop icon, her screen was taken over by a text box. Jomsviking71 sent his usual greeting – "Good morning, pretty lady."

A smile lighting up her face, Audra quickly typed back in response. "'Good morning :-)," she wrote back, and their daily morning conversation was off to its usual start. At first, it was just a simple exchange of generic or obvious questions and statements such as 'you're certainly up early' and 'any plans for today,' but that was fine. Their conversations had a way of starting her day on a good foot, so as she answered his questions, telling him that her big plan for the day was to stand behind the pine and dream of going out on the town with him again, he replied that his day was basically more of the same – sitting around his flat and keeping his sanity through a steady diet of television, spy novels, and aimless walks around the city. The only difference in his routine that day was lunch with his uncle in Senatgrad. To Audra, that sounded mostly wonderful, for she was naturally an introvert, and sometimes the thought of standing behind the bar, hearing drunken tales of exaggerated glory and tired pickup lines, sounded unbearable. However, Aleksey lamented his situation, stating that it was a lonely way to be, especially when the day he'd have to return to active duty was fast approaching.

"It would be lovely to see you again," he wrote suddenly. "It sounds like you could use a couple of days away from the bar, too."

Sighing, for she certainly wanted to see him again, she didn't think she could. Of course, she carefully explained the unfortunate situation she found herself in. "I'd love to, I really would, but this stupid bar rules my life anymore," she said. "Honestly, getting up early and having these chats is what gets me out of bed some days."

"That's too bad," Aleksey replied. "On the same token, I'm honored to be the sunshine in your morning. Just don't work yourself too hard. You deserve time for your art and friends."

Yes, friends, Audra thought to herself, for she didn't have too many of those anymore thanks to the combined efforts of her time sink of a job, her idiot ex-boyfriend, and her brother running off most of her friends. Those who remained weren't exactly people she considered much beyond associates anymore, but she tried not to dwell on her own loneliness. Instead, she pivoted toward talking about the things closest to her heart.

"I finished a new painting the other day," she typed joyfully, though her emotions didn't quite show in the text box. "I'd love for you to see it."

"And I'd love to see it. Snap a picture and send it over," he wrote, but she declined.

"I don't have a digital camera," she said. "Perhaps you could come and see it in person ^_~."

"That would be fantastic, but I'm not allowed to leave the country for the duration of my recovery. Not my choice, of course. The government let me ride out my recovery at home in exchange for my silence on the incident."

Although Aleksey hadn't divulged the exact details of what had led to his suffering from a nasty infection that threatened his arm with amputation, she was aware that it was a training accident. Why the government would buy his silence piqued her curiosity, but she knew better than to press him for further information. She didn't want to get him in trouble, so she tried to raise his spirit instead.

"You know, there are worse places to be laid up," she said. "Honestly, if I could drop everything I'm doing and go back out there to be with you, I would in a heartbeat. I'm sure there's so much cool stuff to see in Gdansk, but I don't see a vacation happening anytime soon."

"What if I paid your way?" he asked, and while she appreciated his generosity, she had to decline.

"I own a bar, Aleksey. As much as I'd like to go, I can't just up and leave. Maybe in a few months, though. I'm interviewing someone to be my assistant manager this afternoon."

"Well, that's exciting. Perhaps things will get better," he wrote with hope in his heart.

"Perhaps, but we'll have to wait and see. Until then, I'm stuck in an endless cycle of work and sleep with a little bit of time for a hobby and talking with this cute guy I met on vacation."

"Then don't let me keep you," he wrote, but the lack of emotion in the text left her unsure if he was being kind or if he was annoyed with her.

"I'm talking about you, silly," she said. "I'd really like to see you again. I hope you know that."

"I know," he replied. "Is there really no way you can get away, even for a weekend?"

Sitting back in her chair, she pondered his insistence that she go out and see him. For a moment, she wondered if he really wanted her company or if he was being a creep, but she had never gotten an awkward vibe from him. He always presented himself as a decent person, so hoping to drop the subject without causing unnecessary friction, she wrote back.

"Give me some time. Maybe I can work something out. This candidate sounds promising," she replied. "But hey, I have about an hour before I have to head out. Would you mind if we talk again tonight? I'd like to paint a little before I go."

"Yes, of course. Talk to you later," he replied. "And good luck with your interview. I hope they work out for you."

"Me too, thank you. Enjoy your time with your uncle. You're fortunate to have family that cares to see you."

"I'm fortunate to know you care, too," he said, but the message came just moments before she logged off. This left her feeling a little sheepish, but he tended to carry on after the conversation had come to its logical conclusion. Of course, there were worse character flaws to have, so she didn't mind it so much. However, she wasn't lying about wanting to get some painting done before heading down to the bar for twelve hours before the pine. So, logging off her computer, she took her empty plate and coffee mug to the kitchen sink and headed back to her living room, which now doubled as her studio. However, when she looked upon the empty canvas before her, she found her inspiration was lacking. Wanting to save face, though, she rejected the idea of logging back onto the computer and chatting some more or even wasting her time with an internet flash game. Instead, she went out for a nice, long walk before work. She would use the time to think about her conversation with Aleksey and her growing feelings for him.

After wandering around the city for a while, Audra walked through the alley shared by the bar and the music shop next door. Entering through the side door that led directly into the storeroom, she stepped inside to find the lights on and music playing. Confused, for she didn't recall leaving the radio on when she closed the night before, she moved quickly into the public space of the building. It was here that she found a blonde woman about her age standing behind the pine dressed in the exact uniform Audra and the other bartenders wore. However, she had never seen this woman in her life and was surprised to learn that this woman, who introduced herself as Klaudia, was apparently her new assistant manager.

"Assistant manager? Since when? I don't think I've ever seen you before," Audra said, truly puzzled by this woman's words, especially her sincerity and calmness.

"Since the owner assigned me here," Klaudia said, but Audra smiled and shook her head.

"That's impossible. I'm the owner," she said, and Klaudia reacted with genuine confusion.

"Strange. It was my understanding that this was a property of Mr. Rozek."

Her eyes widened for a moment, Audra had a feeling that something strange was at play. Her brother was no stranger to elbowing his way into situations and taking control. Therefore, something told her Richard's uncharacteristic generosity in buying the bar for her was nothing more than a thinly veiled business venture.

"Excuse me," she said quickly. "I need to make a phone call in the back."

Leaving Klaudia at the bar, Audra went into the back room and walked down a short, narrow hallway that led to the office. Closing the door behind her, she dropped into the worn leather office chair and grabbed the phone atop its receiver on the equally worn-out wooden desk that had been there since before she was first hired.

Dialing her brother's cell phone from memory, Audra leaned back into the chair and felt it dip back as she waited for the ringing to stop. When she heard her brother answer, she went on the offensive.

"Who the hell do you think you are?" she asked sharply, and judging from the chuckle, he knew exactly why she was so riled up. "Who is that woman behind my bar?"

"The lovely Klaudia Pesch," Richard said calmly, and without hesitation. "Not to worry, she's one of my best. She managed the Kitty Kat for the last two years."

"I don't give a shit!" Audra snarled. "This is my bar. You have no right to hire people on my behalf."

"You're working way too much for your own good. You need time to yourself, so I took the necessary steps to alleviate that problem. If I were you, I'd be more grateful."

"You have no right—"

"On the contrary, I do," Richard said coolly. "Until the debt is settled, you're leasing the property from me."

"You said you're a silent partner!"

"I will be... once the debt is paid," Richard replied, so Audra groaned her regrets for accepting his generosity.

"There's always an ulterior motive with you, Richard. Even with your own sister. You're such a bastard!"

"Calm down, you're blowing this out of proportion. She's very good at what she does and will help you turn that place from a shithole into a goldmine. Trust me, I know a lot about making money."

"Fine, but if you want to be involved, then at least tell me next time. I had an interview scheduled for that position."

"Hire them on, too. You could use the help. Your bar is about to become a neighborhood hot spot, I guarantee it."

"I wish I could, but I can only afford one assistant manager," she said, but Richard was quick to state that Klaudia was still on his payroll and would remain so until the debt was paid. Although Audra should have been grateful, she remained cautious.

"I can't allow that, Richard. If people found out you're involved, the authorities might think this is a front."

"The authorities will think that regardless. You're a Rozek, are you not?"

"Unfortunately," she replied, and Richard snickered.

"I can't help but feel like you resent me," Richard said. "Perhaps you should take a good, hard look at your current situation and learn to show a little gratitude. Did I not take on the burden of helping Aunt Astrid raise you when Jens couldn't be bothered? Did I not help you with your schoolwork and get you on the path of success? Dammit,

Audra, I've done so much for you over the years, and this is how you treat me? You think I'm some two-bit conman?"

"Richard, I—"

"You'd better shape up or you'll be finding a new place to live. Oh, and as far as your boyfriend goes, he'd better pray you don't piss me off further. He's damn lucky I'm willing to bail him out again to make you happy. And yet here you are, ungrateful as ever."

Richard's reference to Gustav's predicament reopened the wound of their breakup, and his dig at her apparent ungratefulness stung sharply. Audra wanted to shout at her brother for even bringing him up, but she relented. Instead, she quickly recalled that no one in Berlin knew that they had broken up, and for a moment she thought of challenging Richard's threat, but her curiosity and lingering care for Gustav overpowered her.

"What do you mean you'll bail him out?"

"I don't talk business of that nature over the phone," Richard said, but Audra didn't sigh. Instead, she asked where he was at that moment. "The club, where else would I be?"

"I'll be there in ten minutes."

Marching down to the club, Audra slipped past the team of bouncers guarding the front entrance and made her way through the dimly lit gentlemen's club. Heading up a red-carpeted staircase, she came to a brief halt at the doors leading into the second-floor VIP suite that served as her brother's private office. The exchange between her and the guard was brief. She was almost immediately allowed entry as if the guard had been ordered to allow her through without question.

Stepping through the double doors to the office suite, Audra spotted her brother leaving his private lounge with a drink in hand. As was always the case for anyone in his organization above the status of a common thug, Richard was dressed sharply in a pricy designer suit, but she paid no attention to this. She was there to get answers, not admire her brother's keen sense of style.

Looking at his watch, Richard remarked that she might have set a new land speed record for stomping over from Heinrich's Platz, but she wasn't amused.

"Tell me what new business you have with Gustav," she said firmly, so he held out his hand and asked her to take a seat.

Complying with her brother's request, she took a seat across from his desk about the same moment that he sat down. However, he took his time answering the question. Instead, he savored his drink and eased back into his seat, causing her to grow impatient.

"Today, Richard," she groaned, and he smirked.

"You seem tense. Would you like a drink?"

"Stop stalling," she commanded.

"I got a call out of the blue from Gustav. Apparently, he's desperate enough to ask me for another favor."

"Is that so?" she asked, crossing her arms. "What has he gotten himself into now?"

"Why would I know something you wouldn't?" he asked, but she rolled her eyes. "Well?"

"Because I broke up with him a month ago," she said. "But that's beyond the point. What has him so desperate that he'd turn to you?"

"He tried to join the Foreign Auxiliaries and failed to make the cut," Richard said. "He's desperate to come home and apparently suicidal. Good work, you broke the poor bastard."

"He brought this on himself," Audra said, unmoved by the revelation that Gustav may be considering ending his life. "You still didn't answer my original question, by the way."

"He asked for the money to pay his debt to Poland," Richard said, but Audra remained unmoved. "You're really not worried about him?"

"No, he's nothing to me at this point," Audra said bitterly, and Richard nodded.

"Well, you're going to have to pretend that's not the case. I need you to go out there and make sure the money gets into the right hands."

"Yeah, that's not going to happen," Audra said quickly. "I'm done with him. He can rot for all I care."

"Such anger, he must have really messed up," Richard said, and Audra shook her head, whispering that he had no idea. "Regardless, you're the only one who can ensure he isn't going to run off with the money."□

"What about Jens?"

"Jens made a questionable decision during his last visit to Senatgrad. Let's leave it that," Richard replied. "With that being said, you're going and that's that."

"I'm not doing it," Audra said, quite resolutely.

"Well, that's the problem, little sister. You're in no place to deny me. You owe me for the bar, and until I'm paid in full, I can and will make your life a living hell."

"I own the fucking place! My name is on the land contract," Audra argued, but Richard shrugged.

"Sure, but you're also living in my apartment complex rent-free. Unless you feel like living in your dingy little office, I suggest you play ball."

"Let me get this straight. You're telling me my options are to screw my ex-boyfriend into debt slavery or end up homeless," she asked, and he nodded mischievously. "Where did our mother go wrong with you?"

"You're making this harder than it has to be," Richard said, ignoring her jab. "Gustav made a deal, fully understanding that I don't do this sort of thing out of the goodness of my heart. I reserve my kindness for you."

"I think you should look up the definition of kindness," Audra said with a narrow stare. "I'm not a gangster. Send one of your thugs if you want to make your money back."

"All I'm asking for is a small favor in return for the large favor I did for you," Richard said. "Do this for me and I'll ease up on the leverage. I know I'm being a prick, but it's all a matter of righting the balance."

"Yeah, whatever," Audra said, grimacing. "What do I have to do?"

"I just need you to go to Senatgrad, ensure the money goes to the right place, and that he comes home. How you convince him to come back is on you."

Sighing, Audra accepted the burden her brother had thrust upon her, but it came with a condition. "Fine, but I'll need a couple of days."

Nodding, Richard leaned over and opened a cabinet hidden behind his desk. When he sat back up, he tossed her a plane ticket and gave her three days to get the job done.

"Make it four and it's a deal," she said. "And I want someone I can trust to watch over the bar. I don't trust strangers with my property."

"Don't worry, Klaudia is going to amaze you," he said. "There's a reason why I sent her."

"Perhaps she will, but I don't know her," Audra said.

"I'll send Erik to keep an eye on the place," Richard said, referring to one of his bodyguards she was familiar with.

"Fine, it's a deal," she said, and she left shortly thereafter.

Chapter 46

Senatgrad, Federal Special Region, Slavic Federation

Roman had set the dinner reservation for the top of the hour, but wanting to appear punctual, Aleksey took the ferry from Gdansk and arrived in the federal capital more than an hour early. Burning the extra time going about town, he arrived at the restaurant ten minutes earlier than arranged. Heeding his uncle's advice, he went dressed sharply in a newly purchased outfit consisting of black slacks, a glossy red dress shirt, and polished leather loafers. It wasn't quite his style, but he wanted to blend in with the crowd. However, when he walked inside, he found that the good senator was nowhere to be found. Figuring he would arrive within the timespan of a single drink, Aleksey went to the bar and ordered a vodka tonic instead of his usual beer. Never feeling quite comfortable in high-class restaurants, Aleksey kept to himself and drank slowly. As he sat, he thought about all he had been through in Redzikowo, but shook the thought and focused on his lady friend over in Berlin. Thinking about Audra helped him relax as Roman appeared to be running late. However, even fond memories eventually failed to keep him from growing annoyed by his uncle's lateness.

Finishing his drink, Aleksey paid his bill and walked over to the maître d'. Giving his uncle's name, he was informed that he didn't have a reservation. Confused, Aleksey said that was impossible, so he was kindly shown the reservation list. To his surprise, he found his own name on the list. Rather than question this, he nodded and admitted the mistake was his own and was shown to his table. Seated alone, he put in his drink order and began to peruse the menu. Before he could decide, he heard his uncle's voice.

"Well, well, well, if it isn't my favorite nephew," Roman said, prompting Aleksey to set down the menu with a grin. However, as he looked up, he found that his uncle wasn't alone. Standing beside the good senator was Elena Zmarlak of the Office of State Security.

Though it wasn't quite the classic bait and switch, Aleksey wasn't pleased to see the spy handler, for he had a feeling she was there on business. Nonetheless, he offered her a friendly expression and greeted her.

"You remember, Elena, right?" Roman asked as he pulled Elena's seat in a gentlemanly fashion.

"Yes, of course," Aleksey said, reaching over to shake her hand, reaching only her fingers with a feint grip due to the distance between them. "You look lovely as always, Ms. Zmarlak."

"Thank you," Elena said with a toothy smile. "You look well, all things considered."

Easing back into his chair with an uneasy smile on his face, Aleksey's head swiveled between the pair, unsure of who would speak next. For the next few minutes, the group engaged in small talk until their dinner orders were made and their drinks freshened. It was then that the ulterior motive of the meeting was unveiled.

"Elena tells me you managed to survive qualification and were welcomed into the unit. Congratulations."

"Is that what you heard?" Aleksey asked, speaking with a mildly sarcastic tone before taking a long sip of his drink. Though he expected Roman to look at Elena with suspicion, Aleksey's tone didn't seem to register.

"I even heard you made it through the interrogation module while suffering from a burning fever. Well done, my boy," Roman said, clearly impressed. "You know, Elena had a hand in putting together that module. Truly a hellish experience I'd imagine."

"Quite so," Aleksey said, his stare burning into Elena's soul as he seethed over what he had endured. "The interrogation was one of the worst experiences of my life. Thank you for that, Elena."

"That's not where you got that injury, right?" Roman asked, nodding at Aleksey's formerly injured arm.

"No, I got that while crawling through a trench filled with piss and shit," Aleksey said bitterly, still staring at an eerily calm Elena. "Cut my arm on the edge of a drainage pipe and developed a nasty case of sepsis for my troubles. Should I thank you for that, too?"

"No, you can thank Colonel Kozak. Her philosophy behind the program is that war is hell," Elena said coolly, bringing Aleksey to frown at her lack of empathy.

"Her program certainly lived up to that philosophy. Well, at least my war is over, huh?" Aleksey said, putting a fresh drink to his lips, only to be caught by surprise.

"Not quite. You're expected to join your new unit after your next medical exam."

"Excuse me?" Aleksey asked with anger and surprise. "There's no fucking way--"

"Watch your language," Roman interjected, but he was ignored.

"What I went through was nothing short of barbaric. Men were dropping like flies due to the stress and pain inflicted upon us. If that's what is expected of that unit, consider me a washout."

"I understand your frustration, but the course was designed to separate the wheat from the chaff," Elena said, but Aleksey shook his head with disgust. "Don't be so hard on yourself. You proved yourself tougher than most. You earned this."

"I don't want it," Aleksey said defiantly. "Either send me back to my old unit or kick me down to the reserves. I want nothing to do with those maniacs."

"You're making a mistake, Aleksey," Roman warned, but Aleksey remained defiant.

"The only mistake I made was trusting you," he said, snatching his napkin from his lap and throwing it onto the table. "You both can go to hell for all I care."

"Aleksey!" Roman called out, but Aleksey stomped off like a petulant child. However, he wasn't going to let him walk out without explaining what was at stake.

A fast walker, Aleksey easily outpaced his uncle and made it halfway down the block before Roman emerged from the restaurant. Continuing to ignore the furious senator, Aleksey continued his way until he heard the heavy thumping of derby shoes on the pavement. Stopping in his tracks, Aleksey turned to see Roman running his way. Though he wasn't a dishonorable man, the sight of a portly middle-aged man running his way was rather amusing, especially when Roman's lack of an exercise routine was exposed by his exasperation upon reaching him.

"Now you listen... to me... you indignant shit!" Roman snarled between breaths, but Aleksey turned and started off. "Get back here, god damn it!"

"Follow," Aleksey replied simply.

Left with no other choice, Roman sprinted up to Aleksey's side and kept pace with him despite his lungs burning terribly in his chest.

"What the hell is the matter with you? Did your parents forget to teach you respect for your elders?"

"Oh, they did, but you crossed the line back there."

"How? What did I do to deserve such disrespect?"

Stopping suddenly, Aleksey turned to his uncle, anger showing on his face. "You sold me out!" he shouted, before boldly accusing his uncle of impropriety. "You knew what was going to happen out there!"

"I didn't," Roman said, but Aleksey knew he was lying and started off again. Forced to sprint up to his nephew's side once more, Roman gave in to the truth. "Look, this isn't the place to do this. Let's go back to the restaurant, have a good meal, and we'll go somewhere and talk."

"Go fuck yourself," Aleksey said, prompting Roman to grab his nephew by the shirt and twist the fabric in a tight grip.

"Now you listen to me! I'm your only way out of this situation. Disrespect me again and I'll let them know you're on your own," Roman said, quickly finding Aleksey leaning in close, clenching his teeth.

"Are you threatening me right now?" Aleksey questioned fiercely.

"No, I'm warning you. You're in too deep to give the finger to someone like Elena and walk off without consequence. Now come on, I can smooth this over. Just keep that mouth shut unless you're going to be pleasant."

"What the hell's going on?"

"I'll let you know after dinner. Just play it cool. We're on the same side here. You're my nephew, my favorite sister's son. I don't want anything bad to happen to you."

"Well, it's too late for that," Aleksey said, referring to his arm, but Roman shook his head.

"That'll be the least of your worries if you don't listen to me. Now let's go."

Forced to sit through dinner with Elena, Aleksey dodged her questions about what he went through at Redzikowo but remained civil. When the last of their dishes was cleared and the bill was paid, Elena was the first to leave, but she did so with a warning. If Aleksey didn't report back to Redzikowo, he'd lose everything he'd worked for these last ten years. Though taking this as a threat, Aleksey remained calm and assured her that he'd live up to his agreement. What followed was a tense few minutes from the table to the car, for the valet wasn't quite on top of his game that night. All the while, nothing was said between Aleksey and Roman until they climbed into Roman's luxury sedan.

"Look, I want to say that I'm sorry for getting you into this mess," Roman said, but Aleksey just stared out the window with nothing to say. "I know you probably want to punch me in the face right now, and you'd be in the right, but I need you to know that I had your best interest in mind."

Turning to his uncle with determined eyes, Aleksey boldly declared, "I'm not going back."

"I don't think you have a choice," Roman said, keeping his eyes on the road. "They'll take everything you've earned from the service. You'll end up no better off than when you first stepped off the bus at basic training. Do you want that?"

"My father would never allow it," Aleksey said, causing Roman to sigh.

"Aleksey, I'm going to be honest with you. When the secession happens, and it will happen, your father won't have any say in the Polish military."

"What are you talking about?"

"He's a Federalist. What do you think?"

"Bullshit. That's just a façade to keep the Premier off his back," Aleksey said, but Roman shook his head.

"I saw how he voted. He voted to stay," Roman said with disappointment in his voice and heart. "Even if he resigns from his post and claims loyalty to Poland, there won't be a place for him in the new army. He's on the blacklist, and you will be too if you don't listen to me."

"Did you see my vote, too?"

"Yes, and I'm proud of you. I didn't expect you to be a nationalist. Seems there's a bit of Wilczynski spirit in there after all," Roman said with a faint smile. "Nonetheless, you were selected for Poland's answer to Alpha Group, but I'm sure you're already aware of that."

"Indeed," Aleksey said, his eyes staring blankly through the windshield. "So, what's the deal? What do I have to do to keep my name off the blacklist?"

"Right now, the only way is to go through with whatever they say, but I have an idea that just might work."

"Yeah, and what's that?"

"I drafted a non-disclosure agreement," Roman said. "It's in my bag. We'll go over it, you'll sign it, and I'll do what I can to make it stick."

"Wait, what's all this about? You're acting like this is a top-secret program."

"That's because it is," Roman said eerily. "But look, the less you know, the better. Something tells me you're not past the point of no return just yet."

"I'm lost," Aleksey said shruggingly. "Nothing out there that was out of the ordinary. Well, except for the interrogation. That was beyond messed up."

"Right, and if you can agree to keep your mouth shut, I just might be able to smooth it all over."

"I've got nothing to share with anyone. It was just a simple selection program," Aleksey said, and Roman smiled.

"Exactly."

Brought back to his uncle's condo, Aleksey sat on the couch with Roman and looked over the draft of the non-disclosure agreement his uncle had apparently put together. At first, it was just a lot of legal jargon, but after having it explained, Aleksey realized it was an ironclad agreement with severe consequences. In short, in exchange for being allowed to return to his former unit, Aleksey was officially never an attendee at the training camp at Redzikowo; he would never speak to the press or seek legal restitution for his injury; he was an avowed secessionist with no loyalty to the Slavic Federation post-secession, including a vow to abandon his citizenship; he would serve his remaining ten years of military service unless rendered physically unable; he would never seek political office or officer candidacy. Any violation of this agreement would have severe legal consequences, including loss of military benefits and imprisonment.

While it was certainly a hard pill to swallow, especially considering Aleksey felt that the agreement was far too severe for what he had seen, he willingly signed. Though knowing there was a chance that the agreement would be tossed into the fire, and he would be forced to serve with Rapid Response regardless, Aleksey figured it was worth a try. Another ten years in the service wasn't as bad as it sounded, so long as he could transfer to the reserves at some point. Also, giving up his citizenship in the Slavic Federation wouldn't be a problem since he had already planned to stay in Gdansk post-service. However, the threat of imprisonment and loss of benefits didn't sit well. He couldn't understand what was so secretive that he had to be threatened with financial and social ruin, but that was the price he had to pay to get out of this situation. However, signing the agreement didn't give him the relief he had expected, and when he left his uncle's home and boarded the ferry back to Gdansk, he felt no better.

Halfway across the bay, Aleksey had purchased an overpriced beer from the bar and was leaning on the railing, staring at the water below. He took a long drink from the bottle and stared out toward the horizon. Gdansk was in view, and if it were light out, he'd have a great view of the bay and the surrounding city. Regardless, the city lights were beautiful, but they got him to think about how things have changed for him. He used to sit out on the balcony like this with Tatiana and stargaze, but now there was just an empty seat beside him whenever he went outside. He wondered if that seat would ever be filled and if it was, would it be Audra? He chuckled at the thought, for he found it ridiculous that he was falling in love with a woman over the internet, but the moment was quickly dashed when his eardrums were bombarded by a sudden roar. Believing someone had opened fire or a bomb had gone off, Aleksey hit the deck, but quickly realized the ferry was fine, but the explosions continued.

Taking to his feet and looking out at the water, Aleksey saw a massive series of orange fireballs lighting up the darkness over the bay far in the distance. Though caught off guard, it was painfully obvious that a ship had just exploded. Whether it was a military or civilian vessel was unknown, but whatever it was, it was a large ship, and it likely happened near Gdynia. A cold feeling of dread suddenly ran down his spine as he wondered if this had something to do with the secession - a black swan event, or perhaps even a false flag.

Chapter 47

Senatgrad, Federal Special Region, Slavic Federation

Nearly a full day after an explosion aboard a ship in the Bay of Gdansk, citizens and politicians alike were gathered for the Premier's press conference. In Senatgrad, members of the Polish Liberation Party sat silently as they watched a television screen airing a live broadcast from the Premier's briefing room in Moscow. With no one at the podium, the image dominating the screen was that of the seal of the Premier of the Federation. Behind the podium stood three flags: the Republic of Russia, the Slavic Federation, and the royal coat of arms of the defunct Russian Empire. Though the flag of the Federation should have been centered with the others flanking it, both men took notice of the fact that the coat of arms held the center position. This made Roman chuckle when he first noticed it, but his amusement was short-lived, for it wasn't long before the Premier appeared from stage left and took to the podium. As always, he was perfectly groomed and sharply dressed in a black suit with a red tie, but this time he had a naval insignia pin on his lapel. This, too, caught the eye of the Polish senators and was met with silent scrutiny as the Premier began his speech.

"Good evening," Sergei began, speaking in Russian but with Polish subtitles displayed at the bottom of the screen. "I've come before you all to address the tragic incident aboard the Russian naval ship Varyag. At my personal command, the incident is undergoing a close, surgical investigation by the very best within the shared Military Intelligence apparatus and the Department of the Navy. Thus far, it has been found that the ship had suffered a series of devastating explosions within one of the ship's forward magazines while undergoing inspection. The explosions have been determined to have begun in the front-most magazine, creating a chain reaction due to an improperly sealed bulkhead. Despite media reports around the world, there is no evidence that this was an act of terror or sabotage. However, should this prove to be an act of terror or sabotage, it is my solemn vow that we will find those responsible and bring them to justice."

Roman smirked at the Premier's mentioning of the shared military intelligence apparatus, for as far as he was aware, it was only the Russian GRU and FSB that were involved. As well, he couldn't help but silently accuse the man of lying when he declared the cause of the explosion as anything but an act of terror or sabotage. After all, the Varyag was the flagship of the Russian Baltic Fleet. Ceding it to Poland in an apparent show of goodwill was no doubt a sore subject in Russia.

While the Premier continued to speak, neither man remained invested in his discussion of the geopolitical situation, or the state of Polish secession.

"It was sabotage," Roman said immediately

"No doubt," Bednarz said. "I never expected them to play fair."

With a tired gaze, Bednarz turned his attention back to the television set and listened to the Press badger the Premier with questions regarding the incident, secession, and the like. Nothing stood out until one bold reporter asked about rumors that the Varyag had been sabotaged.

"Mr. Premier, is there any truth behind the claims that this was the work of Polish separatists? Perhaps the so-called Polish Liberation Army?" the reporter asked.

The question grabbed their attention by the throat, and Roman felt his body become hot as the Premier answered. Though inactive at the moment, the Polish Liberation Army was a top-secret endeavor that only a handful of people were aware of. How this reporter knew about it was shocking, and he could feel the President-elect's ire as if he believed Roman was responsible for the leaking of their contingency plan to the media.

"The Polish Liberation Army? I'm not aware of any such organization," Sergei said, though Roman wasn't sure if that was a lie. Of course, the Premier's expression and tense body language made it appear so, especially as he dodged a follow-up question. "Next question, please."

"Mr. Premier, Moscow Times," another reporter asked, and the Premier nodded. "Will the bombing of the Varyag have any effect on the upcoming Special Session of the Senate?"

"First and foremost, this has not been ruled a bombing, an act of sabotage, or an act of terror," Sergei said firmly. "Secondly, unless there was an outright assault on the Senate, the Special Session will go on as planned."

"Then, considering the incident's proximity to the federal capital, will there be a military presence in Senatgrad ahead of the Special Session? If so, what forces will be involved?"

"While the incident is presently being treated as a tragic accident, there will most certainly be a strong military presence in the days leading up to and through the Special Session. This decision comes at the recommendation of my top military advisors and will be handled in unison by local police forces and the nearby army garrison."

The questions would continue flooding in, and most, if not all, seemed to revolve around the idea that the explosion aboard the Varyag was an act of terror or sabotage. Despite Sergei's insistence that the government was treating it as an accident until evidence proved otherwise, Bednarz and Roman read between the lines. They could see the Premier was playing sleight of hand, and his regime had ordered the reporters to ask these questions to put the idea of terrorism into the public's psyche. This gave them both a feeling that another attack would follow to justify the deployment of military forces in and around Senatgrad, and perhaps to even cancel the Special Session in the name of state security. If that were truly the case, they needed to ensure that his contingency plan wasn't compromised. Everything needed to go to plan if he was going to ensure that the government didn't steal his country's best chance at freedom.

Turning to Roman, Bednarz looked at him with cool, inquisitive eyes. "I surely hope you didn't let anything slip about our contingency plan," Bednarz muttered, clearly referencing Roman's assurance that Aleksander could be trusted. "I told you he wasn't our ally."

"I told him nothing of the sort," Roman defended, but Bednarz grimaced.

"We took a massive risk trusting a federalist—"

"He's not a federalist," Roman said, but Bednarz snapped back.

"Well, he sure isn't a secessionist, and it wasn't me that told him about the contingency, I'm certain it wasn't Krupa."

"Are you seriously accusing me of leaking our plans to the federals? Family or not, there are some things I keep close to my chest, and operational security is one such thing."

"Well, someone talked, and it's a small cadre of people with the knowledge of what Squadron C is up to," Bednarz said. After a few seconds, his eyes lit up as if he had a eureka moment. "Your nephew. He was part of the program, wasn't he?"

"He doesn't know any more than anyone else who went through the program. As far as he knows, the whole thing was just selection for a new unit," Roman said calmly. "Besides, it's been taken care of. I had dinner with him last night and made sure he's kept quiet."

"Then you better hope the federals don't actually know anything, or there's going to be hell to pay."

"He's headed back to Squadron B and will be out of the way," Roman said, but he soon pointed his index finger at Bednarz and clenched his teeth. "But let's be very clear here. President-elect or not, no one threatens my family, Filip."

His gaze morphing from cool to almost terrifyingly cold, Bednarz responded in kind. "If it means keeping the movement on track, I'll cut down your entire family tree."

Stunned by his colleague's Sergei Medvedev-like comment, Roman knew better than to cross the former general and nodded slowly. He then vowed to ensure that Aleksey stayed quiet and that his brother-in-law knew what was at stake. This was enough to appease Bednarz, but it left Roman feeling uncertain and fearful of his own movement.

Chapter 48

Moscow, Republic of Russia, Slavic Federation

Uninterested in the Premier's speech, Katrin and Lena were in the kitchen preparing dinner when the phone rang. Passing the stirring spoon to her daughter, Katrin walked over to the phone and answered it. Though she was fully expecting it to be Aleksander calling to tell her he would be late for dinner, she heard the voice of her brother.

"Katarzyna, my dear, sweet sister," Roman said cheerfully. "How are you doing this evening?"

"Roman, my dear brother. What did I do to earn the honor of this most unexpected call?" Katrin said sarcastically, for she had a feeling about the nature of the call.

"Did you watch the bastard's speech?" he asked, groaning with disdain.

Katrin rolled her eyes. "No, I have more important things to do," she replied. "And no, I don't need to be filled in. I'm sure it was the usual crock of bullshit. Federation good, Poland bad."

"Indeed," Roman said coolly. "Regardless, I have a favor to ask."

"No," she said immediately. "I'm in the middle of cooking dinner."

"Your dinner can wait. This involves us all," Roman said, speaking out of fear that she might hang up. "This was a false flag. I can feel it."

"I don't know what that is, and I don't care."

"Don't play dumb, you know what that means," Roman said, so Katrin got firm.

"Look, my husband is General of the Army, and you're a senator. You're playing with fire and threatening to burn us all."

"Proving this was an inside job is integral to our cause," Roman said, but Katrin was done.

"I'm not going to jail for you, Roman. Sorry, but don't call again if this is what you want to talk about. Goodbye," she said, and a moment later she slammed down the phone in anger.

"Mom?" Lena asked, still standing before the stove. "Is everything alright?"

Sighing as her body shook from the adrenaline flowing through her veins. "No, I'm afraid your uncle is trying to get himself killed."

"What?" Lena asked in surprise, but Katrin was quick to calm her with just a raise of her hand.

"Not literally," she said. "He's convinced that the ship that blew up last night was done by the government."

"That's crazy," Lena said, and Katrin nodded, but Lena's fear got the best of her. "Wait, can you get in trouble for even suggesting that on the phone?"

"No, we'll be fine," Katrin said calmly. "Your father refuses to talk to him anymore because of all this. If they're listening, they'll know that fact."

"Ok, good, but there's definitely something rotten with that incident," Lena said, pausing nervously for a moment. "Uncle Roman is a smart man, and he's on the intelligence committee. Why would he think the government would do such a thing without proof? Surely, he knows something, right?"

"Perhaps, but I think the stress is getting to him. It's making him go mad," Katrin said, though she was truly inclined to believe the idea of a false flag attack. She just didn't want to get involved for the sake of her own family.

"I hope he doesn't get himself into trouble. He's a huge asset to the Cause," Lena said, and though Katrin voiced her agreement, the sound of the garage door's motor alarmed her.

"Ok, new subject. Your father's home."

Doing as she was told, Lena turned back to stir the sauce while her mother set the table. Not long after, Aleksander stepped into the house through the garage, which fed into the living room. The moment the door was closed behind him, all eyes were on him. He furrowed his brow at this, but Katrin was quick to welcome him home with a hug and a kiss while Lena pulled the roast from the oven with two mittened hands.

Happy to see his wife, Aleksander embraced her a bit longer than usual before walking to the front hall of the house to remove his jacket. He returned a few moments later to sit down to dinner with his wife and daughter. For the first few minutes, everything was calm and happy, but Lena couldn't contain herself for long and asked if there was anything new about the bombing of the Varyag.

"It was an accident, not a bombing," Aleksander said coolly. "There was probably a gas leak in the magazine, and some poor sailor tried to sneak a cigarette."

"That's strange, wouldn't someone notice that before lighting a cigarette?"

"I don't know, but it's a problem for the Department of the Navy and Military Intelligence to solve," Aleksander said, clearly sick of the subject after poring over documents and sitting through meetings related to the incident most of the day. "Can we just enjoy dinner without bringing up military affairs?"

"Sorry," Lena said sheepishly. "I'm just taken with the whole thing."

"It's alright, I just have a feeling there's another reason you're asking," Aleksander said, his eyes shifting to his wife. "He called, didn't he?"

"Yes, but I didn't give him the time of day," Katrin said, and Aleksander nodded.

"Good. The further we get from the fiasco back home, the better," Aleksander said, before turning his attention back to the slice of roast on his plate. "How was your day, love?"

There was an awkward silence for a few moments, so Aleksander looked up to see that his wife was contemplating something. He sighed at this and chose to end the conversation with a firm statement. "If this was the work of extremists, they only hurt their own cause."

"Our cause," Katrin said, but Aleksander shook his head. "Are you not Polish anymore?"

"Until the day I no longer wear this uniform, I'm a senior officer of the Slavic Federation," he said calmly, "Besides, you know where I stand."

Katrin nodded, and the dinner continued in silence for several minutes until Lena changed the subject to Aleksey and her belief that he might have a secret girlfriend. This brought a smile to Katrin's face, and though Aleksander couldn't care less about his son's personal life at that moment, he feigned interest in hopes the subject of the Varyag and secession was dead for the day.

Chapter 49

Senatgrad, Federal Special Region, Slavic Federation

It was late in the evening, and the Senatorial Palace was mostly empty. Though there were a few offices lit up against an array of blacked-out windows, no one of prominence was still on the grounds. Rather, the lights were either left on by accident or a night cleaner taking out the daily trash as they made their rounds. However, typically the cleaning duties were done by now, but a sick call left an unlucky Gustav to clean the entire building himself. What was normally a four-hour job turned into eight, but he was at least fortunate enough to be paid by the hour rather than a fixed salary. Still, Gustav was working two jobs to keep his head above water, and he was keen on getting back to the hostel as soon as possible to catch up on sleep.

Negating basic security procedures to get the job done faster, Gustav was making record time as he made his way through the building with that in mind. As a result, he didn't check his corners as much as he should, nor did he make his presence known before entering rooms. This typically wasn't a problem, considering the place would be deserted until the next morning. However, when he stepped out of the elevator and into the basement, he was surprised to hear two men talking.

Curious as to who could be down in the basement at this time of night, if at all, considering the space was nothing more than a storage space for janitorial supplies and a shelter for times of extreme weather. Though he should have retreated and called the authorities, Gustav was driven by curiosity to abandon his mop and bucket in the elevator and investigate for himself.

Creeping down the hall toward the source of the voices, he stopped short of the small bathroom near a secondary storage room filled with old furniture. As he drew closer, the conversation at hand became much clearer, giving him no doubt that the intruders were inside. Unsurprisingly, they spoke in Polish, but his command of the language was limited, so all he could understand was bits and pieces. Regardless, what he was hearing piqued his interest, bringing him to creep a few paces toward the door to better eavesdrop on the conversation at hand. What he was hearing caused his heart to beat intensely, but he couldn't pull himself away.

"... all I'm ... is something feels off ... this one," he heard a voice say.

"I feel you, man, but ... is what we do," said the second speaker, his accent thicker than the other, making him harder to follow for Gustav. "We .... get paid .... the Lord's work ... you ..."

"Yes, but I ... can't .... this is a setup. This is .... government. We blow ... and ... all dead."

Realizing he had to get out of there, and fast, Gustav carefully turned on his heels to sneak away, but he soon heard the click of the lock on the bathroom door. His brain commanded his legs to launch into a sprint, but his body wouldn't react. All he could do was tense up and raise his hands, for just moments after he heard the lock disengage, he heard a gasp and the distinctive clicking of a pistol. He had no doubt it was pointed right at his back, but before he could turn around, he felt a strong tug at his collar and felt himself falling. However, he was soon in an embrace that was anything but loving. A pistol poking against his neck, he heard a grunted command and was forced first to his feet and then into the bathroom.

Now pinned against the wall of the cramped space, Gustav felt a terrible strain as he craned his neck to lessen the pressure of the pistol held to his neck. Though he tried to avert his eyes, he could see that they were wearing security uniforms, but he had never seen either of them before.

"What the fuck did you hear?" asked the man he believed to be the first speaker, though the language barrier was made apparent when Gustav blurted out in German. The man smirked and repeated the question in almost perfect German.

"I didn't hear anything," Gustav choked out through the tension. "I'm just a cleaner. Just let me go. I won't say a word."

"No dice," said the Gunman, while his compatriot stood back silently. "We're going for a walk and then we'll have a little chat."

"Please don't kill me," Gustav pleaded, but the men said nothing. "Please, I just want to go home."

Looking down at the identification badge worn at Gustav's chest, the Gunman took the card between his fingers and looked it over. "Gustav Hagen, Civil Service," he muttered. "What kind of clearance do you have, Gustav?"

"If I tell you, can I go?" Gustav asked, but the gun was suddenly pressed harder into his neck, making it feel like his artery was going to explode.

"I'm asking the questions!" snarled the Gunman.

"All-access," Gustav said quickly. "I can get you anywhere you want to be. Now please."

"Help us out and we'll see to it you get at least one more sauerkraut and bacon sandwich in your belly."

Swallowing hard, Gustav nodded quickly and agreed to whatever they wanted. In turn, the Gunman put the weapon away.

"Then here's the plan, Gustav Hagen. The three of us are going to walk out of here together. We're then going to have a little chat with our boss, and figure things out from there. If you try to run or call out for help, we'll grease you right then and there. You got it?"

"Got it," Gustav said with a quick, nervous nod of his head.

"Let's go."

Brought to a rented flat in a town outside of Senatgrad, Gustav was confined to a bedroom with one man guarding the door from the inside while the two from the Senate basement talked things over with the apparent man in charge. Though he could hear an argument through the door, he couldn't make out a single word. Then again, even if he could hear them in perfect clarity, he would have had trouble understanding the boss at all. The man's thick accent and slang-riddled vocabulary would have kept a native speaker on their toes. However, they would have been able to accurately guess him as a soldier, for much of his slang was army jargon. Yet, even if he knew anything of that, Gustav didn't care what they were saying so long as it resulted in him living to see another day.

Secured only by the armed man at the door, Gustav got as comfortable as he could in the stiff armchair on which he was seated. His knees bent at a right angle and his elbows set on his thighs, his face was buried in his hands, and his eyes were clenched shut. He was sure he wasn't going to make it out alive, so he contemplated his life up to that point and tried to think of better days. His concentration would only be broken by the thumping of heavy boots on the hardwood floor. The leader, a man known to his men as Captain Sobczak but referred to only as Zero, soon entered. His first word was a simple 'out' to his subordinate standing watch. The door was then closed, and Sobczak stood before him in a pose common among military officers.

"Alright, German, let's talk," Sobczak said, his voice gruff but his German good. "I just had a good, long talk with my men. They say you might be of some service to our mission here."

"I'll do whatever you need," Gustav said, and Sobczak grinned.

"That's good, very good," he said. "I'm told you have full access to the Senate complex. Is that right?"

"Correct, sir."

Nodding, Sobczak stroked his bald chin, running his thumb down the prominent crease in the center. "You ever been in a fight before?"

"I'm a semi-professional kickboxer," Gustav replied, lighting up the soldier's face.

"Is that right?" he asked, and Gustav nodded. "Maybe you are more useful than I thought."

"What do I have to do?"

"You'll find out soon enough," Sobczak said. "For now, we need to come to an understanding. You were never here, you never saw me or my men, and you know nothing about nothing, understood?"

"Ok, then what?"

"You go back to whatever hole you call home and wait for the day we scoop you up for your big, important job," Sobczak said. "Just let it be known that we'll be watching. If we catch wind of you talking to the authorities, the press, or just acting off, we'll make you disappear."

Chapter 50

Senatgrad, Federal Special Region, Slavic Federation

A few days had passed since Gustav had his run-in with the men plotting against the government in Senatgrad, but nothing had happened yet. In fact, he hadn't even seen a single sign of someone watching or following him at all. He wondered if they had second thoughts about whatever they were planning and called it off. Whatever the case, he went about his life as if nothing had transpired by reporting in each day for his morning janitorial duties at the Senate offices and returning to the hostel to catch a few hours of sleep before lunch. However, when he stepped into the lobby of the building, he was caught by complete surprise – there sitting on a chair, seemingly waiting for him to return, was the last person he thought he'd ever see again.

His heart pounding as he made eye contact with Audra, Gustav was overcome by surprise and joy. However, when he tried to speak, his tongue was tied, and he could only babble like a fool. Though he expected a smile at his clumsy words, she remained stoic even as she approached.

"Hello Gustav," Audra said, speaking without much emotion. "Is there somewhere we can talk?"

His hopes running wild that she would come to work things out, Gustav nodded quickly and told her to follow him. He soon took her to his dorm, but when the door was closed and he tried to embrace her, she thrust him back in apparent anger and disgust.

"What the hell are you doing? Back off!" she scolded. "I'm not here because I want to be."

Surprised by her actions and hurt by her words, Gustav took a few steps back without breaking eye contact. He then asked why she bothered to see him.

"My brother sent me," she said. "Apparently, you didn't learn your lesson the first time."

"Oh, fuck you!" Gustav snarled, but Audra was unfazed. "Does it look like I have a choice here?"

"Look, I just want to get this over with," Audra said, before turning her attention to the messenger bag she was carrying, which doubled as an overnight bag and purse. She soon produced a cashier's check written out to Gustav from one of Richard's front companies.

"I was expecting cash," Gustav said, but Audra shrugged.

"I guess it's a matter of security," she said, bringing Gustav to roll his eyes. "Do you have time to go down to the bank and make a deposit, or should I come back later?"

"Yeah, let's go," Gustav said bitterly, for though he was being bailed out, he knew this wasn't a grant. Richard Rozek was going to add the sum on the check to his overall debt. Regardless, he led Audra out of the hostel and to the nearest bank.

Standing back with her arms crossed as Gustav deposited the check, Audra had an expression that showed she was impatient and terribly unhappy with being there. Throughout her time at the bank, she occasionally looked around the room and toward the door as if she was feeling uneasy or suspicious. In time, she was getting unwanted attention from bank tellers and the security guard posted at the door. Considering the nature of the transaction, she approached Gustav and touched his shoulder as a lover might do. She then asked what the hold-up was.

"Give it time, this is a secure international transaction," Gustav said as he stood at the teller's desk. "She needs to confirm things, you know."

"Fine, whatever," Audra said with mild frustration in her voice. "Just hurry up. I want to go home."

"You know, you don't need to stick around. The government garnishes my wages and deposits automatically."

"I need to see proof of deposit," Audra said, knowing Gustav might just take the money and run.

"Suit yourself," he said, and he turned his attention back to the teller who was still on the phone with the bank manager.

Stepping back a few paces, Audra waited until the teller returned and confirmed to Gustav that the check was legitimate and that the transaction could be completed. About a minute later, the transaction was finally completed, and Audra had her proof in the form of a banking receipt that showed the money had been transferred to the account Gustav had specified.

Seemingly satisfied, Audra turned to leave, but Gustav asked where she was going. Turning back to him with an annoyed expression, she asked why he needed to know.

"I was hoping that maybe we could get lunch, and well, you know."

"No," Audra said bluntly, so Gustav shook his head.

"I didn't mean it like that. I just wanted to talk. Maybe figure out what went wrong and how we can fix it."

"There's nothing to talk about, Gustav. We're through, and nothing is going to change that."

Sighing at her response, Gustav pitifully asked if he could at least have one last hug. Audra grimaced at the thought of letting him touch her, for her anger and sadness over their failed relationship had given way to disgust and contempt. However, rather than outright decline, she turned her back to him once more and walked out, leaving him to accept that she truly was done with him.

Feeling defiant for a while, Audra walked down the street and made her way back to the very same hotel she stayed at during her last visit. However, it was a long walk, and as she got further along the avenue her adrenaline rush faded, and her defiance went with it. The hard expression she held the entire time she was near Gustav softened, and her buried emotions began to surface. As much as she wanted Gustav out of her life and to move on to happier days, seeing him among the dregs of society and treating him so poorly out of spite only reminded her that there were still some lingering feelings in her heart. Though she wouldn't say that the lingering feeling was love, for that feeling had died long ago, she couldn't help but feel bad for him. He was a professional screw-up, and no one made him take money from gangsters, but she couldn't help but feel partially responsible. Had she argued against going to Senatgrad, he might have been spared this troubling fate. Yet, at the same time, had she not been supportive of his dreams, she'd still be stuck in a loveless relationship with an uncertain future. So, as she reached for the handle on the front door of the hotel, she quietly accepted that perhaps his deal with Richard was inevitable, and quite possibly the best thing that could have happened to her. After all, she was free from a loveless relationship and was a business owner now. She even had a cute guy waiting for her at the hotel bar for a quick drink before a day in town. If she played her cards right, she might snag herself a love affair with a man far better than Gustav could ever hope to be. Still, she was an emotional mess, and she couldn't dare face Aleksey with smeared makeup and a much too casual outfit. She needed to go up to her room to freshen up and get a hold of herself if she was going to make the right impression.

☐

Wiping away a tear brought on by an involuntary trip down memory lane, Audra did her best to compose herself before stepping into the hotel, but it was a struggle. The best she could hope for was for Aleksey to be waiting at the bar as promised, allowing her to sneak off upstairs and fix her makeup. Fortunately, that would be the case, so heading up to the suite her brother had rented on her behalf, Audra went to the bathroom and got to work.

Stripping out of her jeans, hooded sweatshirt, and t-shirt, she replaced them with something tasteful but sexy enough to get a man's attention. Her choice of outfit consisted of a black and white argyle skirt, black stockings, and a grey sweater that accentuated her curves without being revealing. Next, she redid her makeup, and when she was through, she looked at herself in the mirror and smiled. While her confidence hadn't quite risen to the point that she'd consider herself a knockout, she thought she looked good. However, when she started pulling on a pair of leather boots, she wondered if she was overdressed. Ultimately, she decided to run with her look, and she had no regrets. She wasn't expecting much from this day. She just wanted to have a bit of fun and forget her troubles.

Chapter 51

Senatgrad, Federal Special Region, Slavic Federation

At Sobczak's orders, a pair of ultranationalists always kept an eye on Gustav, no matter how mundane his routine proved to be. While the day started as any other, the appearance of a moderately attractive woman at their quarry's side was suspicious.

Following the pair to the bank, the ultranationalists observed Audra as she watched Gustav make a bank deposit before mysteriously parting ways with him. This raised internal alarms for the men, and it was silently decided that someone had to break off and follow Audra.

Closer to the door, the man who went by the code name Duch Trzy left without question. A well-trained reconnaissance specialist, Trzy followed Audra without being noticed. Tracking her back to the hotel, he didn't follow her upstairs, but he knew she'd return. She had stopped in the lobby and looked into the bar, as if she were looking for someone. So, entering the bar, he ordered a drink and took a seat at a high-top table in the corner that gave him the best view of the room.

As he had surmised, Audra entered the bar sometime later and approached a handsome man sitting at the bar. The pair embraced like friends rather than lovers, giving him concern. His fears heightened when he heard Aleksey translate the drink menu from Russian and smoothly transition to Polish. At first, their conversation was casual, but his ears perked at the mention of Gustav and the business she had with him. It was at this point that Trzy believed Aleksey was FSB, and Audra was his agent, or perhaps a Polish intelligence officer with federalist sympathies. Whatever the case, he needed to call this in, but to keep his cover, he finished his drink and walked out slowly. Once in the lobby, he called his commander and informed him he was returning home for a family emergency – a code phrase that surely set off Sobczak's internal alarms.

Seemingly panicked by the phone call, Sobczak was pacing alone in the kitchen when Trzy stepped into the flat. Without letting his subordinate say a word first, Sobczak marched up and demanded to know what was going on and if the mission was compromised.

"I'm not sure yet," Trzy said calmly, but that wasn't enough for his commander.

"What do you mean you don't know? You don't call me on the burner unless it's for a damn good reason!"

"It was a good reason, I assure you."

"Then spit it out."

"I was on my shift, watching the Kraut. He went to the bank with a woman. I don't know who she is. I've never seen her before."

"What does she look like?" Sobczak asked.

"Eh, kind of tall for a woman, sort of cute, a bit chubby around the waist, nice rack as far as I could tell."

"The hell is wrong with you? You're a reconnaissance specialist, and the best you can give me is your search box query?"

"I didn't get a good look at her, sir. She was wearing sunglasses and a hooded sweatshirt for the most part. I think she might be working with the GRU or FSB."

"What makes you think that?" Sobczak asked. "Did you hear her speaking Russian?"

"No, she spoke Polish, but the guy she was with did. He translated a cocktail menu--"

"Wait, hold on a damn second here. There's a guy, too?"

"Yeah, but she didn't link up with him until later. They met at a hotel bar and went out on the town. Looked like how they'd set up a spy meeting. He's got himself a native accent, so maybe he's a local desk for special intelligence and she's just a honey pot, I don't know."

"Ah, fuck me running! This can't go sideways already. We're too close!"

"I don't know, but maybe this is a sign. Perhaps we should drop the plan for the gala and go with the Senate."

"What's this now?" Sobczak asked. "I thought the German worked at the Senate complex. Why are you worried about the gala suddenly?"

"Don't you find it a little strange that we come across this German and a few days later we might have a government operative sniffing around that same German?"

"You're right, that's a hell of a coincidence," Sobczak said. "But what's this about quitting the gala job. If anything's a setup, it's the Senate operation. Unless someone told the German something he shouldn't know, no one outside of this group would know a thing about that operation."

"Maybe it's just my nerves talking," Trzy said out of frustration. "Shit never seemed right from the start."

"Don't go getting cold feet on me now. We're in deep, and our country is counting on us."

"I know, but we're running a huge risk here. We're a small team and we're going to try to pull off two major jobs on the same night, miles apart. You can't tell me you don't feel like something is off here."

"This all came down from the Marshal himself. He wouldn't call for this kind of action if he didn't believe we could pull it off right," Sobczak said. "Besides, the Senate is just a diversion. The gala is the big prize. And that's only if they decide to play games."

"You know they will," Trzy said. "There's no way in hell they'll let us go free without a fight."

"Then a fight they'll get," Sobczak said with a smirk. "And we'll kill their queen."

Swallowing hard at the thought of carrying out an operation that was likely a suicide mission and the flashpoint for an invasion, Trzy couldn't help but voice his concern.

"Listen to yourself, sir. They want us to kill the First Lady!" Trzy cried. "There's no way we can pull this off, especially with a government agent sniffing around."

"What makes you think we can't pull this off?" Sobczak asked curiously. "Are we not elite? Were we not hand-selected by the Marshal himself?"

"We're going after one of the most important people in the world, sir. There's no way anyone is getting close to her and getting the job done without getting caught or killed."

"If you don't like our odds, then find someone on the riot squad willing to trade places."

"What difference would that make? No one is walking away from that operation," Trzy said, but Sobczak was undeterred.

"We have a duty to serve the needs of our country. We're doing this job whether you like it or not, so shut and do it, or find someone willing to take your place."

"Look, I just don't feel good about this one."

"I understand that, but you knew what you were getting yourself into when you chose to side with the patriots over the fascists," Sobczak said firmly. "You're a good man and an excellent soldier, but I'm becoming concerned. I need to know I can count on you to carry out your duties, even if it is a suicide mission."

"You know you can count on me to do my job, but this is ridiculous. We need to abort."

"We're not aborting unless we're set free on the Senate floor!" Sobczak snarled. "You can pray to your lucky star that it happens, but you know damn well the bastard in Moscow wants his empire whole."

Sighing through his nose, Trzy asked what would happen if he couldn't find a man willing to take his place on the gala squad. Sobczak replied with an offer to put him on the rear guard, to which Trzy likely smirked as he made a snide remark.

"Funny, I thought you would have saved that for yourself," Trzy said, for the man on the rear guard in such a mission had the highest chance of survival, or at least immediate escape.

Ignoring the remark, Sobczak replied with pride and determination. "If there's anything the army taught me, it's that I don't need cheap tactics to survive a suicide mission. All I need is a reliable gun, a bit of luck, and a few good men to watch my six," Sobczak said. "You, on the other hand. I'm starting to wonder about you. Hopefully, you can remember your oath and pull that trigger when the time comes."

Chapter 52

Senatgrad, Federal Special Region, Slavic Federation

Spending the day together, Audra and Aleksey stopped first at a café for lunch and then hit the town for a day of window shopping, followed by a lovely dinner together, eventually finding themselves wandering along the waterfront. Growing tired from so much walking, they found a bench to sit on and look out onto the picturesque scene of the Vistula Lagoon before them. Finding comfort in his presence, Audra wrapped her hands around Aleksey's right arm and rested her head on his shoulder as if they were lovers and not friends contemplating their feelings for one another. While they were largely silent from the moment they took their seat, Audra let off a relaxed sigh and spoke to him.

"This was nice," she said. "You really know how to make a girl feel special."

"Well, it's my pleasure," Aleksey said warmly. "It's always a joy spending time with you."

Touched by the sincerity in his voice, Audra bowed her head and looked back at him with a smile. "I'm really happy we ran into each other that day at the museum," she said. "We really made a connection since then, haven't we?"

"I can't help but agree," Aleksey said with a bashful smile. "I just didn't expect you to feel the same way."

"Why would you think that?" Audra asked curiously, but he shrugged.

"I guess I was worried that I shared my troubles a bit too much," he said, but she rubbed his arms in a caring fashion. "Honestly, I'm surprised I didn't scare you off with all my whining. Not very soldierly of me, right?"

"I wouldn't call it whining. Your life got turned upside down, and then you ended up injured. Besides, I felt your pain. You weren't the only one dealing with a broken heart," she said, sighing at the thought of everything Gustav put her through, but she smiled just then. "Honestly, in a weird way, hearing about your horrible experience was somehow uplifting."

"I'm glad my pain helped you through your own," Aleksey said with a laugh, but Audra was quick to explain her meaning.

"No, that came out wrong. What I mean was that hearing about what you experienced made me realize my life didn't suck nearly as bad as I thought."

"Getting stuck with a bar you didn't want isn't so bad when you could be a soldier with sepsis, huh?" Aleksey said with a grin, as Audra shook her head at her perceived failure to avoid sounding like a fool. Of course, he took no offense to her words, so in a bid to preserve the good vibes they had shared up to this point, he touched her leg and gained her attention once more. "Thank you for being there for me. A friend like you is just what I needed to get through all this."

"You're very welcome," she said, her heart swelling as she gazed into his eyes. "Everyone deserves to be happy, so thank you for being there for me just the same. And thank you for such a wonderful date. I really needed this."

Her use of the word 'date' ringing in his ear, Aleksey smiled, giving her face a rosy tint as she looked away bashfully. Having realized she may have misunderstood his intentions in seeing her, she tried to backpedal, but he gripped her leg a little tighter and spoke to ease the tension.

"I'm glad you feel the same as I do," Aleksey said. A magnetic feeling came over him just then as he felt himself gravitating toward her. Feeling the same way, she moved in, and their lips touched in a tender kiss for a few brief seconds. When they parted, Audra appeared flustered while Aleksey seemed satisfied.

"Well then," Audra said, smiling brightly. "I suppose there's no hiding it anymore. We have some real chemistry brewing between us."

"I think so," he said. Just then, she wrapped her hands around his arm once more and leaned onto his shoulder. Neither said a word for a few moments, and Aleksey just enjoyed the moment until Audra sat up and looked at him with a serious expression.

"What happens now?" she asked carefully.

"Well, that depends on you, my dear."

"Well, the sun is starting to set, and it'll be dark soon. Perhaps we could keep things going a bit longer? Unless you're sick of me by now."

"Sick of you? How could I be sick of you? I've been dreaming about seeing you for weeks."

"Is that right?"

"Honest to God. I haven't been able to get you out of my mind since we first met," he said, bringing a bright smile to her face as she silently contemplated her next few words.

"Well, in that case... what are you doing for breakfast tomorrow? I hear my hotel has a nice restaurant," she said with a racing heart, for the words were completely out of character and she could hardly believe what she had just said.

His heart racing just as quickly as hers, Aleksey recognized the hint she had just dropped in his lap. Yet, while he would have loved to take her up on that offer, he was bound to his duties, and he didn't want to appear too eager.

"Unfortunately, I'll be having breakfast in the mess hall," Aleksey said. "Powdered eggs, freeze-dried potatoes, and coffee as tasty as mud; the breakfast of the Polish military elite."

"Oh, well, when are you due back?" Audra said, sounding a bit deflated.

"0900 at the very latest," he said, and she nodded. She was clearly downtrodden by this fact, for she rightfully assumed that Gdansk wasn't just a short train ride away. "What's wrong?"

"Oh, it's nothing. I was just having such a nice time," she said. "I'd hate for the night to be cut short, but I guess that's life."

"I never said I couldn't stay the night," Aleksey said with a sly smile. "It's a two-and-a-half-hour ride. I could wake up at five, catch the train by six, and be on base with enough time to check in and have some quick chow," Aleksey was quick to say, but again, he didn't want to appear eager. "However, that would all hinge on me finding a hotel room for the night."

"Seriously?" she asked with a sly smile of her own. "I think it's pretty clear that we're more than just friends at this point, yeah?"

"Yeah, but I wouldn't want to intrude," he said, bringing her to roll her eyes and pull him in by his collar for another, more thorough kiss. When they parted again, she looked deeply into his eyes. "I'm not going to beg you, but I have a nice bottle of wine in the fridge and my suite has a balcony with a really nice view of the city."

"That sounds lovely," Aleksey said, enchanted by the light shimmering in her eyes. "If you'll have me over, I'll be a perfect gentleman."

Chuckling, she told him it was a deal. She then took him by the wrist and took to her feet. "Come now, it's getting dark, and I couldn't possibly make it back to my hotel alone."

Finding amusement in her faux innocence, Aleksey held out his arm and waited for her to wrap her hands around his bicep and forearm so that he could escort her like a gentleman of the past. The pair then headed off, eventually dropping the charade in favor of holding hands.

Sitting on the balcony as proposed, Aleksey was sprawled on a couch-like Cleopatra chair with Audra lying back against him, resting her head on his chest. Sipping wine, they talked about their lives and their dreams, but both could feel the tension building up between them. In time, she sat up and turned to him at an odd angle. Their eyes locked, she then leaned toward him and kissed him gently as lovers do. Instead of pulling away as she had done at the park, she let her passion take control, and a tender kiss soon became vigorous and passionate. However, wanting to go at her own pace, she pushed off and lay back down, pulling his arm across her chest and placing his hand over her breast, holding his hand in place with her own. She felt safe and warm in his arms. She hadn't felt like this toward a man in a very long time. She appreciated how respectful he was of her boundaries, but his unwillingness to make a move until that point had her feeling concerned.

Staring out at the city with a blank expression for a short while, Audra tried to figure out what the problem could be. She had been more than proactive with him, both physically and verbally, yet he hadn't made his move. She was starting to wonder if he was getting cold feet, but she didn't want to be the one to make the big move. After all, she felt she had made her intentions known well enough, and she feared appearing a bit too eager. After all, she couldn't help but feel like he was out of her league.

Annoyed by these intrusive thoughts, Audra sighed through her nose. Taking notice, Aleksey asked what was on her mind. Still staring at the horizon, she asked him why he was there. Aleksey's thoughts raced as a result. Unsure if she was drunk and somehow forgotten she had invited him over, or if she was just frustrated that he hadn't made a move, he played it safe.

"You invited me here," he said, and Audra rolled her eyes at this.

"You know what I mean. Why did you come here? Be honest."

"Because I didn't want our time together to end," he said, but his words only caused her to sit up and face him with concern and suspicion.

"Is there something wrong? Did I say something to offend you? Am I coming on too strong?"

"No, everything is fine," Aleksey said, but it still wasn't enough.

"You don't find me all that attractive, do you? Am I not pretty enough? Too thick? What?"

"None of that's true at all," Aleksey said, his voice calm and his eyes cool. "In fact, I think you're very pretty and you have a lovely body. Dare I say, you're gorgeous."

"Then what's the problem? Are you getting cold feet? Do you not have a condom? We can always trade favors, you know?"

"It's none of that, but what's with the questions? We were having a nice time," Aleksey asked, seemingly offended that she even felt the need to question his intentions or feelings toward her.

"I feel like something is keeping you from making your move, so just be honest with me," she said, bringing him to furrow his brow.

"Let me be clear, I didn't come over here solely to sleep with you. Honestly, I'd be perfectly happy if things didn't go any further."

"So, it's cold feet," she asked, but he shrugged. "It's nothing to be ashamed of. I get it, you're still hurting."

"It's not cold feet. I'm just afraid of blowing this. I guess I'm out of practice," he said, and she nodded. "But why didn't you make a move?"

"I have been. In fact, I thought I was being pushy," she said, but he shook his head, so she sighed. "Alright, just tell me this. Do you want me or not?"

"I think you know where I stand on that," Aleksey said, giving her an anxious expression, but before he could better explain himself, she stood up and faced the door.

"I'll be right back," she said, but her tone told him he had blown it.□

"Audra, wait!" Aleksey cried, but she assured him that she just needed to use the bathroom. Feeling like he had really screwed up, he sat up and perched on the edge of the chair. Ridiculing himself for not being forthright with his feelings, he took a long pull from his remaining wine and contemplated the situation for several minutes.

He'd be lying if he said he didn't want to sleep with her, but his hangup was the fact that he didn't want to have her for just one night. She had him by heartstrings, hence his unwillingness to push the envelope too much for fear she'd perceive him as too eager. The last thing he wanted was to spoil the night and possibly ruin their friendship by asking for something she wasn't comfortable with doing or crossing a line by making an awkward move. Yet, as he thought about the many hints dropped that night, it was clear she was waiting patiently for him to make a move and growing agitated. She obviously wanted him badly, and while that humbled him, he couldn't seem to make up his mind.

He liked her very much and knew he could have her if he just went in after her, but he was conflicted. He wanted her just as badly, but he didn't want to give her the wrong impression. He wasn't there for a quick rendezvous. He was a romantic who dreamed of a wife and children, not empty sex with strangers. However, he wasn't so sure if she felt the same way. Sure, she had her heartbroken recently, too, but he wasn't convinced this wasn't just a means of boosting her deflated confidence.

Deeply conflicted, Aleksey finished his wine and set the glass aside. Looking over his shoulder toward the patio door, he wondered if she was coming back. Though the lights were off inside, and he couldn't hear her, he didn't think she had left. It was her room after all. So, deciding it was best for him to swallow his pride and finally make his move, he got up and headed for the door.

Sliding the patio door shut behind him, Aleksey quickly noticed a beam of light reaching out from beneath the bathroom door. Assuming she was doing some thinking of her own, he reached for the light switch and turned on the lights. Walking over to bed, he took a seat and waited until he heard the door unlock and open. When he looked up, he was surprised to see that she was stripped down to just her underwear. While her figure was typically masked by her choice of clothing, he knew she was curvy and a bit heavier than average. Still, even half-naked, she carried her weight well, and he couldn't bring himself to look away.

Locking eyes with him, Audra walked slowly, stopping about midway between the bathroom and the bed. Adjusting her bra strap, she looked nervous, but she carried out her plan as intended. "Do I still look gorgeous?"

"You look incredible," Aleksey said, taking to his feet as he was overcome by temptation. He slowly closed the gap between them, and they soon embraced with her wrists crossed behind his neck and his hands at her hips. "My god, you have an amazing body."

"You don't mind the imperfections?" she asked, self-conscious of the stretch marks lining her waist after a rapid weight gain during her last year at university.

"We all have scars," he said, looking deeply into her eyes. "Would you like to see mine?"

"I would," she said, and while she kissed him tenderly, she began to unbutton his shirt while his hands remained at her hips. After getting to the bottom, she opened his shirt and laid eyes on his sculpted abdomen for the first time. Though she should have been awash with desire, her anxiety took hold as her hands touched his belt, and she backed off.

"What am I doing?" she asked, hanging her head low to avoid eye contact.

"What's wrong?"

"I don't know. I... I guess I'm the one getting cold feet now," she said, continuing to hang her head in apparent fear and shame. She was silent for several moments before sighing hard and looking up at him. "I'm sorry things got so awkward all of a sudden."

"Just take your time and think it all through. We don't have to do anything if you don't want to."

"That's the problem, I do want to do something here. I've been thinking about this all day, but now my stupid fucking brain has to get in the way."

"What do you mean?"

"Look, I'm just going to be honest here. I have intimacy issues, but I'm trying to get through it."

"Do you want to talk about it?"

"No, I want to take you to bed and have my way with you," she said, quickly cringing at her own words before shaking her head in embarrassment. "I'm blowing this, aren't I?"

"You're not. Just tell me what I can do to make you feel at ease."

"Just make a move already. It's the only way I'm going to be able to do this," she said, but Aleksey was hesitant.

"Audra, I don't want to take advantage—"

"I'm not drunk, I'm just having trouble coming to terms with everything, ok?" she said, looking up at him with sadness in her eyes. "I know it might sound stupid, but Gustav made me almost hate sex."

"I'm sorry," he said, but she shook her head.

"You know what? To hell with Gustav! He was then, and you're now," she said, her voice trembling from nervousness. "This is my chance to make everything right again, so come on. Make your move already. Better yet, take it out and tell me what you want me to do with it. Just do something, anything."

Allowing his desire to finally overcome his anxiety, Aleksey walked the short distance between them and placed his hands at her hips once more. Kissing her tenderly at first, he ran his hand up her sides and around her back. Working her bra hooks, he released the straps with relative ease. She backed off slightly to slip off her bra, and he was invigorated by what he saw, so much so that he pulled her in tightly and lifted her off her feet. She responded by smiling brightly and wrapping her legs tightly around his waist as he buried his face in her heavy breasts. She let off a pleasured laugh as he let his instincts run wild with her, but before long, he carried her over to bed and laid her down gently.

Lifting her legs straight into the air, he eased off her panties and began kissing her ankle before working his way down her inner thigh until he reached the end. Though he sent pleasurable shivers through her body, Audra didn't need foreplay at this moment. She wanted him inside her, so touching one hand to his forehead, she eased him back, and with a lustful whisper, she invited him inside. Willing to oblige, he watched as she crawled backwards up to the headboard as he undressed. When he was bare, he climbed onto the bed and crawled over toward her until he was in position. Kneeling before her, he began to lay a trail of kisses that started at her navel, ran up her abdomen, crossed each breast, and ended at her mouth. Almost demandingly, she whispered into his ear for him to begin.

Ready to cross the threshold at last, he placed his hands on either side of her head and propped himself up so that he could look into her eyes. Gently easing into her, he kissed her tenderly and felt her nails sink into his back. As their lovemaking became more vigorous, he turned his attention to her neck and kissed the sensitive skin beneath her earlobe as she softly moaned in his ear. All at once, their anxieties washed away as they became lost in the liberating act.

Lying under the covers, Audra felt awash with satisfaction and comfort. Though she could have told him she loved him at that moment, she knew it was just the hormones running wild. Regardless, she had no regrets about taking him to her hotel room and giving herself to him. Yet, as he held her close, she felt her crippling self-doubt rearing its ugly head once more, threatening her with renewed feelings of regret and anxiety.

Rolling over to face him, Audra accepted a short kiss but placed her hand over his lips to stop him from embracing her further. She had something on her mind, and she wanted to discuss it without delay.

"This wasn't a mistake, was it?" she asked, causing him to furrow his brow.

"How could this be a mistake?"

"Tell me we're going to see each other again. This wasn't a one-time thing. I'm not just another notch on your belt, right?"

"Audra—"

"Just tell me this meant more to you than a cheap thrill."

"Before you, there was only Tatiana," Aleksey said. "You're not a rebound, and this wasn't a one-time thing. We'll see each other again, I swear."

"Then where do we go from here? Do we go back to being friends? Are we lovers with no strings attached?"

"At the very least, we're lovers, but I'd like you all to myself if I could."

"I'd like that, but how would that work?"

"I'm based and live in Gdansk. That's a six-hour trip to Berlin. I can get a weekend off every month and visit you, or you could visit me. We could even go on trips or have a week or two together alone at my flat," he said, bringing a smile to her face.

"I'd like that," she said sweetly. "So, you want me to be your girlfriend?"

"I'd love for you to be my girlfriend," he said, but she sighed. "What?"

"I'd like that too, but would you really want to bring a bartender home to your mother?"

"I'd be bringing home an artist and entrepreneur," Aleksey said warmly. "You're more interesting than you give yourself credit for."

"If you really mean that, then I'm all yours," she said, drawing closer until the tips of their noses touched. "But don't you dare make a fool out of me. I've had enough pain in my life."

"You're in good hands. I'm going to treasure you."

Touched by his words, she pushed him so that he was flat on his back. She then cuddled up to him, placing her head on his shoulder. "I hope we can make this work."

"We will," he said, kissing the top of her head. "You have a good man in your life now. We're going to see each other as much as we can, and when my contract is up, we'll have a nice life together. Just you, me—"

"And a couple of kids with a dog and a cat in the suburbs?" she asked with a smile.

Though he couldn't tell if she was joking, he smiled back. "If that's what you want, then that's what you'll get," he said, but she couldn't help but chuckle just a bit.

"Listen to us. We sleep together once, and we're already talking about marriage and kids."

"Some might call it fate."

"I call it really good sex," she said, and they shared a laugh. She then adjusted herself so that she was hovering over him, propped up by her forearms. "Jokes aside, I'm excited about this. I don't know if we'll last, but I'm not going to miss my chance to have you at least for a little while. You're everything I could want in a man."

"Just don't make a fool out of me, and everything will work out fine," he said, mirroring her words from earlier. Smiling and sharing one last kiss, she lay back down on her side with her head on a pillow of her own. Pulling the covers over their naked bodies, she reached out and held his hands in her own and just enjoyed the silence as they eventually fell asleep together.

Chapter 53

Senatgrad, Federal Special Region, Slavic Federation

Alone in the sole bedroom at the safe house, Sobczak was sitting at an old desk with a chipped top. Unnerved by what Trzy had come to him with the previous night, he anxiously awaited a scheduled call from the man he referred to as the Marshal.

Normally a calm and reserved individual hardened by countless engagements and black operations, Sobczak was visibly disturbed by the worries brought to him by one of his most reliable men. Making matters worse, the Marshal was late for the call. This got his blood running, and he feared that Trzy's fears were valid. Perhaps the FSB had somehow learned of their plot and was investigating. So driven by growing paranoia, Sobczak wandered the small room and pressed his body against the wall to peer outside unnoticed. Nothing appeared out of the ordinary to his trained eyes. He didn't see any indication from the pedestrians that there was a force of police special tactics units parked out of view of the window. He didn't see anyone looking up at the flat either. There was nothing, but that didn't mean there wasn't anything. The FSB's Special Intelligence division and their attack dogs in Alpha Group were highly trained and more than able to blend into their surroundings to make a high-risk arrest or assassination without the public knowing it ever happened. This sent a fresh wave of worry over the grizzled commando, but then the phone rang.

"Yes, Marshal," Sobczak said, his voice distorted by a modulator, per usual.

Wasting no time with apologies for the lateness of his call, enigmatic Marshal spoke with a distorted voice just the same. "Are we all set for the operation?"

"Yes... we're all set," Sobczak said, but the short pause in the sentence told the Marshal otherwise.

"Is there something I need to be aware of?"

"No... well, yes... we ran into another snag," Sobczak chugged. "One of the men found a new variable to the op in the Grad. He spotted an unknown woman with the German. She was dressed for concealment, so we didn't have a good idea of what she looked like at first, but she was spotted later with a man who carries himself like a soldier," Sobczak continued, pausing for a few moments. "We're working on figuring out who they are."

"We don't have time for that. The fate of our country will be decided in less than twenty-four hours," the Marshal said gruffly, but then he sighed as he began to share Sobczak's concerns of an FSB investigation. "Alright, what do you know about the woman and the man?"

"We have a physical description of both, but we don't know much else just yet. We just know the woman made the German put some money in the bank and linked up with that man at a luxury hotel. As for the man, well, you're going to get a kick out of this one."

"Amuse me," the Marshal said.

"He looks a lot like the son of a certain General of the Army," Sobczak said with a grin. "We're working on figuring out if it's him."

"Good, but the girl is your primary objective," the Marshal said suddenly, for he knew Aleksander Rybinski far too well to believe his son would be involved with the Russians in any way, shape, or fashion. "Confirm his identity but put your best effort into the girl."

"We're working on it. I have Jeden and Cztery on her trail. They were last seen at the hotel after a day in town. They haven't come out since, so we assumed they stayed the night."

"Tell your men to make their move when they're separated. If he is a Rybinski, we can't afford to get him involved," the Marshal said, but Sobczak, ever the strategist on his feet, had an idea.

"Why don't we take care of them both? They're not going anywhere, and they're cornered."

"Absolutely not!" the Marshal thundered. "We can't afford to skirt this operation. We're on the cusp of victory. Make any move on that man, and this all goes down in flames. Just focus on the woman. Lean on the German if you must."

"Yes, sir."

"Good luck and godspeed," said the Marshal. "I look forward to seeing the results of this operation. Hopefully, we can quietly abort, and no one gets hurt."

"I won't hold my breath," Sobczak said, and the Marshal seemed to concur.

"Regardless, this will be the last time I contact you before the job is done," he said, and the line went dead.

When he heard the dial tone, Sobczak was left with an uneasy feeling, for he hadn't been entirely truthful with the Marshal. The soldier had already been identified as Aleksey

Rybinski, but their plan for him had to change. Being a man of conviction, Sobczak dialed the number for his right-hand man in the operation. A few moments later, he heard the modulated voice of the operative known as Jeden.

"The game has changed. Wait until the guard is gone and rescue the princess. The troll stays in his cage until I say otherwise," he said, speaking in coded language that only his team understood. "Be silent and effective."

"Always."

Chapter 54

Gdansk, Republic of Poland, Slavic Federation

For the first time since returning from the Balkans, Aleksey was feeling like his old self again. Audra had captured his heart, so with a smile rarely leaving his face, he rode the early morning ferry back to Gdansk. From the civilian port, he took a short taxi ride to the naval yard. Upon reaching the front gate, he signed in and headed toward the barracks on foot as if he had never left this place with the intention of never returning. Thankfully, once he stepped inside, no one questioned his return, and more than a few welcomed him back as if he had merely been on leave. This warmed Aleksey's heart, for over the years, he had come to view many of the men of Squadron B as like the brothers he never had, but he couldn't help but notice more than a few of the bunks were empty. Far more than just the two that Zielinski and himself would have occupied. It was just a few moments later that he learned that something terrible had happened, and it had claimed the lives of many GROM operators. Many of whom were good friends of his.

Though stunned by the news that the explosion in the bay he had seen from the ferry was a series of explosions aboard a newly acquired Soviet-era aircraft carrier, Aleksey kept his emotions in check. In fact, he was a bit grateful, for had he never left the unit, he very well might have been one of the fallen. Nonetheless, he mourned his fallen compatriots in his own way and quietly ate breakfast at the mess with what remained of his team. When breakfast was over, they marched out to the parade grounds and fell into formation as if it were any other day. But, considering it wasn't any other day, they were met by their commanding and executive officers, respectively. However, Lieutenant Colonel Kulig spoke only for a short while to explain the situation from an official point of view.

"Gentlemen, official word has come in regarding the incident aboard the Varyag," Kulig said. "There was a malfunction in the forward battery, causing catastrophic failure and a chain reaction that resulted in the explosion that decimated the ship and this unit."

Stunned by what he had just heard, Aleksey's mind blanked out, and he didn't hear the rest of Kulig's briefing. He only saw his lips moving, and his expression remained grim until he stepped back and ceded the floor to his second-in-command, Major Wronka.

"While I concur with Colonel Kulig that we should be spending this day mourning the loss of our friends and colleagues, unfortunately, duty calls as it so often does," Wronka said. "While the Varyag incident is officially being treated as an accident, the High Command is treating it as a potential act of political extremism. With that in mind, we've been tasked with providing additional security at the Senatorial Palace for the upcoming special session of the Senate. Also, a select detachment will provide security for a gala at the Premier's Manor. Both sites are considered high-value targets for extremists, so stay sharp and keep an eye out for anything and everything. This could very well be your finest hour, gentlemen."

Like that of the Kulig, Wronka's words hit Aleksey hard. The thought of the Varyag incident being the work of extremists felt right, but at the same time, he couldn't see the point. Poland was about to have its moment before the Senate. There was absolutely no reason to blow up a ship at this moment in time unless the extremists were Federalists. Shaking his head, Aleksey cast the thought away as Wronka continued.

"As it stands, our transport over to Baltiysk is being prepared and I've been told they should be ready to fly in roughly an hour. Get your gear packed, your phone calls made, and your mind on the mission. I want you all back here in fifty minutes or less. Fall out!"

Aleksey followed the group back to the barracks as an hour really wasn't much time for anything. While he could have gone off to the gym, which was one of the few facilities open at that time, he chose to just lie on his cot. He spent the time thinking not about whatever mission lay ahead but about the day he had with Audra. He tried to reason with himself that he just had to stay alive and in contact for the duration of his contract. After that, he could weigh his options as to where he would go from there. Hopefully, things would work out better than they did with Tatiana. This got him to think about how his previous relationship had blown up in his face, but he didn't get to dwell too long. He had a mission to worry about, so he shifted gears and worked to get his mind off his love life and onto the mission.

Chapter 55

Senatgrad, Federal Special Region, Slavic Federation

Kissing Aleksey goodbye felt like the hardest thing Audra had done since she finally ended things with Gustav. Their lovemaking that morning and the previous evening was passionate yet gentle, and the satisfaction she felt afterward was invigorating. She hadn't been in such high spirits in a very long time, and she felt no regret about taking a chance and bringing him back to her hotel. He not only made her feel good about herself with his kind, often flattering words, but she never felt like he was lying to her. Despite a lingering doubt that they'd see each other again, she believed that he was sincere in his promise that this wasn't just a one-time fling. So, when she was alone, she told herself that so long as they stayed in contact, there might be a chance, and she welcomed that. Truly, the only thing she worried about was the time until they saw each other next. While she found it relatively easy to abstain from giving in to her urge for romance, she didn't know him well enough to be sure if he wouldn't just forget about her over time. All she had was his word, and while she wanted to believe he would keep himself for her, it was just a girlish fantasy. After all, he was a handsome man who traveled the world for a living. There was no doubt in her mind that he had many opportunities to get his needs taken care of. Fortunately, she was able to keep regret at bay by convincing herself that he was a good man through and through. He had a steady, though unfaithful, girlfriend for a decade or more, and the way he made love suggested he was not only a romantic but not as adventurous as someone who couldn't get enough. This all gave her hope that she had made the right choice in pursuing him.

With a smile on her face, Audra went downstairs to the hotel's restaurant for a quiet breakfast alone. After finishing, she returned to her room and made a cup of tea to enjoy alongside a good book and a hot bath. Taking advantage of her clear schedule, she stayed in the tub until the water ran cold and her eyes felt tired from so much reading.

Setting her book aside on the toilet lid, she pulled the plug for the drain and stood up. Stepping out of the tub, she grabbed a nearby towel from the shelf above the toilet and dried herself off. As she did so, she glanced up at herself in the mirror and smiled sheepishly. She wasn't so sure what Aleksey saw in her, but she was happy he saw what he did. After all, she didn't see herself as anything special to write home about. She had a curvy figure, which turned heads from time to time, but she saw more flaws than advantages in herself, particularly her slightly above-average height and the extra pounds she carried around her waist and thighs. But rather than bring herself down like she always did, she stood tall and thought positively about herself. After all, Aleksey thought she was gorgeous and didn't seem to want to leave. So, with a smile on her face, she readied herself for the day, brushing her teeth, slipping into a comfortable outfit, and putting on a bit of makeup. She was just about to leave when she heard a knock at her door.

Knowing Aleksey had to be in an entirely different city by then, she froze with fear. She had no reason to believe the hotel staff would be bothering her, and there was a chance that Gustav had followed her. If the latter was the case, she feared what he might do, but then she heard a stranger's voice from behind the door. It was too muffled to understand, though it was certainly a man and sounded faintly like Aleksey.

Moving closer to the door to investigate, she stopped herself just short of unlocking and opening the door without checking who was on the other side first. Using the peephole, she spied two men, each somewhere in the late twenties to mid-thirties. Judging by their attire, they appeared to be police officers, which sent a chill down her spine. So, when they knocked again and called out her name, she asked who they were. Seemingly aware that she was there, one of the men reached into his coat and flashed a badge proving he was an undercover police officer.

"It's the police. Please open the door, Ms. Rozek," the officer said, her identity known to them thanks to the efforts of a set of compatriots tasked with watching Gustav.

"Just a moment," she called out. Despite her raging nerves, she slowly opened the door with the chain still on just in case these men weren't who they claimed to be. After all, anyone could falsify a police badge. "Can I help you?" she asked nervously.

"Sorry to bother you, but there's been an incident involving your boyfriend," an officer said, his accent very similar to Aleksey's, but she wasn't ready to let her guard down.

"What's his name?"

"Gustav Hagen," the Officer said, and Audra rolled her eyes, but refrained from correcting her status with Gustav.

"What happened?"

"He attempted suicide, I'm afraid," the Officer said. "He's in critical condition and asked to see you."

Her heart racing, Audra felt instant responsibility for what Gustav may have done. The Officer offered his deepest condolences while his partner remained mute. Audra was then asked if she would be so kind as to go with them to the hospital, as it was urgent.

"Yes, just let me get my shoes and purse," Audra said, and she closed the door.

Her back to the door, Audra was awash with grief and remorse. She knew Gustav was in a bad way, but she never expected him to do such a thing. So, hurrying to grab her purse and pull on her shoes, she left with the officers. However, she was taken out of the building through a rear door, and when she didn't see a squad car or even something that resembled a police cruiser, she was forced upon from behind with a thick cloth quickly wrapped around her mouth so tight that any attempt to scream was almost completely muted. She was soon grabbed in a bear hug and lifted off her feet. Though she thrashed her legs, it was no use, and she was quickly forced into the back seat of a car. Given that she was unrestrained, she tried for the door handle, but the child locks were engaged. When she tried to maneuver to the front, the two men appeared at the driver's and passenger's side doors. Both were brandishing pistols, but it was the one who spoke German that had assured her that she wouldn't be harmed so long as she didn't make a scene.

Doing as she was told, Audra kept quiet and was brought to a flat on a working-class side of the city. Her gag removed in confidence, Audra marched up a set of steel stairs leading to a second-floor flat. Once inside, she found herself among several men, none of whom she knew, save for one.

"You son of a bitch!" she snarled, upon spotting Gustav seated on the couch. Unable to resist the urge to walk over and punch him in the face with all her might, it took two men to keep her from continuing the assault.

"Easy there, sweetheart," Sobczak said with a hearty laugh, before looking at Gustav with a wide grin. "She's a firecracker."

Saying nothing at first, Gustav just rubbed his face and worked his jaw around, but Audra continued to thrash and curse them for kidnapping her. His eyes then turned to Duch Trzy and spoke in German. "Her brother is going to kill us all. I hope you know that."

Trzy translated Gustav's words into Polish for the others, and Sobczak laughed.

"Yeah, I'm not so sure about that," Sobczak said, aware of Richard Rozek and his Marzahn Syndicate. He then looked at Audra and asked if she spoke Polish. When she nodded, he asked if she was fluent. When she nodded again, he asked her to calm down a bit so he could explain the situation.

Unable to move at that point and knowing that kicking the burly commando in the balls would only make problems worse, Audra calmed down enough for Sobczak to get down to business.

"So, this is your boyfriend, yes?"

"He's not my boyfriend," Audra said with apparent disgust.

"Well, whatever this kraut-eater is to you, he knows too much about us, and we want to know what he told you."

"He didn't tell me anything. I don't even know who you people are."

"Well, that's a good start, but I don't quite believe you," Sobczak said. "Why don't you tell me what you two were doing at the bank yesterday. Receipts tell quite the story."

"I was making sure he paid his debt."

"His debt to whom? And why?" Sobczak challenged.

"This idiot owes your government a lot of money, and even more to gangsters back in Berlin."

"That's quite the situation. Where do you come in?"

"This idiot used to be my boyfriend, but what does it matter?"

"It matters because he knows what we're up to. We're just covering our bases," Sobczak said firmly. "Now again, what did he tell you?"

"He told me nothing," Audra said, just as firmly. "I came here to make sure the money went where it was supposed to, then I left."

"Where'd you go after that?" Sobczak asked, but Audra didn't want to say, so Sobczak got firm. "Answer me."

"Fine, you want to know what I did after that? I met with my new boyfriend at our hotel, we went to the town, had a good time, and then we went back to my hotel and had great sex. Would you like to know more?"

"Your new boyfriend?" Gustav asked in German, for he was able to understand just that small bit, causing his heart to wrench at the thought of Audra with someone else.

"Shut up!" Sobczak said, an index finger pointed at his heart like a dagger. He turned back to Audra. "This boyfriend of yours. Was that the one that we saw leaving your hotel this morning? Where did he go?"

"Back to his base," Audra said with a shallow smirk. "He's a soldier... special forces."

"His name isn't Aleksey, is it?" Sobczak asked, unmoved by Audra's words, in turn causing her stomach to sink and her smirk to fade in an instant.

For a moment, Audra feared that her entire relationship with Aleksey up to this point was some sort of scheme, but she didn't want to believe it. Regardless, she had to know how he was involved with them.□

"He's not involved, but he will be unless you cooperate," Sobczak warned. "Tell me what you told him."

"I didn't tell him anything. I don't know anything about what's going on here. I'm just a bartender from Berlin with an idiot ex who got himself in deep shit. Just let me go. I won't say a thing, I swear."

"Nice try, sweetheart," Sobczak said with a smirk. He then fished out his burner phone from his pocket and handed it to her. "You're going to call him right now and you're going to tell him you're just fine, but you're going to cancel any plans you have for the next twenty-four hours."

"That won't be necessary. He's already back on base. I won't be able to contact him," Audra said calmly. "I'm nothing to worry about, I assure you. Gustav didn't say anything to me, and I still have no idea who you people are or what you're up to. Just let me go and I'll be on the next train home."

"Alright then," Sobczak said, seemingly believing her, but then he looked at Trzy. "Get on the line with the Marshal and find out if there are any special troops in the area. If there is, find out what they're up to. I don't believe this is a coincidence."

"On it," Trzy said, and he disappeared into a bedroom shortly after.

Looking back at Audra, Sobczak spoke with a cool but sincere tone. "My compatriot is going to look into things. What he finds out will determine what we do with you."

"You can't be serious. I didn't do anything. Why would you kill me?"

"Easy there, Ms. Rozek. I didn't say anything about killing you. I'm just trying to determine if you're going to be spending the night or if you'll be going on your way," Sobczak said. "Either way, you won't be harmed. You're just an unexpected variable."

"So, what's going to happen?"

"For now, you sit tight and stay out of the way," Sobczak said. "Oh, and no more beating on the ex. You've got a mean hook, but we need him looking halfway decent if we're going to pull this off."

Nodding, Audra looked at a terribly confused Gustav and assured them that they would be alright. Gustav nodded slowly, for despite her anger toward him, it wasn't in her character to lie to him like that.

Chapter 56

Senatgrad, Federal Special Region, Slavic Federation

Like all his fellow senators, Roman left his home in the city while the sun was just barely rising, and the air was still cool with a thick fog rolling in from the sea. When his limousine arrived at the Senatorial Plaza, his heart was warmed by the sight of encampments along the sidewalks and the plaza itself. The pride of Poland was on full display, and though most of the people camped out were still asleep in their tents and sleeping bags, a few were awake and alert. However, his limousine was unmarked and lacked government plates for the sake of security that day; he received his fair share of smiles and cheers, but also a few middle fingers from those who stood openly against secession. A man who truly believed in democracy, this did little to upset him, for he had always viewed the opposition, or loyalists as they were known in a derogatory sense, as a tiny minority. After all, the will of the people to secede was represented by a massive majority. He found it hard to believe anyone with a passion for their country would have stayed home, so he stood by the belief that a vast majority of the nation wished to be free and independent. This warmed his heart and allowed him to enter the Senate Palace with pride and high hopes that he would leave that evening a victorious hero of his people.

Hoping to spend much of the morning taking advantage of the empty offices, Roman made his way from the parking lot without the escort of bodyguards. Entering the building through a pair of double doors, he stepped into a security room manned by a pair of uniformed police officers. Though a familiar face to the pair, he still flashed his identification badge and placed his briefcase on a short conveyor belt. When his briefcase went through the X-ray machine, he was asked to step through a metal detector. Doing as he was asked, Roman was quickly cleared by security and allowed to carry on his way.

Leaving the security room, Roman made his way down a long hallway that led to a T-section. Following the path straight ahead would lead to the lobby where public tours always began, but he took a right. This led him down a short hall, past the bathrooms, and to a secure door opened only with a magnetic strip on his identification badge.

Through the security door, Roman was now in the east wing of the Senatorial Palace and was just a short journey away from his personal office. As expected, the wing was dim, and very few offices were lit. Even so, each one he passed on the way to his own office was simply illuminated by a reading lamp left on overnight. It didn't seem that any of his fellow senators had arrived yet, and for good reason. It was two hours before the Senate would hold its session for the day, and there was little reason anyone would want to arrive so early when the average workday could last half a day or more. However, Roman had good reason to be there so early. He wanted to look over his notes, particularly the list of potential senatorial allies he had acquired since being tasked with doing so, as well as his speech. He planned to refresh his mind on the promises made between each ally and approach them within minutes of their arrival. As for his speech, he was a perfectionist and would be tweaking his word choice and grammar until the moment he was required in the Senate Chamber unless distracted with something more important.

Left to his own devices for close to an hour, Roman was able to accomplish his primary goal before he was unexpectedly interrupted by Filip Bednarz. Given the man's status as both President-elect and Poland's most senior senator, Roman gave him the audience he requested. Fortunately, Bednarz wished to keep things brief.

"I've gone through this novel of yours," Bednarz said, clearly in reference to Roman's lengthy speech. "Are you planning on delivering a filibuster, or do you actually have that much to say?"

Folding his hands on his desktop, Roman looked his compatriot in the eye with a calm expression. "I'm preparing for the worst," he said. "Something tells me we're not going to get the cut-and-dry victory we're hoping for."

"This is no time for talk like that," Bednarz warned. "We need you to appear cool and confident."

"Not to worry," Roman said with a show of confidence that the President-Elect desired.

"But are you confident? We only have one shot at this," Bednarz said.

"I came here hours before today's session to prepare myself and remind our allies of what they stand to gain by siding with us," Roman said. "I'm not saying we won't take the day, but I have prepared a surprise or two. Surely you understand that the people we knew as allies yesterday could have been swayed overnight by the fascists to vote against us."

"I do understand, but what good is this massive speech if we don't get the votes?" Bednarz asked, but Roman was hesitant to say. "Well? What's the reason, Roman?"

"It's the last stand of our legal approach," Roman said. "If it goes down to a tiebreaker, I'll do my absolute best to make the bastard see things our way or go down fighting."

Nodding, Bednarz, though appearing reserved, had his concerns that his country's champion in the Senate was already preparing for failure. He didn't want to believe that, but he hadn't slept well the previous night – kept awake by dreams of an astounding defeat by way of failure to achieve a majority vote or even a tie. However, just as he had said, they couldn't afford to show weakness before the Senate. They needed to prove Poland was not only prepared to go independent and succeed on its own, but that it had wise and confident leaders prepared to take the reins.

"Just let me prepare, Filip. Every second counts."

Nodding, Bednarz wished his associate luck and left him to his work. Roman would then go back to his perfectionist ways, and when he took notice of the first senator on his list, he left his office and prepared to convince them to keep their word. He would go on like this until he either ran out of allies to speak with or he was summoned to take his seat amongst his peers in the Senate Chamber.

Chapter 57

Senatgrad, Federal Special Region, Slavic Federation

Unrestrained and seated on the couch, a full cushion away from Gustav, Audra watched a news program covering the special session of the Senate with bored eyes. Meanwhile, all around her stood the remaining half of the 'Ghost soldiers' - all of them were dressed in the uniform of Senatorial Palace security personnel. Though she had no idea what they were planning, Audra didn't bother to ask, nor did she want to know. These men were very obviously dedicated terrorists, so she wouldn't be surprised if there was bloodshed later that night. As to who would benefit from their actions, she could only guess, but she really didn't want to think about that. So rather than ask questions of the apparent squad leader – a man called Jeden – she continued to watch the opening procedure of the Senate's special session. All the while, Jeden watched with his arms crossed and a frown on his grizzled yet still youthful face. She wondered what he was thinking about, but the moment she heard the Speaker of the Federation call Senator Roman Wilczynski to the floor, the terrorist broke his long silence.

"That's our cue, boys. Let's move out," Jeden said, and as all but one of his men started toward the door, he looked to Gustav with an annoyed scowl. "You too, Kraut-eater. Let's go," he commanded.

"What? Me?" Gustav asked, looking to Audra for help, but she looked away.

"What are you waiting for? A formal invitation? Get your kraut ass up and out that door, double quick!" Jeden commanded.

"But I'm not even dressed like one of you," Gustav said, but Jeden didn't care.

"You don't need to be. Now let's go."

"But why me?"

"Son of a bitch," Jeden muttered under his breath, before becoming forceful. "The boss says you're going, so you go. Now move out!"

"But I'm not even Polish," Gustav said defensively, before looking to Audra again for a moment. "But she is. She even speaks the language!"

"Get fucked!" Audra snarled, but Jeden was intent on Gustav, as evidenced by the drawing of his sidearm.

"I'm running out of patience," Jeden said, the gun held tightly in his hand. "Get up or we'll drag you out."

Looking to Audra again, Gustav whispered a plea for help, but she ignored him and stared at the television. This prompted Jeden to give up on Gustav going freely and ordered someone to pull him to his feet. This sparked the necessary flame under Gustav's rear, and he jumped to his feet.

"Okay, I'm going. Shit!" Gustav exclaimed. "Just tell me what you want from me already."

Rolling his eyes, Jeden told him his job was simple. When the official word that secession had been denied, he will scream out 'śmierć faszyście!' This made Audra chuckle, so Gustav demanded to know what he was going to be forced to shout.

"It means 'death to the fascists,'" Audra said.

"Why would they want me to say that?"

"We'll cover that on the way. Now move!" Jeden shouted, grabbing Gustav by the shirt and pulling him to his feet.

Forced along by Jeden, Gustav left the flat and was followed by the others until only Audra and a single man remained. The sole remaining terrorist then locked the door and looked out the window to ensure his compatriots drove off without a tail. When he was assured that they were clear, he reached into his pocket and removed a phone. Dialing a number committed to memory, he waited several seconds for an answer.

"Boss, this Osiem. The band is on their way to the club."

"Copy that," Sobczak replied. "Security is tight, and we are good to go. Enjoy the party."

"Copy that," Osiem replied, closing his phone a moment later. He then turned to Audra with a grim expression.

"Well, it looks like it's just the two of us for the foreseeable future."

"Don't get any funny ideas," Audra warned, but the terrorist smiled sarcastically.

"Don't kid yourself, I don't much fancy the ladies," Osiem said. "Besides, I don't dig on soft serve."

"Prick," Audra muttered under her breath, sulking into the couch.

Chapter 58

Senatgrad, Federal Special Region, Slavic Federation

Speaking nearly nonstop for almost an hour, Roman was only beginning to hit his stride. He was firing on all cylinders, calling out the detractors to the secessionist cause within his own country's government while speaking about the value of a free and independent nation. All the while, he took opportune swipes at the Medvedev administration, declaring the Premier an autocrat posing as an elected head of state. His fiery rhetoric and bold choice of words earned him much applause from a variety of senators. However, while he surely managed to win a few hearts and minds from the anti-secession camp, it could be said with confidence that he only strengthened the resolve of his opposition.

Roman was a political maverick who took to the floor like a highly trained soldier fighting on home territory. He knew just where to set his crosshairs and what munitions to unleash and where. However, even at his highest points, he couldn't keep the attention of his primary detractor. Whether this was due to sheer boredom or simple malice, he didn't know, nor did he care. But when he noticed the man who claimed to be the head of state for the Slavic Federation had fallen asleep, he took the opportunity to deliver a decisive blow at his nemesis sitting in the highest seat in the chamber.

"And this right here is why we are seeking our independence!" Roman thundered, his hand outstretched toward the snoozing Premier. "This man ... this so-called leader of the Slavic people, is sleeping on the job. He clearly cares not for the plight of his people or the means by which this government operates. He sees himself as higher and mightier than us all. A man so important that he doesn't even have to be awake for this proceeding. A man so vital in his own mind that I may dare accuse him of believing himself as our Tsar without scandal. What do you say, my liege? Are you the lord of these people, or are you their humble, duly elected head of state until the genius of term limits forces you back to Moscow to be forgotten in the dustbin of history?"

The sharpness of Roman's tongue as he lashed out at the Premier echoed through the chamber, stunning his allies and detractors alike. However, his words did not have the effect many would have expected from the man suffering such a berating. Rather, it caused a roar of laughter, for Sergei had fallen into such a deep sleep that a bodyguard had to nudge him awake. However, rather than answer with humility, the Premier recovered expertly with a short counteroffensive.

"I'm sorry, were you still talking, Senator?" Sergei asked, looking at his watch in a comical manner. "It's been more than an hour, surely you're through wasting our time."

"Oh, I've only just begun, Mr. Premier," Roman called back, pointing to a thick stack of papers atop his podium. "Perhaps I should start over since you couldn't give me your full attention the first go around."

"No, I don't think that would be necessary. You've made your primary points, Senator. The vote can begin," Sergei said, but Roman ignored him and attempted to continue his speech. "Senator! I said the vote may begin."

"I'm not yet through," Roman said through gritted teeth, but Sergei refused to allow him to continue and pounded his fist with a thunderous echo heard throughout the chamber.

"Step down from the podium or you will be removed," Sergei snarled.

Though he stood in grim defiance, appearing willing to be removed by force to make one final point, Roman ultimately retired from the podium. As he marched back to his rightful chair among his fellow Polish senators, he wore a reserved grin. Despite appearing to have surrendered to the whim of the man he blatantly called out as a dictator, he felt he had accomplished what he had come to do. So, when the voting began, tradition allowed his nation to have its say first. As expected, the Polish senators stood in solidarity, voting in favor of secession. This was not only a symbolic gesture but a powerful push toward victory. Poland was the third most populous republic in the federation, giving it a sizeable share of senatorial representation. However, Russia, by far the most populous of the seven republics, tripling Poland in both population and senatorial representation, also voted in solidarity. This left many feeling that the cause was lost before the final vote was cast, but Roman's words proved to have a powerful effect. More than half of the Czech and Ukrainian senators voted in Poland's favor, greatly closing the gap. In the end, it would come down to the smaller republics of Bulgaria, Belarus, and Slovakia to vote heavily in favor of Poland to ensure victory. This made the air thick with tension as the votes began to roll in and the pro-secession votes tallied up to rival the Russian-led anti-secession votes.

In the end, the fate of Poland rested on the shoulders of Slovakia, but Roman held onto hope. He had made Slovakia a prime objective in his quest to accrue allies ahead of the vote, and he refused to believe it was for nothing.

One by one, Roman and his countrymen listened as the final batch of senators cast their vote either in favor or against Poland's secession. It seemed as though every second senator voted against them, but when it came down to the final senator, victory was just a single vote in favor away. However, this hard-nosed Slovakian, despite knowing the power of his vote cast against secession, cast his vote quickly and decisively. The result of the vote was a tie.

In Roman's mind, likewise in the mind of his entire country, that one vote signaled the death knell for peaceful secession. The fate of Polish independence was not firmly in the hands of the man Roman had so willingly declared a dictator and publicly embarrassed before the world. As expected, Roman's arrogance would cost him dearly.

Stepping up to the podium with a reserved expression, Sergei Medvedev had already made his choice long before entering the chamber and taking his seat among the Senate. However, rather than cast the tiebreaking vote and put an end to Poland's bid to secede, he took the time to deliver a speech.

"While I certainly admire the courage and bravado of Senator Wilczynski, I cannot in good faith see things his way," the Premier began. "You see, I was skeptical of the intention of the secessionists, even after their country voted quite proudly to leave our beloved federation. While I was stunned by this decision and quite personally disappointed, I respected the collective decision of the Polish people. However, not wanting to see such a lovely nation fall into ruin from a lack of forward-thinking, I extended the olive branch and offered the Polish Liberation Party a generous amount of time to develop their social and economic plans for an independent Poland. Unfortunately, a deal could not be met between the presumptive government of the Free Republic of Poland and the legitimate government of the Polish Republic aligned with the Slavic Federation. Yet, I extended the olive branch again and allowed them to make their case before this very special session of the Senate. And as you can see, you all have had your say, and the results are quite remarkable. Therefore, I applaud you, Senator Wilczynski, as well as Senator Bednarz. While you both worked very hard to prove Poland is worthy to stand on its own, I'm afraid Senator Wilczynski wasted far too much time finding ways to assassinate my character instead of winning over your peers, and it shows. Regardless, I must vote with my conscience, not ego, though the result is the same. As Premier of the Slavic Federation, I hereby cast the tiebreaking vote against Poland's secession from the Slavic Federation."

The moment the Premier took to the podium, Roman felt his stomach sink and the acid churn within. He could taste the bitter flavor of defeat on his tongue as Sergei gave his speech before finally driving the nail into the coffin that now contained the idea of peaceful secession. For though he always stood firmly against plots of violence, he could not stand the thought of his country staying under the boot of a tyrant like Sergei Medvedev without a fight. So, in one final desperate show of patriotic defiance, he stood up and boldly cried out to Sergei with a challenge.

"Prove me wrong, Mr. Premier!" Roman called out. "Prove you're not the tyrant I accused you of being by resigning this instant. Show the people that this is truly a federal union of free republics and not a dictatorship ruled over by a fascist with dreams of a Russian Empire reborn!"

"I have nothing to prove, Senator," Sergei said with a smile. "The people voted me into this office, and they will surely vote me out if they see fit. Nothing short of scandal will remove me from this position a moment sooner."

"Then you've proven my point, Mr. Premier," Roman said strongly. "But don't let your arrogance get the best of you. Sooner or later, the people will see you for what you really are."

In a bold move, Roman turned to his shocked compatriots, nodded his head, and headed back onto the floor. But rather than take to the podium, he headed for the doors that would lead to the main hall.

"And where do you think you're going, Senator?" Sergei called after Roman.

"To address my people."

When Roman stepped out onto the steps of the Senatorial Palace, Roman found the plaza brimming with life. Men and women of all ages had shown up to show their support for either secession or the status quo. While the sight of Polish flags waving in the air warmed his heart, he wasn't quite sure how the crowd would take the news. Nonetheless, he took to the podium and scanned the crowd with the cool eyes of a veteran politician. Fully aware that ultranationalists were lying in wait, fully prepared to turn the city upside down, he swallowed hard as he took to an empty podium. Clearing his throat quietly, he gripped the sides of the podium and lowered his head for a moment of silence. His action spoke louder than the words to come, for the crowd hushed, save for a few ecstatic loyalists.

"My beloved countrymen, I apologize for the length of time you have waited for this moment, but I had a great deal to say to secure the freedom of our great nation once and for all," Roman began, sparking hope in the hearts of his constituents. "However, despite a valiant effort, the vote ultimately went down to a tie, and the Premier had his way--"

"Death to the fascists!" Gustav shouted out from somewhere in the crowd, but confusion only spread as Roman appeared to agree with the uncouth statement.

"Though crude, I'm inclined to agree, good sir," Roman said in response, despite being cut off mid-sentence. "The will of the Polish people was heard loud and clear when we voted as a nation to free ourselves from the bondage of this corrupt federation. We were denied our decision under false pretenses so that a man who will surely be our Premier for life could stomp out the last fading embers of our hope, but this isn't over, my friends. My fellow patriots and I will not take this disrespect lying down. We will fight tooth and claw until we see our great nation set free. While Poland may not be seceding tonight, I will continue this great crusade so that one day our nation and our people will have the freedom our brothers and fathers fought and bled for not even a generation ago. Until then, go home, reflect on our situation, and wake up tomorrow refreshed and ready to take this fight to the next level."

With nothing more to say, Roman thanked them all for their valiant efforts to get their countrymen to the voting polls and their undying support of the cause and then turned to head back inside. But just as he took his first steps toward the doors back inside, he heard chants of 'śmierć faszyście!' echoing throughout the plaza. While Roman was inclined to agree and even wanted to address the crowd again, his bodyguards urged him onward. Feeling their anger, he threw aside his bodyguard's hand and broke free of their collective grasp as the group attempted to seize him for his own good.

Hurrying back to the podium, Roman spoke as he stared out onto the rowdy crowd with anger in his face. Though he spared them the venom he had unleashed upon the Premier, his words were just as calculated and vindictive.

"I hear your anger, my friends. Let it out. Show them our pride. Show them that our voices will not be silenced. Rise up against your oppressors and show them your anger. Let there be no peace until we have had our way!" Roman cried out, and though he had more to say, his bodyguards grabbed him in a tight grip and pulled him back.

Forced along, Roman was able to break free for just long enough to turn to the crowd and raise a defiant fist - a symbol of revolutionary spirit. As if his gesture was a cue, a flurry of loud pops not unlike gunshots echoed through the plaza. Before he could even react, his bodyguards flocked around him and ushered him inside as the crowd panicked. Further pops could be heard as fighting broke out between opposing sides. Riot police moved in quickly to control the situation before it could spiral out of control, but they were soon pelted with rocks and bottles. A vicious melee soon broke out, and eventually a riot officer crossed the line when he smashed a young woman in the face with a baton. Their collective anger centered on the offending officer; a mob quickly enveloped and beat down the officer without mercy. His compatriots could do little to save him from the vengeful crowd, for every officer had become fair game, and the riot was quickly growing out of their control.

While no one was sure who opened fire first, the riot quickly turned into an un-quenchable maelstrom of street violence bordering on insurrection as angry and violent protestors ultimately overwhelmed the police lines and attempted to storm the Senate before being beaten back with tear gas and rubber bullets. The Senate had to be evacuated as a result, and the blame was laid solely on Roman's shoulders. All the while, the ultra-nationalists truly responsible for the riot made their escape with their objective complete, while the riot spread across the city like a firestorm. The fighting in the streets would capture the attention of law enforcement from around the region, providing the perfect opportunity for the grand finale of the ultranationalist plan to kick off a campaign of violent revolution.

Chapter 59

Senatgrad, Federal Special Region, Slavic Federation

Leaving the Gdansk naval yard for the naval base at Baltiysk that morning, Aleksey learned his battered unit was assigned to the Premier's Manor in the countryside north of the federal capital. Traveling there was about forty minutes and though the grounds were prepped for a splendid gala, the party wouldn't begin for hours. So, after a briefing session with the FSB's Alpha Group operators serving as primary security, Aleksey caught a few hours of much-needed rest in one of the many guest rooms found within the spacious Russian Revival-style mansion that sat atop a hill at the center of the property. When he was on duty, he found himself assigned to a twelve-hour patrol that would see him split his time between overwatch on the roof and wandering the grounds on patrol. Unfortunately, his patrol route was focused on the gardens on the east side of the property. This would leave him isolated from the gala, which was meant to be contained to the south lawn and the ballroom.

It was going to be a long and grueling shift, but it had its perks. Being isolated for six of the twelve hours meant he could openly carry his weapon while the men from Alpha Group wandering the gala had to keep a low profile. Regardless, he was kept to the same standards as the others and was allowed to carry no more than a suppressed pistol and a small utility knife. This left Aleksey wondering if there was a threat at all, but he didn't dare question his orders. He simply dressed in the fine tuxedo he was issued at the request of the First Lady and carried out his shift with high hopes that it would be nothing more than a splendid night for high society.

Eight hours into his shift, Aleksey was walking his patrol route through the gardens, and aside from coming across a naval officer receiving a party favor from a waiter, there was nothing out of the ordinary to report. It was a posh event with dozens of high-ranking citizens and dignitaries mingling between sips of champagne or top-shelf spirits. This was a who's who affair, but it was also dreadfully boring for a man like Aleksey. Having spent his teen years among the affluent, he could easily guess what the small talk consisted of and none of it interested him. While they all cared for high fashion, business, and politics, he was more interested in heavy metal and adventure, and little has changed for him. Of course, Aleksey wasn't there to mingle or partake in elitist debauchery, he was there to ensure no one shot up the place in a bold act of extremism. After all, the fate of Polish secession was on the table at the Senate at that very moment.

Walking a copper-colored stone footpath that snaked along the perimeter and through the garden, Aleksey made his way along his usual route. Eventually, he turned onto a paved path that ran down a few steps and along a babbling brook that crossed the property into a pond hidden by an untouched meadow at the very edge of the property.

As with the other times he had made his way along this part of his route, he expected that there would be nothing to report. However, this time would prove to be different, for as he made his way down the path, he spotted a figure in the distance. The path was dimly lit by design, so Aleksey couldn't get a good look at the person, but he knew the rules – all areas of the grounds are restricted aside from the south lawn, the patio, and the ballroom. If a Rear Admiral couldn't get a blowjob on his watch, no one was getting a pass.

Living up to his duty, Aleksey quickened his pace and prepared to intercept the intruder. While he assumed this could have been a guest getting some air or a risky adventure, their reason didn't matter. Only security personnel were allowed there, making him a little anxious. This could very well be a hostile encounter, so to ensure his own safety, he quietly unbuttoned his holster and drew his service weapon. Taking a moment to check the slide, he held it low and closed the distance with both hands gripping the weapon. Never did his eyes stray from the advancing intruder, but it didn't seem like he realized that he was even there. Regardless, Aleksey held out one hand in a universal gesture and made his command in Russian.

"Hey! This is a restricted area," Aleksey called out, but the intruder didn't respond. He repeated himself, this time in Polish, and he soon heard a reply.

"Settle down, we're on the same team," he heard the shadowy figure say. A few moments later the mysterious stranger transformed from a shadowy figure into a middle-aged man bearing the very same outfit as his unit and the Alphas. However, Aleksey didn't recognize him, but that was understandable. He was given precious little time to meet with the men from Squadron A before deployment, so this could have been one of the few men he missed. However, he had to be certain. It wasn't the Russians who were seceding, after all.

Keeping his composure and sticking to protocol, Aleksey kept a blank face as he approached the suspicious GROM soldier. When they were no more than a short dash apart, he watched as a military identification card was presented. Right away, Aleksey noticed he was who he suspected him to be, so he nodded and told him to carry on. The soldier didn't say anything, though he kept right on his path as if Aleksey was in the wrong.

Shrugging off the encounter, Aleksey continued his patrol, but for a moment he thought to turn back and question why he hadn't responded when he first spoke in Russian, though he ultimately chose against it. For all he knew, the man was listening to orders streaming through his earpiece and didn't hear him, so he just kept on his way. He would soon spot a familiar pergola a short distance from his path and decide to have a quick sit to rest his legs after walking for so long without rest.

Sitting at a wooden table situated just a few feet from the rocky embankment of the brook, Aleksey could have gone for the quick nicotine rush of a cigarette, but like anything that could be considered mind-altering, cigarettes were contraband while on duty. Though it wasn't the worst policy, kicking that dirty habit he picked up early on in his career wasn't as easy as he had hoped. The trick was getting his mind off the craving, but he was too tired to think about much else. Even his memories of Audra were blurred. Letting off a sigh, he just leaned back onto the table and stared at the concrete platform beneath him. After a short while, he caught notice of a faint red light flashing every couple of seconds.

Intrigued by what he was seeing, Aleksey squinted his eyes and leaned forward to see if he was really seeing a dull red flash or if it was just the product of his imagination. After about twenty seconds he realized it was no illusion, there was indeed a dull red light strobing nearby. The question was where it came from and what was causing it.

Climbing off from the bench situated before the table and taking two steps back, Aleksey stared between the bench and the table. He could still see the light blinking every two or three seconds, but it wasn't coming from beneath the table nor was the source found along the roof slats of the pergola. For a moment he was perplexed and considered his mind really was playing tricks, but something told him to kneel. When he did, he spotted the source beneath the very bench he had been sitting on. While he felt the need to investigate more closely, he heard a strange, almost confirming beep emitted from the device. His heart began to race, as his brain screamed for him to run. That thing was just armed!

Dashing out from the pergola, Aleksey had the terrible feeling that the device under the bench could blow at any moment. The will to survive demanded he find cover quickly. However, the brook was far too rocky to safely dive for lower terrain, but there was a low wall built before a short hedge just a few feet away but on the opposite side of the paved path.

His legs pumping as hard as they could, Aleksey felt like he was running in slow motion, but when he reached the wall, he dove hands-first through the air and heard a deafening roar followed almost immediately by a sharp pain across his body. Luckily, his survival instincts were in firm control, and he landed harmlessly in a perfect shoulder roll.

When his body came to a halt after a single rotation, he felt the searing pain return. His jaw clenched he fought through it as he crawled toward the hedge he had just vaulted. Tucking himself as close to the hedge as he could, he covered his head with his torn jacket as debris rained down. He tried to control the oncoming panic and clear his head so that he could listen for an approaching hostile, but then came another explosion, and then another. By the time the explosions stopped, he counted four, but the screams of terror were quickly overwhelmed by the sound of automatic gunfire. Judging by the distinct snarl of the weapon, it was the Skorpion machine pistol – a favorite of Alpha Group.

Sitting silently for a few moments, Aleksey tried to calm his nerves and get a hold of the situation, but there was no time. Someone was on the footpath and attempting to approach quietly. His pistol drawn and readied, Aleksey eased himself onto his feet and crept low and slowly along the hedge away from the ravaged pergola. Doing well to keep his head down and his steps quiet, he followed the footsteps on the footpath, stopping when they stopped and moving only when they moved. While a less disciplined mind would have panicked by now, Aleksey had shifted from simple survival mode to hunter. Whoever was on the other side of that hedge was his enemy and had a part to play in the massacre unfolding elsewhere on the property. First and foremost, he had to take this son of a bitch down, but his next few moves were critical. One wrong decision would determine if he lived or died, and he was intent on seeing his sweetheart again.

Like the well-trained killing machine that he was, Aleksey calmly but surely made his way along the hedge and to the farthest edge of the wall. With his finger ready to cover the trigger at any moment he licked his lips and took a chance by peering around the corner. The terrorist was out of sight, but he could hear his footsteps, though they were quite faint. This told him he had moved on, but he couldn't risk calling in for help or making a run for safety until he was either spotted at a safe distance or neutralized. He preferred the former, but the latter was suddenly chosen for him as he realized the footsteps were echoing off the gravel path that led to the grassy lawn behind the hedge and wall.

"Shit!" Aleksey screamed in his head, doing well not to speak the word aloud, but he was quick enough around the wall to avoid the terrorist's line of sight.

Once more on opposite sides of the wall, Aleksey felt like no progress had been made. Rather, he was more exposed than ever. If he stayed against the exterior of the wall, he would be an easy target for anyone coming through the meadow. He had to find better cover and the only option it seemed was the wreckage of the pergola. This proved to be a wise choice, for within moments of taking refuge behind a support beam of the wrecked structure, the terrorist took his chance and sprang up from behind the wall in hopes of taking him down with a quick barrage of bullets from his machine pistol.

Thanks to the darkness of the area – caused by a power outage that struck about the same time the bombs went off – Aleksey was able to hide in almost plain sight as the sharp-dressed terrorist checked his surroundings. It appeared he was considering investigating the pergola once more, but after a few seconds had passed, he turned on his heels and started off toward the party in a hurried crouch. He would only take a few steps before grass and dirt shot up ahead of him and he heard Aleksey shouting at him.

"Drop the weapon! Get on your knees!" Aleksey shouted with his gun drawn and steady. "Do it! Do it now!"

Seemingly accepting that he was caught in a compromising position, the terrorist tossed the gun aside and raised his hands to show he was no longer a threat. He then slowly lowered to his knees and rested atop his bent legs as if he was attending a karate class, but his hands were placed on his lap giving Aleksey reason to worry.

"Let me see your hands!" Aleksey barked while slowly closing the distance. "Do it!"

His command ignored, Aleksey moved his finger over the trigger and prepared to open fire if necessary. He wanted to take this man alive but the way his arms and shoulders were moving slightly told him he was up to something.

"Last chance. Show me your hands or I'll shoot!" Aleksey said, but the terrorist twisted his body suddenly and sent something thin in Aleksey's direction with a flick of his wrist.

While he certainly expected something like this to happen, Aleksey was barely able to react as a slender throwing knife cut through the air and narrowly missed the diving commando. But even before Aleksey hit the ground his pistol barked four times in rapid secession. All but one of the bullets met their mark as the terrorist jumped to his feet and tried to run off to find cover or join his compatriots in the mellowing slaughter.

Quickly recovering from another hard collision with the ground, Aleksey stood his ground as the terrorist lay sprawled out on the footpath. From what he could see there was nothing in his hands, but the knife seemingly came out of nowhere, so taking no chances he held his ground. More than thirty seconds passed; Aleksey's arms were growing tired, but he refused to move. The only thing that managed to break his concentration was a sudden communication in his ear.

"This is Wronka. All units report in if you can," he heard the Major call out over the radio.

Keeping his weapon steady and his eyes on the downed enemy, Aleksey touched his earpiece with his index finger. "This is Rybinski. I took down a hostile in the east garden. Holding position," he said, but the voices of others began to echo in his head. It seemed the whole unit was accounted for, but no one seemed to know what was going on and was awaiting further orders.

"Copy that," Major Wronka said, before a long period of silence was ultimately broken by the Alpha commander.

"All units, the Iron Lady is secure and waiting to evacuate. Fall back to your designated rendezvous point," the Alpha Commander said, and Aleksey sighed in relief.

"Copy that," he said, but he couldn't move out just yet. He had to ensure the terrorist before him was dead and not waiting for him to turn his back for an easy kill.

Moving in slowly, both hands gripping his weapon as before, Aleksey kept his pistol steady and his eyes locked on the target. With each nervous step, the picture became clearer. The imposter had taken a bullet in his right arm and shoulder, crippling him if he were right-handed. As he drew even closer, he spotted a sizeable bloodstain at the exact center of his back. By some miracle, the man had forgone a bulletproof vest, allowing for one lucky bullet to strike him straight through the heart.

Hurrying through the garden while keeping close to whatever cover he could, Aleksey made his way through the winding and somewhat confusing garden paths. Ducking behind statues, stone planters, and benches, his journey was slow but methodical. Just because the shooting had stopped and all his team was accounted for didn't mean the threat was gone. The last thing he could do before regrouping was let his guard down.

So careful as always, he made his way through the darkened gardens, prepared to defend himself with deadly force.

Coming up near the junction that would lead to the east patio and a wrought iron service gate that led out onto the south lawn where the party had been hosted, Aleksey crept slowly. This was the perfect place for an ambush, but in time enough he found the area was clear. Flushed with relief, he kept toward the gate and carefully pulled open the door to his right. While the door creaked, he didn't hear anything in the immediate area. It seemed the coast was clear, but when he stepped out onto the south lawn, his stomach dropped.

The main patio was akin to his worst experience in Yugoslavia. There were bodies everywhere. Servants, military officers, government officials, businessmen all lay crumpled on the ground. They had been caught by surprise and slaughtered with little hope of survival. To make matters worse, Aleksey had no choice but to pass through the macabre scene. Fortunately, he had a strong stomach, but he could barely hold onto his dinner as he walked through the rows of dead victims. As he moved, he kept his body low and his weapon ready, allowing him to notice that several bombs had gone off there, too. He quickly surmised that these were the bombs he heard after the one in the garden. The pergola was likely part of a diversion to draw away security personnel to allow for the gunmen to swoop in and maximize casualties after blowing their primary charges.

Hoping his compatriots survived and were planning to hunt down and punish those responsible for this atrocity, Aleksey continued to move with a strong determination to avenge the fallen. Though cover was sparse, he worked with what he had and slowly made his way toward the stone steps that would lead up to a raised section of the patio off the back of the house. Knowing this point was prime for an ambush, he took cover behind an overturned table. Steadying his breathing, he listened for movement, and for a moment, he could have sworn he heard his name.

Fearful of an ambush, Aleksey drew his weapon and checked the magazine. With his body fully covered by the table, he peered out from hiding. His eyes scanning the area, he spotted a hand reaching up from a thicket of bodies a few feet from his position. Knowing there was no way anyone would have died in such a position, he leaned his head toward his shoulder radio and spoke into the receiver. "Anyone upstairs with eyes on the lower patio?"

"Who's that?" he heard a member of GROM ask.

"Rybinski. I have eyes on a survivor, I need cover. Copy?"

"What's your location? I don't see anyone down there."

"I'm on the lower level, behind an overturned table. I'll raise my hand."

"Copy, I see you. I've got your six."

Confident that the sniper would have him covered, Aleksey checked his surroundings before leaving the safety of the table. Moving out in a low crouch, he weaved through the dead until he laid eyes on a man he hadn't expected to see there.

"Wolski!" Aleksey cried out at the sight of a badly wounded GROM operator, Stefan Wolski.

As he approached, Aleksey found him clenching his abdomen with one crimson hand. His instincts in control, Aleksey dashed the remaining distance and dropped to his knees beside his fallen friend. Staring up at him in anguish as he clenched his abdomen, it was immediately clear that Wolski had taken a hit to the midsection. Despite his pain and looming death, he croaked out a simple question regarding Aleksey's presence, but it was ignored as Aleksey checked him over for life-threatening wounds.

Though he wasn't equipped for first aid, all members of GROM learned enough battlefield medicine to know how to treat a bullet or shrapnel wound on the fly. However, without a first aid kit, there was little he could do for him other than what Wolski was already doing. Nevertheless, Aleksey was resolute in saving his friend and vowed to get help. Yet, when he tried to stand upright, Wolski grabbed him by the sleeve with one hand.

"I'm not going to make it," Wolski said, but Aleksey told him to keep his hope alive long enough for a medic to see to him, but Wolski weakly shook his head. "Is she alive?"

"Is who alive?" Aleksey asked, confused by the question.

Suddenly, Aleksey's radio came to life just as he heard the whining of a helicopter's engine firing up. "The Iron Lady is secure and making her exit. Prepare for anything," he heard a Russian voice declare.

"Dammit," Wolski said with a bitter sigh, flinching as the pain grew more intense. Despite the pain it caused, he reached into his pocket and pulled out a tightly folded square of paper. "Here, make sure this gets to my parents. It'll explain everything."

"I'm not taking some death letter. Just wait here, I'll be back soon," Aleksey said, but Wolski kept his grip and forced the paper into Aleksey's hand.

"I'm not going to make it, but I can't let them take me in."

"What?" Aleksey asked, as confused as ever. "What are you talking about?"

Just as the words left Aleksey's mouth, he heard the distinct hiss of a shoulder-fired missile. Turning on his heels with his eyes to the sky, his blood ran cold as he saw a small surface-to-air missile racing toward the helicopter. Seconds later, the aircraft deployed countermeasures, but the flares were launched too late, and the helicopter erupted in a magnificent fireball. Aleksey's heart just about stopped as he saw a fiery wreck descend to the ground. There was no chance anyone aboard was still alive, but strangely, there was no frantic chatter. Not even the Alphas were in a panic. It was almost as if they allowed the First Lady to be killed.

Though unsure what to make of all of this, he didn't have time to waste. He looked at Wolski and saw that he was fading fast. Knowing he didn't have much time, Aleksey had to accept the risk that came with moving him.

"Listen, I have to get you to the rendezvous point, but you're going to be in a lot of pain."

"Just leave me," Wolski said, but Aleksey refused.

"It's not far. I just need to get you down to the garage in the basement. Doc will patch you up," Aleksey said, but as he tried to pull Wolski to a sitting position, the wounded soldier made a sudden and unexpected move for his sidearm, but the weapon fell from his grasp. He was weak from blood loss.

Unsure what was going through his wounded friend's mind, but knowing the clock was ticking ever faster, Aleksey forced Wolski to a sitting position before hoisting him over his shoulders and carrying him off as they had all been trained.

Following a slow but unremarkable journey from the back lawn to the rendezvous point in the basement, Aleksey arrived to find his team standing by and watching as Major Wronka engaged in a heated discussion with his Alpha Group equivalent. While he was sure they were arguing over the downing of the helicopter, Aleksey boldly interrupted them declaring he had a survivor in need of immediate medical attention. As a result, both men and their subordinates turned their attention to Aleksey as he laid Wolski down on the floor.

"Who the hell is this?" the Alpha Commander asked, for despite his attire, Wolski was immediately seen as an imposter.

"Is that Wolski?" Wronka asked, but neither man got an answer, for as the GROM operator known simply as Doc checked over the wounded solider, he made a grim discovery.

"This man's dead," Doc declared.

Aleksey's heart swelled in his chest as he looked down at Wolski's lifeless eyes as he lay sprawled on the floor. This man was one of his best friends since joining the squadron and now here he was, dead before his eyes, and he blamed himself. Had he just left him behind and brought Doc back, he might have survived. However, the Alpha Commander didn't give him more than a few seconds to mourn, for with a cold expression, he pointed his index finger at Wronka like it were a knife.

"You know this man? He's one of yours?"

"Yes, of course, but no. He's not part of this detachment," Wronka said, confused by Wolski's presence and the Alpha Commander's aggression.

"This man is a terrorist!" the Alpha Commander shouted, and without a second thought, he drew his sidearm instigating a tense standoff between GROM and Alpha Group. Tensions flared as the Alpha leader declared Wolski a terrorist and Wronka being a co-conspirator. While Wronka did not take kindly to being called a terrorist himself, he chalked this all up to a case of mistaken identity. So, to prevent further violence, he boldly lowered his weapon.

"Enough of this shit!" Wronka said. "We need to secure the grounds."

Glaring at Wronka, the Alpha Commander held his position for a tense few seconds before disengaging his weapon and slipping it back into his hip holster.

"He's right. We need to secure the grounds. I want a priority on capture over kill. Fall out!"

Chapter 60

Federal Special Region, Slavic Federation

Still at the terrorist safe house, watching the Senate's live broadcast, Audra was sitting as far from the man tasked with guarding her as possible. While Roman was certainly passionate throughout his speech, she found herself fading in and out due to the length of the speech and general disinterest. Still, she couldn't allow herself to fall asleep out of fear of the soldier watching, even though his snoring was loud enough to block out the volume of the broadcast at times.

Bored and on the verge of falling asleep, Audra pinched her eyelids, making a tiny pop as the air escaped. This always seemed to give her a small boost, but to help matters, she sat up and tried to focus on what was being said by the passionate senator. However, despite her best effort, she eventually lost control and nodded off. Sometime later, she woke up to a concerned voice, and when she opened her eyes, she saw a young field reporter broadcasting from a chaotic scene at the Senate Plaza. Though her tired brain struggled to follow what was being said, a picture proved to be worth a thousand words, for it was obvious from the fire, yelling, and general chaos happening behind the reporter that a riot was in progress. The point was driven home when a well-aimed rock struck the camera directly in the lens, prompting the cameraman to break professional etiquette and swear loudly before the reporter finally ordered her crew to cut the scene and run. This all drew Audra in, but the report cut shortly after to the main broadcast back at the station. For a moment, Audra prepared to settle in for a boring run-of-the-mill news segment, but she was met with a breaking news story – a gun battle had erupted at the Premier's Manor north of the city. However, before Audra could become engrossed in the story, the soldier, whom Audra hadn't realized was missing until this point, stepped out of the kitchen with a phone in hand.

"Time to go," he said calmly.

Fearful of him, Audra carefully asked where they were headed, but the soldier wasn't willing to divulge much. He simply told her that it didn't matter and that she had best go quietly and without incident. Taking this as a sign that she wouldn't be harmed, she went quietly and was taken to a work van parked along the street. While she was allowed to ride shotgun, this only lasted until they reached a rendezvous point outside of the city. It was at this point that matters took a dark, though somewhat expected, turn.

Taken from the vehicle, Audra marched to the back of the van that was waiting for their arrival. Told to relax and that they were doing it purely for her own safety, she was gagged with a bandana and restrained at the wrists with plastic zip ties. She was then loaded into the cargo area with the vague promise that it wouldn't be too long a ride and that she had nothing to fear. Regardless, Audra was terrified and didn't expect to survive.

Roughly an hour after leaving their safehouse in Senatgrad, Sobczak was riding in an inconspicuous sedan when the burner phone in his pocket began to ring. Knowing that the caller could be only one person, he answered with a simple remark of 'Yes, Colonel?'

"The city is aflame, and it seems someone shot up the Premier's Manor," Colonel Kozak said with a tone that bordered between displeased and bemused. "Your orders were clear, Captain. Your men were to disrupt the gala and kidnap the First Lady, not shoot up the place and get your men slaughtered. What were you thinking?"

"We walked into an ambush. Someone rolled on us," Sobczak replied, but that did little to ease the frustration coming from the other end of the line. "Besides, a few of the men had a score to settle over the Varyag."

"Don't bullshit me! You had your orders, and you chose to disobey them," Kozak snarled. "Do you have any idea what you have done?"

"Yes, I got a handful of good men killed, but we killed the First Lady," Sobczak said, masking his emotion well. "We showed them that there are consequences for their actions, and we're not afraid to give it all for the cause."

"All true, but you don't seem to understand that your actions tonight could very well have started a war," Kozak declared, but Sobczak was unmoved. In fact, he was resolute, even questioning the second-in-command of the Polish Liberation Army.

"War is what we signed up for, Colonel. This is no time to get cold feet—"

"You watch your mouth!" Kozak snapped. "We spent months planning out this campaign, and you threw it all out the window by going rogue."

"I accept that I failed tonight, but again, it was an ambush. They were waiting for us to launch the attack. But rest assured, it's all going to work itself out," Sobczak said with cool confidence. "We accounted for every liability, even losing most of the squad. It's going to be fine, ma'am."

"I still don't think you understand the gravity of the situation," Kozak shot back. "You commando types may know how to cover your tracks, but you're overlooking a very simple fact about war."

"Oh, and what's that?"

"The fact that the fascists are going to use this to justify invading," Kozak declared, and Sobczak had no recourse. He simply remained silent, so the Colonel sighed. "At least tell me the foreigners are accounted for."

"I'm dealing with it as we speak," Sobczak said. "They won't be a problem after tonight. I can assure you that."

"After what you just pulled, I'm not sure I can trust you on that," Kozak said, but Sobczak shrugged. "I want those liabilities eliminated with extreme prejudice."

"I'll handle the liabilities, but if you want them to disappear, that'll cost you," Sobczak replied. "These are German citizens, you know."

Enraged, Kozak declared that he'd be hearing from the Marshal himself before ending the call abruptly. This only made Sobczak chuckle, for he had no fear of the Marshal. After all, it was Marshal Krupa himself who ordered the audible. Had he not been told to kill the First Lady, he would have carried out Kozak's plan flawlessly. So, given that the contract was fulfilled, he knew the Colonel threw the phone out the window. A few minutes later, he ordered the driver to pull over.

Stepping out of the vehicle, Sobczak walked along the shoulder of a deserted country highway, passing alongside a work van driven. Walking to the back, he unlocked the back door, prompting the cargo light to turn on. Inside, he found Audra curled up against the back wall with her mouth still gagged and her hands tied. When their eyes met, she started to scream, but her voice was muffled. Sobczak responded by raising one finger to his mouth and quietly declared that he had no intention of hurting her, but it had little effect. In fact, she only tried harder to be heard when Sobczak climbed into the van and partially closed the door to avoid a situation should someone happen to pass by. When he began approaching her in a low crouch, she became hysterical, pleading for mercy through her gag. When he was close enough, she kicked her legs, but he easily outmaneuvered her and took hold of her wrists as she attempted to smash him over the head with one big fist.

"Look, I know you're scared, so I'm going to level with you. I'm going to send you on your way, and if you keep your mouth shut, you will never see me or my men again. Do you understand?" he said, but while Audra stopped trying to scream, she was breathing heavily and moaning fearfully. So, to calm her down, Sobczak cut to the chase and reached into his pocket. He soon presented her with her own government identification. "I have a copy of this, so I know where you live, but so long as you don't tell a soul about what happened out here, you're going to be fine. Nod your head if you understand."

Seeing her nod quickly, Sobczak thanked her for her cooperation. "Now, if you can be a good girl, I'll take off those restraints. I'll even let you ride up front. Can I trust you to do that?"

Seeing her nod again, Sobczak drew a boxcutter from his pocket, and Audra became hysterical again, but showing that he was a man of his word, he cut the plastic restraints at her wrists and ankles. He then put the blade away and reached for the bandana wrapped tightly around her head.

"Do yourself a favor and don't scream. I don't like loud noises in confined spaces."

Seeing the edge of the knife glistening in the artificial light as it poked out from his pocket, Audra nodded slowly. She was then freed of the gag, but she didn't say a word. She just stared into the beady black eyes sunken behind Sobczak's grizzled face.

"Good girl," Sobczak replied, putting the knife away. "Now just follow me out, nice and easy. We'll get you to the train station real soon. This will all be over so long as you keep your word."

"I won't say a word to anyone," Audra said, breaking her silence.

"Good," Sobczak said, and he turned to leave, but then he smirked and turned back. "Curious thought. Aren't you worried about your boyfriend?"

"He's not my boyfriend," Audra said firmly, but Sobczak just smiled.

"That's not how he tells it."

"He's delusional, but whatever. I just want to go home," Audra said.

"Then right this way."

Doing as she had been ordered, Audra carefully climbed out of the van. Scanning the area, she found that they were in the middle of nowhere with wheat fields flanking the highway they were on. Seemingly trusting of her, Sobczak walked ahead toward the car idling behind the van. Though her instincts told her to take her chances and run into the wheat, she resisted. They would likely find her, and they would probably kill her for such a stunt. So, taking her chances in trusting them, she joined Sobczak by the car and climbed into the back seat. Where they were going was known only to the driver, and perhaps Sobczak, but so long as this night ended with her safely on a train home, she didn't care.

Chapter 61

Senatgrad, Federal Special Region, Slavic Federation

A man gripped with sorrow after having his nation's independence stolen from him with a smile, Roman returned home against the advice of his security detail. Truthfully, he didn't care if the riot threatened his building. He did all he could do to free his homeland, but everything he did appeared to be nothing more than dust in the wind.

Wanting nothing more than a stiff drink and some time alone on the balcony to reflect on the situation, Roman stepped into the condo and passed his wife without a word. Heading to the wet bar, he fixed himself a drink from the finest English gin he had ever tasted – the very same he planned to drink to celebrate Poland's freedom. However, considering the turnout of the night, the thought of his original intention for the spirit robbed him of his will to drink.

Passing on his gin, Roman went outside with nothing in hand. Leaning on the steel railing, he looked down at the streets below. It was a long fall, certainly long enough to guarantee a successful suicide, but killing himself was the last thing he would ever consider. He may have been lost to sorrow, but he had not lost his mind or his will to live. He was grappling with the fact that, despite his best efforts, he had lost the good fight and had to accept that the only way to free his homeland once more was by way of the sword. However, he did not have the heart to do such things. He was a politician, and a maverick at that. He hadn't carried a gun in decades, but even amidst a revolution, it never felt right in his hands. His mind was his weapon, but it appeared to be as effective as a bayonet against a machine gun. He just hoped this war wouldn't be as costly as the last, but he knew that was wishful thinking. Just like the last war, they were up against a superpower led by a man who would stop at nothing for complete and total victory. Their only hope for victory this time around would be foreign intervention, yet he feared nothing had changed in the decades since the world watched the Kremlin burn and the Soviet Empire collapse under the weight of popular revolution. NATO didn't help then, so who's to say they would help now?

Leaving the railing and sulking on a patio chair, Roman dreaded the thought of his country becoming a battleground for the fourth time in a century, so he tried to put the thought from his mind and enjoy the cityscape while he still could. For all he knew, he was a marked man for what he had done on the Senate floor. So long as they left his family alone, he didn't care. He was more than willing to die for his country, even if his crime was nothing more than telling a bitter truth with the whole world watching.

Suddenly deciding that perhaps he did need that drink, Roman pushed himself up from his chair and slid the patio door open. Upon stepping inside, he found his wife pouring a drink. When she turned around, he saw that she had two highball glasses in her hands. It was clear that she wanted to talk, so he met her halfway, but she passed him the drink as she headed for the door. Following her closely, he joined her on the patio.

Holding his drink close to his chest, Roman looked to his wife as she took a long sip. She then blew the burning air from her nose and looked at him with compassion in her eyes. "Why don't you tell me what's on your mind?"

"The future of our country," he said, but she shrugged.

"What about it?"

"I'm worried what will happen now that we've lost."

"Just let it go, Roman. It's done and over with."

"It's not that easy. I'm a national hero. The people expect me to do something."

"And you did," his wife said. "There's nothing more for you to do. You gave it your all, but their minds were set."

"And what did it give us? Certainly not our freedom."

"It inspired the next generation to follow your example and fight for change in the right ways," she said. "Your work was not in vain, sweetheart. You'll be remembered for what you did tonight."

"I'd rather be dead than be remembered for that," Roman said loathingly. "I failed, Paula. Heroes don't fail in their finest hour."

"So, your career is over, so what? What matters is that you took a stand and you fought for what you believe in. You made that painfully clear to the whole world."

"But what good does that do? Sure, I inspired the next generation, but is that all we can tell our people? I believe Poland deserves more than that."

"Then what do you suggest?"

"I don't know," Roman said, clearly deflated. "I guess I'm just pissed with myself for letting this happen."

"It's not your fault," Paula said. "We all knew at the start of this whole ordeal that we were going against the odds. The fact that a vast majority of our people voted for independence is proof enough that you're not a failure."

"You're right, but I still failed in the end," Roman said. "I failed to deliver our independence the right way."

"What do you mean?" Paula asked, perplexed by her husband's choice of words.

"This fight isn't over. It's just going to get ugly now. What's going on in the streets... what happened at the Premier's Manor... it's just a taste of things to come, and I'm afraid there's nothing I can do to stop it."

A chill ran down Paula's spine as she listened to her husband speak. She didn't want to believe he was privy to some violent plot, but she had to know.

"I had nothing to do with it," Roman said honestly and calmly. "I just have no doubt in my mind that what happened out there was the work of the ultranationalists within our own ranks."

"As long as you had nothing to do with it, I don't care," Paula said. "My heart goes out to the victims, but you can't blame yourself for the actions of a few extremists."

"I can and I will," Roman declared. "I didn't push back hard enough at the suggestions for war. I thought we were destined for victory, but now that we lost, I'm scared.... no, I'm terrified that we'll all pay the price for what the radicals might do."

"It's not your problem anymore, Roman. We can go home and put this all behind us."

"Sure, we can go home, but can we run away from war?"

"There won't be war. This was an act of terrorism perpetrated by a small group of extremists that will be brought to justice before they can hurt another soul."

"God willing," Roman said, but his hopes weren't high. "I can already see the propaganda in my head. They'll use this incident as a bludgeon against the entire damn independence movement."

"But as I said, it's not your concern anymore," Paula said, but Roman couldn't let it go.

"You just don't get it. What happened on the Senate floor, at the gala, and now out in the streets... this is just the tip of the spear. The people have had enough, and when Moscow strikes back, the extremists are going to hit even harder."

"If you have nothing to hide, then you have nothing to worry about," Paula said, blissfully unaware of how bad things could turn for them if the Premier took Roman's verbal assault personally.

"Maybe you're right. I'm just over-thinking things," Roman said, though he didn't believe his own words. He only wanted to end the discussion. "Perhaps once things cool down a bit, we should consider going home."

"There's nothing to consider. Nothing is keeping us here. This city isn't our home. We belong back in Poland. You said it yourself many times," Paula said, and Roman seemed to agree this time.

"You're right again. This isn't our home. This is where Senators live, and I won't be a senator much longer," Roman said bitterly. "Whether that means I'll be allowed to serve out my term in peace or thrown in some godforsaken prison, I don't know. Perhaps going home and leaving this all behind is the best course of action." Roman soon stood up and leaned on the railing. Staring out at the city, listening to the emergency sirens and the occasional pop of gunfire, he shuddered and hoped the munitions were less lethal, riot control ammunition. Unfortunately, he wouldn't be surprised if live munitions had been deployed. After all, someone went against the odds and turned the First Lady's gala into a shooting gallery. That thought alone had him thinking about his own safety.

While the tower in which he stood was a secure building, even against the most determined rioter, it was still a government building. With a quick phone call or even hacking of the security system, there was nothing Sergei Medvedev or one of his lackeys from ordering a late-night raid on the building to kill him and his fellow senators. After all, there was a city-wide riot in progress, and a terrorist attack had already taken place at a highly secured location. Blaming it on radicals wouldn't be a hard sell. This got him thinking that perhaps it was best that they got out of the city as quickly as possible and just went back home to Gorzów Wielkopolski, but he quickly perished the thought. "You know what? No!" he said firmly. "We're not going anywhere."

"What are you talking about?" Paula asked, as her husband looked out onto the city with determination in his face.

"Do you hear that, Paula? The people are out in force. They're making their anger known to the world," Roman said. "I can't abandon them. Not now. We can turn this around. The fight isn't over, my dear."

Admiring her husband's spirit, though not so much his choice of words at that moment, Paula joined him by the railing. Alongside her husband, she looked out upon the city and listened to the riot ripping through the streets. While she couldn't bring herself to admire the symphony of destruction playing in her ears, she could see the beauty in what her fellow Poles were doing. Like her husband, they were making a bold stand against the government. She just hoped that this patriotic crusade could be solved with words rather than blood, and Roman felt just the same. However, he was a realist. He knew he'd be forced to take the blame for the riots ripping the federal capital, for his speech was nothing short of divisive and easily misconstrued as a call to arms. Therefore, it wasn't if but when they came for him, but he'd accept the shackles with dignity. He'd gladly become a political martyr, for behind bars, he'd be more than a disgraced politician. He would be a living symbol of Poland's subjugation by the tyrant in Moscow.

Chapter 62

Senatgrad, Federal Special Region, Slavic Federation

While most of the men of GROM were unaware of the standoff in the basement between the two unit commanders, those who had been involved carried on, unsure if they could fully trust their Russian counterparts. Regardless, they carried out the task at hand, sweeping the southern half of the grounds of the Premier's Manor and the guest houses. All the while, the Alphas cleared the main house, but neither side had it easy. Everywhere someone could have possibly hidden themselves, a body or signs of violence were found. As quickly as the attack had unfolded, the terrorists had been thorough, but so were the defenders. Every so often, in a bullet-riddled room or somewhere on the grounds, they found the body of a terrorist. Sometimes they were dressed in black fatigues, other times they appeared as members of the security team. How anyone was able to tell legitimate security from an imposter without killing a friend was anyone's guess, but somehow casualties were low. This seemed highly suspicious to many, but no one spoke of it. Their primary focus was clearing the grounds and making it back to Gdansk alive.

While the buildings were few, going room by room took time, but nothing was slower and more nerve-wracking than combing the grounds. With each step, Aleksey feared he'd feel the searing hot kiss of a sniper's bullet or have the sudden realization he had tripped a well-hidden improvised explosive device. By the grace of God, their slow, exhaustive search was completed without incident, but they had no surviving enemy to drag back to the main house either. Though they failed to find any evidence of surviving gunmen or even an obvious point of entry, they could rest easy knowing at least their portion of the ground was clear of hostiles. However, as they waited for the Alphas to report their section clear, the men got to talking. Some openly wonder if this was an inside job carried out by a handful of ultranationalists walking among their ranks, or if it was a false flag put into motion by the Alphas themselves. Whatever the case, they were all happy to be alive, and eventually a few started cracking jokes.

Having witnessed the carnage of the attacks firsthand, Aleksey knew he wouldn't be sleeping that night and had no heart for joking at that moment in time. However, he would have preferred lying awake in his bunk over assisting in the cleanup operation once Alpha Group declared their section secure. After all, he joined the military to serve his people, not put their bodies in bags after failing to protect them from harm. However, he didn't have a choice, so with a grim expression never leaving his face, he waited for the Alphas. Once the order came through, Aleksey spent the next few hours helping to comb the lawn and patio where the party was largely situated.

One by one, the bodies were laid out on the lawn in long rows of shiny black ovals. It was a long, grueling job that offered no satisfaction, but it had to be done, and no one complained. In time, the grounds began to resemble the famous scene of the wounded soldiers from Gone with the Wind.

Despite the mental toughness required of a GROM operator, not one of the men would be able to easily put aside what they had gone through that night. It was one thing to face such horrors on a battlefield or in a foreign land where such violence was commonplace. It was absolutely devastating for it to happen at the Premier's official residence, just a short drive away from the capital of the entire federation. However, for Aleksey, the night was about to get a few shades darker, for coming his way was the Alpha Commander.

"You!" the Alpha leader said, his finger pointed at Aleksey. "You speak good Russian, yes?"

Looking around, Aleksey realized no one was paying the Alpha Commander any attention, so he nodded. The Alpha closed the distance and thrust a piece of paper toward Aleksey's chest. "Translate this. We found it on one of the terrorists."

Furrowing his brow, Aleksey stretched the paper to smooth the creases down the center. Reading it, his expression morphed from mildly annoyed to disturbed and angry. The massacre was the work of Polish ultranationalists, and the man in question was someone he trained with at Redzikowo.

"What does it say?" the Alpha asked.

"It's a confession and declaration of intent," Aleksey said. "In short, he declares himself a patriot of Poland and an enemy of the fascist-controlled Slavic Federation. He says his mission this night is the beginning of Poland's latest war for independence."

His expression remaining cold and unreadable, the Alpha Commander murmured to himself. After a short pause, he grunted and ordered Aleksey to follow. Unsure if he should, he looked for Wronka, but the GROM commander was nowhere to be found. Considering they were part of a joint unit for the duration of the mission, Aleksey had no choice but to follow the Alpha to wherever he was going.

Following the Alpha Commander to an exterior entrance to the basement, Aleksey felt the cool, stale air on his skin as he stepped inside. Something felt off about this, but the Alpha Commander always remained ahead of him and hadn't said a word since ordering him to follow.

Winding through the basement and into the wine cellar, Aleksey saw two Alphas standing in front of a door. What horrors were hidden behind the door was unknown to him, and though he should have felt as though he was among friends, he was terrified. What the Alpha Commander said to him next left him feeling quite uneasy.

"I'm going to be frank with you, Sergeant. We caught ourselves a live one, but he's not long for this world. We need your help, and we need it fast."

Nodding quietly, Aleksey watched as a guard reached over and opened the door. What lay within was hidden from his sight by the mass of the Alpha Commander's broad trunk, but when he finally stepped aside, Aleksey was taken back to his last day at Redzikowo.

A lone man sat naked upon a chair, his bare chest soaked with blood and his head hanging low. From what he could tell, the man was already dead, but a swift backhand from the Alpha Commander proved he was still alive.

"This is your last chance, you son of a bitch. Tell us what you know," the Alpha Commander ordered, but the naked man stared back with a distant stare from behind swollen eyes. His lips curled as if he was going to say something, but he boldly spat blood at the Alpha Commander, earning himself a solid punch to his already broken nose. "Talk, god damn it!"

"You'll have to kill me," the prisoner said in Polish, exhaustion in his voice. "I don't talk to fascist scum."

Frustrated, the Alpha Commander looked at Aleksey for answers. "Do you recognize this man?" he asked, and though Aleksey did, he shook his head simply out of disbelief.

"I'm afraid I can't tell. You've done a number on his face," Aleksey lied, for even through the blood, he knew the man he was staring at was Miko Zielinski.

"He's the same man who wrote that letter of intent."

"Then he must be Sergeant Mikolaj Zielinski, GROM Squadron B, Fifth Platoon, Delta Squad."

"Aleksey? Is that you?"

"Yeah, it's me."

"Then suck a cock, traitor!" Zielinski snarled at Aleksey before spitting at his feet, likely unaware of who he was berating due to the blood in his eyes.

The captive terrorist was suddenly gripped by his jaw, and his head was pulled back with force. He soon had a knife held to his throat as the Alpha Commander stared into his eyes.

"Do that again and I'll slit your throat ear to ear," the Alpha Commander threatened, but Zielinski remained defiant, causing further harm.

"Cut the crap, Miko. They've beaten you half to death," Aleksey cried, barely able to bear the barbarism before him. "Just tell them what you know and get this over with."

"Go to hell!" Zielinski said, so Aleksey tried to reason with him.

"Think of your sister and your nephews. Do you want to die in this place? Don't you want to see them again?" Aleksey asked, but Zielinski was silent. "Miko! Listen to me. It's me, Aleksey--"

"Unless there's a heaven, I'll never see them again," Zielinski said. "Now just get it over with. I won't say a word."

Clearly a man of his word, the Alpha Commander pressed the knife harder against Miko's throat, drawing blood.

"Tell him this is his last chance. Tell us who sent you, or I'll send you on your way to whatever's next for your miserable soul," the Alpha Commander said firmly, but the bloodied commando stared back with determined eyes and an unbroken spirit.

"Back off and let him speak," Aleksey said, and the Alpha Commander did as he was asked. Aleksey then turned his attention back to his friend. "Miko, listen to me. They're going to kill you if you don't talk. It doesn't have to end like this."

"You know what? Fine. I'll tell you something," Miko said with a defeated tone. "I'll tell you why we did what we did tonight. It's because you fascist bastards stole our freedom. You ignored the will of the people. This is what you get."

"I understand your anger, but those people you helped kill tonight were innocent," Aleksey said, but Miko stared back at him with an expression of strong disagreement.

"Those people were the social and government elite. The parasites that give these tyrants power over us. They deserved what they got," Zielinski choked out painfully, before suffering an agonizing coughing fit and spitting up blood. "Just get this over with already. I'm ready."

Sighing, Aleksey apologized for what was about to happen, but Miko said nothing. He didn't even hang his head. He just stared into Aleksey's eyes as the Alpha Commander stomped over, a pistol now in hand. A moment later, a pistol was thrust against his head, and the trigger was pulled without a second thought. The sight of his friend's brain and skull fragments erupting from the side of his head was sickening, and Aleksey couldn't bear to see more. He turned on his heels and headed for the door, but the Alpha Commander called out to him. He stopped and slowly faced his friend's executioner.

"Well done," the Alpha Commander said. "We put that man through hell. He refused to break. I suppose talking to one of his own loosened his tongue."

With no words to say and a flurry of emotion swirling inside over everything he had been through that night, Aleksey could only nod. He left the cellar a conflicted man. Yet, not once did he show any sign of weakness before either the Alphas or GROM, only strength and professionalism. Not even when he was confronted by Wronka about where he had gone did he break. He just answered honestly and went about his work until the job was done, and they boarded a helicopter headed for the naval yard in Gdansk. He just hoped the nightmare would stay behind in Senatgrad, but he knew that was unlikely. Miko Zielinski was right; this was the opening skirmish of another bloody war for Poland's independence.

Chapter 63

Elblag, Republic of Poland, Slavic Federation

Driven from Senatgrad in the backseat of a passenger car, Audra was quiet but untrusting of her captors. Her eyes always stared straight forward; never once did she turn her head to appreciate the shifting landscape from urban to rural to semi-rural to urban once more. In all, the trip took a little over an hour and a half, but it felt so much longer. Despite the promise that she'd be taken to safety and allowed to go free under threatening conditions, she wasn't holding onto hope. She thought for sure she was being taken to some quiet, out-of-the-way place where she might be assaulted and killed. Much to her surprise, the terrorists kept their word.

The car came to a halt in the passenger drop-off lane before a sizeable train station. The engine was still running, and the doors remained locked, but she tried the door anyway. This prompted Sobczak to turn in his seat and break the silence in the vehicle since the journey began.

"Here we are, Audra Johanna Rozek of Berlin," he said, likely as a means of intimidation. "Remember the agreement. I know who you are, and I know where you live. Keep that pretty mouth shut and you'll live your life without ever seeing me again."

"Unlock the door, please," Audra said distantly.

"Give me your word and I'll let you go," Sobczak said coolly.

"Yes, I won't say anything. Now let me go, please."

"You'd best keep your word. This war doesn't have to involve you," Sobczak said, before turning to face forward. "Unlock the door. She's free to go."

Set free by terrorists that had played a role in the murder of dozens that night, Audra went straight into the train station with no more than the clothes on her back and the messenger bag she had brought along for the trip. Buying a ticket for the earliest train with a connection to Germany, she made her way to the train and joined a line where she patiently waited her turn to climb aboard. Unfortunately, when she stepped into the nearest car, she found Gustav sitting alone in a seat. As much as she wanted to avoid him, she was facing him, so it was impossible not to cross his line of sight. Yet, she passed him by as if he wasn't even there and took a seat at the back of the car.

Sitting beside the window, she placed her bag on the empty seat beside her to ward off any unwanted guests. However, in due time, she felt a presence and heard someone clear their throat. She didn't need to turn and look to know it was Gustav.

"Leave me alone," she said, staring out the window, but she knew it wouldn't be that easy.

"Can we talk?"

"No, absolutely not," she said firmly. When he tried to apologize anyway, she turned to face him and cut him off sharply. "Get the hell away from me, Gustav."

Not backing down, he again tried to apologize for the ordeal she had just gone through, but she refused to sit there and listen. She took to her feet and grabbed him by the shirt, clenching it tightly in her hand.

"Listen closely, you son of a bitch. I never want to see you again. From this moment forward, you are dead to me. Do you understand?" Audra snarled through her teeth.

"You don't mean that," he said, but she glared at him with cold fury in her eyes. "You're angry, I get it, but--"

"But nothing!" Audra barked, gritting her teeth again. "You turned my life upside down, and then you put me through a living hell only to act like it was nothing unforgivable?"

"What do you want me to say?" he asked in frustration. "I didn't ask for you to come out here."

"I don't want you to say anything. I want you to get the hell out of my life and stay out," she said, releasing his shirt at last. "Now go find a seat elsewhere! I don't want to even look at you."

"How can you say that? You were my girl. The love of my life."

"Yeah, I was, but that was then, and this is now," she said, still seething. "If you really think I could forgive you for this, you're a hopeless fool."

"Maybe I am, but you can't just walk away from someone you love."

"I fell out of love with you a long time ago, Gustav. It's time to move on. I certainly did, and he's so much better for me," she said coldly, causing his lips to quiver as her words hit like a gut punch.

"You're just saying that to be cruel," he said, struggling desperately to keep his emotions in check, but she stood firm.

"I meant every word," she said, and that was all he needed to hear for his heart to sink and his stomach to twist in agony.

"Fine," he choked. "I'll go, but don't cry if you never see me again." He then turned toward the front of the car and headed toward the exit.

Gustav walked halfway to the exit and stopped, expecting her to come to her senses and call after him, or even chase him down out of regret. But when he turned to see, she remained in her seat, staring out the window. She was dead serious, so with no plan in mind, he stepped off the train and walked down the platform.

Never moving a muscle, Audra stared into the station as Gustav marched by with his shoulders square and his chin raised. She knew he was trying to appear macho to disguise his agony, but she knew she had broken his heart for a second time. Perhaps he'd finally accept that it was over, and do what was necessary to set his life straight, but she doubted it. Gustav was a stubborn soul, but so long as he left her alone, she didn't care if he disappeared that night, never to be seen again if she could help it. She just wanted to go home and put this all behind her – Aleksey being the sole exception. She could have used his kind words and loving embrace right about then.

Chapter 64
Gdansk, Republic of Poland, Slavic Federation

The ride back to Gdansk was long and tense. While they were all grateful to have made it out of Senatgrad alive, emotions varied among the men of GROM Squadron B. While some of the men cracked jokes as if nothing had happened, others stared blankly as the weight of the night's events pressed on their souls. Aleksey was in the latter camp, but it wasn't the horror of nearly being killed in a terrorist attack that gripped his mind. It was the peculiarity of it all. For one, he couldn't understand how a security force comprised of two tier one military units could have allowed a massacre to unfold on their watch. That whole scenario was highly suspect, but the more he thought about it, the more it made sense. The Rapid Response unit and the brutal selection program he suffered through at Redzikowo were clearly part of an ultranationalist plot, and Wolski and Miko were somehow convinced to take part. This hit him hard because in all the years he'd known both Wolski and Miko, neither had ever given him the impression of a political extremist. In fact, they were among the most level-headed soldiers he had ever known.

As the ride home dragged on, Aleksey thought more about what he had seen in the basement and the way Miko carried himself, even as he faced certain death. The man he saw in that room wasn't the Miko Zielinski he knew. That got him thinking about what might have happened in those few weeks between Aleksey's departure from Redzikowo and that night to radicalize him. He could recall seeing something about the Varyag in the manifesto the Alpha officer had given him, but he didn't dare pull it out in front of anyone else to read it in full. However, he had his theory that what happened to their team aboard the Varyag played a role in the attack, and that the answers were in Miko's manifesto.

The moment the helicopter touched down on the pad at the naval yard where GROM was based in Gdansk, Aleksey and his unit headed for the showers. Seeing his chance to break away for a few minutes, he fell to the back of the group and dropped to his knee. Not a single man stopped to see what he was doing, but he pretended to retie his boot regardless. When the group was far enough ahead, he slipped off the main path and onto a more dimly lit path between some buildings. Turning a corner, he ducked behind an air conditioning unit and pulled out the manifesto received in Senatgrad. Though the light was dim, he was able to make out the writing and knew quickly enough that it was written by Zielinski. It read as follows:

If you're reading this, it's because I'm dead, but rest assured, I died fighting for my country and I didn't let the bastards take me alive. Because I'm dead, there's no point in keeping secrets, so allow me to explain to you just why I had to go out like this:

My name is Mikolaj Zielinski, Sergeant of the Polish Army, a proud member of the elite GROM, Squadron B, the Silent Unseen. Until a few weeks ago, I was a candidate for a new unit in the Special Troops – a unit they claimed would be the most elite, most revered unit in the whole country. With a few of my compatriots, I left my compatriots in Gdansk and went to Redzikowo where we would endure a hellish selection experience.

Like my friends and compatriots, I pushed my limits and battled the pain and self-doubt. While Aleksey washed out despite passing the final test, which was no fault of his own, I made it my duty to carry on in his honor. With the handful of frogmen that made it through, I carried out my duty with pride and excellence. Compared to what came before, the next phase test was nothing special. It was just a mock sabotage mission on an enemy vessel carried out in the middle of a lake. For weeks, we carried out this same mission between hours-long classes aimed at honing our patriotism and dedication to the cause. Eventually, we were dispatched to the Bay of Gdansk. We were informed that a Kuznetsov-class aircraft carrier was headed to Gdynia for transfer, should secession pass, but the ship stopped halfway and was abandoned.

Believing something was wrong, GROM was sent to secure the ship, and my team was tasked with inspecting the hull for sabotage. It was clear that this was the final test, and our mission was simple. If there were explosives on the hull, we'd disarm them. As expected, the bitter bastards rigged that ship to blow. They were going to scuttle the damn thing. Whether they intended for our people to be aboard, I don't know. What I do know is that I went into the water that night, determined to derail any fascist plans for that ship. As far as I could tell, we did our job. We disarmed every bomb we found, but something went wrong.

As I waded in the water, waiting for pickup, I witnessed the destruction of the Varyag firsthand. What I saw should have been impossible. We disarmed every last ordinance, but then it clicked. The sons of bitches planted some inside and hid them so thoroughly that even the canines couldn't sniff them out. Again, I don't know if they planned to blow up the ship with our boys aboard, but that's what happened.

The news I heard the next day left me fucking sick. The fascist media accused my countrymen of attacking and blowing up the ship. Their bastard propagandists smeared us as terrorists, calling it a failed false flag aimed at winning support in the Senate. Worse yet, that excuse for a leader in Moscow declared that justice would be swiftly dealt with on the Senate floor. Knowing what really happened out there, I felt hatred in my heart. I wanted action. I wanted blood. The sinking of the Varyag and the murder of my brothers were the catalyst for action.

With my fellow patriots, I prepared for war while I prayed for peace. Every day, I carried out my duties and followed the drills perfectly. Every night, I prepared for my finest hour with hope in my heart that it would never come. Yet, on the eve of this war, I watched as my country was officially stolen from my people once again, but I did not stay silent. I did not stay unseen. I carried out my orders in the name of the fatherland, and I made the tyrants pay for what they've done. My only regret is that I'll never see my nephews grow up into men, nor will I ever see my dear sister again. But that is the sacrifice I chose to make. Hopefully, what my brothers and I did this night ignited the flames of revolution, and every patriot with a drop of Polish blood in their veins takes up arms to take back what was stolen from us. I will only rest in peace once Poland is free again.

Long live the Republic!

Sgt. Mikolaj Zielinski, Polish Liberation Army

Left breathless by what he had just read, Aleksey was stunned. What happened on the Varyag was a tragedy, but the official narrative declared the tragedy the result of an explosion in munitions storage. He had heard some rumblings of a Polish false flag, but that was largely from Russian and federalist media. However, there was always a chance that Zielinski was right, but to take it to such an extreme was unfathomable. This left Aleksey terribly conflicted. While he wanted to burn the manifesto and protect Miko's name from further damage, he knew there was no point. The Russians had executed him, and it wouldn't be long before he was branded a traitor by the media. The right thing to do was to bring the manifesto to a superior officer and try his best to wash his hands of this mess before he, too, was branded a traitor.

Sitting nervously in an office chair with his hands clasped around the corners, Aleksey watched as Major Wronka read through Zielinski's manifesto. When he was done, Wronka clenched his eyes shut as if in terrible pain. Let off a long, frustrated sigh before looking at Aleksey with renewed composure.

"You said you received this from one of the Russians?"

"An Alpha Group officer, sir," Aleksey said, and Wronka nodded silently. "I'm afraid to admit, but Sergeant Zielinski is—"

"He's dead," Wronka said, quite matter-of-factly. There was a long pause before Wronka spoke again, and when he did, it was grim. "Let me ask you something, and I want the truth."

"Yes, sir," Aleksey said, not quite sure what he was about to be asked.

"Were you really in Redzikowo with Sergeant Zielinski?"

"Yes, sir, I was," Aleksey said, stopping himself from saying more when he saw the officer grimace. "His actions are unfathomable, I assure you."

"Indeed," Wronka said lowly. "Unfortunately, he didn't act alone, and I'm afraid there's a pattern."

"A pattern?"

"A pattern," Wronka said, turning in his chair to retrieve a piece of paper sitting atop a black file holder. He turned back and handed the paper to Aleksey. It was a list of names and ranks. "Recognize any of these names?" He asked, and Aleksey nodded. "Which?"

"Cieślak, Wysocki, Hanko, Wolski, and Zielinski," Aleksey said, recognizing just five names from the list of fifteen. "They were all GROM Squadron B at one point."

"Yes, and they were among the dead at the manor," Wronka said, giving Aleksey an uneasy feeling. "You left this unit for the reserves. How did you manage to get yourself recruited for that new unit forming at Redzikowo?"

"My uncle is on the Senate Intelligence Committee. He offered me an opportunity to work for the Office of State Protection as an embassy guard. I was led to believe the training at Redzikowo would serve as basic training, but it was, in fact, a selection program for some new elite unit."

"I see," Wronka said coolly. "So, this new unit had no name?"

"Rapid Response, but I believe that was just a cover," Aleksey said, quickly surmising it referred to itself as the Polish Liberation Army. He soon found himself involuntarily defending himself. "I never once got the feeling it was a terrorist training camp."

"I don't believe it was intended to be," Wronka said honestly. "I think everything changed after the Varyag incident." There was an uneasy silence for a few moments before Wronka continued. "I know emotions are high after tonight, but I need to know where you stand politically at this moment. Are you a federalist or a secessionist?"

"I'm neither," Aleksey said, and Wronka raised an eyebrow. "I'm a soldier of the Republic of Poland. My politics are meaningless so long as I am in the service of my country."

"Good, that's what I was hoping to hear," Wronka said before sighing deeply. "Unfortunately, tough times are ahead, so let me be very clear with you. The fanatics that carried out the massacre tonight are no friends of GRCM or the republic it stands for. They are as much an enemy of our nation as any invader. Is that clear, Sergeant?"

"Yes, sir."

"Then I have one small task for you to carry out. After which, you are free to clean yourself up and turn in for the night."

"Very well, sir. What is the task?" Aleksey asked, and he was quickly given the manifesto.

"Dispose of this and never speak another word about its existence."

Quietly accepting his duty, Aleksey was dismissed, so he stood up and snapped a salute. Upon returning the salute, he left the office and headed to a latrine across the base. It was there that he read the manifesto one last time before tearfully tearing it apart and flushing it down the toilet.

Lying in bed, unable to sleep without seeing the faces of the dead whenever he closed his eyes, Aleksey stared at the ceiling. Try as he may to clear his head and not think of anything, he was haunted by the sight of Zielinski tied down to that chair, naked, and bloodied. The defiance in his voice echoed the soul of a hardened extremist and the seething anger of his manifesto. While he understood his desire for vengeance, he couldn't justify it. Miko had a girlfriend and nephews who adored him, but he threw all that away for petty vengeance. He went from a good and honorable soldier to a terrorist in a matter of weeks. That got Aleksey wondering if he had been there to see the Varyag go down after believing he had disarmed a bomb, if he would have done the same.

Clenching his eyes, Aleksey tried to push it all from his mind. He tried to think of better things. He tried to think of his own family, of Audra, even Tatiana, but nothing came through to save him from the madness invading his mind. Even as he tried his hardest to think of Audra lying under him, lost in the heat of passion as they made love for the first time, nothing would pierce the veil of darkness surrounding his brain. All he could see were scenes of death and vengeance.

His mind eventually grew tired, and the terrible memories of the night began to fade from exhaustion. While pleasant memories began to slip through, sleep didn't come easily. He was worried about his own safety at this point. Would this so-called Polish Liberation Army come for him? Would it be the FSB or an agent from the Office of State Protection that did him in? Had they already tried? Despite sleep drawing nearer, he couldn't let go of the thought that he was purposefully targeted that night and that it wouldn't be the last attempt on his life by the terrorist wing of Poland's intelligence service. All he could do now was pray the worst scenarios never came true and that what happened that night was the worst of it all. He didn't want to fight a war, and he certainly didn't want to kill any more of his countrymen. He just wanted to hang up his uniform and one day go home to a loving wife and children. But until he was facing the decision whether to reenlist or go off into the sunset, he'd be living on the edge, praying that the war Miko Zielinski had promised never came to fruition and that he'd be back in Audra's loving arms sooner rather than later. However, deep down, he knew that was all just fantasy.

While the extremist faction calling itself the Polish Liberation Army tried to have its vengeance for the Varyag and the denial of independence in killing the First Lady, their bold attempt only made a long, bloody conflict an eventuality. One thing they didn't count on was for men like Major Wronka and himself to reject their radicalism and stand firmly for the rule of law. While this did little to ease his worry or his sorrow, he took solace in knowing that Audra was far from it all, and if by some chance they made things work amidst an armed conflict, he'd have his second chance at the new chapter in life he dreamed of for so long. He just had to survive the coming storm.

Brett Kihlmire is an American author from the Midwestern United States. An avid reader and cinephile, his works range from political thrillers and spy fiction to comedy and horror. He began writing his first finished novel while still in high school, finishing what would become Killer Instinct by his freshman year of college. He would follow-up on Killer Instinct with numerous novels, short stories, and novellas as he sharpened his skills in journalism school and beyond.

Aside from writing, Brett has studied multiple martial arts, visited many of America's many state and national parks, and is a lifelong fan of heavy metal music. His passion for heavy metal tends to show in all his works, particularly his Smash! series, while his knowledge of martial arts and history shines brightly in At All Costs.

www.ingramcontent.com/pod-product-compliance
Lightning Source LLC
Chambersburg PA
CBHW071154100726
47908CB00002B/380